A Secret Splendor
&
Above & Beyond

SANDRA BROWN

A Secret Splendor
&
Above & Beyond

MIRA®

Recycling programs for this product may not exist in your area.

ISBN-13: 978-0-7783-2945-9

A SECRET SPLENDOR & ABOVE AND BEYOND

Copyright © 2011 by MIRA Books

The publisher acknowledges the copyright holder of the individual works as follows:

A SECRET SPLENDOR
Copyright © 1983 by Sandra Brown

ABOVE AND BEYOND
Copyright © 1986 by Sandra Brown

For questions and comments about the quality of this book please contact us at Customer_eCare@Harlequin.ca.

www.MIRABooks.com

Printed in U.S.A.

CONTENTS

A Secret Splendor

Chapter 1

She's here again, Drew McCasslin thought as he slammed his racket against the tennis ball. For the third time that week she was sitting at the same table, the one nearest the ledge overlooking the tennis courts. The table's brightly striped umbrella partially shaded her face.

She hadn't been there when he and Gary started playing, but he'd known the moment she walked out onto the patio, which was an extension of the club's outdoor snack and cocktail bar. He had missed a ball when he let his attention wander to the graceful way she smoothed her skirt beneath her hips and thighs as she sat down.

"Better every day," Gary said to him as they met at the net to catch their breath, take a swig of Gatorade and towel mop rivers of sweat that saturated sweatbands couldn't absorb.

"Not good enough," Drew replied before taking a long pull at the bottle of lemon drink. Over the bottle's length, he eyed the woman sitting on the patio above them. Ever since the first day he had seen her there, she had inspired his curiosity.

She was bent over the table tapping a pencil against a tablet in a manner that he now associated with her. What the devil was she always writing down?

Slowly, he lowered the bottle from his mouth, and his blue eyes narrowed with suspicion. Could she be another blood-sucking reporter? God forbid. But it wouldn't be unlike an enterprising tabloid publication to send bait like that to trap him into an interview.

"Drew? Did you hear me?"

"Huh?" He swung his eyes back to his tennis opponent. A friendly opponent for once. "I'm sorry. What did you say?"

"I said your stamina has improved since last week. You're running my ass all over the court, and you're barely winded."

Drew's eyes crinkled at the corners as he smiled, obscuring the tiny white lines in his bronzed face. It was a smile reminiscent of the days before he had learned the definition of tragedy. "You're good, but you're not Gerulaitis *or* Borg *or* McEnroe *or* Tanner. Sorry, chum, but I have to be a helluva lot better than you before I'm ready again for the big fellows. And I'm not there by a long shot. No pun intended." The once-famous grin flashed again in the Hawaiian sunlight.

"Thanks," Gary said dryly. "I can't wait for the day I'm stumbling over my tongue and you've still got enough energy to jump the net when the match is over."

Drew slapped him on the shoulder. "That's the spirit," he gibed goadingly. He picked up his racket and twirled it with the absentminded finesse that had come from years of thinking of it as an extension of his hand.

A cheer and hearty applause erupted from a group of female spectators. They were clustered on the other side of the fence surrounding the courts. Their vocal approval increased as Drew walked back to the baseline.

"Your fans are out in full force today," Gary said with a taunting inflection.

"Damn groupies," Drew grumbled as he turned around and glared at the women who clung to the fence like hungry zoo animals at mealtime. And he was the feast. He scowled at them angrily, but that only seemed to stir them rather than to repel them. They called outrageous endearments to him and flirted shamelessly. One, wearing a brief halter top, peeled the side back to flaunt a heavy breast with his name, decorated with flowers and hearts and lovebirds, tattooed on it. Another had a bandanna, the kind he wore as a trademark sweatband around his forehead every time he played, tied high around the top of her thigh. He looked away in disgust.

He forced himself to concentrate on the ball as he bounced it idly, planning his serve, plotting to fire the ball across the net to bounce in the back corner of the serve box and spin out to the left, Gary's weak backhand side. One of Drew's "fans" called out a lewd invitation, and he gritted his teeth. Didn't they know that the last thing he was interested in was a woman? My God, Ellie had only been dead…

Dammit, McCasslin, don't think about Ellie, he warned himself. He couldn't think about Ellie when he tried to play or his game went straight to hell….

"Mr. McCasslin?"

"You've got him," he had said cheerfully into the telephone receiver that sunny day in paradise when the last thing a man would expect was for his wife to die in the tangle of metal and glass of a car crash.

"Are you alone?"

Drew had pulled the receiver from his ear and looked at it in puzzled amusement. He laughed out loud. "Yes, I'm alone except for my son. Is this going to be an obscene phone call?" He'd meant it as a joke. He'd had no idea how obscene the call would actually be.

"Mr. McCasslin, I'm Lieutenant Scott with Honolulu P.D. There's been an accident."

He didn't remember much after that....

Now he took up the ball and bounced it in his hand as though weighing it. Actually, he was trying to erase his mind, to wipe it clean of memories that made his insides churn. His eyes gravitated to the woman still sitting at the patio table. Her cheek was resting on her palm as she stared vacantly into space. She seemed impervious to everything going on around her. Didn't she hear all the commotion from the women at the fence? Wasn't she the least bit curious about him?

Apparently not. She hadn't so much as glanced at the tennis court. Unaccountably, he resented her indifference, which was irrational, since all he'd wanted for the year since Ellie's death was to be left alone.

"Hey, Drew," called out a singsong voice from the gathered fans, "when you're through playing with your balls, you can play with something of mine."

The *double entendre* was so blatant and so crudely bold that Drew's blood boiled, and when his serve sliced through the air, it was but a blur. For the rest of the set, he kept up that kind of anger-inspired play. When it was over, he'd granted Gary only two points.

Draping a towel around his neck, Gary wheezed, "If I'd known that all it took to get you to play championship tennis was a dirty suggestion from one of your groupies, I'd have rented them by the hour weeks ago."

Drew had already gathered up his tennis bag, zipped his racket into its holder and was heading toward the stairs that led to the patio overlooking the courts. "Most of them could be rented by the hour, I'm sure."

"Don't be too hard on them. They're your fans."

"I could do with more fans who are sports writers or commentators. Among them, I don't have one. All they do is tell the world that I'm washed up. Finished. Drunk all the time."

"You *were* drunk all the time."

Drew stopped on the step above Gary and whipped around to confront him angrily. His friend's face was guileless, open and damnably honest. What he'd said was true. Drew's anger dissolved in the face of such forthright friendship. "I was, wasn't I?" he asked on an embarrassed sigh.

"But not anymore. Today you were the old Drew. Blistering serves. Damn! Every time one came near me, I saw my life flash before my eyes." Drew laughed. "Well-thought-out maneuvers, strategy to take advantage of my weak left side."

A grin split Drew's mobile mouth. "I didn't think you'd notice."

"Like hell."

They were laughing companionably as they took the last few stairs up to the patio. Drew saw at once that she was still there, a sheaf of papers strewn over the table top, a glass of mineral water at her right hand. She was scribbling furiously on a yellow legal pad. He was going to walk past her table. It was on his way to the lockers, and he would only call attention to himself if he avoided passing where she was sitting.

They were almost beside her when she glanced up at them. The glance was a reflex action, as though they had disturbed her train of thought and she was looking up involuntarily to determine the source of that interruption. But she looked directly at Drew, directly into his eyes, and the impact of her gaze made his eyes narrow on her and his ears close to Gary's chatter.

Her eyes dropped immediately back to her paper, but not before Drew had seen that they were incredibly green and surrounded by dark, bristly lashes.

That was when he made up his mind. He'd make a wager with himself. If she was still there when he came out of the locker room, he'd speak to her. If not, well, nothing was lost. He wasn't really interested in meeting a woman, any woman. It was just that this one intrigued him. If he was honest with himself, he'd have to admit that the main reason she piqued his curiosity was because she was so *un*curious about him.

Yes, he'd leave it to chance. If she was still there when he came out of the locker room, he'd at least say hello. No harm in that.

One other thing, he reminded himself. *Don't linger in the shower.*

Arden's heart was booming like a kettledrum.

It had been a full five minutes since he'd walked within touching distance, since she'd seen his face up close and in the flesh for the first time, and still her heart hadn't quieted. She blotted her palms with the damp napkin knotted in her fists. Ice rattled in her glass when she took a sip of her lime-refreshed mineral water.

He had looked straight at her. Their eyes had met. Briefly, briefly. Yet it had been like lightning striking her to see Drew McCasslin for the first time, knowing the bond that linked them together. Total strangers to each other, yet with a common secret they would share throughout their lives.

She looked down at the court where he had just played with such brilliance. A few months before, she'd known little about tennis, especially professional tennis. Now she was almost expert in her wealth of knowledge on the subject. Certainly she had a vast amount of knowledge on the career of Drew McCasslin.

A group of four ladies came onto the court, looking ridiculous in their designer tennis clothes and extravagant gold and diamond jewelry. She smiled at them indulgently, remembering Ronald's urging that she join the tennis league at their club in Los Angeles.

"That's not me, Ron. I'm not athletic. I'm not a participator, a joiner."

"You'd rather sit in the house all day writing those little verses that you lock away and don't let anyone see. For God's sake, Arden, you don't have to play *well*. I don't care if you can play tennis or not. It's just good for my professional image, not to mention the valuable contacts you could make if you're an active member of the club. Socialize with the other doctors' wives."

He'd settled for bridge. She never was a master of the game, but she played well enough to be invited to all the tournaments sponsored by the country club, and that satisfied Ronald's demands that she mix and mingle with what he considered suitable friends for a prominent doctor's wife.

Then Joey had come along and provided her with a viable excuse for curtailing her social activities. Joey had provided her with excuses for many things. Some, she wished she could forget. Would her son, her adorable, painfully sweet, innocent son, have understood that one life-altering decision? Would he have forgiven what she couldn't forgive herself?

She'd asked his forgiveness the day the pitifully small casket was lowered into the short grave. She'd asked God's forgiveness, too, for the bitterness she felt at watching an intelligent, beautiful child waste away in a hospital bed while other robust children played and ran and got into mischief.

Shaking herself out of her emotional reverie, she took another sip of water and mentally toasted herself for playing it just right with Drew McCasslin. It was public knowledge that since he'd retreated to his carefully guarded estate on this island, he'd avoided interviews and shunned publicity of any kind.

For days, Arden had occupied herself with thinking of a way to approach him. On the long flight over from the mainland and even after her arrival on Maui, she had discarded one plan after another. The only positive thing she'd done was to acquire a room at the resort and club where he worked out every day. His privacy had been guaranteed him by the management. This was the first day since she'd been watching him that he hadn't entered the locker room from the metal door that opened directly onto the courts.

Her only option had been to play it subtly, to make herself visible and see what happened. She would pretend to ignore him. It wasn't hard to see that his more forward fans irritated him.

And today he'd noticed her. Instinctively, she knew it. She'd given an impression of casual disinterest, but she'd been aware of every move he made. He'd glanced in her direction several times, especially after executing an outstanding move. He'd never caught her eyes on him. A famous personality like Drew McCasslin wasn't used to being ignored.

In his case, such conceit was justifiable. His blond hair was too long, but it suited his dashing good looks. His trim physique didn't show the ravages of his recent bout with alcohol. The tropically tanned arms and legs, which moved with the precision and power of a well-oiled machine, were the epitome of masculine grace, and contrasting with the bronzed skin was an eye-catching dusting of tawny body hair. He was somewhat broader of chest than most tennis players, but that flaw was readily forgiven by anyone who watched the play of those muscles under his tailored white T-shirts.

It was obvious that since the tragic death of his wife, Drew McCasslin had just as soon women not notice his virile appeal. No, she had played it just right, Arden congratulated herself. Today he had looked at her. Maybe tomorrow—

"You must have a lot of friends and relatives."

Startled by the masculine voice, Arden swiveled around; to her dismay, she found herself staring into the fly of a pair of white shorts. The sculpted bulge behind that fly could only be produced by either very brief and very tight underwear or a jock strap. Either possibility sent a hot current rushing through her body.

She dragged her eyes away from Drew McCasslin's crotch and let them scale the long torso, which was clothed in a royal-blue nylon windbreaker zipped only halfway up to reveal a coppery chest furred with golden hair. His smile was an orthodontist's dream. Straight white teeth were set in a jaw too strong to be anything but stubborn. The blue eyes were as dazzling as they were reported to be.

"I beg your pardon?" she asked in a voice she hoped didn't betray her disabling nervousness.

"You're busy writing an awful lot of something. I thought it might be postcards home. 'Wish you were here.' That sort of thing."

His voice was clear, a true baritone in pitch, unaccented, his tone strangely intimate.

She smiled, remembering her act of nonchalant indifference. "No. Not postcards. There really is no one home to miss me."

"Then no one could mind if I joined you."

"*I* could mind."

"Do you?"

Elated but not daring to show it, she paused only a heartbeat before saying, "No. I guess not."

He tossed his canvas bag beneath the chair opposite hers and sat down. Reaching across the paper-strewn table, he said, "Drew McCasslin."

She took the extended hand into her own. "Arden Gentry." She was touching him! Looking at their clasped hands, at his flesh against hers, she marveled over the wonder of this being their first physical contact when—

"Are you on vacation?" he asked politely.

She released his hand and sat back in her chair, trying to dispel a feeling of lightheadedness. "Partially. A mixture of business and pleasure."

He signaled the waiter from behind the outdoor bar. "Do you care for another?" he asked, indicating her glass.

"Pineapple juice this time," she said, smiling.

"You're a foreigner, all right. You haven't had time to grow sick of the stuff."

She wished he weren't quite so attractive when he smiled. His blatant sex appeal distracted her from the reason why she had wanted to make his acquaintance, gain his confidence, if possible, become his friend.

"The lady wants pineapple juice, and I want about four glasses of water, please," he told the waiter.

"Yessir, Mr. McCasslin. You were playing well today."

"Thank you. Hurry with the water. I'm all sweated out."

"Yessir."

"You did play well," Arden said when the waiter hurried off to get Drew's order.

He studied her face for a time before he said, "I didn't think you noticed the match at all."

"I would have to be blind and deaf not to. I don't know much about tennis, but I know you're playing better now than you were several months ago."

"Then you knew who I was?"

"Yes. I'd seen you on television once or twice." He seemed boyishly crestfallen, and Arden's smile widened. "You're a celebrity, Mr. McCasslin," she whispered reassuringly. "People all over the world know your name."

"And most of those people don't make any bones about staring at me when I'm in public." It was a gently spoken challenge.

"Like your cheerleading section down there?" She nodded toward the fenced-off area where the groupies had collected. They had since dispersed.

He groaned. "Would you believe I began working out here because I was promised anonymity and privacy? It's also about the best court on Maui. But we didn't take into account the fact that guests of the resort have access to the courts. When word gets out that I'm practicing—" He sighed in exasperation. "Well, you see what happens."

"Most men would be flattered by such adoration."

He scoffed at that and quickly changed the subject. "What is all this, anyway?" he asked of the papers scattered across the table.

"Notes. I'm a free-lance writer."

His retreat was instantaneous and physical, though he didn't move. His eyes became cold and implacable. The sensuous curve of his lips thinned into a line of aggravation. Around the frosted glass of water the waiter had just delivered, his fingers flexed in anger. "I see," he said tersely.

She lowered her eyes and picked at the paper doily under her glass of juice. "I don't think you do. I'm a writer, not a reporter. I'm not after an interview. You initiated this conversation, not I, Mr. McCasslin."

When he didn't respond, she lifted her thick, dark lashes and looked at him. He was as he had been before, smiling slightly, friendly, yet guarded, just as she was. "Call me Drew, please."

He had laid down the terms of the truce, and she accepted it. "All right, Drew. And I'm Arden."

"What kind of writer? Novelist?"

She laughed. "Not yet. Maybe someday. Right now I'm trying to peddle anything and everything until I find my niche. I'd always wanted to come to the islands but never had. I lined up several articles to write to help subsidize my trip. This way I can stay longer, see more and not have to worry about the drain on my bank account."

He liked the sound of her voice, the way her head tilted first one way then another as she talked. It made her dark hair move against her neck and bare shoulders. The wind off the ocean lifted sun-reddened strands and tossed them playfully about her face before letting them rest against skin that had been in the islands long enough to be tinted a beautiful apricot but not long enough to take on that lined, leathery look that he found repulsive. Arden Gentry had exceedingly touchable skin. And hair. And lips.

He cleared his throat. "Articles on what?"

She went on to explain that she was doing one for the travel section of the *Los Angeles Times,* another for a fashion magazine. She was also going to interview a local botanist and do an article for a gardening publication. He barely listened.

For the first time since he'd met Ellie, he was interested in a woman. It surprised him because he had never thought he'd want to be deeply involved with a woman again. Not that this would go beyond sharing a drink or casual conversation. But having met Arden, he felt that he might one day get over Ellie's death and actually seek another female companion.

He couldn't help being conscious of Arden Gentry physically. He'd have to be a blind eunuch not to be. She was a beautiful woman. And she had a serenity about her that he found appealing. He tried to concentrate on that and on her soft voice and keep his mind off other aspects of her.

From the moment he'd sat down, he'd tried not to look at her breasts and speculate whether that firm shape came from a strapless bra beneath her green cotton sundress or whether she had such a figure naturally. *What the hell. Go ahead and look.*

He voted strongly in favor of the latter theory. For with the caress of the cool wind, he could detect the merest puckering of her nipples. He felt stirrings of desire that he thought had been buried with Ellie and didn't know if he was ashamed or glad to feel them again.

He hadn't admired a woman's body since the last time he'd made love with Ellie. Gross displays of flesh did nothing to turn him on. He had the same interest in a woman's body as any man, but this...this was something different. It wasn't merely the flesh he found himself liking about Arden, but a personality, an evident intelligence, a certain disregard for his fame.

A spark of his old mischievousness flared. It made him wonder what she'd do if he leaned toward her and said, "Arden, please don't take offense, but for the first time since my wife died, I'm not disgusted by the way my body is responding to a woman."

There had been women. Bodies. Nothing more. Procured for him by well-intentioned friends who thought that erotically talented hands and mouths would cure him of all ills. If he could remember the drunken encounters later, he'd become sick with disgust for himself.

One night in Paris, where he'd publicly disgraced himself with a humiliating defeat on the courts, he'd found his own woman. She was the most sordid of whores. She was the punishment he doled out to himself. His penance. Later, when he was sober enough, he'd wept and hoped to God he hadn't been infected with something he'd have to be terribly embarrassed about.

That had been the turning point. The last chapter in the suicidal dissipation of Drew McCasslin. No one could save him but himself.

And then, besides himself, there was Matt to consider.

"How long have you lived in the islands?"

Arden's question yanked him back into the much brighter present. "Most of my adult life. After I began winning and making money on endorsements, it seemed like the ideal place for a bachelor to live. I was living in Honolulu when I met Ellie. She—"

His words came to an abrupt halt. He looked down into his water glass, and his shoulders assumed a defensive hunch. "I know about your wife, Drew," Arden said softly. "You don't have to apologize for mentioning her."

He saw in her eyes a compassion that was unlike the morbid curiosity he was accustomed to reading in inquiring faces. That alone compelled him to continue. "Her father was a naval officer stationed at Pearl. Eleanor Elizabeth Davidson. I told her it was too much for a woman her size—she was petite—to carry the name of a first lady and a queen."

"So you dubbed her Ellie." Arden was smiling encouragingly.

He answered with a chuckle. "Yeah, much to the irritation of her parents." He took a sip of water and drew idle circles in the condensation on the side of the glass. "Anyway, after she was killed, I wanted a change of scenery, so I moved here to Maui where it's much more isolated. I wanted to protect my privacy and shelter Matt from all the curiosity seekers."

Arden's whole body went still. "Matt?"

"My son." Drew beamed.

Her throat throbbed with the thudding of her heart, but she managed to reply. "Oh, yes. I've read about him, too."

"He's terrific. Smartest, cutest kid in the world. This morning, he—" Drew bit off his sentence. "Forgive me. I get carried away when I talk about him."

"You won't bore me," she said quickly.

"Given half a chance, yes, I will. Suffice it to say that he's been the one thing in my life recently that I could take pride in. We live right on the beach. He loves it."

Arden, striving for control, stared out at the horizon. The sun was a brassy reflection on the surface of the ocean. It hurt one's eyes to look at it from this angle. The island of Molokai was a gray-blue shadow against the northwestern horizon. Palm trees swayed with rhythmic grace in the gentle wind. Frothy white waves rolled in to kiss the sandy beach before receding.

"I can see why you'd want to live here. It's lovely."

"It's been great for me. A healing place, both mentally and physically."

He wondered why he was talking so openly to this woman. But he knew why. She inspired confidence and radiated understanding. A thick, sun-bleached brow arched quizzically over one of his eyes as a thought struck him. "You said there was no one at home to miss you. You aren't married?"

"I was. I'm divorced."

"No children?"

"A son. Joey." She faced him squarely. "He died."

He muttered an expletive before he sighed and said, "I'm sorry. I know how painful inadvertent reminders can be."

"Don't be sorry. The only thing I hate is when friends *won't* talk about him, as though he didn't exist."

"I've run into that, too. People avoid speaking Ellie's name, almost as though they're afraid I'll collapse into tears and embarrass them or something."

"Yes," Arden said. "I want Joey to be remembered. He was a beautiful child. Fun. Sweet."

"What happened? Accident?"

"No. When he was four months old, he contracted meningitis. It damaged his kidneys. He was on dialysis from then on, and I thought he'd live a fairly normal life, but…" Her voice faded into nothingness, and they were quiet for long moments, not even aware of the peripheral noises around them—laughter from a table on the other side of the patio, the whirring of the blender the bartender was using, a gleeful shout from the tennis courts below. "He got worse. There were complications, and before a suitable organ became available for a transplant, he died."

"Your husband?" Drew asked softly.

When had he taken her hand? She didn't remember. But suddenly she became aware of his holding it, rubbing the back of her knuckles with his thumb. "We were divorced before Joey's death. He more or less left Joey in my care."

"Mr. Gentry sounds like a real son of a bitch."

Arden laughed. His name wasn't Gentry, but she couldn't agree with Drew more. "You're right, he is."

They laughed softly and privately until they became aware of it. With the awareness came a flustered embarrassment. He released her hand promptly and leaned down to pick up his gear. "I've distracted you from your work long enough. Besides, I promised to baby-sit this afternoon so my housekeeper can go shopping."

"You have a housekeeper who tends to Matt? Is she...good with him?" Anxiety made her voice breathless.

"I don't know what I'd do without her. We had Mrs. Laani before Matt came along. When Ellie died, she took over and moved here with me. I trust her completely."

Arden could feel the taut muscles of her body easing with relief. "It's fortunate you have someone like her."

He stood and extended his hand. "I've enjoyed it, Arden."

She shook his hand. "So have I."

He seemed reluctant to let go of her hand. When he did, his fingertips lightly dragged against her palm. He wanted to do that to her cheek, to the underside of her arm, to her shoulder. He wanted to do what her hair did, sweep the skin of her neck and chest with seductive caresses. "I hope you enjoy the rest of your trip."

Her heartbeat had accelerated; there was a tickling sensation in the back of her throat. "I'm sure I will."

"Well, goodbye."

"Goodbye, Drew."

He took three steps away from her before coming to a stop. He weighed his decision for a few seconds before turning back. He was going to do something he hadn't done since he'd met Ellie Davidson. He was going to ask for a date.

"Uh, listen, I was wondering if you'd be around tomorrow."

"I don't know," Arden said with cool tact. Actually, she was holding her breath, offering up a silent prayer. "Why?"

"Well, Gary and I play tomorrow morning." He shifted from one sneakered foot to the other. "And I was thinking that if you were going to be around, maybe you could watch a game or two and then we could have lunch somewhere here at the resort."

She lowered her eyes, almost closing them in jubilation.

"If you'd rather not—" he began.

"No," she said quickly, lifting her head again. "I mean, yes, that would be...I'd like that."

"Great!" he said, his confidence flooding back. Why the hell did it matter so much that she'd consented? He could have a woman anytime he wanted one. And not for lunch. But it had been damned important for Arden to say yes. "Then I'll see you here sometime around noon?" he asked, trying to steal a glance at the legs primly crossed beneath the table. Maybe she had thick ankles.

"I'll be here."

Her ankles were gorgeous. "'Bye." His lips opened wide over a devastating smile.

"'Bye." She hoped her own lips weren't visibly trembling when she returned it.

His easy, athletic stride carried him quickly across the patio. She watched him go, admiring the effortless way he moved and the athletic shape of his body.

She liked him! And she was so glad she did. He was a nice man. An extraordinary man, to be sure, but a man. Not a faceless, nameless question mark in her mind any longer. A man with an identity and a personality. A man who had experienced love and pain and bore them both well.

She had won his trust, and that gave her a twinge of guilt. Would he have invited her to lunch if she'd told him who she was? Would he have been as eager to see her again if he knew she had been the woman artificially impregnated with his semen? Would he have confided in her so openly if she had come right out and said, "I'm the surrogate mother you and Ellie hired. I bore your son"?

Chapter 2

In her absence, the maid had cleaned her room and left the air conditioner going full blast. Dropping her purse and notebook on a table, Arden first adjusted the thermostat on the wall, then slid open the wide glass door that led out to her private ocean-front terrace. The room was exorbitantly expensive, but the view was well worth every penny.

She drew in a great breath, and as she quelled it, breathed a name: Drew McCasslin. Her quarry. At last she had met him, talked to him, heard him speak her son's name. Matt.

It didn't take her long to peel off the sundress and wrap herself in a terry robe. She stepped out into the embracing Hawaiian warmth and sat down in one of two chairs on the terrace. Propping her heels against the seat of the chair, she rested her chin on her knees as she stared out at the seascape.

Drew had assumed that Gentry was her married name. What he didn't know was that she'd thrown off that name like an animal shedding old skin as soon as she had filed for divorce. She wanted nothing to do with Ronald Lowery, even his hateful name.

Just when she'd think the anger was finally gone, it would sneak up and grab her, as it was doing now. It was as silent and intangible as a fog, but just as blanketing, just as blinding, just as suffocating.

Would she never forget the humiliation of that night he had first broached the subject? She had been in the kitchen of their Beverly Hills home preparing dinner. It was a rare evening when Ron came home directly after office hours. But that afternoon he'd called saying that no babies were due, he'd made hospital rounds early and he'd be leaving the office in time to have dinner with her. In a marriage that had quickly proved disappointing for Arden, even having dinner together was an event. If Ron was going to try to make things better, Arden would do her part.

"What's the occasion?" she had asked when he came in carrying a bottle of vintage wine.

He kissed her peremptorily on the cheek. "A celebration of sorts," he said offhandedly. She knew from experience that he liked to keep secrets, not for the pleasure they would eventually bring someone else, but because they gave him a sense of superiority. She'd learned long ago not to press him for information. More often than not, his surprises were unpleasant.

"The pot roast will be done in a minute. Why don't you go in and see Joey? He's in the den watching 'Sesame Street.'"

"For God's sake, Arden. I just got home. The last thing I want to do is listen to Joey's chatter. Fix me a drink."

Stupidly, she had obeyed. As was her habit. "Joey's your son, Ron," she said as she handed him his Scotch and water. "He worships you, but you do so few things together."

"He can't do normal things."

She hated the way he dashed down his drink and then shoved the glass toward her with an unspoken command to refill it. "That's why it's even more important that you find—"

"Christ! I should have known that if I came home with good news, you'd have to spoil it with your bitching. I'll be in the living room. Call me when dinner's ready. *Our* dinner. I want to talk to you about something important, so feed Joey ahead of time and put him to bed."

With that, he had stalked out of the room, and Arden had taken immense pleasure in noting that his pants bagged in the seat. When she had met Ron as a medical student, he'd been proud of his athletic physique. Too many cocktail parties later, his stomach was no longer flat and trim. His buttocks were getting flatter and his hips wider. He wasn't nearly as suave and debonair as he used to be. And he knew it. All he had to fall back on now was the gynecological practice that he had sacrificed everything else for. Even her love.

She made an effort that night to be congenial and attractive when she called him into the dining room for dinner. Joey had been shuttled away after a hasty and insincere kiss from his father. The meal she'd prepared was sumptuous. In those days, she had taken pleasure in cooking.

"Well, now," she said, smiling across the table at her husband as he finished his second slice of apple pie, "are you going to tell me what we're celebrating?"

"The end to all our problems," he said expansively.

The end to all her problems would be to see Joey completely well and living the normal life of a three-year-old. But she asked politely, "What problems? The clinic's going well, isn't it?"

"Yeah, but..." He sighed. "Arden, you know lately I've

needed to…relax, have some fun. All I hear day in and day out is women griping about cramps or screaming in labor."

Arden swallowed a tart rebuke. Her father hadn't felt that way about the practice he'd spent a lifetime making one of the finest in Los Angeles. He hadn't felt intolerance of his patients' pain, imagined or not, the way Ron did.

"I've been gambling a little, and well…" He shrugged and grinned at her with what he considered to be boyish appeal. "I'm busted. In debt up to my armpits."

It took her a moment or two to absorb what he'd just said. Then a full minute to fight down her panic. Her first thought was Joey. His medical care was incredibly expensive. "How…how much in debt?"

"Enough that I might have to sell the practice or put it in hock so deep I'd never get it out no matter how many brats I deliver."

The dinner she'd just eaten almost came up. "Oh, my God. My father's practice."

"Goddammit!" Ron roared, slamming his fist down on the table so hard that china and crystal clattered. "It's not *his,* it's *mine.* Mine, do you hear me? He was a country doctor with outmoded methods until I converted that women's clinic into a modernized—"

"Factory. That's how you run it. Without compassion or feeling for the women you treat."

"I help them."

"Oh, granted, you're a fine doctor. One of the best. But you have no emotion, Ron. You don't see that woman you're treating as a person. You only care about her checkbook."

"You don't mind living here and being a member of the grandest country club—"

"*You* wanted the house and the club, not me."

"When a woman leaves my office, she feels on top of the world."

"You have a terrific bedside manner. I know that, Ron. I'm not stupid. But it's all for show. You can charm a person into thinking you care for them."

He settled back in his chair, his legs stretched out in front of him, ankles crossed. His expression was sly. "Speaking from experience?" he drawled.

She lowered her eyes to her plate. It hadn't taken long after their marriage for her to realize that all his romancing and professions of love had been to gain himself, not a loving wife, but a well-established, well-paying practice. "Yes. I know why you married me. You wanted my father's clinic. I think you purposely badgered him until he had his stroke and died. Now you have everything you want." Her anger had been building up to this point. Now she ended on a shout. "And now you're telling me that you're about to lose it all because you've gambled it away!"

"As usual, you're jumping to conclusions and not listening to half of what I'm saying." He poured a generous glass of wine and downed it. "I've been given an opportunity to make a lot of money."

"How? Drugs?"

He glowered at her but continued. "Do you remember when I got that baby for a couple to adopt about a year ago? They wanted no hassle, no red tape, just a baby with legal documents."

"I remember," she said cautiously. What was he considering? Black-market babies? It wouldn't be beyond him. She shuddered.

"I had an appointment with friends of theirs today. A *secret* appointment. Very hush-hush. Because they're celebrities." He paused dramatically, and she knew he wanted her to beg him for their identity. Later, she would regret that she hadn't. "This couple wants a baby more than any I've seen. They've tried everything for her to get pregnant. Nothing's worked, but he's been checked out. A loaded pistol if I've ever seen one," he said lewdly. Arden listened stoically, with no change of expression. "I said I'd see what I could do about finding them a baby to adopt with no hassle. But the woman said no dice. She wants this to be her husband's baby."

"I'm not sure I follow you."

"The fruit of his loins, his seed," he intoned theatrically. "They want me to find them a suitable surrogate mother and impregnate her with his sperm. *Presto!* They have a baby."

"I've heard of surrogate mothers. How do you feel about it? Can it work? Would you do it for them?"

He laughed. "Hell, yes, I'll do it for them for the money they're talking about. One hundred thousand dollars. Fifty for the mother. Fifty for me."

Arden gasped. "One hundred... They must be *wealthy* celebrities."

"All they demand is a healthy baby and absolute secrecy. Secrecy, Arden. Nonreportable income. They've said they'll pay me in cash."

It was unethical, if not illegal. She couldn't imagine any woman consenting to such subterfuge. "Where will you find a woman willing to have a baby, only to give it up?"

His eyes bored into hers, and a chill slithered down her spine. For ponderous moments, they stared at each other over the corner of the table. "I don't think I'll have to look too far," he said.

Her face drained of all color. Surely he couldn't mean *her.* His own wife! "Ron," she said, hating the note of desperation and panic in her voice, "you're not suggesting that I—"

"Exactly."

She bolted out of her chair and spun away, but he was a step behind her, nearly wrenching her arm out of its socket when he spun her around to face him. His face was florid, and he showered her with spittle as he growled, "Think for once, Arden. If you do this for me, we get all the money. I... we don't have to divide it with anyone."

"I'll try to forget we ever had this conversation, Ron. Please let go of my arm. You're hurting me."

"You'll hurt even more if your sweet tush gets booted out of this house you love to seclude yourself in. And what about Joey? His treatments are eating us alive. And your precious father's legacy. Are you going to let it go down the tubes because of your sterling principles?"

She yanked her arm free and would have run from him, but what he'd said made her think despite the insanity of it all. She couldn't let Ron gamble away her father's life's work. And Joey! What would they do if they couldn't afford his medical bills?

"I'm sure this...this couple didn't have their doctor's wife in mind when they sought you out."

"They'd never know. They don't want to know the mother and don't want her to know them. They intend to pass the kid off as their own. All they want is a healthy woman to deliver them a healthy baby. A vessel."

"Is that all I am to you, Ron? A means of bailing you out? A money-making *vessel?*"

"Take it from one who knows. You're not using that equipment for anything else. You might just as well have a baby with it."

Her whole body sagged under the weight of his insult. It was true. The infrequency of sex between them was an ongoing argument. Arden didn't have an aversion to sex. She had grown up educated to it by her father's frankness, with a respect for its sanctity, with a healthy anticipation for it. What she did have an aversion to was Ron's kind of sex. It was without foreplay, without tenderness, without love. She had submitted for years until she couldn't stand any more and had begun to make frequent excuses.

Rather than begin that stale argument, which invariably led to his near raping her, she said, "I don't want to have a baby. Another man's baby. I have Joey to consider. I'm worn out half the time when I come in from the hospital. I don't think I'm physically up to it. Certainly not psychologically."

"You're up to it if you make up your mind that you are. And forget that crap about another man's baby. It's a biological process. Sperm and egg. Slam, bam, one baby coming up."

She turned away in revulsion. How could he be so callous about a miracle he witnessed every day? She didn't know why she was even standing there discussing this with him, except that maybe she saw it as her way out, too.

"What would we tell people? I mean, when I came home from the hospital without a baby."

"We'd tell them that the baby had been stillborn, that we were devastated and wanted no funeral service, no memorial. Nothing."

"But what about the hospital staff? There are strict rules forbidding doctors to treat family members. How do you make the switch, give my...the baby to a woman who wasn't pregnant and pass mine off as dead?"

"Don't worry about any of that, Arden," he said impatiently. "I'll take care of all those details. Money shuts people up. The delivery-room nurses are loyal. They'll do what I tell them to do."

Apparently, he was accustomed to such intrigue, pulling

off deals. Such things were foreign to Arden, and the scope of possible repercussions made her uncomfortable.

"How do we…do it?"

Now that he thought she was going to comply, his excitement heightened. "First we have to make sure you're not pregnant." He smirked a nasty grin. "But then that would be almost impossible, wouldn't it? I'll show them your medical history, which is without blemish. You had no trouble with your first pregnancy. We sign a contract. I do the procedure at the office."

"What if I don't conceive?"

"You'll conceive. I'll see to it."

She shivered. "I have to think about this, Ron."

"What's to think—" he began on a shout. But when he saw her chin lift stubbornly, he softened his approach and relied on his charm. "Sure. I know. Give yourself a few days, but they want an answer by the end of the week."

She told him her answer the next morning. He was thrilled. Then she stated her conditions.

"You *what?*" he snarled.

"I said that I want half the money upon delivery, along with divorce papers, signed, sealed and delivered. There will be no intimacies between us until I deliver. As soon as I leave the hospital with my money, I never want to see you again."

"You won't leave me, baby. If anyone gets dumped around here, it will be you! You care too much about the clinic's reputation to leave me."

"I did. While Father was alive, it was everything it was supposed to be. I strongly suspect that under your auspices it will gradually begin to crumble. I won't be there to see it. It's no longer something I can take pride in." She drew herself up straight. "You used me to get the clinic. Now do with it as you will. I'll have this baby because the money will allow me and Joey to be free of you. You've used me for the last time, Dr. Ronald Lowery."

He'd met all her terms. He never told her, but Arden was fairly certain that his creditors were pressuring him. A desperate man didn't have any choice but to accept conditions. When she left the hospital that day, feeling soiled and used and empty, but free, she hadn't regretted her decision. The money her nine months' job had earned her would enable her to take better care of Joey.

But now, almost two years later, she had ambivalent feelings about her decision to bear the child of a stranger. The McCasslins had had their heartfelt wish granted when she bore a baby boy. He had enriched their lives and given Drew an anchor to cling to, a reason for living when the rest of his world fell apart. Shouldn't that alone absolve Arden of any guilt she felt? Why did she continue to fault herself? In any event, it was too late now to alter history.

She hadn't moved as she reviewed the event that had finally brought her to that lovely island. Now she stood up and stretched muscles that were stiff from having been in one position so long. She spent a quiet evening in her room, writing some, mostly wondering when she would tell Drew McCasslin who she was and how she could ask him to let her see her son.

"Hi." He jogged over to the edge of the court and looked up at her where she sat at her customary table near the ledge. "You look as cool as a cucumber."

"And you look as hot as hell."

He laughed, surprised. "And that's exactly how I feel. Gary's giving me a run for my money."

"I'd say he's getting his money's worth, too." Arden had been watching the strenuous match for the last two games, and Drew was playing at what she knew must have been his full potential before grief and too much alcohol crippled his game.

He seemed pleased that she'd noticed. "Yeah, well, I've managed to get in a few good shots," he conceded humbly. "I'm working up a hearty appetite for lunch."

"Don't rush on my account. I'm enjoying the exhibition."

He bowed at the waist and trotted back onto the court, calling to an exhausted-looking Gary that rest time was over. Drew took the next game without granting a point. On Gary's serve, however, the club pro came back with a vengeance. The game went to deuce several times before Drew took two points in a row to win the match.

Ignoring the cheering girls who had again collected like bright butterflies against the fence, he comically staggered over to the wall and looked up at Arden. "Isn't the matador supposed to throw the lady the bull's ear or tail or something to dedicate the bullfight to her?"

She laughed. "I think so, yes. But please don't cut off Gary's ear."

"I don't have anything to throw you except a tennis ball. Or a sweaty towel."

"I prefer the ball."

He tossed it up to her, and she caught it deftly, bowing her head over it in regal acceptance. "Order me four glasses of water and I'll be with you in a minute."

Arden watched as he slung his bag over his shoulder and loped off in the direction of the locker room. He waved at her once before disappearing through the thick metal doors.

Had he ever thought about the woman who had borne his child? she wondered as she signaled the waiter and ordered his water and another glass of iced tea for herself. Had he ever considered how she must have felt carrying a part of him in her body? Intimacy without intimacy.

The day Ron determined she was fertile—he had taken her temperature with a specialized thermometer for several days in a row—he told her to come to his office after hours. Naked and vulnerable, she had lain on the examination table, her feet propped in stirrups while he inserted what he called a cervical cup. Then he injected the frozen seminal fluid into the receptacle. It would hold the fluid against the door of her womb until she painlessly extracted it at home. With any luck, the results would be positive.

"You're getting no more excited over this than you do over the real thing, Arden," he said, leering down at her.

"Just hurry and finish," she said wearily. His lurid jokes no longer had the power to provoke her.

"Aren't you the least bit curious? Hmm? Don't you wonder what he looks like? Who he is? I have to admit he's a handsome fellow. Are you wishing you could get a little turned on beforehand so it would seem more official?" His hand grasped her breast and squeezed painfully. "I could accommodate you. Everyone's gone home."

She slapped his hand away, and he laughed cruelly. Did he truly think that slack-lipped, insinuating smile was going to send her into the throes of passion? She looked away as a lone tear rolled down her temple. "Just finish, please."

"We do it again tomorrow," he said when she sat up.

"Tomorrow?"

"And the next day. Three days while you could be ovulating." He leaned against the table and stroked her thigh. "Then we sit back and wait and see."

She prayed that she'd conceive on that first attempt. After subjecting herself to Ron's lewdness, she didn't think she could stand to go through with it again next month. Her prayers had been answered. Within six weeks, Ron was certain that she was pregnant. He informed the couple that their surrogate mother had conceived. He told Arden they were ecstatic.

"You be damn sure to take care of yourself," he warned. "I don't want anything to mess this up now."

"Nor do I," she had said, closing the door to the bedroom in his face.

She didn't think about the life she was carrying as a baby, a personality, a human being. She thought of it only as a means to let her and Joey have a better chance at happiness, free of Ron's greed and selfishness.

During the weeks of morning sickness and on the long, exhausting days she drove Joey to and from the hospital, she tried not to resent the fetus she could never let herself love. When friends congratulated her and Ron on the pregnancy, she forced herself to smile and accept their good wishes and Ron's proprietary arm around her shoulders.

The day she first felt the infant move, she knew a moment of incredible joy. It was quickly suppressed, pushed aside, hidden in some secret corner of her mind. Only at night, alone in her room, as she spread soothing lotion on her distended abdomen did she allow herself to wonder about the child. Would it be male or female? Blue eyed or brown? Or would it inherit her green eyes?

And that was when she'd begun to wonder about the father, about whose seed she carried. What was he like? Was he kind? Would he be a good parent? Did he love his wife? Surely he did. She loved him enough to let another woman bear his child. Had they been lying together when he collected—

★ ★ ★

"Penny for them."

"Oh!" Arden gasped, flattened her hand over her chest and whirled around to see the subject of her thoughts leaning down over her, smiling. His hand was on the top of her chair, close to her bare back.

"I'm sorry," he said, genuinely contrite. "I didn't mean to scare you."

"No, no. It's okay." She knew her cheeks were burning and that she looked as disconcerted as she felt. "I was a million miles away."

"I hope the daydream was worth the trip."

His eyes were unbelievably blue against his dark tan, and they were ringed with thick, brown lashes, gilded on the tips. His teeth flashed whitely. He smelled wonderfully of soap and an elusive and expensive cologne. Apparently he intended to let the sun dry his hair. Damp strands lay rakishly on his forehead.

Because of what she'd been thinking, Arden didn't want to see him as a man with a face and a body. A handsome face. A sexy body. Her cheeks burned as she thought of that life-generating injection Ron had made into her body. She looked away, wetting her lips nervously. "It wasn't really a daydream," she said lightly, dismissively, she hoped. "Just musings. The surroundings are hypnotic. The lull of the surf. The sighing of the wind. You know."

He relaxed in the chair across from hers. He was wearing ivory-colored slacks and a navy polo shirt. He took a long drink from one of the glasses of ice water and said, "Sometimes I can go down to the beach in front of my house, particularly in the evenings, and sit for an hour or more without ever knowing that time has passed. It's like sleeping, except I'm not asleep."

"I think our minds have a way of shutting down when they know we need escape."

"Ah-ha, so that's what you were doing? Trying to escape me."

Arden laughed, thinking that no woman in her right mind would want to escape a man who looked like him when he smiled. "No. Not before you buy my lunch, anyway," she teased.

"That sounds like Matt. He demands a treat before he grants a hug and a kiss." When he saw her startled expression, he cursed under his breath. "Arden, ah...hell. Arden, I didn't mean that the way it sounded. There are no strings attached to this lunch. I mean..."

"I know what you meant," she said, smiling again. "And I didn't take offense. Truly."

He partially lowered one eyelid as he assessed her mouth, making no secret of the fact that it appealed to him. "It bears thinking about, though, doesn't it? Kissing, that is."

"I don't know," she said gruffly.

She had debated all morning over what to wear. Now she wished she hadn't been quite so adventurous. For months after Joey's death, she had wallowed in misery, letting herself become slovenly. Before she embarked on this mission, she had exercised diligently, begun eating right, worked on her nails, her complexion, had her hair cut and bought a new wardrobe of coordinates that stretched her limited budget. She was amazed at the results. Had Ron repressed her that much? She looked better than she ever had. That day was no exception.

The black, elasticized, strapless tube top clung provocatively to her breasts, detailing every nuance of their shape. The trim white skirt was fashionably cut and buttoned down the left side from waist to hem. She'd left the buttons undone halfway up her thigh. Her legs looked tanned and silky against the white cloth. Her sandals were flat-heeled black patent leather and had thongs that wrapped around her ankles. Her only jewelry was a white bangle bracelet and large white hoops in her ears.

Standing in front of the mirror in her room, she had thought she looked smart. Smart and chic. Why was she now feeling she had dressed seductively?

Because Drew's eyes, taking a long, appraising tour with evident appreciation for everything he saw, made her feel seductive. She knew he could detect the hardening of her nipples. She'd never thought of herself as a sensual person, but now, with those azure eyes lazily tracking her, every sensory receptor in her body seemed to be going wild.

"Maybe we should start with lunch and go on from there," he said when his eyes eventually returned to hers.

"All right."

Chapter 3

He escorted her to one of the restaurants in the resort. With a deference reserved for VIPs, the maître d' seated them at an ocean-view table. Though the luncheon diners were dressed in casual clothes for the most part, there was an underlying elegance to the room with its mint-green and peach décor, black lacquered chairs and vases of fresh flowers scattered throughout.

"Cocktails, sir?" the waiter asked.

"Arden?"

"A virgin Mary, please."

"Perrier and lime," Drew said to the waiter, who backed away with a silent nod.

Drew reached for a bread stick, snapped it in two and handed her one half. "Did you order that on my account?" he asked in clipped tones.

"What?" She bristled at his curtness. "The drink?"

"The drink that isn't really a 'drink.' If you want something else, order it." He had the appearance of a tightly wound coil about to spring. "I promise not to grab it from you and guzzle it down. I'm past the sweating-and-shaking stage." As though to prove that, he was taking inordinate care in buttering his half of the bread stick.

Arden set her bread stick on the plate and folded her clenched hands in her lap. "I'll order what I please, Mr. Mc-Casslin." Her frigid declaration brought his head up. "If anyone knows your name, he knows you had a drinking problem. But please don't talk to me like I'm some missionary who has appointed herself to rescue you from demon rum. If I didn't think you were past your sweating-and-shaking stage, I wouldn't be here with you in the first place."

"I've made you mad."

"Yes, you have. And I'll thank you never to do my thinking for me again."

The waiter brought their drinks and placed menus in front of them. Arden stared levelly at Drew across the table. She was nettled and was making no secret of it.

"I'm sorry," he said when the waiter withdrew. "I'm sensitive to criticism, even though lately I've deserved every word of it. I've become the classic paranoid, looking for slights when none are there."

She was studying the pattern of the silver and cursing herself for being so prickly. Did she want to win his friendship or scare him off? When she lifted her green eyes, they had softened considerably. "I'm sorry, too. For years I let my husband do my thinking and speaking for me. It's a dangerous rut for a woman, or anyone, to get into. I think we touched sore spots at the same time." Diplomatically, she smiled and lifted her glass. "Besides, I *like* tomato juice."

Laughing, he raised his own glass and clinked it against hers. "To the loveliest lady on the island. From now on, I'll take everything you say or do at face value."

She wished he had composed another toast, one that had less to do with honesty, but she smiled back at him.

"What do you like to eat?" He opened the embossed menu.

"Name it."

"Liver."

She burst out with a spontaneous laugh. "That's the one thing I *won't* eat in any form or fashion."

His grin was wide and white and wonderful. "Good. I can't stand the stuff, either. I think this friendship was predestined."

As Arden scanned the menu, she couldn't help thinking that Matt would probably grow up hating liver, too.

She ordered a shrimp salad that was served in a fresh pineapple boat garnished with avocado and orchids. It was almost too pretty to eat. Drew had a small fillet and garden salad. During lunch, they got acquainted. When asked, Arden told him that her parents were dead, that her mother had died while Arden was studying creative writing at UCLA and that her doctor father had died of a stroke a few years after that. She went into no details, especially on her father's gynecological practice.

Drew had grown up in Oregon, where his mother still lived. His father had died some years before. Drew had begun playing tennis in junior high school.

"That was before very many public schools had tennis teams. When the coach saw that I had a knack for the game, he asked me to be on the new team he was setting up. I really preferred baseball, but he kept pressuring me, so I gave in. I soon became obsessed with getting better. By the time I got to high school, I was winning local tournaments."

"But you went on to college."

"Yes, much to the consternation of my manager, Ham

Davis, who took me on in my sophomore year. Exams were always getting in the way of practice and play, but I knew my body wouldn't let me play tennis, at least not competitively, the rest of my life, so I thought I'd better prepare for the day when I couldn't."

"You caught up, though, didn't you? Once you started playing the circuits, you were an instant winner." She plopped the last chunk of papaya into her mouth. They had ordered fresh fruit compotes for dessert and were finishing them and sipping coffee.

"I had some good years." He shrugged modestly. "I had the advantage of a few years' maturity, too, and didn't stay out all night and carouse like some players do the first time they tour." He took a sip of coffee. "The system is unbalanced. When you first start out, it's expensive as hell. Transportation, lodging, food. Then, when you make it, when you're winning prize money and getting endorsement contracts, everything's paid for."

He shook his head, laughing. "I risked losing some valuable contracts when even the best of tennis shoes couldn't keep me from stumbling onto the court after a drinking binge."

"You'll get them back."

His head came up to search her eyes. "That's what Ham says. Do you really think so?"

Was her opinion so important to him, or did he need any form of encouragement? "Yes. Once they see you play the way you've been playing, once you've won a tournament or two, you'll be back on top."

"There are younger guys every day to take my place."

"Can't hold a candle," she said with a dismissive wave of her hand.

He smiled crookedly. "I wish I had your confidence in me."

"Uh, Mr. McCasslin, excuse us, but…"

A dark scowl wrinkled Drew's thick blond brows as he turned in his chair to see the couple standing timorously behind him. They wore matching Hawaiian shirts in a gaudy floral print and labeled themselves tourists in myriad, unmistakable ways. "Yes?" At best, Drew's greeting was chilly.

"We…uh…" The lady hesitated. "We were wondering if you'd give us your autograph for our son. We're from Albuquerque, and he's just now getting into tennis, and he thinks you're wonderful."

"He has a poster of you in his room," the man said. "He—"

"I don't have anything to write on," Drew said, and rudely turned his back on them.

"I do," Arden chimed in, noticing the embarrassed, discomfited expressions on their sunburned faces. She reached into her bag and took out the tennis ball Drew had tossed her from the court. "Why don't you sign this for them, Drew?" she suggested softly, extending the ball to him.

At first, his eyes were hooded and rebellious, and she thought he might very well tell her to mind her own damn business. But when he saw the gentle chastisement in her eyes, he smiled and reached for the ball. Taking the pen the woman had found in her purse, he scrawled his signature on the fuzzy surface of the tennis ball.

"Thank you so much, Mr. McCasslin. I can't tell you what this souvenir will mean to our son. He—"

"Come on, Lois, and let the man enjoy his lunch. We hated to bother you, Mr. McCasslin, but we just wanted to tell you we can't wait to see you play again. Good luck."

Drew stood and shook hands with the man and kissed the

lady's hand, an action that almost caused her to faint, if her fluttering eyelashes were any indication. "Good luck to your son, too. Have a nice vacation."

They ambled away, studying their precious souvenir and murmuring how nice he'd been and that all those reporters who said he was nasty and belligerent were wrong.

Drew looked over at Arden, and she prepared herself for a blistering put-down. Instead, his voice was husky when he asked, "Are you finished?" When she nodded, he put his hand under her elbow and helped her from her chair. They left the restaurant and didn't speak until they were wending their way through the landscaped pathways that connected the various buildings of the resort.

"Thank you," he said simply.

She stopped on the path and looked up at him. "For what?"

"For subtly warning me that I was behaving like a bastard."

She found his eyes too compelling to look into, so she studied the third button on his shirt, but was instantly distracted by the wedge of chest hair above it. "I shouldn't have interfered."

"I'm damn glad you did. You see, that's another thing I'm overly sensitive about. For months after Ellie died, I was hounded by reporters for a 'comment' every time I stuck my nose out the door. Soon I became furious whenever someone even recognized me in public."

"I can imagine that having such a high public profile can be trying." What did that hair feel like to touch? It was a gorgeous golden color against his tanned skin.

"Under the best of circumstances it's trying. Under the worst, it's hell. When I was at my lowest, I had crowds jeering at me from the spectator stands, throwing things at me because I was playing so badly. Irrationally, I blamed them. My fans were deserting me because I drank, and I drank because my fans were deserting me. It was a vicious cycle. I'm still wary when people approach me, thinking they may very well have an insult to throw in my face."

"What I just witnessed was nothing short of unabashed hero worship." Forcing her eyes away from his chest and her mind from the erotic thoughts it incurred, she looked up at him. "You've still got thousands of fans just waiting for you to get back on the circuit."

He stared down into her sincere face for a long while and almost got lost in the swirling green depths of her eyes. She smelled of flowers. She looked both cool and assured, yet warm and giving. He raised his hand, intending to touch the sable hair that blew gently against her cheek, but changed his mind and dropped it back to his side. At last, he said, "Meeting you is one of the nicest things that's happened to me in a long time, Arden."

"I'm glad," she said, meaning it.

"I'll walk you to your room."

They went through the lobby of the main building. At the elevator, he said, "Wait here for me. I'll be right back."

Before she could wonder what he was doing, he had dashed off. She punched the up button but had to let two empty elevators go before he came running back carrying something wrapped in white paper. "Sorry," he said breathlessly. "Which floor?"

They took the elevator up, and Arden's female curiosity over his package was killing her. His eyes were dancing. If this was to be a surprise, she wasn't going to spoil it for him.

At her door, she stuck out her hand. "Thank you for a lovely lunch."

He didn't take her hand. He unwrapped the paper and

shook out a plumeria and orchid lei. Dropping the wrapping negligently on the hallway floor, he held the lei over her head.

"You've probably been presented with dozens of these since you've been here, but I wanted to give you one."

The heady fragrance of the flowers and his nearness made oxygen scarce. Her senses reeled. Emotion congested her throat, but she managed to strangle out, "No. I've never had one. Thank you. The flowers are beautiful."

"You enhance the flowers."

He slipped the ring of perfect blossoms over her head and settled it gently on her bare shoulders. The fragile petals were dewy and cool against her skin. He didn't withdraw his hands but laid them lightly on her shoulders. Confusion and conflicting emotions swamped her, and she bowed her head.

The man and everything about him overwhelmed her, filled her head, her heart. He subjected her body to a lethargy that was foreign, but so delicious. She longed to succumb to it and sag against his hardness. The flowers lying on her breast trembled with her erratic heartbeat. Tentatively, she touched them with palsied fingers.

In her peripheral vision, she saw his fingers reaching toward hers, and then they brushed, touched, entwined. His were dark with springy golden hairs on the knuckles. They were warm, sure, strong. She raised her head and looked at him with eyes as dew-sparkled as the flowers.

"Aloha," he whispered. He leaned down and kissed her first on one cheek, then the other. He rested his lips against the corner of hers. There, with his beard-roughened cheek lightly touching her, he sighed her name. "Arden."

His thumbs traveled over her collarbone, while his breath fanned her temple and teased her ear. "Now that lunch has been dispensed with..."

Oh, no! she groaned silently as her heart sank. *Here comes the sleazy proposition.*

He pulled back and released her shoulders. "How about dinner?"

Even as she dressed for the evening, she knew she should have begged off when Drew asked her for the date. It would have been logical for her to have said, "I'm sorry, and it sounds wonderful, but I should stay here tonight and work on an article."

Instead, she had heard herself say, "I'd love to, Drew." He had smiled and turned toward the elevator. She had entered her room in a cloud of romantic feeling. It hadn't taken long, however, for her to remember why she had contrived to meet Drew.

For a few minutes, while his hands had been touching her and his breath stirring her hair, she had forgotten her son. She had been thinking of Drew not as her son's father but solely as a man, a man she realized she was dangerously attracted to.

After her dismal marriage and hideous sex life with Ron, she had thought she'd never be interested in having a relationship with a man again. It came as a shock to her how much she was anticipating another few hours in Drew's company. And for all the wrong reasons.

It would have served her purpose better had Drew not been so sexually appealing…and widowed…and lonely himself. Wouldn't it have made her task less complicated to find her child's parents both alive and well, the father a jolly sort? Short, soft, round and balding? At the outset, the looks and personalities of the couple hadn't been a factor. She'd been interested only in locating the child she'd given birth to but had never seen. It hadn't been easy.

It was like opening a wound every time she remembered the gray, rainy day she had buried Joey. Never in her life, not even after the deaths of her father and mother, had she felt so alone. After obtaining her divorce, she had devoted herself to taking care of Joey. For the last few months of his life, he had been hospitalized. She watched him deteriorate with each day and struggled against praying for the death of another child so Joey might have the needed kidney. God couldn't be expected to grant such a prayer, so she never actually verbalized it.

When at last the time came, he had died as sweetly as he had lived, asking her please not to cry, saying that he would save her a bed next to his in heaven. For hours after he'd breathed his last, she held his thin hand in hers and stared into his peaceful face, memorizing it.

Ron had put on a performance of abject grief at the funeral service for those few of his friends who had attended. Arden was sickened by his hypocrisy. Valiantly, Joey had hid his disappointment each time Ron failed to come to the hospital to see him, as promised.

After the funeral, Ron cornered her. "Do you still have any of that money you screwed me out of?"

"That's none of your business. I earned that money."

"Goddam you, I need it."

She couldn't help noticing that the ravages of dissipation were becoming more and more pronounced. He wore desperation like a banner. It generated not the least amount of compassion in her.

"That's your problem."

"For God's sake, Arden. Help me. Just this once, and I promise—"

She had slammed the limousine door in his face and demanded that the driver leave immediately. Even at his son's funeral, Ron's thoughts were only for himself.

For the next several months, she was so immersed in grief that she didn't know one day from the next. She lived in a vacuum of despair. Only on paper could she communicate her feelings, reconcile herself to them. An essay she wrote on losing a child was sold to a ladies' magazine, and it won public acclaim. She was asked to write others but had no ambition to do so. She felt that she was only filling time until her own death, for she had nothing else to live for.

Except that other child.

It came to her quietly one day. She *did* have a reason for living. Somewhere in the world, she had another child. It was at that point she made up her mind to find it. Never was it her intention to disrupt the child's life. She wouldn't be that cruel to parents who had gone to such great lengths to get that child. She only wanted to see it. To know its name, its sex. She had asked Ron to give her anesthesia just before the moment of delivery so she'd never remember the birth itself or inadvertently learn anything about the child she had borne for someone else.

"What do you mean there are no records?" she had demanded in frustration on her first attempt to gain information.

The administrator's face remained unperturbed. "I mean, Mrs. Lowery, that your records seem to have been misplaced and I've yet to locate them. In a hospital this size, these things happen."

"Especially when an influential doctor asks you or pays you to 'misplace' a file. And my name is Ms. Gentry!"

It was the same story everywhere. Birth records both at city hall and at the hospital had mysteriously disappeared.

But to Arden it was no mystery at all who was responsible for such a puzzling loss of efficiency.

She didn't know the attorney who had drawn up the official papers. But he had to have been hired by Ron and therefore wouldn't tell her a thing if she found him. Ron, guessing correctly that after Joey's death she'd feel compelled to locate her second child, had gone before her, putting everyone involved on guard against feeding her one scrap of information.

The obstetric nurse who had helped her through her labor was her last resort. She found the nurse working in a charity clinic that specialized in abortions.

Arden could detect her fear immediately when the nurse spotted her as she left the clinic one afternoon. "Do you remember me?" Arden began without preface.

The nurse's furtive eyes darted around the parking lot as though looking for some means of escape. "Yes," she whispered fearfully.

"You know what happened to my baby," Arden guessed, intuitively knowing the statement to be a fact.

"No!" Earnest as the answer was, Arden knew she was lying.

"Miss Hancock," she pleaded, "please tell me anything you know. A name. Please. That's all I ask. Just a name."

"I can't," the woman cried, and covered her face with her hands. "I can't. He…he watches me, told me that if I ever said anything to you, he'd tell them about me."

"Who watches you? My ex-husband?" The woman jerked her head up and down in confirmation. "What is he using to blackmail you? Don't be afraid of him. I can help you. We can turn him over to the police—"

"No! My God, no. You don't…" She choked back racking sobs. "You don't understand. I was on…I had a little trouble with Percodan. He found out about it. He had me fired from the hospital, but got me a job here. And…" Her narrow shoulders shook. "And he said if I ever told you anything, he'd turn me over to the police."

"But if you're clean now. If you…" Arden's voice trailed off when she read the guilty admission in the woman's shattered face.

"Not just me. My old man would die without…his medicine. I have to get it for him."

It was useless to pursue that channel. Arden sank back into a black pit of self-pity and despair. One day bled into another with no real differences between them. That was why she was sitting on her living-room sofa staring vacantly into the television screen one Saturday afternoon. How long she'd been there, she didn't know. What she was watching, she couldn't have said.

But suddenly something caught her attention. A face. A familiar face the camera loomed toward. And just as closely, Arden's brain focused on it. Shaking off the leaden depression, she turned up the volume on the set. The program was a sports show. The day's featured event was a tennis tournament. Atlanta? Somewhere. Men's singles match.

She knew that face! Handsome. Blond. Broad white grin. Where? When? The hospital? Yes, yes! The day she left with nothing but a purse with fifty thousand dollars cash in it. There had been a commotion on the outside steps. Reporters with microphones and cameras. Television crews crawling over the marble steps for better vantage points.

They were all there to see the beautiful couple leaving the hospital with their new baby. The tall blond man with the dazzling smile had a protective arm around his petite, equally blond wife, who was holding a squirming bundle of flannel. Arden remembered the joy they radiated and had known a stab of envy at the loving way the man smiled down at the woman and child. Tears had blurred her eyes as she shoved her way through the crowd toward the taxi that had been called for her. She had refused Ron's offer to take her home.

She hadn't thought of that scene until then. And *this* was the man. She listened to what the commentator was saying as the man's body arched into his serve.

"Drew McCasslin seems to be making a heroic effort here today after his crushing defeat in Memphis last week. We've seen a steady decline in his performance over the past several months."

"Much of that has to do with the personal tragedy he suffered this year," another off-camera voice said charitably.

"No doubt."

Drew McCasslin lost the point, and Arden read on his lips a vile expletive that should never have been televised. Apparently the director thought so, too. He picked up another camera angle that showed McCasslin at the baseline, concentrating on the ball he was bouncing methodically. The serve was brilliantly executed, but the line referee called it out.

McCasslin axed his aluminum racket against the court and lunged toward the referee's high chair shouting vicious curses and insults. The television network judiciously went into a commercial break. After the virtues of an American-made car had been touted, they rejoined the match.

Arden hung on to every word as the commentators smugly excused McCasslin's behavior as a result of his grief over losing his wife in a grisly automobile accident in Honolulu, where the couple lived with their infant son. McCasslin played, surly and belligerent, and lost the match.

Arden went to bed that night thinking about the professional tennis player and wondering why she was so intrigued by him, having only seen him once. It came to her in the middle of the night that she *had* seen him more than once. She sat bolt upright in bed, her heart racing, her mind spinning out of control. She couldn't grasp the thoughts before they eluded her.

Slinging off the covers, she paced the room, pounding her temples with agitated fists. "Think, Arden," she commanded herself. "Think." For some reason, it was terribly important that she remember.

With agonizing slowness, the pieces fell into place. She'd been in pain. Lights, moving lights. That was it! She was being rolled down a hospital corridor on a gurney, and lights flashed by overhead. She'd been on her way to the delivery room. It was almost over. All she had to do was deliver the baby and she'd be free of Ron forever.

She'd seen the couple out of the corner of her eye as she was pushed past a shadowed hallway. The light had caught on their two blond heads. She'd turned her head slightly. Neither of them noticed her. They were smiling, clinging to each other happily, whispering excitedly and secretively. What was wrong with that picture? Something, but what? *What?*

"Remember, Arden," she whispered as she slumped down on the side of the bed and clasped her head with both hands. "They were happy just like any other couple having a baby. They—"

Everything stopped at once. Her breathing. Her heartbeat. Her whirling thoughts. Then they started up again, sluggishly, gaining momentum as the dot of light at the end of a dark tunnel grew larger until the conclusion blasted into her mind. *The woman hadn't been pregnant!*

She hadn't been in labor. She'd been standing out in the hall talking in excited whispers with her husband. They had

had about them an air of secrecy, like children plotting a marvelous prank.

The McCasslins were wealthy. They were recognized worldwide. He was handsome, as Ron had said the father of her baby was. They had left the hospital with a newborn child the same day Arden had left.

She had had their baby.

Arden wrapped her arms around herself and rolled back and forth on the bed in solitary celebration. She knew she was right. She had to be. All the pieces fit.

She sobered considerably as she remembered the other fact she'd learned that day. Mrs. McCasslin was dead. Arden's son—the sports announcers had said Drew McCasslin had an infant son—was being reared without the loving care of a mother and by a father who wasn't mentally or physically stable.

Drew McCasslin became Arden's obsession. For months, she read everything she could about him, past and present, spending hours in the public library poring over microfilms of sports pages that featured stories about his heyday. Daily, she read of his decline.

Then, one day, she read that he had gone into semiretirement. His manager was quoted as having said, "Drew knows his game has slipped. He's going to concentrate on restoring it and spending time with his son at their new home on Maui."

That was when Arden had begun planning to go to Hawaii to somehow meet Drew McCasslin.

"And now that you've met him, what are you going to do about him?" she asked her mirror image.

She hadn't counted on being susceptible to his charm and good looks. "Remember why you're here, Arden. Stay objective," she told her reflection.

But it mocked her from the mirror. She didn't look like a woman striving for objectivity. The strapless jade silk dress did nothing to disguise her figure. The fuchsia belt encircled a trim waist and drew attention to the round curves above and below it. The cream-colored blazer she wore over the sheath only made more suggestive the expanse of bare shoulders it covered. She was wearing the lei instead of jewelry. The flowers almost matched the color of her belt. She had pulled her hair back into a neat chignon, but its severity was compromised by wavy tendrils that had escaped to lie on her neck and to form a soft brush of bangs over her forehead.

The woman who looked back at her with smoky green eyes looked like a prime candidate for a tempestuous love affair.

"My God," she whispered as she pressed cold, trembling fingers to her forehead. "I've got to stop thinking of him this way. I'll ruin everything. And I've got to stop him from thinking of me as a…a…woman."

He would need discouraging. She knew that with every feminine instinct she possessed.

He had loved his wife. Probably still did. But everything about him spoke of intense virility. He wasn't the kind of man who could live without a complementing feminine presence for long.

The electricity between them—and she could no longer convince herself that it wasn't there—threatened her plan. The plan had been to meet him and win his confidence as a friend. When she had proved she didn't mean to threaten his relationship with his son, she would tell him who she was and make her request. "I would be forever grateful if you'd let me see my son now and then."

Hold that thought, she told herself when she heard his knock on her door. *Objectivity,* she reminded herself, and resolved to put away any other thoughts about Drew McCasslin.

It was impossible, however, to keep that promise to herself when he looked so handsome in tailored navy slacks, a beige sport coat that was almost the same color as his collar-length hair and a baby-blue shirt that matched his eyes.

Those eyes were doing their fair share of looking. They went all the way from the top of her head to the heels of her lizard sandals and back up again. They stopped short of her face and paused in the vicinity of the lei. Arden got the distinct impression they weren't looking at the blossoms but at the shape of her breasts beneath them.

"You do a lot for those flowers," he said in a gravelly voice that confirmed what she had suspected.

"Thank you."

"You're welcome." Only then did he lift his eyes to hers and smile. "Ready?"

Chapter 4

They had dinner dates each night after that for the next three. Arden knew she was making the difficult impossible, but couldn't bring herself to refuse his invitations. She and Drew were growing closer, true, but in the wrong way. There was no room in her scheme for romance. So, on the fourth night, she begged off, using the lame excuse of working on her article about the chances of tropical-plant survival in less tropical climes, an article she'd already mailed.

Instead of directing her thoughts away from Drew, she spent that evening wondering where and with whom he was having dinner. Was he home with Matt? With a friend? With another woman? She doubted it was the last. When they were together, she held his undivided attention.

"Am I moving too fast, monopolizing your vacation time, horning in on someone else's territory?" he had asked when she declined his dinner invitation. The question was spoken lightly, almost jokingly, but she knew by the frown wrinkling his eyebrows that he was serious.

"No, Drew, it's nothing like that. I told you the day I met you, there is no one I'm accountable to. It's just that I think we might need a night away from each other. I don't want to monopolize your time, either. And I really do have work to do." Skeptically, grudgingly, he had accepted her refusal.

She was terrified of what was happening to her each time they were together. She was flirting with disaster and knew it well, but the hours she wasn't with him had become colorless and monotonous. He had never kissed her except for that one time when he gave her the lei. Beyond common courtesies, he never touched her. Yet he made her feel giddy and young and beautiful. All those emotions were symptoms of falling in love. And that simply couldn't be. She had come to Maui to see her son. That was her main goal, and Drew McCasslin was only the means to that end.

Still…

The morning after their evening apart, she meandered in the direction of the tennis courts, swearing to herself that she wasn't going there to see him. He might not even be playing.

He was guzzling Gatorade when he spotted her. He tossed the bottle to Gary and trotted over to her.

"Hi. I was going to call you later. Dinner tonight? Please."

"Yes."

His rapid-fire invitation and her spontaneous acceptance surprised and delighted them both. They laughed together softly, shyly, all the while drinking in the sight of each other.

"I'll pick you up at seven-thirty."

"Fine."

"Are you going to watch me play?"

"For a while, then I must go back to my room to work."

"And I promised Matt I'd play with him on the beach."

Whenever he mentioned the boy's name, her heart lurched with eagerness. "I'm not keeping you away from him too much, am I?"

"I don't leave in the evenings until he's bedded down for the night. He doesn't miss me. He makes sure I'm the second one in the house awake every morning."

She laughed. "Joey used to do that, too. He'd come into my bedroom and peel open my eyelids, asking if I was awake."

"I thought only Matt knew that trick!" They laughed together again; then he said, "I'm losing momentum. I need to get back, but I'll see you tonight."

"Play well."

"I'm trying."

"You *are*."

He winked at her before rejoining the patient Gary, who hadn't wasted his time, but had been flirting with their covey of spectators. Arden wondered if she looked like just another groupie to anyone observing her and Drew. The thought made her uneasy. *Was* she just another groupie?

She wasn't quite ready when Drew knocked on her door. Despite her subconscious thoughts about him all afternoon, she had become inspired and had worked fast and furiously on one of her articles. She'd barely allowed time for a bath and shampoo before he arrived.

She was still zipping the back of her dress as she raced for the door. "I'm sorry," she said breathlessly as she pulled it open. He was leaning indolently against the jamb as though she hadn't kept him waiting a full minute already.

He took in her flushed cheeks, stockinged feet and general appearance of disarray and smiled. "It was worth the wait."

"Come in. I'll be ready as soon as I get on my shoes and jewelry. Did you make reservations? I hope we don't lose—"

"Arden," he said, closing the door behind him and catching her by both shoulders. "It's okay. We've got plenty of time."

She took a deep breath. "Right. I'll slow down."

"Good." He laughed and released her. He took a cursory look around the room, finally focusing his gaze on her as she stepped into high-heeled sandals. Flattening one hand against the wall to brace herself, she lifted one slender foot to adjust the strap. Her movement was graceful, innately feminine and unconsciously provocative.

He took in the smooth length of silk-encased legs. The muscles of her calves were clearly, but softly, defined as she stood on the balls of her feet. They would fit in the palm of his hand perfectly, he thought.

Catching a glimpse of the weblike lace that bordered the hem of her slip, he smiled at the sheer womanliness of it. And as she leaned down, he couldn't help noticing the precious weight of her breasts filling and pulling taut the bodice of her dress. The deep V neckline revealed the shadowy velvet cleft between her breasts. Mentally, he placed his lips there and pressed them against the fullness on each side of it. Immediately aroused, he ordered his unwilling eyes to safer ground.

Her hair always seemed soft and touchable even when it was pulled back. That night she'd worn it loose, and his fingers tingled with the desire to caress the dark strands, to test their silkiness and then to see if her complexion was as soft as it looked. All over.

"There," she said, pushing herself away from the wall and going to the long, low bureau opposite the king-size bed.

Drew hadn't allowed himself to think about the bed, to

think about the alluring body he was examining so closely lying naked on that bed.

"Jewelry." She was rummaging through a satin travel jewelry carrier.

Her sleeveless dress was of some clingy, soft aqua material that conformed to nicely rounded but not overdeveloped hips. Anything she wore looked terrific, no matter how dressy or casual. He thought she could be wearing jeans and a sweatshirt and give them as much class as an *haute couture* ensemble. She'd also look great in nothing at all.

Damn! He was thinking about what he'd promised himself he wasn't going to think about.

Her fingers worked deftly to clip gold earrings onto lobes he now fantasized about touching with his tongue. His heart began to hammer when her breasts lifted and swelled above her dress as she raised her arms to clasp a slender gold chain around her neck.

"Here. Let me," he said unsteadily. He moved up behind her. For a moment, before his fingers took the ends of the chain from hers, they stared at each other in the mirror. Her arms were still raised, her breasts still high and voluptuous, the tender undersides of her arms displayed, making her pose both wanton and vulnerable.

She lowered her arms slowly as he took the chain from her hands and ducked his head to work the intricate clasp. When it was fastened, she hurried to move away.

"Wait." His hands gently held her. "Your zipper's stuck."

"Oh." She barely had enough air to utter the word. In her effort to make the sound, it came out as a soft exclamation.

With tantalizing slowness, he eased the zipper down. Air cooled the flushed skin of her back. Motionless, not daring to draw a breath and break the sensuous spell, she stood, letting him draw the tab of the zipper all the way to her waist.

His eyes, matching the leisureliness of his hand, charted its descent. The bare expanse of smooth skin let him know that there was no bra between her and the bodice of the dress.

Again, his eyes met hers in the mirror. They were dark and smoldering, like the purest of blue flame. And in her own eyes was the glassy sheen of desire.

His tense body radiated silent sexual messages. She knew that if she moved back but a fraction of an inch and let her hips brush the front of his trousers, she'd feel him hard and primed with passion. She doubted they would go to dinner. It was her decision.

But going to bed with Drew was out of the question. Bringing sexual involvement into this already untenable situation would be lunacy. And in some secret corner of her mind, she feared she might be disappointed. Or worse, he might be. Ron's scathing criticism of her sexual prowess haunted her.

It would be best to keep things on an even footing. Friendly. Wasn't it possible for a male and female to be nothing more than platonic friends? Wasn't that what she'd originally wanted from Drew McCasslin?

Wisely, judiciously, with cowardice, she lowered her head and shook it slightly. He got the message and pulled the zipper up. "A loose thread got caught. All done."

"Thank you," she said, stepping away.

She wasn't going to get off that easily.

"Arden?"

She picked up her purse before turning to face him. "Yes?"

"It's been a long time since I've been around feminine clutter, watched a woman I care for dress. I didn't realize until now how much I've missed living with a woman."

She looked away, out the wide windows where palm trees

were blackly etched silhouettes against an indigo sky. "Living alone has disadvantages for a woman, too."

He took a step closer. "Like what?" It was a low, urgent whisper.

This had to stop. And it was up to her to see that it did. She raised her eyes to his, forced them to twinkle mischievously and determinedly grinned a gamine smile. "Like not having someone around to unstick a zipper."

His disappointment in her answer showed in the slight relaxing of his shoulders, but he smiled a gracious surrender, alleviating the crackling tension in the room. "See? What would all you liberated women do without us?"

That cheerful, bantering mood stayed with them as he drove his Seville along Maui's narrow highways. The Kaanapali Beach area was one of the few developed regions on the island. It was studded with elegant hotels, restaurants and clubs.

Drew brought his car to a stop under the porte cochere of the Hyatt.

"Ever been in here?" he asked as he joined her on the curb after a valet had assisted her out of the car.

"No, but I wanted to see it before I went home."

"Prepare yourself. It's like no other hotel in the world."

That was readily apparent. Most other hotel lobbies had ceilings. This one did not. The ceiling of the lobby, which was many stories high, was a starry sky. The lobby was landscaped to represent a rain forest, profuse with tropical trees and blooming plants. When it did rain, the effect was true to life. The areas that were covered were elegantly decorated with huge Chinese vases that dwarfed even Drew. Priceless rugs and oriental antiques gave the hotel a palatial aspect without detracting from the casual, homey atmosphere.

They crossed the immense lobby, Drew giving her far too

little time to gaze into the elaborate shops and galleries before whisking her down a curved staircase into the Swan Court.

"I feel like a country bumpkin in the city for the first time. Is my mouth hanging open?"

"I like bumpkins," he said, and squeezed her waist. "And your mouth, like the rest of you tonight, looks delectable."

She was glad the maître d' chose that moment to escort them to a candlelit table beside the pond, where swans glided across the surface with the haughty disdain of royalty. As were most of the restaurants on the island, this one was open-air. It looked out on a small lake complete with waterfall and lava rocks.

The patrons were dressed in evening clothes, and Arden was glad she'd selected her dressiest dress to wear. Drew seemed to guess her thoughts. "Don't be too impressed," he whispered from behind his menu. "In the mornings, this room is swarming with people in swimsuits and thongs at the breakfast buffet."

She let the ambience of the room soak into her and was only vaguely aware of Drew signaling the waiter.

"Would you like wine with dinner, Arden?"

She met his challenging stare levelly. "Yes, thank you."

He ordered an expensive bottle of white wine. She refused to show her surprise. In all the time they'd been together, he'd never drunk anything alcoholic.

"I drink an occasional glass of wine at dinner," he said.

"I didn't ask."

"No, but you were probably wondering if I can handle it."

"I asked you once before not to do my thinking for me. You're a big boy. You know if you can 'handle' it or not."

"You're not afraid that I'll go on a binge and become drunk and disorderly?" He was teasing.

She tossed down her own gauntlet. Leaning toward him, she whispered, "Maybe I'd like you to become a little disorderly." Moths had an instinct for flying directly into flames.

Drew's eyes narrowed seductively. "It wouldn't take even a sip of wine to make me completely unruly."

She backed off before her wings could be singed. "But I trust you not to."

He allowed her retreat. The tone of his voice told her he was willing to change the subject. "You have every reason to be concerned. I've been drunk and disorderly more this last year than I've been sober. I don't think I'll ever live it down." He clenched his teeth as strongly as he clenched the fist that lightly thumped the tabletop. "God, I'd give anything to undo some of the things I did."

Arden was well acquainted with the frustration and self-loathing he was feeling. Decisions were made; decisions were regretted. Most were irrevocable. "We all make mistakes, Drew, and later wish we could redo it all. We can't. We have to live with our decisions." Her voice became painfully introspective when she added, "Sometimes for life."

He chuckled softly. "That sounds so defeatist, hopeless. Don't you think we're given second chances to make things right again?"

"Yes. Thank God, yes. I think we *make* our second chances. We either try to turn our mistakes around or learn to live with them."

"That's the loser's way. To give in."

"Yes. And you're a winner."

"I couldn't live with the garbage I'd made of my life. I had to do something about it."

"So did I," she muttered to herself.

"Pardon?"

Should she tell him now? Now? He'd brought up the

subject of personal failures and attempts to rectify them. He was doing that in his own life. Surely he'd understand her own desire to correct her mistakes. Wouldn't he? What if he didn't? What if he stormed out and left her alone and she never saw him again? She would never see Matt, either. No. Better to wait until after she'd at least seen her son once. Then she'd tell Drew she was Matt's mother. Then, not now.

She sat up straighter and flashed him a brilliant smile. "Why are we having this gloomy conversation? Here comes the wine. Let's not dwell on past mistakes tonight."

Their veal was scrumptious, as were all the dishes that went with it. They had only the one bottle of wine, and half of it was left when they finally brought the two-hour dinner to an end. Full and satisfied, yet feeling as light as a feather, Arden seemed to float up the staircase. She wasn't drunk on wine but on the romantic atmosphere and the magnetism of the man beside her.

At the lobby cocktail bar, a pianist was playing love ballads on a white baby grand. An ocean breeze swept through the lobby, stirring the leaves of the trees and carrying with it the perfume of pikaki and plumeria.

They paused beneath a softly glowing lamp. "Enjoy the dinner?" he asked, taking both her hands in his and swinging them back and forth.

"Um-huh." She was looking at his hair and wondering what it would feel like to run her hands through it, to twist it around her fingers when passion rendered her mindless. She contemplated his mouth. The most erotic scene she'd ever seen in a motion picture was a camera-close view of a man's mouth on a woman's breast. She remembered vividly the tender flicking of his tongue as it circled a dusky areola, the flexing of his cheeks as he gently sucked the nipple, the moist caress of his lips on the soft flesh. That was what looking at Drew's mouth brought to mind, and her whole body flushed hotly with the fantasy.

Ron had never taken time for such foreplay, and never asked what she'd like. She probably wouldn't have liked it with Ron. She thought she'd like it very much with Drew.

"What?"

"What?"

"Did you say something?" Drew asked. His eyes were scanning the features of her face, lingering on one a long while before moving to another.

"No," she whispered. "I didn't say anything."

"Oh. I thought you said something." He was studying her mouth now, and if she had blushed at her own fantasy, she would have disintegrated with embarrassment had she known where *his* fantasy placed *her* mouth. To safeguard his sanity, he pulled a curtain over the erotically detailed mental picture. "What would you like to do?"

"Do? I don't know. What do you want to do?"

Oh, God, don't ask! "Go dancing?"

"That sounds fun," she said, coughing lightly and making an unnecessary straightening gesture down the front of her dress. Activity. That was what they needed. When they stood still, they became absorbed in each other to the exclusion of everything else.

"There's a club downstairs. I've never been there, but we can give it a try."

"Fine."

He led her down yet another staircase, this one brass banistered and reminiscent of the turn of the century. Pushing open the tufted leather door, they were greeted by a smiling hostess, a blast of disco music, a rumble of conversation and laughter and a cloud of tobacco smoke.

Drew looked down at her in silent query. She looked up with the same question in her eyes. Simultaneously, they turned on their heels and went back up the stairs. They were laughing by the time they reached the lobby.

"We must be getting old," Drew said. "The music of that single piano sounds better to me."

"To me, too."

"And I don't want to shout to be heard." He leaned down and placed his lips on her ear to whisper, "I may say something I wouldn't want anyone else to hear." When he pulled back, the burning glow in his eyes reinforced the intimacy of his words. A shiver of excitement feathered up Arden's spine. "Would you like something to drink?"

She shook her head. "Why don't you show me the pool?"

Clasping her hand and linking their fingers, he led her out onto the terraced rock pathways that wound through a veritable Garden of Eden. The paths were lit by widely spaced torches. Their flames flickered drastically in the wind. The swimming pools were an architectural masterpiece built on several levels around a lava-rock grotto.

Arden responded appreciatively to everything he pointed out, but she didn't really care what he said or what she saw. It was marvelous to hear his voice near her ear, to catch the fragrance of his warm breath, to feel the protective strength of his hard body as he directed her footsteps with subtle movements. Her pulse seemed to beat with the pagan rhythm of the surf as it pounded the shore only yards away.

Lovers lurked in the shadows, embracing, whispering. It was tacitly understood that privacy was the goal of anyone walking through the garden at that time of night. And when Drew stopped and pulled her behind a sheltering rock draped with a clinging vine, she made no protest.

"May I have this dance?" he asked with mock formality.

She laughed, trying to keep a straight face as she answered, "Yes, you may." She walked into his arms, and for the first time since they met, she knew the thrill of holding him, of being held.

He held her in the traditional waltz position, his arm around her waist and their joined palms at shoulder level. Her hand rested on his other shoulder. They couldn't move much without sacrificing this precious, private space, and both knew the invitation to dance had been issued only to provide them with an excuse to hold each other. So they swayed to the rhythm of the mood music wafting from the piano in the lobby bar.

Minutes ticked by, and one song drifted into another, and still they clung together, their eyes never wavering from each other's face. Their bodies, looking deceptively serene, were raging on the inside, clamoring for closer contact, yearning and straining until finally her breasts brushed against his chest.

He uttered a small groan and closed his eyes in exquisite pleasure. When they opened again, hers had been shuttered by the most fragile, lavishly fringed eyelids he'd ever seen. He wanted to kiss them. Instead, he brought his hand up from her waist and increased the pressure on her back until first the delicate crests, then the full mounds of her breasts were flattened against his chest.

Her eyes opened slumberously, and she moved her hand from his shoulder to the back of his neck. Her fingers threaded through the adorably shaggy blond hair that lay on his collar. Never taking his eyes from hers, he brought the hand he held to his mouth and brushed the knuckles with his lips. Back and forth, he caressed that dainty ridge, leaving it moist with the vapor of his breath.

Gradually, he lifted her arm and placed it over his shoulder

and behind his neck. Then his hand glided down the underside of her arm, down her ribs and around to her back. He
drew her close.

"You know how hard it's been for me to keep my hands
off you, don't you?"

"Yes," she said throatily, responsively arching her body to
meet his.

"I've wanted so badly to hold you, Arden."

"And I've wanted so badly to be held."

"All you had to do was ask," he whispered before he
buried his face in her hair, nuzzling her with his nose and
chin and mouth. "You smell so good, feel wonderful. Your
complexion is beautiful. Honest to God, I've imagined every
inch of it. I've wanted to see you, touch you, taste you."

A tremulous sigh shook her whole body as she nestled her
face in the curve of his throat. Her hands tightened around
his neck, and she took a step closer. His rasping groan of ecstasy was emitted through tightly clamped jaws. One of his
hands stole down her back, paused briefly at her waist, then
lowered to conform to the curve of her buttocks. Without
separating himself from her, he managed to alternate their
feet until one of his legs rested between hers, one of hers
between his.

He was hard. And warm. So warm. Arden felt his heat
searing through their clothes, burning into her body and
melting it against his. Holding her still with one hand on her
hip, he rubbed himself against her. Her sharp, startled cry
was muffled against his shirtfront.

"I'm sorry, Arden. I don't mean to be crude, but God, it
feels so good."

"Drew—"

"Do you want me to stop?"

"Drew." She threw her head back to look boldly into his

face. "No." She shuddered. "No." Then, a bit hysterically, a bit deliriously, and quite desperately, she begged, "Kiss me."

His mouth came down on hers with the same kind of desperation she had voiced. It was a violent kiss, an explosive release of pent-up longing and withheld emotion. His lips ground into hers almost brutally, but she welcomed the rough caress, for she'd never felt more alive. She was a butterfly bursting free of a dreary chrysalis, a prisoner of despair and dark unhappiness seeing the light of life for the first time.

He lifted his head and looked down at her with shining blue eyes. His breath was ragged, labored. It matched hers. She could feel his rigid virility against that part of her that seemed to be throbbing with joy.

By an act of will, he controlled his raging impulses and let his hand come up to cradle her jaw with heartfelt tenderness. He ran the pad of his thumb along her bruised lower lip and frowned his regret. She smiled her forgiveness.

When next his lips met hers, it was with the merest touch. He skimmed over them with soft, moist lips whose comforting caresses became a gently building torment.

"Drew." His name was a plea from the bottom of her soul.

"I was rough. I didn't mean to be."

"I know."

"You make me wild with need of you."

"Take what you want."

A moan of animal pleasure rumbled in his chest as his mouth descended once again. His tongue was a sweet aggressor. It traced her bottom lip, bathing it with the nectar of his own mouth. She picked it up with her own tongue and murmured her approval. He placed his mouth against hers and opened his lips slowly. She did the same. For long moments, they waited there, savoring their expectation, their accelerated pulses, their aroused sexes.

Then his tongue pressed home, embedding itself snugly in her mouth. He withdrew, pressed again. Again and again, until Arden thought for certain she would die. She could feel her body flowering open, preparing for love. Her nipples grew hard and sensitive against the cool, sensuous cloth of her dress.

His kiss became playful. His tongue darted around her mouth. He teased, explored, stroked, probed, at varying tempos and angles and with such skill that she clung to him weakly and called his name softly when she had to tear her mouth free to breathe.

The heels of his hands inched up her ribs to find the sides of her breasts. With soft pressure, he squeezed them together. They nearly overflowed the V of her neckline, and he whispered accolades to them. He pressed hot kisses into the fragrant flesh. His tongue delved into the deep cleavage in a caress so evocative that Arden's body was washed with a delightful sense of shame.

She had needed this all her adult life. She had needed a man to show her what it was to be adored, loved for what she was, admired for her femininity. Not until she met Drew had she thought of herself as an attractive woman. From the beginning, his every look, every gesture, had told her he thought she was extremely sexy and desirable. He'd been honest and forthright about it from the beginning.

But she hadn't been.

What she was feeling now was pure and honest, but would he believe that later? When he learned she was Matt's mother, she would have so many things to answer for. Did she want to add luring him sexually to that list? The thought sickened her. She had to reverse this headlong plunge into sexual involvement immediately or forever be the object of his scorn.

"Drew," she murmured against his lips, which had returned to hers.

"Hmm?" He was lost in his caress.

"Drew," she repeated more stridently, and placed her hands against his shoulders. "Don't—" His hand was sliding beneath the strap of her dress, easing it down. She panicked. If she didn't stop this now, she wouldn't be able to. Her only resource was to make him angry. He was beyond reasoning with.

"Stop it!" She slapped his hand away and yanked herself free of his embrace.

His face registered total bewilderment. He blinked his eyes rapidly until he could focus on her clearly. She watched as his initial befuddlement changed to irritation. "All right," he said tightly, "you don't have to treat me like a disobedient child. I had every right to think you were enjoying my kisses."

She avoided looking at him. "Kisses, yes, but I'm not one of the groupies you—"

"Is that all you think this is?" He raked a hand through his hair and worked with frustrated, ineffectual fingers at his necktie. "Is it?" he demanded.

Angering him had been her intent, but she hadn't counted on contending with such a volatile temper. She stammered to explain. "I...I—"

"Well, okay, then, but what sets you apart from the others? Huh? You've been more than available, and there were no strings attached. What else was I supposed to think? Or are you different because you never intended to go 'all the way'? No sex, just spiritual support for my much-publicized lost soul." He was furious. "Was that it? Was I a charitable case you took on?"

Arden was finding it difficult to keep a leash on her own temper. "As I pointed out to you the first day, you approached me, not the other way around. As for taking you on as a 'case,' I don't care if you go straight to hell or drink yourself to death or stumble and fall on every tennis court in the world. I frankly doubt if you're worth saving."

He ignored her, cocking his head to one side as if seeing her in a new light. "Maybe you're not so different, after all. Groupies want to sleep with a celebrity to elevate their own egos. Was sleeping with me going to shore up your shattered confidence after a failed marriage?" He thrust his face to within an inch of hers. "What's the matter? Chicken out?"

Fury bathed her world red. "You conceited ass. I'm not some frustrated divorcée. I was all too glad to get rid of the man I had. And I'll think long and hard before wanting another one. And if my confidence *were* shattered, which it's not, it would take a lot more than sleeping with a washed-up tennis bum to restore it. You can keep what's in your pants, Mr. McCasslin. I've lived without it for thirty-one years. I think I can go at least another thirty-one."

She whirled away from him and stumbled down the darkened path. He caught up with her and growled, "You're going the wrong way."

She tried to wrench her arm free, but he wouldn't let her. She wasn't going to engage in an undignified tug-of-war, so she let herself be escorted through the lobby. They waited in hostile silence for his car to be brought around. Not one word was said on the drive back to the resort where she was staying.

"I can find my way, thank you," she said as she pushed open the door the instant he braked the car to a stop. Not looking back, she rushed to the elevator and to her room. He didn't follow her.

Only when her anger had been spent in a fit of door slamming, drawer rattling and cursing did she realize what she'd done.

Matt!

She had ruined all chances of meeting him now. Tears rolled down her cheeks in torrents, and she pledged to herself repeatedly that it wasn't for losing Drew but only for losing her son again.

Her eyes were puffy and burning when she tried to pry them open the next morning. She rolled over and burrowed her face in the pillow. When the second loud knock sounded on her door, she groaned, "Go away, maid."

A third knock, more imperious, shook the whole room. Arden cursed the maid's ambition. She saw that her only option was to go to the door and tell the maid to come back later.

She rolled out of bed, groping for the walls, since her eyes seemed to have been glued shut with tears. They came open wide when she peered through the peephole and saw Drew standing on the other side of the door. She watched as he knocked again. This time, he said, "Arden, open this door."

"Not on your life."

"So you *are* awake."

She appreciated his cheerful tone of voice as much as she would appreciate a splinter under her thumbnail. "I don't want to see you, Drew."

"Well, I want to see you. To apologize. Now open the door or everyone on this floor is going to hear an apology that will wake them up faster than a good strong cup of coffee."

She gnawed at her bottom lip while she weighed her options. She wasn't up to seeing him. The night before, he had been insulting, and she wasn't ready to forgive him. And even if she were, she knew she looked like the devil. Her eyes were probably red and swollen and her hair tangled. When she met him face-to-face again, she wanted to be at her haughtiest best.

On the other hand, she'd deliberately made him angry. No man, no matter how easygoing normally, could be expected to be in the best of humor after being sexually thwarted. She had spent half the night tearfully berating herself for letting her relationship with Drew jeopardize her chances of seeing Matt. Swallowing her pride was a small price to pay for that, wasn't it?

She flipped open the dead-bolt lock and opened the door a crack. "I'm not dressed."

"You're dressed," he said, taking in the collar and sleeves of her blue-and-white striped oxford-cloth nightshirt.

"If you insist on seeing me, I'll meet you in the lobby. Give me——"

"Haven't got the time." His grin was both devilish and winning. "Come on, Arden. Let me in."

Reluctantly, she opened the door and preceded him into the room. The door was closed softly behind him. He took in her dishabille in one lazy glance. Her bare feet and legs made her feel nervous and uncomfortable. The nightshirt wasn't revealing, but she suddenly wished the hem fell below the middle of her thighs. Self-consciously, she crossed her arms over her chest and tried to look bored.

"You're right. I'm a conceited ass." He brushed past her and went to the window, opening the drapes without her permission and flooding the room with a blinding sunlight that made her squint.

"I was acting like a horny teenager, grappling and grop-ing in the dark. Hell——" He sighed, rubbing the back of his neck "—no wonder you thought I saw you as no more than a groupie. That's how I was treating you. And when you said no, I don't know why I said the things I did. I didn't mean them. They weren't accurate, and I knew it." He glanced over his shoulder to see that her militant stance hadn't relaxed one iota.

"The only excuse I can offer," he went on, "is that soon after Ellie died, I was surrounded by women who thought they could cure me of my grief. I got the impression they saw themselves as some kind of sexual social workers out to save me from my self-destruction. And to them I'd be no more than a notch on the bedpost."

Arden lowered her arms and relaxed her posture. She'd had that same kind of response from men after her divorce. Friends of Ron's, divorced themselves, began calling, offering her their "help." "No, thank you," she had said until they finally gave up.

"Anyway," Drew was saying, "that's why I had to see you first thing this morning. The minute I pulled away from here last night, I knew I'd acted like a jerk. You should have kicked me in the groin or something."

"I thought about it."

He laughed. "Well, it might not have changed my mind immediately, but you would have gotten my attention."

She laughed, too.

"Now that we're friends again," he said hurriedly, clapping his hands together, "why don't you go over to Oahu with me for a few days."

"What—"

"Just a minute," he said, holding up both hands to ward off her objections. "There are still no strings attached. I'll only be there a few days. I've got a suite of rooms reserved. Maybe you'll get an idea for an article." It was a weak argument, but he was in a rush to convince her.

"But I can't just move out of here. I—"

"I'm not suggesting you do. Pack only what you'll need. We'll tell the manager that you'll be gone for a few days but want to keep the room."

He stepped closer and clasped her hands. "I like the way you look in that nightshirt," he said in a sexy drawl, "with your hair all mussed up and your cheeks blushing pink. You have the sweetest mouth I've ever tasted. And I really can't believe I was stupid enough to let a good thing like last night end so badly."

"You're a bully, did you know that? You have your nerve coming in here this morning after the things you said to me last night, telling me how good I look when I know I must look like hell." Her outburst made him smile, and that fueled her anger. "Do you always get your way?"

"I'm a competitor, Arden, and I like to win." The fierceness in his eyes told her she was his next goal. While she was held dumbstruck by his handsome appeal and the earnestness of his expression, he urged softly, "Come to Honolulu with me. We'll get to know each other better."

She wanted nothing more, but knew she was only letting herself in for more trouble. Taking a deep breath, she shook her head. "Drew, I don't think—"

"Please. Besides, it'll give you a chance to know Matt."

Chapter 5

Seconds ticked by while she stared at him speechlessly. The arsenal of arguments she had been stockpiling in her mind tumbled. Finally, she stammered, "M-Matt's going?"

"Yeah, he's the main reason we're going. It's time for a checkup at the pediatrician. He needs a booster shot. And Mrs. Laani was complaining the other day that he's growing so fast he doesn't have any clothes. She's planning an extensive shopping trip."

Arden's mind was thrown into chaos. It was going to happen! She was going to see her son, spend time, *days,* with him. For months, she had waited for this moment, dreamed about it, imagined how she'd feel. But the panic that seized her now was unpredicted. That was all she felt—cold, blind panic. Now that what she'd prayed for was here, she was terrified of it.

She began trying to talk her way out of it. "This is a family trip, and I wouldn't want to interfere. He…Matt might not like me. Mrs., uh, Laani, is it? She might resent your bringing a...me along."

"It *is* a family trip, but I happen to be the head of the family. Mrs. Laani lectures me on just about everything, including the deficiency of a nice—and I stress nice—lady in my life. She's eager to meet you. And Matt's only twenty months old. He loves anyone who feeds him." His hands cupped her head. "Please come, Arden. If I didn't think it was a good idea, I wouldn't have asked." His voice deepened perceptibly. "I don't want to be away from you even for a few days."

Oh, God, why wasn't she jumping up and down with glee? Why was she hesitating? Did she feel guilty? Was that the emotion that had a stranglehold on her heart and wouldn't let go to make room for others? Drew was gazing down at her with naked longing. He was looking at her as a woman he was growing romantically attached to, not as the surrogate mother he and his beloved wife had hired. How long could she go on tricking him?

"Drew, I'm not sure going with you is a good idea."

"Are you still angry about last night?"

"No, but—"

"I don't blame you for being mad. I said terrible, insulting things." His thumb stroked her cheekbone. "I was wrong, but everything you said was true. I behaved like an ass. I am conceited. I am accustomed to getting my way and am likely to throw temper tantrums if I don't. I am a washed-up tennis bum."

"No! That's not true. I said that to deliberately hurt. No other reason."

He sighed. "Whether it's true or not remains to be seen. What I am is a man who finds himself attracted to a woman when he never thought he'd feel that way again. I'm scared as hell of you, Arden, and of what I'm feeling. Don't make it so damn hard on me. I'm trying to adjust to being a human being again, to act like one and not like a wounded animal. Sometimes I have lapses. Last night was one of those times."

"I'm not playing coy, Drew."

"I know that."

"I wasn't last night, either."

He kissed her gently. "I know that, too."

"There's a reason why I shouldn't go."

"You've given me no reason. I don't think there is one. Not a valid one, anyway. Come with us. The plane leaves in an hour."

"What?" she gasped, shoving him aside and checking the digital clock on the bedside table. "An hour! Oh, Drew...I can't... Why didn't you say...I'll never get ready—" She stopped abruptly when she realized she'd just consented.

He laughed at her startled expression, and dropping down on the bed, picked up the telephone. "You'd better hurry. I'll call down for coffee."

By the time she stepped out of the shower, he was tapping on the bathroom door. "Room service." She eased the door open a crack and took a cup of coffee from him. "Thirty minutes," he said. "Want me to toss a few things in a suitcase for you?"

The thought of his handling her intimate garments set off a chain reaction that ended in a flush of warmth between her thighs. "No. I'll be out in a jiffy."

She sipped the coffee and tried to keep her hands from shaking while she applied her makeup. She told herself her jittery nerves were the result of a short, virtually sleepless night. But not a little of her tenseness had to do with standing naked only a few feet and one door away from Drew. And most of it had to do with the fact that in less than an hour she'd meet the son she'd carried for nine months but had never seen.

Drew was dressed in a pair of casual khaki slacks and a loosely woven white cotton sweater with wide sleeves that he'd pushed up to his elbows. Arden had taken a pair of raw silk slacks and a matching top with dolman sleeves into the bathroom with her. She wound her hair into a loose French braid down the back of her head and tucked the ends under at the nape. Not great, but the best she could do in a hurry.

When she came out of the steamy bathroom, she looked nervously toward Drew, who was slouched in a chair near the glass terrace door perusing the morning newspaper. He tipped down a corner of the paper to look at her and whistled long and low. "How'd you do that so fast? Take casual clothes, shorts, swimsuit, something to wear to dinner, but nothing fancy."

She began folding things into a shoulder bag, her mind clicking off the accessories that went with each outfit. She became all thumbs and butterfingers when she began packing her underwear into the bag. Though he still held the paper up in front of him, Drew's eyes weren't on the print. Arden could feel him watching her every move as she packed lacy panties and flimsy brassieres. When she shot him an accusing glare, he flashed her a broad, guileless grin.

"All set," she said as she zipped the bag, in which she'd managed to cram not only clothes but also makeup, jewelry caches and shoes.

"Amazing," he said, standing up and glancing at his wafer-thin watch. "And just on time. We're meeting Mrs. Laani and Matt at the airport. Mo, who takes care of the grounds of the house, is going to drive them. We'll take the resort's limo, if that's okay. I hated to leave my car at the airport for that long."

"That's fine." She set a natural-straw hat with a wide, floppy brim over her head and slid on large square sunglasses. "Remember, I'm accustomed to traveling on a shoestring budget."

"You certainly don't look like it," he said as he carried her bag down the hall toward the elevator. He took in every fashionable detail as they waited for the elevator. "I approve," he said softly.

"Thank you," she whispered back.

Once inside the cubicle, he said, "I forgot something."

"You left something in the room?"

"No. I forgot this." He bent his knees to put his height on a level with hers, tilted his head under the brim of her hat and slanted his mouth over hers.

His lips moved but a little, but she felt their sweet pressure all along her body. His tongue barely breached her lips to touch the tip of hers, but he could have been teasing her fingertips, her nipples, secret places deep inside her, for she felt the titillating caress in all those places.

When he pulled back, she was exceedingly warm and tingling. "You fogged up my sunglasses," she said in a husky voice.

"Sorry?"

She shook her head. He was well into a second kiss when the elevator door whooshed open. Flustered, Arden said, "I've got to make arrangements about my room."

"I'll save us a place in the limo."

She waded through the crowd at the concierge's desk. Naturally, it was jammed that time of day, with guests either checking out or checking in or making reservations for various excursions via land, sea or air to other parts of the island. She cast several anxious glances over her shoulder toward the front doors before it was finally her turn.

Hastily, she explained that she wanted to pay for the days she had occupied her room but wanted to keep it until she returned in three days. After repeating her request several times, she finally made herself understood over the hubbub. The harried clerk found her registration card, ran her credit card through his machine, smiled at her toothily, wished her a good trip and expressed his gratitude for her business. She felt uneasily that she'd been dismissed, but before she could get the clerk's attention again, Drew was calling to her.

"Arden, the limo's waiting."

"I'm coming," she called back, and made her way through the crowd until he clasped her hand and pulled her toward the door.

"No problems?"

"No."

"Good. We're barely going to make it."

Once they were seated in the limo and speeding toward the airport, she realized that in just a few minutes she would see her son. Her heart was pounding in her chest, and her breathing was shallow.

"You're not scared of flying, are you?" Drew asked, mistaking the source of her obvious nervousness.

"No. I don't mind flying, although I prefer the larger jets."

"I like the smaller airplanes because I can see more. Besides, this airport, such as it is, is only five minutes from home. And it's a good commuter airline. I know just about everyone on staff by now."

Kaanapali Airport, as Drew had said, wasn't much compared to major-city airports. The building was about the size of a self-service gas station. But it was a beehive of activity. As each plane landed and disgorged its nine passengers, another would be taking off.

The resort's van pulled up with a jarring halt. Drew hauled her bag onto his shoulder, stepped out ahead of her and offered her a hand to help her down.

"They should be somewhere... Ah, there they are." His chin lifted, indicating that Arden should look behind her. She drew in a great amount of air, squeezed her eyes shut momentarily and turned around. She had to lock her trembling knees to keep them from buckling under her. Drew hadn't noticed. He was walking away from her toward a grove of trees. "Matt," he shouted.

Arden saw him, and her heart turned over.

He was wearing a white shirt and a pair of bright red shorts with a bib and shoulder straps that crisscrossed over his back. White knee socks encased stocky calves. He had on white high-topped shoes. The pumping chubby legs came to a weaving halt when Matt heard his father's voice, and he turned around, squealed and came racing back in the opposite direction toward Drew. A woman in a white uniform, who was as wide as she was tall, came huffing along behind him on amazingly small feet for someone her size.

Arden had eyes only for the blond boy who almost toppled over in his excitement before he barreled into his father's legs and was swooped over the tall man's head.

"Hey, you little dynamo, slow down or you're going to skin your knees again," Drew said, shaking the boy, whose peals of laughter filled the morning air.

"Up, up," he shouted.

"Later," Drew said, swinging him down to hold him in the crook of his arm. "I want you to meet a lady. Arden," he said, turning to the pale, transfixed woman beside him, "this is Matt."

Her eyes were rapacious, trying to devour as much of him as she could. She searched for something familiar but found little. His coloring was his father's: blond hair, blue eyes. There was a squareness to his chin that reminded her a little of her father.

She saw none of herself, but she could not have been more certain that this was her son. She knew by the way her breasts expanded, as though filling with the milk that had never been allowed to come. She knew by the contracting of her womb as she remembered each time she felt the movement of a fist or a foot or laughed at a case of prenatal hiccups that echoed through her own body. She knew because of her yearning to touch him, to clutch his sweet, young, healthy body to her.

"Hi, Matt," she rasped out.

The child stared back at her with candid curiosity. "Say *aloha,* Matt," his father directed him, nudging his stomach.

"O-ha," he mumbled before turning in Drew's arms and shyly burying his face against his father's neck.

Drew closed his arms tight around his son and rubbed his back. He looked at Arden over Matt's blond curls. "We're still working on etiquette," he said, smiling apologetically.

"Mr. McCasslin, I thought I'd let him run off some energy before the airplane ride," the nurse panted as she came up to them.

"Good idea. Mrs. Laani, I want you to meet Ms. Gentry. She's our guest for the next several days."

"*Aloha,* Mrs. Laani," Arden said, dragging her eyes away from the soft skin on her son's nape. She used to tickle Joey there with her mouth. "Getting sugar," she called it.

The middle-aged Polynesian woman was eyeing her with open curiosity. She seemed to like what she saw, for her round, unlined face split into a broad grin.

"*Aloha,* Ms. Gentry. I'm glad you're coming with us. Sometimes two men are too much for me to handle."

"Fine," Drew said. "Your job is to handle Matt. Let Arden handle me."

Arden blushed beneath her hat, but Mrs. Laani laughed gustily. Arden liked her instantly. Despite her size, she was neat to a fault, her uniform crisply starched. Her hair was cut short and permanently curled to form a dark, silver-threaded wreath around her head.

One of the employees of the commuter airline stepped out onto the porch. "Mr. McCasslin, we're ready for your party to board now."

"Did you get all the luggage on board?" Drew asked the attendant, who checked them off the passenger list.

"Yes, sir, we sure did."

"Add this," he said, handing the man Arden's bag.

"I don't mind carrying it on board," she offered.

"No, ma'am," the attendant said. "The seats are too small. All luggage has to go in the back."

A man in shirtsleeves, whom Arden determined was their pilot, slapped Drew on the back. "When are you going to treat me to another match? I finally recovered from the last one." As they chatted, they made their way onto the tarmac to the waiting plane. Drew was still carrying Matt on his shoulders. Arden had yet to take her eyes off him. She was grateful that the confusion of boarding the airplane provided her with an opportunity to stare at him without anyone noticing.

Mrs. Laani's bulk could barely squeeze through the narrow door of the aircraft. She sank into one of the seats in the back so she wouldn't have to wedge herself through the aisle.

"Care to ride in the copilot's chair this morning?" the pilot asked Drew.

He grinned boyishly. "You know that's my favorite seat." He turned to Arden. "Do you mind sitting beside Matt?"

She shook her head, not trusting herself to speak. She took the window seat so Matt wouldn't feel so confined. Drew buckled him into the seat beside hers and just behind his. "There we go, hotshot. You can be the navigator, okay?"

Matt smiled, revealing eight pearly teeth. His excitement wavered when the pilot started the noisy engines. His back went ramrod straight, his eyes widened, and his lower lip began to tremble. Arden placed her hand on his knee, and when he looked up at her fearfully, she smiled. Drew turned around, winked at the boy and reached back to pat him on the head.

Matt sat still and stiff until the plane gained altitude and he was convinced he was in no immediate danger. Only one stranger had boarded the plane with them, and he had fallen asleep immediately. As had Mrs. Laani. Matt grew restless and strained against his seat belt. After first checking with Drew and the pilot, Arden released it.

"Just don't let him crawl around too much," Drew told her. "If he gets too rambunctious, pass him up here."

"No. He'll be fine." Drew went back to his conversation with the pilot, and she devoted her attention to Matt, as she had longed to do. In typical little-boy fashion he couldn't sit still. He twisted and turned in his seat, tried to stand up, wobbled unsteadily and sat back down. He investigated everything.

Arden watched each movement, adored it and savored it for the time when she'd have to leave him again. She hadn't made plans beyond this point, beyond getting to see her son. But she knew she couldn't uproot him from the life he had. She couldn't do that to his father, and she knew it wouldn't be best for Matt, either. For right now, she only wanted to love Matt, silently and secretly, but love him as only a mother could.

When she patted her lap, he paused for only a moment before climbing up into it. He studied her closely and reached out and poked the lens of her glasses with a damp fist.

"Thanks," she joked as she took the glasses off to clean the smudged lens. "Between you and your dad, I'm having a hard time seeing out of these."

He grinned and pointed toward the back of Drew's head. "Dad."

"Yes," she exclaimed, laughing. She touched his cheek and marveled at how soft it was. His hair, too, curled softly around her fingers. It was only several shades away from platinum, and as he grew older, it would darken to the wheat color of Drew's. Lovingly, she ran her hands over his dimpled arms and let him wrap tight, damp fists around her fingers. Quoting a nonsense rhyme, she made a game of squeezing his knees until he giggled. "A good child, a good child / As I suppose you be, / Will neither laugh nor cry / At the tickling of your knee."

When he didn't resist, she pulled him into her arms and held him close. She hugged him as tight as he'd allow. He smelled of baby soap and clean clothes and sunshine. Mrs. Laani took good care of him. He was spotless; his fingernails were well trimmed. Arden loved the sturdiness of his body. Joey had been so pitifully frail. When she left Matt, she'd leave knowing that he was healthy and normal.

And like any normal, healthy little boy, he rebelled against so much affection. He squirmed away from her, taking her hat off in the process. Playfully, she placed the hat on his head, and it all but swallowed him. They played peekaboo from under the floppy brim for a while. Inspired, she put the glasses on his nose. He had to hold his head still to keep them from slipping off, and she could see his eyes rolling back and forth behind the lenses to watch her as she took a compact from her purse. When she held the mirror up to him, he crowed with glee.

"Dad, Dad," he called, getting to his feet in Arden's lap and hitting Drew on the head. The hat and glasses were knocked askew, but Matt didn't notice.

Drew turned around and burst out laughing at the comical sight. "You look worse than E.T. in the wedding dress," he hooted. Matt bobbed up and down until he became a little too wild and had to be calmed down. When he eventually tired of the hat and glasses, Arden placed them in his chair and took him back on her lap.

The droning motors of the plane and her gentle maternal stroking of his hair lulled him, and soon his head was resting heavily on her breasts. She couldn't believe that she'd been blessed with this moment. It was more than she had allowed herself to hope for. He liked her, trusted her instinctively, enough to fall asleep against her.

She could feel the rapid beating of his heart against hers and thought of the irrevocable and eternal bond that bound them. There was none other like it in the universe, that between mother and child. Her body had nourished him, breathed for him, sheltered him. Emotion such as she'd never known welled up inside.

Drew glanced at them and did a double take when he saw the rapt attention Arden was giving his son. She was absorbed in the small hand she held in hers, massaging the tiny knuckles. As though she sensed him watching her, she raised her head, and he was further startled to see tears pooling in her eyes. She smiled at him tremulously, then once again lowered her eyes to the boy sleeping on her bosom.

The pilot landed the plane expertly and taxied toward the terminal. As soon as he cut the engines, he excused himself and hurried to the back of the aircraft to assist Mrs. Laani out. The other passenger left as soon as he located his briefcase.

Drew eased himself down on the edge of the seat next to Arden's. He studied her for a moment with probing blue eyes before he spoke. "I see you two have taken to each other."

"I hope so. He's dear, Drew. So dear. A wonderful little boy."

"I think so."

Lightly, she ruffled the blond curls. "Was he a good baby?"

"Ellie and I didn't have anything to compare him to, but we thought so. He was hard to come by. We wouldn't have cared if he'd squalled all the time."

Her next question would be like stepping off a high diving board into a vat of fire. The quantity of adrenaline that pumped through her veins was the same as if she were. "Ellie had a difficult time having him?"

There followed a significant pause. She continued to stare down at the sleeping child, noting each eyelash that rested on his flushed cheeks.

"Not exactly," Drew said slowly. "She had a hard time conceiving him."

"Oh." It relieved her conscience somewhat to know that Drew had chosen to lie, also. How far could she fish before he became suspicious? "Does he look like his mother?"

"Ellie was blond," he answered noncommittally. "I think he takes more after me, though."

Arden looked up at him then and smiled, though there were still tears in her eyes. "As a proud father, you're biased."

"I'm sure that has a lot to do with it," he answered with a hint of self-mockery. "I can't really tell how much he looks like his...mother."

Arden looked away again, quickly, before he could see her wounded expression. But he saw the tear that rolled down her cheek. Raising her head with a gentle fist under her chin, he lifted away the tear with his fingertip.

"Because of the son you lost?" The question was asked with such tenderness and compassion that a new, unnamed emotion blossomed in her chest. She was stunned by it. Stunned and frightened.

Now, now, she said to herself. He had presented her with the perfect opportunity to tell him that she had just now *found* her son, that she had borne this boy whose life Drew treasured. But the words wouldn't come. He might yank her son away and never let her see him again. He might think that she'd been using him all this time to get to her son.

Wasn't that what she had done?

No, no! She cared as much for the father now as she did for her child. She couldn't hurt Drew, not when he had just gotten his life back in order and regained his self-confidence. No. She couldn't tell him yet. Later. When the time was right, she'd know it.

"Yes," she said. "Because of the son I lost."

Drew nodded in understanding. Matt's breath whistled through his cherubic mouth. He had left a trickle of saliva on Arden's top.

"He's getting your blouse wet," Drew whispered in the still silence. He couldn't have honestly said which he found the most captivating, his son's sweet mouth or the sweet place it rested against. Her breast was plumped out from the weight of Matt's head and looked maternal and comforting, and he longed to touch it, to stroke its full softness.

"I don't mind." And she didn't. She didn't care if the child irreparably stained every garment she owned as long as she could continue to hold him.

Entranced, she watched as Drew's index finger reached toward his son's cheek. He brushed it lovingly, then moved toward the open baby lips and picked up the beads of moisture that lingered there. Fascinated both by what she was seeing and the love that was bubbling inside her, she watched the finger trail slowly from the child's mouth to the wet spot on her breast. He touched it, but had she not been watching, she might not have known it, so light was that touch. Then, moving with excruciating slowness, he turned his hands and cradled his son's head, placing the back of his hand against Arden's breast.

A shudder of emotion rippled through her, and a soft half sob escaped her trembling lips. Her eyes were made blind by collecting tears. Drew's head snapped up, and his blue eyes pierced into her wide green ones.

"Arden, don't cry anymore." Without moving anything but his head, he joined their mouths together. This kiss wasn't restrained like the one in the elevator earlier that morning. This one was rife with emotions, any one of which would have been sufficient to tear down all their defenses.

His tongue delved deeply and was received into the snug warmth of her mouth. Without thinking about it, her hand came up and pressed Matt's head to her breast, trapping Drew's hand between them. Now she was holding them both. The son. The father. So long dreamed about, speculated on. Ever elusive. Now her flesh could feel them both; her senses could luxuriate in the sounds, smells and sights of them. Their bodies were the most beautiful in the world to her. With one, she had created the other.

Drew groaned softly, and his lips twisted over hers. With his fingers, he caressed his son's head. It wasn't accidental that his fingers were also moving against Arden's nipple with the same pressure his tongue applied inside her mouth. His passion coursed through her, down her throat and straight into her body until it touched her femininity and bathed it with liquid heat. And she knew then what it would have been like had they made Matt in the conventional way, and she felt cheated, bereft at not having had the full knowledge of that miracle.

"God," Drew moaned as he pulled away at last, lifting the still-sleeping Matt into his arms. "If you go on kissing me like that, I'll start crying myself. And for an entirely different reason."

He helped her out of the airplane into the balmy sunlight. The sleeping Matt was draped over his shoulder. With his free hand, Drew clasped hers, and they made their way to the terminal.

Their suite of rooms at the Sheraton was spacious and faced the ocean with an unrestricted view of Diamond Head. There was a sitting room that separated the room Mrs. Laani and Matt would share from Drew's bedroom. Arden had the room across the hall from his.

"Here's a key to the suite if you should need one," he said on their way up in the elevator. "Make yourself at home any-time." He pressed the key into her palm, making his mean-ing implicitly clear. When Arden had the nerve to glance at Mrs. Laani, she saw that the woman was beaming a smile. Arden knew they'd both be disappointed if they expected her to use the key.

They got the worst over first. As soon as they had eaten lunch and Matt had taken a short nap, Drew and Mrs. Laani left with him for his appointment with the pediatrician.

Under the hotel's wide breezeway, as they were getting into the car Drew had leased at the airport, he clasped Arden's hand. "We'll be back in about an hour. You're sure you'll be all right?"

"Yes, but I wouldn't mind going along." In fact, she wanted desperately to go with them but knew it would seem unnatural to press the issue.

"That's generous of you, but I wouldn't force this on anyone." Drew laughed. "Matt's not the most cooperative of patients. Shop, sightsee and we'll meet you back in the suite by five o'clock."

"Okay," she said resignedly. He kissed her quickly on the cheek, and they sped away.

Matt was obviously miffed at both Mrs. Laani and his father when they brought him back to the hotel. He treated them as enemies who had put him through a terrible ordeal. He would have nothing to do with either of them during the early dinner they ate at one of the coffee shops in the hotel complex. Only Arden was allowed to cater to him.

"You're only making it worse," Drew said as she fed ice cream to Matt after his dinner. "He'll think you're his fairy godmother or something."

Arden almost dropped the spoon but managed to recover. She looked pleadingly at Mrs. Laani and Drew. "Let me spoil him. He's had a hard day."

The child was querulous with everyone by the time dinner was over, and Drew firmly suggested they make it an early night.

"As soon as Matt's in bed," Mrs. Laani said, "I'd like to go out for a while. My sister wanted me to come see her and meet my niece's fiancé."

"That's fine with me," Drew said.

"Why don't you go on now," Arden rushed to say. "I don't mind putting Matt to bed. In fact, I'd love to. There's no sense in your postponing your visit."

"Are you sure you know what you're letting yourself in for?" Drew asked her, his brows creasing over skeptical eyes.

"Yes." Arden turned to Mrs. Laani. "Go on. Matt and I will get along fine."

It was settled, and Mrs. Laani left a few minutes later. Between the two of them, Drew and Arden managed to get the cross little boy bathed and snapped into pajamas. Arden almost regretted that he was so fractious and sleepy. She would have loved to have played with him longer.

It was she who laid him in the portable crib the hotel had provided and patted his back until he fell asleep. Drew had already withdrawn into the other room. She stayed by the crib until Drew called to her.

When she joined him in the sitting room, he was leaning back in the sofa with his feet stretched out in front of him. He had changed into a pair of shorts and a T-shirt. He was barefoot. Arden admired the bunched muscles in his arms and legs, the rippling ridges of muscle on his chest. She loved, too, the way his body hair shone golden against his bronzed skin in the soft lamplight.

"Come here and crash," he said, extending his hand. "I'd get up and come get you, but I'm pooped."

She laughed and sank down beside him on the sofa. "A big strapping boy like you being worn out by one twenty-month-old!" she teased.

He grunted. "He can wear me out faster than a tennis match. Incidentally, I've got to practice while I'm here. Want to watch me tomorrow morning?"

"Of course."

"We'll make good our escape before Matt realizes we're gone. Mrs. Laani can take him to the park or something. Right now I'm feeling very jealous of my son for absorbing so much of your attention." He turned to face her, letting his eyes take in her pleasantly rumpled appearance. As he had been sure she would, she made even domesticity look elegant.

"You shouldn't," she said, wishing she had the courage to brush the wayward strands of hair from his forehead. "The reason I like him so much is because he's related to you."

His eyes gleamed with pleasure. "Is that right?"

"That's right." It was true. She loved Matt not only because he was her son but also because he was Drew's. It only stood to reason that she loved Drew, as well. But what kind of love? Was it merely because he was Matt's father? No. She was in love with this man, and it had nothing to do with Matt.

He was looking at her in the same intense way she was surveying him. "This is twice today my son has gotten you wet." His finger traced the damp patterns that Matt's body, wet from his bath, had left on the casual blouse that had replaced her traveling clothes.

His hand paused at the top curve of her breast, and his eyes met hers. "From the very beginning, you were no casual pickup, no quick lay. Tell me you know that."

Shaking her head and closing her eyes briefly, she said, "Yes, I know that." She dared to meet his gaze again, knowing as she did that she was making an error in judgment. Her conscience screamed at her, but she ignored it because she wanted him so badly. "Last night, I was afraid."

"Of me?"

"Of…this."

"And now?"

She shook her head, and his face tightened with emotion. His hand moved down, over the swelling mound of her breast. He looked at what he touched in a way that endeared him to her. She got as much pleasure from watching the delight in his eyes as she did from the stirring way his hand caressed her. When he raised his head, his eyes were smoldering with desire, and he held her captive in that swirling inferno. He was looking directly into her eyes when his fingertip grazed the tip of her breast. It ripened beneath his touch. They cried each other's names simultaneously.

His mouth came down hard on hers as his arms enfolded her. She locked her hands behind his neck and opened her lips to his tongue. It mated with hers, rubbing and pressing and thrusting, intimating the most primitive of lovemaking.

"God, but you're sweet," he whispered against her throat. He nuzzled her neck, left tiny love bites on the fragile skin, tasted her with the tip of his tongue.

He palmed the generous fullness of her breast, kneaded it tenderly, then sought the nipple with his thumb. He worried it to tight perfection before ducking his head and taking it between his lips. Even through her clothes, the moist fury of his mouth surrounded her, drove her mad with its sensuous tugging cadence.

She lay back against the cushions, urged down by his reclining weight. His desire strained against the cloth of his shorts. She felt it against her thigh and thrilled to it. Her hands slipped under his T-shirt and began working it up even as he began to unbutton her blouse. His mouth returned to hers for quick sipping kisses. "I want to love you. Now, Ellie, now."

Arden froze.

Drew jerked upright when he heard the words leave his mouth. *What had he said?* It took only one look at Arden's chalky face to know.

He vaulted off the couch to his feet. The heels of his hands

Chapter 6

They were petrified by shock. Drew's blasting curse had left a vacuum of silence behind it, like the absence of oxygen immediately following an explosion, like the sulfurous charge in the air after lightning has struck. They were held paralyzed in that deadly quiet void.

When at last he spoke, his voice carried a great weariness with it. "I'm sorry, Arden." He raised his arms in helpless appeal. "Dammit, what else can I say but that I'm sorry?"

Arden stood like a somnambulist, swayed slightly, but at last was able to propel herself toward the door, rearranging her clothes as she went.

"Arden." He said her name softly, apologetically, but when she didn't turn around, he repeated it with more force. When she didn't stop then, he lunged after her. "Arden," he said, grabbing her arm and turning her around. "Listen—"

"Let me go, Drew." She kept her head averted, her voice iron hard and cold.

"Not until you've listened to an explanation."

She laughed without humor. It was a hollow, lifeless sound. "I think this poignant scene is self-explanatory." She struggled against his tenacious hold. Had she not been so civilized, she would have clawed, kicked. She was frantic to get away. "Let me go," she shouted. "I don't belong here. I don't know why I'm here. It's wrong. Let me go." She was bordering on hysteria but couldn't contain it and fought the manacle of his hand around her upper arm.

"You *do* belong here because I invited you. I want you here with me and Matt."

"You want Ellie here!" she screamed up at him.

His face, which had been working with anger at himself and frustration over her misunderstanding, went completely blank. Her cruel words erased all expression. The steely fingers around her arm relaxed, and his arm fell to his side. "Ellie *is* here," he whispered. "That's the problem."

He returned to the sofa with trudging footsteps. Slumping down onto it, he laid his head against the back cushions and closed his eyes.

The moment Arden flung her hateful accusation in his face, she would have given heaven and earth to recall it. As he turned away from her, she reached out a comforting hand, but pulled it back. The last thing he would want now was her pity. But she couldn't leave without saying something.

"What I said was unforgivable, Drew."

He scoffed with the same bitterness she had shown only moments before. "What *I* said was unforgivable. I know you feel insulted. Don't. You should feel flattered." He opened his eyes and looked at her. "I'd like to explain."

"You don't have to."

"I want to." His tone was determined. She nodded.

He stood up and walked to the wide glass door. Sliding it

open, he let the scent and sound of the Pacific Ocean fill the suddenly stifling room. "Honolulu is where Ellie and I met, where we lived when we were married. I can't come back here without having a million places and things remind me of her or something she said or something we did."

"I know what that's like. After Joey died, sometimes the memories were so strong, I would think I'd hear his voice."

He shook his head in aggravation. "She's been on my mind since we arrived. We used to take Matt to the pediatrician together, you see. Tomorrow I'm taking him to visit her parents." Arden didn't want to acknowledge the stab of envy that pierced through her. "And all day, I've felt like...like I was being unfaithful to Ellie."

"Because of me?"

"Yes."

Sorry as she was about what she'd said to him, she felt he'd slapped her in the face again. "Is that supposed to make me feel better?" she asked scathingly. He pivoted around, and she saw again that flicker of impatience in his eyes. Actually, she preferred it to the haunted vacancy that had been there moments before.

"It might if you wouldn't fly off the handle, if you'd let me tell you a few things before you jump to conclusions."

"You make me sound like an unscrupulous home wrecker."

"Dammit, will you *listen?*" He muttered a curse and shoved strands of hair off his forehead. "There have been other women, Arden. Since Ellie and before you."

"I'm feeling better all the time."

He frowned at her sarcasm before going on. "Too many women. One-night stands. Faceless, nameless women that I was later glad I couldn't remember." He closed the distance between them and peered closely into her eyes to emphasize his next point. "They meant nothing. Nothing," he said, slicing the air with his hands. "My desire for them was a biological function, nothing more. What I did with those women could be described in the coarsest of terms because that's all it was. I didn't feel I had betrayed Ellie, at least not our love, because there was no emotional involvement for me."

He took a breath that expanded his chest almost enough to touch her. His voice lowered in pitch and volume. "You're the first woman I've felt guilty about."

Her outrage receding, she wet her lips nervously. "Why?"

"Because with you there *is* an emotional involvement. With you it wouldn't be just..." He searched for a less abrasive word, shrugged and said bluntly, "Screwing." He placed his hands on her shoulders and drew her closer. "It would be loving. I'm falling in love with you, Arden. I'm surprised by it. Actually dismayed. And I don't quite know how to handle it."

She swallowed the knot in her throat. "You still love Ellie." There was no inquiry in her voice; it was a simple statement of fact.

"I'll always love her. She was a part of my life. But I swear to God I'm not trying to replace her with you. The two of you are too totally different. Nothing alike. So please don't think that because I spoke her name while I was loving you, I superimposed her image over your body. I wasn't thinking of her. I was immersed in you, only you."

He brought his hands up to her face and alternately stroked her cheekbones with his thumbs. "It's just that this is the first time since her death that my heart has been an integral part of having sex. Speaking her name was a conditioned reflex, because I haven't felt that emotional and spiritual rush since

I last held Ellie. Not until you. Don't assign any Freudian implications to it, please."

"I reacted out of conditioned reflex, too. My pride was stung," she cried. "Any woman's would have been."

"Or any man's. I'm not diminishing my error. Believe me, I know I was ghastly. I just want you to know where it was coming from. Tell me you understand."

When he was close like this, she couldn't think, so she stepped away from him and stared out the glass door herself. She wondered if he would be telling her all this if he knew who she was. If she identified herself as the surrogate mother he and Ellie had hired, would he still want to make love to her? How could she ever hurt him and risk losing him by telling him the truth?

"I do understand, Drew. You and Ellie had a rare and special marriage." She could have added, "She loved you enough to let another woman have your child."

"Yes, we did. I was faithful to our vows." He laughed softly. "On tour, that's not always easy. There are opportunities every day. Whatever you want, it's available."

He came to stand beside her, propping himself in the doorframe by leaning into it with his shoulder. "Ellie traveled with me when she could, but not all the time. Sometimes I wanted sex. Badly. And there were plenty of women who would have obliged. But I knew how rotten I'd feel afterward. And it would be more than just feeling guilty for being unfaithful. After having experienced sex as a part of love, I really didn't want it any other way. I didn't want it reduced to a merely physical exercise."

He glanced at her quickly. "I'm not a saint. There were times when I was strongly tempted. Particularly if I'd played well, won a match and wanted to celebrate. The adrenaline would be pumping, and I'd want...want to make love."

She looked away, out over the ceaseless surf. Quietly, she said, "I can see how one would go with the other. How physical stamina would give you more energy...make you..."

His laughter this time was genuine, and he cupped her chin with his hand and turned her face back to his. "I know what you're thinking, Ms. Gentry."

"I'm not thinking—"

"You're thinking that since I was playing well that first day we met and since you were sitting there on that patio all cool and serene and appealing as hell, I automatically wanted to hop in the sack with you and work off some excess energy."

She blushed and hated herself for being so transparent. Drew smiled wider, knowing he'd been right on target. "Well, I'll admit I was aroused from that first day. I've given making love to you a lot of thought since we met, particularly after our first lunch date. You looked so untouchably sophisticated, yet you nearly drove me to distraction in that little black top that fit like a second skin over your breasts."

She gasped softly in surprise, but he continued. "Arden, here," he touched the fly of his shorts, "I've been ready to make love since I first saw you. Here," he touched his temple, "I know it's time I loved again. It's here," he said, indicating his heart, "that I'm in conflict."

"You don't hold a monopoly on that," she said, brushing past him and going back into the room. "Hasn't it occurred to you that this might be different for me, too?" She whirled on him. "I'm not accustomed to accompanying men on three-day vacations." Her eyes darted past him as she said in a quieter tone, "The only man I've slept with was my husband. Before or after we were married. It was a lousy marriage. In every way." She hazarded a look toward him. He was listening closely, his eyes trained on her.

"He and I didn't love each other the way you and Ellie

were lucky enough to. And when the marriage was over, I gave all the love I had to give to Joey. When I lost him, too, I felt empty, depleted of emotion, a shell with no soul inside. Until…" She raked her bottom lip with her teeth and cautioned herself not to reveal too much.

"Anyway, I'm not ready to gamble with my heart, either. I've lost my parents, my husband, such as he was, and my son. I don't know that I'm ready to risk loving anyone else."

"The odds don't look particularly promising when you're risking it on a has-been tennis bum and his orphaned son."

"Don't say that about yourself," she said fiercely. "You're *not* a has-been and certainly not a bum. And Matt is—"

She broke off when she saw the grin tilting up one side of Drew's lips. "You've just put your foot in it, Arden. You care more than you want to admit."

She lowered her eyes in chagrin. When she raised her eyes again, he could see that they were brimming with tears. "I'm afraid, Drew."

He went to her and wrapped his arms around her. His large, strong hand cradled her head and pressed it into his shoulder. "What are you afraid of?"

Afraid that if you find out who I am you won't believe how much I've come to love you. I wanted my son, but now I think I want you more, and that's wrong of me. Isn't it? I don't know. I don't know.

"I'm afraid to let myself love again."

He pulled away only far enough to look down into her face. He squeezed his hand between their bodies and placed it over her heart. "You have so much love to give. I can feel it, beating here, trying to get out. Don't be afraid to let it go." He lowered his head, and his lips made a pass across her brow as his hand cupped her breast and made a caressing circular motion. "God, Arden, but it would be easy and right for us to love each other."

Yes, it would be so easy. Her body gravitated toward his as naturally as the river flowed toward the falls. And just as perilously, she wanted to hurl herself over the cliff of conscience and principle.

But would it be *right?* Would he feel it was right if he knew that their meeting hadn't been dictated by fate but had been contrived by her for the purpose of finding her son? She tamped out the fires of desire that were already rekindling.

His lips hovered above hers, but she placed her fingers over them. "Don't, Drew. Not now. If we ever make love, I want everything to be perfect. It wasn't that way for me with my husband." Before she could say more, his mouth stopped her. It was a kiss that promised loving him would be beyond her previous experience and her wildest imagination.

Shakily, she went on when he lifted his lips from hers. "Until such a time, we have our private wars to wage. I don't want you to blame me for any guilt feelings you might have over Ellie."

"You're not to blame," he whispered into her hair. "I blame only myself."

She maneuvered her mouth away from the seductive persuasion of his. "Let's continue being just close friends for the present. Please?"

He sighed his disappointment, but she knew he was going to agree. His smile was wry. "You're making it hard on me." His nose nuzzled her ear. "In case you didn't catch it, there's a pun in there."

"I caught it," she said dryly, pushing him away. "It was in exceedingly bad taste."

"I told you I wasn't a saint."

"Then I'd better clear out while my virtue is still intact. What time do you practice in the morning?" They arranged to meet and have a quick cup of coffee before driving to the courts.

At the door, he caught her waist with both hands. They were indomitably possessive as they squeezed lightly. His eyes swept her breasts and lingered. She focused on the hollow of his throat.

"Arden, do you honestly believe we're going to remain just good friends?"

Her eyes took in the sensuous shape of his mouth. "No."

His voice was slurred with longing when he replied, "Neither do I."

They were friendly the next morning when they met, the tension of the evening before having been dispelled. Drew kissed her briefly on the mouth as he cheerfully greeted her. When they arrived at the courts at the appointed time, he introduced her to his opponent. Bart Samson was a retired professional, Drew's senior by fifteen years, but he could still play a mean game of tennis.

They played on municipal courts, which surprised Arden, but she didn't remark on it. She sat on the splintery bleachers and watched the match. She had brought along a tablet and pen, should she want to work on an article, but took very few notes. Drew's superb game held her attention.

"Thanks for the workout, Bart," Drew said to the man as they strolled toward the parking lot when they were through.

The older man ran a towel over his face and around the back of his neck. "Thank *you*. You whipped me, but it was great tennis." He looked at Arden before he said, "Why don't you meet me at Waialee tomorrow? This—" he indicated the less than perfect courts "—isn't where someone of your caliber should be playing. Everyone at the country club would love to see you again, Drew."

"Thanks, Bart, but no. Not yet." He took Arden's hand. "If you'd rather not play here with me, I'll understand," he said frostily.

"I don't deserve that," Bart replied quietly and without rancor. "Here, tomorrow morning at eight." He nodded to Arden before sliding into his Mercedes and starting the motor.

They were almost back at the hotel before Arden said, "You and Ellie were members of Waialee Country Club, weren't you?"

"Yes, why?" he asked, momentarily taking his eyes off the rush-hour traffic.

"Nothing. I just wondered."

At the next stoplight, he leaned toward her. "My not wanting to play there has nothing to do with Ellie or you or our old friends seeing you and me together. They'd all be delighted with you, I'm sure. The reason I don't want to play there is because I made a spectacle of myself the last time. I'm not ready to face the club set yet. Okay?"

"Not okay. You should go back and play there with your head held high. Talk to old friends. You've got absolutely nothing to be ashamed of, Drew."

He studied her for a time, grudgingly admiring the wisdom of what she said and appreciating her vote of confidence in him. "Give me a kiss."

"No."

"Because I'm sweaty and stinky?"

"No. Because the light turned green about thirty seconds ago and all the cars behind us are honking."

He cursed softly as he released the brake and continued the drive back to the hotel, scowling at Arden's soft chuckles.

The moment they opened the door of the suite, they knew something was wrong. Matt, tears streaming down his face, came running to his father, arms outstretched.

Drew scooped him up. "What the hell...?"

"Mrs. Laani!" Arden cried, crossing the room swiftly when she saw the woman lying on her back on the sofa, one forearm across her eyes, the other across her stomach. She was moaning pitiably. "Mrs. Laani," Arden repeated, going down on her knees beside the sofa and touching the woman's arm, "are you ill?"

"I'm so sick," she groaned. "The baby, he's hungry and wet...but, I'm sorry, Mr. McCasslin," she said when Drew walked into her range of vision. "I couldn't get up. My stomach." She closed her eyes again in misery.

Matt had stopped crying and was hiccuping against Drew's shoulder. "Do you need to go to the doctor? Could it be appendicitis?"

"No. I had my appendix out years ago. It's...at my sister's house. They all had this virus. I guess I caught it. I don't want Matt to get sick."

Arden was touched over Mrs. Laani's concern for the child. "Don't worry about him. He'll be fine. We need to get you feeling better. Can I get you something?"

"You're a nice *wahine*," she said, squeezing Arden's hand. "Thank you, but I don't want anything except to get out of here and keep all of you from catching this. Mr. McCasslin, I called my sister and asked if I could stay with her until I'm well. My brother-in-law is coming to pick me up. I hate to desert you, but—"

"That's all right," Arden said, intervening again. "I can take care of Matt. When is your brother-in-law coming to get you?"

"He should be downstairs now."

"Drew, give Matt to me and I'll get him some breakfast. You help Mrs. Laani down to the lobby. Is that her bag? Here, carry it for her."

"Yes, ma'am," he said as he followed her instructions. Despite his worry over his able housekeeper, whom he'd never seen in less than perfect health, his eyes were twinkling with amusement at the way Arden was taking charge.

They were still sparkling when he returned after escorting Mrs. Laani down to meet her brother-in-law. Arden was helping Matt eat his cereal. There was a small refrigerator in the suite, and Mrs. Laani had stocked it with juice, milk, fruit, cheese and snacks so Matt wouldn't have to be taken to a restaurant for every meal. The hotel management had provided them with a small assortment of dishes and silverware.

"How is she?" Arden asked.

"Miserable, but relieved that she's separating herself from Matt. He was her main worry. She expects that if she lives for the next twenty-four hours, she'll survive."

"I think so, too. It's probably just a bug."

"And in the meantime—"

"I'll take care of Matt."

"I can't let you do that."

"Why not? Don't you trust me with him?"

He placed his hands on his hips in exasperation. "Yes, I trust you with him, but I didn't bring you along to take over as nursemaid."

Feeling glowingly content, with her child on her lap and his father looking ruggedly handsome in his sweat-damp tennis clothes, she cocked her head to one side and asked impishly, "Why *did* you bring me along?"

"To woo you into bed with me."

She laughed. "Well, before you proceed, would you please go take a shower?"

He looked down at himself, grinned abashedly and said, "Oh, yeah. That might be a good idea."

By the time Drew had showered, she had Matt bathed and dressed. "If you'll give me just a few minutes, I'll be ready, too." She'd told him she needed some things for Matt, and they'd decided to make a short shopping expedition. "Let me pop into my room and I'll be right back."

"I was meaning to talk to you about that."

"About what?" she paused to ask as she was sailing out the door.

"About your room. Wouldn't it be more convenient if you moved in here?"

She fixed him with a doubtful stare. "Convenient for whom?"

His smile fell on her like warm sunshine. "For you. And Matt, of course."

"Oh, of course."

"Think about it," he said, shrugging with feigned non-chalance.

"I already have. The answer is no."

She met them in the designated place in the lobby ten minutes later, looking amazingly well put together after having dressed so quickly. "I like those stretchy little tops you wear," Drew said in her ear as he draped an arm around her shoulders. Matt was walking with independent importance a few steps ahead of them.

"This is a sundress," she said, smiling her pleasure.

"Yeah, but it's made like that top you had on that day at lunch. I loved it because—"

"I know. You've already told me."

"Because it—"

"It's high fashion."

"Because it shows your nipples when they contract. Like now."

"Stop it." She tried to sound indignant and failed.

"It makes me wonder what color they are and how they'll feel against my tongue."

She made a whimpering sound. "Please, Drew, stop talking that way."

"Okay. I will. But only because those two sailors are ogling you in a way that makes me want to knock their heads together. The last thing they need to see is that limpid look in your eyes. It's the biggest come-on I've ever seen, and a man would have to be dead not to notice it." He all but snarled at the two hapless sailors as they walked past them. Then he hissed in her ear, "You've got great legs, too." She laughed.

He was highly irritated that one of the items on the shopping list was disposable diapers. "Matt's supply is running low," Arden explained.

"I want to get him out of diapers, but Mrs. Laani says he's not ready to potty train yet."

"And she's right. It can be traumatic if you try to train a child too early."

"I know," he grumbled, shoving his hands into the pockets of his navy blue shorts. The lean muscles of his thighs looked sculpted. "It's just that he'll seem officially a son when we can go into the men's room together."

She rolled her eyes heavenward. "The male ego. I can't believe it. I've changed him numerous times and seen him in the bathtub twice. He's officially your *son*."

Drew's eyebrows arched wickedly. "You think he inherited something from me?"

Her cheeks flamed scarlet. She spoke over his hearty

laughter. "He might train more quickly if you'd take him into the bathroom with you now and again. Maybe he'd begin to get the idea."

"You're changing the subject."

"You're right."

He kissed her soundly but quickly. "I'll take your suggestion to heart—it sounds like a good idea that I should have thought of myself."

When they returned to the hotel, Arden carrying their parcels and Drew carrying Matt, it was time to clean him up for lunch with Ellie's parents. Arden was dismayed to find that most of her belongings had been moved into the bedroom formerly occupied by Mrs. Laani.

"Remind me to compliment the manager of the hotel on his staff's efficiency."

"Drew," she said, rounding on him, "I won't stay here with you tonight."

"Not with *me*. With Matt. He's in a strange place. He'll feel better with someone in the room with him."

"Then you sleep with him."

He placed an index finger over her lips. "You're too smart for your own good." His eyes followed his finger as it moved over her lips. "Please. Nothing will happen that you don't want to happen. I promise."

In the end, she relented. Actually, being able to spend the night in the same room with her son was like being given a gift.

"You can go with us," Drew repeated for the third time when he and Matt were ready to leave for lunch.

She shook her head as she ran a fine brush through Matt's curls. "No, Drew. I couldn't."

"It wouldn't matter to me. I'd like for them to meet you."

She could tell by his inflection that it was important she believe him. "Thank you for that. But I wouldn't want to spring up from nowhere and probably spoil the visit for them. I know they're looking forward to it."

"They are. Matt's their one-and-only grandchild."

Then they don't really have one, do they? she thought to herself. "Was Ellie an only child?"

"Yes. She moved to the mainland to wait for…until Matt was born. They wanted her to…uh…to have him here, but she wanted to have him in Los Angeles. Anyway, when we brought him home, they were ecstatic. He'll be a demon tonight. They spoil him rotten."

So, even Ellie's parents didn't know that her pregnancy had been a hoax. Did anyone know besides Drew and herself? And Ron, of course.

"What will you do while we're gone?" he asked her.

"Work on an article. I checked with the hotel, and they have a spare typewriter they'll let me use." Drew had discouraged her from carting her portable along. "Or I may go to the pool and work on my tan."

"Wear something modest. I don't want a stray man with dishonorable intentions to get the idea you're available and take it upon himself to make your acquaintance."

She propped her fists on her hips. "That's how I met you."

"That's what scares me."

The sun was hot, baking into her body. It felt marvelous. The breeze off the ocean was cooling, so only her skin, lightly glossed with tanning lotion, was warm from the afternoon sun. She had tuned out the sounds of laughing tourists, playful children, boisterous teenagers, and listened only to the pounding surf. Its rhythm was so hypnotic that she could almost feel her body undulating to the beat.

Was it the surf that caused that restlessness in the lower part of her body? Or was it the thought of Drew's kisses, his caressing hands, his tongue in her mouth and licking her skin? He had introduced her to a world of sensuality she'd never known before. Until she met him, she had thought that sphere existed only in the imaginations of poets and dreamers, romantics who wished life could be better than it was. But this world of sight and sound and smell and taste and breathless excitement did exist. If one was fortunate enough to find the right partner to share it. It wasn't a world that could be experienced alone.

For much of her life, she'd been alone. Now her life was so full it frightened her. She was with her living son. *Her son.* And she loved him as passionately as she had loved Joey. She took advantage of every excuse to touch him, to snuggle him to her, to breathe in his delicious smell, to marvel over his powers of reasoning and his physical dexterity.

And she was coming to love, even more passionately, the man who had fathered him.

She was both joyful and sad. Joyful over having found them and loved them. Sad because she knew she couldn't have them. Everyone she had ever loved, she had lost. They would be lost to her, too. The day would come when she'd have to give them up. But until that day, she'd bask in their presence.

"Oh!" she exclaimed, coming bolt upright on her beach towel and knocking Matt down into the sand on his bottom.

"Code," he shrieked, giggling and shaking another ice cube onto her bare stomach.

She gasped again, sucking in her stomach and reaching

for his cup of ice at the same time. "Yes, it's 'code,' and as smart as you are, I don't think you could have thought up this prank."

She turned around to see Drew squatting on his heels behind her, grinning like a Cheshire cat. The sight of him in light blue swimming trunks took her breath away as effectively as the ice cubes on her burning skin. The breeze tossed his blond hair, making him look wild and reckless and consummately male.

"Guilty as charged," he said, smiling broadly.

"I thought as much."

"But Matt was all for the idea."

"Like father, like son."

He walked around her to sit on the end of her beach towel. Matt had tottered toward the water and was taking tentative steps into the surf. "I thought I told you to wear something modest. If that's your idea of modest, you need a new dictionary."

Out of contrariness, she had put on the most provocative of her swimsuits. It was of black crocheted cotton yarn lined with flesh-colored material. The top was two triangles held together with braided strings. The bottom was brief and narrowed on the sides of her hips to a single strand of braid.

"I'm not going to let you bully me. Besides, no one has bothered me. Until now," she said pointedly.

"Do I bother you?" The seductive pitch of his voice and the way his eyes took in every erogenous part of her body sent her senses into pandemonium.

Before she could voice a suitable comeback, Drew was hailed from the low brick wall that separated the hotel's pool area from the beach.

"Drew! Drew, is that you?"

Drew's eyes searched the crowd to see who had called

to him, and Arden saw a mixture of vexation and caution when he identified the man. Unenthusiastically, he raised his hand and waved. "I'll be right back. Do you mind watching Matt?"

"Not at all," she said, more concerned about the grim shadow on Drew's face than the active little boy.

Drew cursed mentally as he weaved his way through the sunbathers on the beach to the steps leading up to the patio surrounding the pool. Of all the people to spot him. The last person he wanted to see. Jerry Arnold, manager of the tennis program at Waialee Country Club.

"Hello, Jerry," he said, extending his hand.

"Drew—God, man, it's good to see you." The man pumped his hand. "You're looking great since I last saw you."

Drew smiled grimly. "Well, that's not saying a helluva lot, is it? The last time you saw me, you had me by the shirt collar and you were dragging me out of the locker room, asking me not to come back. I wasn't so drunk that I don't remember."

Jerry Arnold was a head shorter than Drew and much stouter. At one time, he'd played on the pro tour, but he knew before coaches or anyone else kindly told him that he didn't have what it took to play competitive tennis. He'd surrendered his dreams graciously and done the next best thing. He worked with those who did. "I'm sorry, Drew. You gave me no choice."

"I don't blame you, Jerry. You should have revoked my membership and whipped my ass."

"I couldn't," the man said, smiling. He rubbed his jaw in remembrance. "You've got a mean right hook."

Drew chuckled softly. "I was violent and abusive. I'm sorry."

"So was I. I hate to see talent like yours going to waste."
His eyes probed Drew's. "I'm hearing terrific things."

"Oh?"

"You're on the way back."

"Yes, I am."

"Prove it."

Drew had been watching Arden and Matt wrestling in the
sand. She had beautifully slender thighs and a nicely rounded
tush. It took a bold challenge like Jerry's to snap his eyes and
his attention away from that. "What did you say?"

"I said prove that you're on the way back up."

"How? By coming back to the club? Bart Samson already
asked me this morning. I told him no."

"By coming back to the club…and playing an exhibition
match. Tomorrow."

Drew's mouth went dry, and his hands involuntarily knotted into fists that matched the knots forming in his stomach.
"I can't," he whispered, terrified.

"You can. I need you to. McEnroe was supposed to be
here to play in a match for charity. Muscular dystrophy. Fifty
dollars a pop for tickets. He sprained his thumb in—"

"I read about it."

"So his coach says no playing. Not even exhibition. I need
you, buddy. And you need this match."

"Like hell I do."

"Like hell you don't. You've got to start sometime, Drew.
Prove to all those who didn't have faith in you that you can
climb right back into that number-one seed."

"Not this year. Next, maybe." He hated the way his insides were churning, the way his hands had become slippery
with sweat, the acrid taste of fear in his mouth.

"As I said, you've got to start sometime. I talked to Bart.
He told me you were here. He said you ran his tail into the

ground this morning, said he couldn't return but half your serves."

"What are you, a cheerleader? Are you asking me to play in this match because you need a warm body on the court to save your face, or do you really care about my floundering career and yet-to-be-seen comeback?"

"Both." The man stared up into Drew's taut face, conceding nothing. He was being brutally honest. At least Drew could appreciate that.

Drew was the first to look away. "I don't know, Jerry."

"Look, if I thought you'd get out there and make a fool of yourself, I wouldn't ask. For both our sakes. You've got your head on straight again. I see you've got a new chick. So—"

"She's not a *chick*," Drew said between his teeth.

Jerry's eyebrows expressed his surprise at Drew's rabid defense. He cast a look at the woman on the beach. She was playing with McCasslin's boy. Jerry returned his gaze to Drew, whose anger was still simmering behind glacial eyes. "I'm sorry. I didn't mean to give offense." His face took on an earnestness that couldn't have been faked. "Drew, I don't care if it's a *guy* you're seeing. I'm glad of whoever or whatever is going to bring you back to where you should be. On top."

Drew let the muscles of his body relax. He was surprised at his possessive, protective attitude toward Arden; it had momentarily overruled his better judgment. He'd been almost ready to kill Jerry for slighting her. In that moment, he realized the extent of his feelings for her. It thrilled him. It also imbued him with confidence.

"Who's playing?"

"Teddy Gonzales."

Drew's curse was terse and explicit. "Thanks, Jerry." He sighed heavily, his flicker of optimism extinguishing.

"Yeah, I know, he's your arch rival."

"And eleven years younger. With eleven years' more stamina."

"And you've got eleven years' more experience. He's a hothead, Drew, an egomaniac. Play with strategy, work on his emotions." Jerry eyed him shrewdly. "Scared?"

Drew stated crudely just how scared he was, and Jerry laughed out loud. "Good. That'll make you play better. Say I can count on you, Drew. You need this match more than I do. If I didn't think so, I wouldn't have asked. I swear to God I wouldn't have."

"Thanks, Jerry." For a brief moment, they looked at each other in honesty and friendship. Drew sought out Arden's graceful form. Just then, she turned toward him and smiled. Matt stumbled in the sand. Her arms were there to help him up. "Can I tell you tonight, Jerry?"

"Sure. I'll call around eight." He clamped his hand on Drew's shoulder and squeezed it tightly. "I hope you'll say yes. Oh, and Drew," he paused to add after he'd taken several steps, "your lady is very pretty."

Drew made his way back to the beach towel and dropped down on it. He tousled Matt's hair and hugged him tightly before the boy toddled off toward the water. Only then did Drew look at Arden. God, she was beautiful. Just looking at her filled him with an assurance that replaced the fear. If he sat and stared at her long enough, would all of it disappear?

"A friend?" she asked softly.

"I wonder." She didn't pry, but he could see the question in her green eyes. "He wants me to play an exhibition match at Waialee for muscular dystrophy. Tomorrow. Against Teddy Gonzales."

"Are you going to play it?"
"Do you think I should?"
"Absolutely."

Chapter 7

He wanted to be talked into it. Arden knew that. He was nervous and keyed up as they left the beach and returned to the suite. He couldn't stand still. While she bathed sand off Matt, Drew paced the bathroom.

"I don't know if I'm ready."

"Maybe you're not." She would play devil's advocate. If she tried to encourage him, he'd only dig in stubbornly and keep refuting every positive thing she said. Then should he be defeated, he'd have her to blame for talking him into playing.

"On the other hand," he contradicted himself, "I'll never know, will I, until I start playing competitively again."

"That's right."

"But *God!* Tomorrow. Why couldn't it be next week?"

"Too bad it's not. Then you'd have all week to stew over it."

He wasn't really listening or he would have caught her caustic tone. Pacing, he was tapping his thumbnail against his front teeth. His brows were creased. "But if I had a week to think about it, I'd probably talk myself out of it."

"Probably," she said, hiding a smile.

"Maybe it's best that I have to make a hasty decision."

"Yes, maybe."

He stalked her as she carried Matt into the bedroom to dress him. "I'll have to call Ham. He's been after me for months to start playing, even in penny-ante tournaments. But he might not think this exhibition match is a good idea."

"No, he might not."

"But I should mention it to him, anyway," Drew said, heading for the phone. "I'll call him right now."

His manager was thrilled and said he'd try to get a plane out of Los Angeles so he'd be there in time for the match the next day.

"It *would* be Gonzales." Drew had ordered a succulent cut of prime rib but had eaten virtually none of it. Arden had ordered for Matt and herself when it became apparent that Drew was too preoccupied to do so. "The last time I played him, he laughed at me. The bastard turned toward the crowd in the bleachers, spread his arms wide in a gesture of dismay and *laughed*."

If Drew was looking for pity, he'd have to look elsewhere. Coddling was the last thing he needed. "It's unfortunate it couldn't have been someone less intimidating than Gonzales. Then people, sports writers and such, could say you were playing it smart and safe, that you weren't biting off more than you could chew."

"They'd say I was a coward," he said, viciously stabbing a piece of meat with his fork and then wagging it in her face as he made his next point. "No, maybe it's a good thing it's Gonzales. At least they can't say I'm afraid to play."

A vengeful light glowed in his eyes, but when he saw

Arden's knowing smile, his face softened, and he lowered the threatening fork to his plate. "What time is your friend calling for your answer?" she asked softly.

"Eight o'clock."

"Then we'd better get back to the suite." She wiped Matt's mouth free of mashed potatoes.

They had eaten early in deference to Matt's bedtime. As soon as they returned to their rooms, his busy day caught up with him, and he was more than ready for bed. Drew's mind was still on his dilemma even as he helped Arden get Matt settled for the night. The telephone was ringing when they walked back into the sitting room after switching off Matt's bedroom light.

Drew froze, staring at the phone for several seconds before purposefully striding across the room and lifting it to his ear. "Hello," he barked. "Oh, hello, Mrs. Laani."

Arden saw his shoulders sag with relief even as she felt her own relax. "That's good to hear. We've missed you, but Arden has a knack for controlling Matt." He glanced over his shoulder and winked at her. "Well, if you're sure you feel well enough. Don't rush back on our account…. No, that will be fine. As a matter of fact, I might be playing a match tomorrow, so it would be convenient if Matt were taken care of…. Okay… Rest tonight and we'll see you then."

He hung up. "She says she can come back tomorrow. She'll be here in the morning to take Matt shopping. Her sister will drive them."

Arden knew a pang of disappointment. She would have loved to be included on the shopping trip. Selecting clothes for her son, as she'd never been able to do before, would have been a joy. But she saw no way she could arrange to go. Besides, if Drew played the match, which she felt sure he would, she wanted to be there.

"I'm going to say good-night, Drew."

He stopped his pacing and looked at her blankly. "Now? It's not even—"

"I know, but you need time alone. To think."

He crossed the room and put his arms around her waist. "I've been acting crazy since I talked to Jerry today. I'm sorry. I haven't meant to ignore you. You're not angry, are you?"

"Of course not! Give me a little credit, Drew. You're trying to make a monumental decision. Your distraction is understandable."

"But I don't want to be distracted from you," he whispered, nuzzling her neck. "I can use your advice and support. Stay with me."

"No. No one can help you make this decision." How well she knew about making pivotal decisions. The night she'd paced her room from dusk until dawn trying to decide whether to go along with Ron's scheme or not had been the loneliest and most frightening night of her life. Responsibility for the decision had rested solely on her shoulders. No one could make Drew's mind up for him. And she wouldn't be his crutch. This time he had to stand alone, or he might never stand again.

"What should I do, Arden?" he asked, pressing his face into her hair.

She pushed him away. "Do you want to play tennis professionally again?"

"Yes, until I can retire on top and not because I can't hack it anymore. Life spans on the professional circuit are short. There is always going to be someone younger and better. I'm resigned to that. But I wanted to finish in a top seed, not in the shadow of ridicule."

"Then I think you know what you should do."

"I should play." A grin broke across his mouth. "I'll play."

The telephone rang again, and this time there was little doubt who was calling. "Good night," Arden said, slipping into the bedroom and closing the door behind her.

She couldn't hear Drew's conversation, but she could detect the assertiveness in his voice. She was smiling as she picked up her tablet and pen and began making notes on the article she was going to do for the food section of the *Los Angeles Times* about simple Polynesian recipes.

When she awoke, Matt's crib was empty. She sat up and blinked rapidly, trying to orient herself in the strange room. Flinging off the covers, she went to the window and peeped through the crack in the draperies. It was before sunrise. The calm ocean was a pink-and-violet reflection of the sky.

The bedroom door was open. She tiptoed through the sitting room to the other side where another bedroom door stood ajar. The room she peered into was rose tinted with the encroaching dawn. Unlike the bedroom she had shared with Matt, this one didn't have two double beds but a king-size one. Matt had curled up beside his father. Both were sleeping soundly.

Compelled by something stronger than common sense or prudence, Arden crept farther into the room toward the bed. Matt was on the far side of it. His rump, looking plump and out of proportion because of the overnight diaper under his pajama bottoms, was nestled against his father's chest. He was snoring softly through slightly parted lips.

Drew's arm was draped over his son's body. The hand that dangled in front of Matt's chest was lean and slender, with long tapering fingers. The faint morning light picked up the fine golden body hair dusting his arm. Even in repose, that arm looked sinewy and capable of tremendous power.

Arden's eyes misted over with high emotion as they traveled up the length of that arm to a set of wide shoulders. He was facing away from her, but she feasted on the beauty of his back. It was a smooth expanse of tanned skin and contoured muscles that she longed to touch with her fingertips... her lips?

His spine curved downward, and she followed its course to the shallow dip of his waist. She could see only a suggestion of his buttocks above the covering sheet. Below his waist, his tan was only a slight shade lighter than over the rest of his body. A ribbon of sensation spiraled up through her center at the thought of the nude sunbathing he must have done to acquire that tan.

His hair was a tumbled mass of blond strands on the butter-colored pillowcase. Moving around the bed to view his face, she admired the well-fashioned length of his nose, the mouth that declared his sensuous nature and the chin that proclaimed masculine authority. His lashes were spiky and thick, lighter on the ends than at the base, where they were almost black. It was a face that made women sit up and take notice whether they knew him by reputation or not.

Each time they went out, Arden could feel the envious stares of other women. Covetous eyes would take in the man, the woman close by his side and the child between them. Arden knew that most guessed they were a family. Biologically, yes, they were a family. But in truth...

Reminded once again that she was an interloper, she turned away silently. She took two steps before she was pulled up short by a swift tug on her floor-length nightgown. Twisting around in alarm, she saw that Drew was awake. He had rolled away from Matt and was facing the edge of the bed, the hem of her nightgown wrapped in his fist.

His eyes were slumberous, lazy, as were his movements as he slowly wound the fabric around and around his fist, reeling her in, shortening the distance between them until her knees bumped into the mattress. His hold on her nightgown was unbreakable. But not nearly as unbreakable as the hold his eyes had on hers. It rendered her motionless while his free hand slowly peeled back the sheet.

Her breath started coming in shallow pants. The sound of her heartbeat, loud and irregular, thundered against her eardrums. A lassitude as heavy and binding as chains claimed her limbs, yet she felt infused with energy.

In one lithe motion, Drew rolled to a sitting position on the edge of the bed, careless of his nakedness. His eyes were still fixed on Arden's, and neither seemed capable of turning away.

He positioned her between his spread knees. His thighs, hard and warm, pressed against the outside of hers. Giving in to an impulse she'd had since she first met him, she raised one hand and let her fingers sift through his sleep-tousled hair. He indulged her for a few moments before catching her hand and bringing it to his mouth.

His kiss was tentative at first, a mere brushing of his lips against the cushion of her palm. Then his tongue tickled the sensitized skin, and she broke out in gooseflesh. Soon his mouth was searing her palm and setting off a chain reaction of startling sensations. Like heat-seeking devices, sensual impulses found the hidden target of her sex, and it exploded under the onslaught.

He nipped and kissed each fingertip, her wrists, sending a wave of heat up her arms and into her breasts. They ached with sexual excitement. They filled and overflowed the ecru lace cups of her nightgown.

After appreciating them with his eyes, Drew let his hands drift across her breasts. His flesh touched hers through the dainty lace, and a wildfire of longing swept Arden's body. His fingers caressed her lightly until her nipples flushed and pouted. Leaning forward, he grazed her breasts with his lips, then rested his head against the lush curves, nuzzling her, breathing in her sleepy, warm scent. His head dropped lower, burrowing into her svelte stomach.

One of his hands went to her back and gathered up a fistful of cloth. He added to it until her nightgown was a tight, revealing nylon sheath that encased her body and made her feel more exposed than nakedness could have made her feel. His eyes flickered over her like tongues of flame. He spotted the indentation of her navel and kissed it, outlining the small crater with an impetuous tongue. She watched the damp spot on her gown grow as he kissed her there again and again. Her knees trembled. Her hands had long since found their way to his shoulders. Now they tangled in his hair as his head moved lower along her sleek feminine form.

She held her breath against a whimper of passion when his index finger traced the diagonal groove above her thigh. Her head fell back, and she instinctively arched into him when he treated the other side of the triangle to the same torturous caress. Then he kissed the spot where they met, and the foundations of her world crumbled and fell away and left her suspended without a foothold. Clutching his hair, she sobbed his name.

The hand at her back released the material of her gown and tunneled through her hair as he stood up. His mouth fell on hers, hot and hungry. But with surprising temperance, his tongue made exquisite love to her mouth.

In one sweeping motion, she was being carried in his arms, through the sitting room toward the other bedroom. She felt his desire against her hips. She had seen it, rooted in a nest of dark gold. Like the rest of him, his sex was splendid.

And she knew the act would be. And just as surely, she knew she couldn't afford it.

She wanted him. Every cell in her body was crying out for surcease from this fever that afflicted her. She ached for him to fill that void that yawned wider each time they touched. Her breasts yearned for the sweet suckling of his lips and the indulgence of his tongue. But this wasn't the time. If they made love now, it could spell disaster for them both.

Unaware of her hesitation, Drew stood her next to the bed and began to caress her anew. His hands closed over her buttocks and urged her forward. Her instinct was to grind herself against him, but she resisted.

There were so many reasons why this couldn't happen now. Would their lovemaking affect the way he played his all-important match that afternoon? What if the act reminded him of Ellie? If making love with her wasn't as good as making love with his wife had been, would he feel only disgust afterward? Or if it were better, would he feel guilty? Either way, he'd be thinking about that and not his game.

Afterward, when she told him who she was, he'd never believe that she hadn't merely bartered her body for the sake of being with her son. No, she couldn't make love to him until he knew everything about her.

Once she had made love to Drew, what then? Supposing he won that afternoon after having had sex with her? He might thank her for helping him get back on his feet and bid her a cheerful farewell. Or if he lost, he might blame her for distracting him. In either case, she'd lose him. She'd lose Matt.

No. No. No. She couldn't gamble everything away, even though she wanted him desperately.

"Beautiful," he was murmuring against her throat as he slid the straps of her nightgown down. "I was dreaming of you, woke up wanting you. Then to see you bending over me, watching while I slept. Oh, God, Arden..."

"Drew...no...ah..." His lips had found her breasts, and his tongue was sponging them. "No, please." Her hands went to his shoulders and pushed. He didn't budge.

"So pretty," he whispered, folding his hand around a breast and lifting it to his mouth. His lips moved back and forth across the nipple. "I knew you'd be beautiful. Let me see all of you," he rasped, trying to peel the nightgown the rest of the way down.

"No," she grated, and pushed herself away from him. Grappling with the slippery nylon, she tried to replace the straps of her nightgown on her shoulders. "No," she said more softly, eyeing him warily. She could tell by his swaying stance and glassy eyes that her negative message hadn't quite registered yet.

"No? What do you mean 'no'?"

She wet her lips and twisted her hands together in front of her. She'd thwarted him once, and the repercussions hadn't been pleasant. "I don't think we...you should...before a match. I've heard it's bad for athletes to...uh, you know... before..."

He laughed and took a step toward her. His finger charted the curve of her cheek. "If that were the case, there would be a helluva lot fewer athletes. Arden—"

"No, Drew, please don't," she said, moving away from the caressing hand he'd placed on her hip.

"What's the matter with you?" For the first time, she noted a touch of asperity in his voice. It sounded tight with rising impatience. "Don't tell me you're not in the mood. I know better." He glanced down at her nipples, and she felt her blush start there and stain the rest of her chest and neck like spilling ink. "Why did you come creeping into my bedroom if you didn't want to make love to me?"

She found the arrogant tilt of his chin and the lordly tone of his voice infuriating. "I was checking on Matt. I was worried when I woke up and he wasn't in his crib."

"You know he can climb out of his crib. Besides, one quick look would have let you know he was in bed with me. You didn't have to stand there at my bedside breathing heavy for five full minutes to confirm that Matt was with me."

"Breathing… You…I…" she sputtered.

"That's right. Admit it. Believe me, if I'd found you naked in bed, I'd have been breathing heavy, too. I don't think we've made any secret of the fact that we find each other sexually attractive. So what's the problem?"

"I've already told you. I don't think it's a good idea when you have that match to play today."

"Why? Are you afraid to commit yourself before you know if you're sleeping with a winner or a loser?"

Rage swept over her in a fiery tide that made the hair on the back of her neck stand on end. She caught him on the cheek with her palm in a cracking slap. The resultant silence reverberated in the room until she regained control of herself enough to say, "That was unfair to me, Drew. Cruel, selfish and unfair."

"Well, you don't exactly play fair, either, Ms. Gentry," he hissed. "Coming on like a nymphomaniac one minute and freezing up like an offended vestal virgin the next—twice, I might add—is not my idea of fair play."

She shook with fury. "Well, then, obviously you're not enjoying this game, and neither am I."

"I'm beginning to think that's all this is to you. A game. What's behind this charade you've been putting on?"

He was so close to the truth that she was seized by panic. She stared at him, genuinely frightened that he might somehow, freakishly, stumble onto the truth. It took her a moment to realize that the knocking that echoed through the suite wasn't her heart but someone at the door.

Drew turned away from her, tearing a towel from the rack in the bathroom and wrapping it around his waist before he went to answer the door. It was Mrs. Laani. Arden rushed into the bathroom and locked herself in before the housekeeper could see her.

In five minutes, she had gathered up those of her belongings that were in Matt's room. Mrs. Laani was alone in the sitting room, watching television until Matt woke up. Arden could hear the shower running in Drew's bathroom.

"I'm glad you're feeling better," Arden said, a plastic smile on her face as she edged toward the door. Mrs. Laani could be gregarious and was usually endearing, but Arden didn't think she could stand the chatter that morning. "Tell Drew I said good luck on his match."

"But Ms. Gentry, he—"

"I'll see you later."

She ducked into the relative safety of her room, showered and dressed quickly in a sundress, took up her straw hat and sunglasses and was on her way in less than fifteen minutes. All morning she poured her energy into the article she was writing, interviewing chefs in several noted restaurants. And all the while she was checking her wristwatch.

Drew had been right. She hadn't played fair that morning. She shouldn't have upset him before his match. What he didn't know was that she hadn't played fair all along. After their first meeting, she should have confided in him, told him who she was. Instead, she had insinuated herself into his life, his personal *and* professional life. She belonged in neither.

But she had fallen so deeply in love with him. That was the factor she hadn't counted on.

Oh, God, what am I going to do about it? she asked herself.

She took a noon break, stopping at a coffee shop and ordering an egg salad sandwich, which she didn't touch, and a glass of iced tea that was becoming watery with melted ice cubes.

There was no solution but to leave. Leave Drew. Leave her son. What good was she doing them? Drew wanted her in his bed but still loved his wife. Arden couldn't settle for that. She'd lived for years with a man who didn't love her. If she ever lived with another, it wouldn't be a one-sided affair. Never that again.

Matt was a happy, well-adjusted, healthy boy who had a mother figure in Mrs. Laani. Drew was dragging himself out of his self-imposed exile and back into the world of championship tennis. He was a good father to her son. She could only cause strife in their lives.

She had what she'd originally set out for. She knew who her son was. Maybe she could call Drew periodically, as a friend, and check up on Matt. He might even come to see her on the mainland and bring Matt with him.

Drew would think she had left over their "lovers'" quarrel. So much the better. If he pursued it, that could be her explanation. Things hadn't worked out. *I'm sorry, Drew, but these things happen all the time. You understand. But I'd still like to be your friend, keep track of you and Matt.* Yes, better to leave now before he learned the truth.

She left the coffee shop with her mind made up. She'd go back to Maui. With only one more article to write, she could return to California within a week. She glanced at her wristwatch, and acting on impulse, hailed a cab. There was one more thing she had to do.

"Waialee Country Club," she said briskly as she slid into the taxi.

The crowd was silent. Collectively they held their breath. The pent-up tension and anxiety were almost palpable. The sun was hot, but no one seemed to notice. Everyone's attention was focused on the tennis court.

The two players were as oblivious to the heat and their soggy clothes as they were to the crowd. They, too, were intent only on the match. It was the third and final set, each having taken one. It was five games to four, and Gonzales was in the lead. It was his serve. If he won the game, he'd take the match.

He had sauntered onto the court to a cheering crowd. His dark, Latin good looks contrasted with the whiteness of a broad, flashy smile. He was a champion and comported himself as one. His attitude toward his opponent as they shook hands at the net was one of cocky self-assurance. He'd swiftly changed his attitude when he'd barely won the first set six to four and then lost the second seven to five.

He was no longer concentrating so much on pleasing the crowd and posing for the sports photographers. He was trying to win the match, and it was requiring all he had to give.

He went up on his toes and fired a stinging serve into the box. The ball came whizzing back. A heated volley ensued. He slammed the ball into the far corner of his opponent's court and took the point.

"Fifteen, love," the umpire intoned.

Arden swallowed hard and dried her hands on the already limp skirt of her sundress. It was full and loose, and she was grateful that she hadn't worn anything more confining. Perspiration rolled in rivulets down her stomach and thighs, and only a portion of it could be attributed to the heat. It was literally a nervous sweat.

Jerry Arnold had hailed her the moment she stepped out of the cab. He had been sent by Drew to take her to the seat reserved for her. "His manager's with him," Jerry informed her excitedly, though she hadn't inquired. "It's like old times. He's calm but angry, you know? That's good. Anyway, he wanted to make sure you were here. If you need anything, ask one of the staff to fetch me."

"Thank you," Arden had said, a trifle confused. Had Drew expected her even after their argument that morning? And who was he angry with? Her?

He had walked onto the court looking breathtakingly handsome in his tennis whites with that familiar logo on the breast pocket and shorts. His trademark bandanna was rolled and tied around his forehead. Blond hair fell over it.

The tennis enthusiasts weren't impressed. He had received desultory applause. The spectators were carefully reserving judgment. They had paid their fifty dollars to see McEnroe and were disappointed. Would this be just another bloodbath for Drew McCasslin?

Drew hadn't seemed affected by the lack of enthusiasm. His eyes had scanned the crowd until he spotted Arden. He had nodded coolly. He hadn't looked at her since.

Drew took the next point, and Arden closed her eyes. *Just two more, Drew, and you've held him. Just two more.* Gonzales aced him on the next serve. "Thirty, fifteen."

Gonzales got overconfident. He didn't expect the next return to come from Drew's lethal backhand. He lunged one way, the ball went the other.

"Thirty all."

The crowd shifted nervously and began to applaud. Arden heard supportive shouts directed to Drew, and her heart swelled with pride. He had been spectacular throughout the match. Even if he lost, he'd played excellent tennis.

Gonzales won the next point. "Forty, thirty. Match point."

An exhausting volley won Drew another point. Gonzales cursed viciously in Spanish. "Deuce."

Arden's knuckles were white, her bottom lip chapped from raking it with her teeth. Gonzales's serve was but a blur. Arden thanked God when Drew found it with the sweet spot of his racket. But he overshot his mark. The ball hit past the baseline.

"Advantage Gonzales. Match point."

Leaning over, Drew braced his hands on his knees. His dripping hair fell over his forehead as he hung his head and breathed deeply. Then he positioned himself for his opponent's next serve. Gonzales put all he had into it. Drew returned it with miraculous precision. They whacked the ball back and forth until the spectators were dizzy with watching. Neither made a mistake. Each outguessed the other, dodging to the far side of the court, then racing to the other. Then a ball caught Gonzales in the corner of the court. His perfect forehand landed on the ball squarely and sent it jetting to the opposite corner.

Drew reacted immediately. With the speed of a cheetah, he propelled himself toward the ball. When he saw he couldn't beat it, he took one final lunge. His body was like a neat arrow slicing horizontally through the air, his racket extended as far as he could reach. That photograph would later win one sports photographer a journalistic prize.

Drew's racket touched the ball, without the necessary momentum. It had enough impetus to reach the net, but touched it and fell back into Drew's court. Landing, he skidded across the court leaving a trail of blood on his elbow and forearm.

No one moved. No one made a sound. With memorable courage, Drew picked himself up and heaved a deep breath. Then, slowly, with dignity, he walked toward the net, his right hand extended for a congratulatory handshake.

Bedlam broke out. Cheers went up, a roar of approval. Not for the victor but for the vanquished. Photographers and tennis enthusiasts of all ages poured onto the court...and they were all headed for Drew!

Arden's eyes filled with tears as she watched while hundreds of people surged around him in celebration. He was back. He was on top again. That last desperate effort proved that he was willing to give whatever it took to be a champion again.

She could leave him now. He'd be all right.

She pushed her way through the crowd, got a cab and had it wait for her at the hotel long enough for her to retrieve her bag before going on to the airport. She caught the same commuter airline that the McCasslin party had flown over on. Tears bathed her cheeks when she remembered the heavy pressure of Matt's head on her breasts and Drew's drugging kiss after they'd landed. She'd always remember that moment when she'd had father and son together.

The concierge's desk at the resort was peculiarly quiet. Then she remembered it was the dinner hour. A young woman greeted her warmly. "Good evening. May I help you?"

"I'm Ms. Gentry. I have a room, though I've been on Oahu for the last couple of days. I'd like my key now. Room 317."

The girl tapped something into a computer terminal. "Room 317?" she asked.

"Yes," Arden responded, feeling all the emotional turmoil of the day like a bag of bricks on her back.

"Just a moment, please."

There was a whispered conference between the girl and the desk manager. They kept glancing over their shoulders at Arden, who was becoming more and more vexed with each passing minute.

"Ms. Gentry?" The man with whom the desk clerk had conferred came up to her.

They were extremely sorry, but there had been some kind of miscommunication. They were under the impression that she had hastily checked out of the resort. She'd paid with her credit card. The things she'd left in the room had been stored at her request in the resort's offices.

"But I didn't check out!" she argued. "I told the man I was coming back. I only paid for my room so you wouldn't think I'd skipped out."

This mistake was entirely their own. They had given that room to another guest who was planning on a two-week stay.

"I liked that room, but if you've already given it to someone else, there's not much I can do about it. I'll take another. I'm very tired—"

There was another unfortunate problem. The resort was full.

"Are you telling me that you don't have one single room to give me after booting me out of the other one?"

They regretted that that seemed to be the case. What they would be happy to do was to call the other hotels and resorts to see if they could find lodging for Ms. Gentry. They would be happy to drive her there in their van.

"Thanks," she said tersely. "I'll wait over there," she said, pointing to a group of chairs that was so visible from the desk that they couldn't pretend to forget her.

A half hour went by, and the reports were becoming repetitive and discouraging. "Every place we've called is full. But we're still trying."

She was resting her head on the back cushion of one of the chairs, going over her options, when her head snapped up. Drew was stalking through the door of the resort with grim determination thinning his mouth. He was dressed in shorts as usual and a windbreaker, unzipped halfway down as usual. His hair had been shampooed since the grueling match, but it had been mussed by the wind. There was a nasty-looking fresh scab on his arm and elbow. He did a double take when he saw Arden sitting in the lobby chair.

He stopped in front of her, put his hands on his hips and glared down at her. "I've been looking all over two islands for you. Where the hell did you go after the match?"

"The answer's obvious, isn't it?"

"Don't play cute with me. Why did you run out?"

"Why? Because we had a fight this morning." She came to her feet and put as much strength behind her glare as he had in his. "I want out from under your bullying ways and bad temper."

His mouth crooked into a smile. "You ought to get mad more often. It does great things for your eyes."

She was ready with another angry outburst but was interrupted. "Ms. Gentry!" The desk manager came trotting up to her waving a piece of paper. "We found you a room—"

"Keep it," Drew snapped, swiveling around to face the luckless man and virtually nailing him to the floor with a blue stare.

The hotel man looked up at Drew cautiously, then glanced

inquiringly toward Arden. "But Ms. Gentry said she needed a room and—"

"I said to keep it." Drew turned to face her again. "She's coming home with me." His eyes softened as they looked into hers. Then he added quietly, "Please."

Chapter 8

He took her stunned silence as consent. Before she knew what was happening, Drew was issuing orders that all her belongings be taken out of storage and put in the trunk of his Seville, which was parked outside. He picked up the shoulder bag she'd taken with her to Oahu, and curving his hand around her arm, escorted her out the door. The staff couldn't have been more accommodating, fetching and carrying for him, repeatedly apologizing for having inconvenienced his friend.

She let herself be settled into the front seat of his car but sat with stiff dignity until they had driven away from the resort's entrance gates and onto the dark highway.

"Drew, I won't argue about this. I'm not going home with you. Please drive me to another hotel. I'll find a room."

"I won't argue about it, either. It's crazy for you to go chasing through the night trying to find a place to sleep when I've got three or four empty bedrooms. Besides, I'll let you have one free."

"Free?" she asked archly, leaving no doubt of her meaning.

He brought the Seville onto the narrow shoulder of the highway with a shower of gravel and a screech of tires. He braked jarringly. The momentum pitched her forward. On her way back, she was caught up against him.

"No. Not free. It's gonna cost you." His hand trapped her jaw, holding her head still. For ponderous moments, his lips hovered over hers. She expected a punishing, brutal kiss. Instead, it was excruciatingly tender. His tongue applied delicate pressure to her lips until they parted. He practiced that evocative thrusting rhythm that splintered her with shards of desire. She felt her body melting along the strength of his, her resolve to leave him dissolving just as surely.

When he lifted his head, he lovingly brushed back silky strands of dark hair from her cheek. "Consider your rent paid for as long as you want to stay."

"No other compensation will be required?"

His eyes coasted over her face, down her throat, back to her mouth. "Not unless you want to give me a gift, a gift you know I want but which I'd never take from you or bargain with you for."

She touched his hair, ran her finger along the brushy bar of his brows. "You played…" Emotion choked back her words as she remembered his brilliant last effort to save the match. "You played stupendously. I was so very proud. I ached with pride."

"Then why did you run away from me, Arden? Didn't you know I'd want to see you more than any person in the world when that match was over?"

"No, I didn't know that. You were so angry after…" She lowered her eyes. It was a gesture that was unconsciously seductive and made his senses reel. "After what happened

this morning," she mumbled, "I thought whatever friendship was developing between us was over. I couldn't bear not
being at the match, but I didn't think you'd want to see me
anymore."

He lifted her hand to his mouth, and pressing it to his lips,
spoke against her fingers "I was mad as hell. But you must
concede that when a man is as…uh…ready to make love as I
was and then it's called off, he can't be expected to be in the
best of moods." He delighted in the shy smile that curved her
mouth upward. "And I wasn't in the best frame of mind to
begin with. Hell, why mince words? I was scared, scared to
death, to face Gonzales in that match."

"By the end of it, Gonzales was afraid of you."

His grin was spontaneous and wide. "Thanks, but that's
not the point right now. The point is, I'm sorry for flying off
the handle this morning. You certainly had every right to say
no."

"I shouldn't have let things go so far before I did."

His eyelids drooped alluringly. "Think about that next
time. I can't say what would have happened if Mrs. Laani
hadn't knocked on the door." His lips took hers once again.
This time, there wasn't even a heartbeat of hesitation in
her response. Her mouth moved against his in generous
reciprocation.

"What will she think about having a houseguest? And I'm
only staying tonight. Tomorrow, I'll have to look for another
room."

"I've got twelve or fourteen hours to convince you otherwise," he said breezily as he slid back under the steering
wheel and turned on the ignition. "As for Mrs. Laani, she's
been throwing daggers at me all day with those beady eyes of
hers, grunting instead of speaking and in every way possible
showing her displeasure with me for making you run away."

"Did she and Matt have a successful day of shopping?"

"By the number of boxes we brought home, I'd say so," he said, laughing. "Which brings up another point. This afternoon, Matt went to the door of the room you'd occupied and began pounding on it shouting, 'Ah-den. Ah-den.' That's when Mrs. Laani started sniffing with indignation every time she looked in my direction."

If there had been any remaining doubts in Arden's mind, they vanished when she heard that her son missed her. How could she turn down this opportunity to live with him for even a brief span of time?

Could she be blamed later? She hadn't manipulated Drew into the invitation; only a martyr would say no to it. Hadn't she earned the privilege of having her son for a little while? Didn't all those months of mental anguish, of wondering who he was and where he was, of having no image of him, entitle her to *something*?

And Drew. She loved him, in a way she'd never imagined loving a man, intellectually, spiritually and physically. Her love encompassed all that Arden Gentry was. It was a love without hope for a future, but that made it no less genuine, no less fierce. The next few days—she didn't really think she'd leave in the morning—would have to last her a lifetime. She'd not refuse them. She deserved a little selfishness.

They entered his estate from the back, since the front of it faced the Pacific Ocean on the western shore of Maui. They drove through iron gates that swung open when he pushed a transmitter and automatically closed and locked behind them.

The sweeping lawn gently sloped downhill several hundred feet toward the beach. It was well past twilight, but Arden could see vast shadows of the banyan trees that mushroomed over the yard like giant umbrellas, their ropelike roots draping from stout limbs. Plumeria trees, with their yellow, pink or white blossoms, perfumed the evening air. Ti plants, wood rose cloaked with yellow blooms, orchid trees and other flowering shrubs banked lush beds of flowers. Giant oleanders provided hedges and lent the estate total privacy.

The house itself—what could be seen of it behind its veil of blooming vines—appeared to be alternating walls of sand-colored brick and glass. Wide verandas led into rooms left open to the evening air and cooled by the ocean breeze.

"It's gorgeous," Arden said, stepping out of the car without waiting for Drew to come around and open her door. The wind flirted with her hair and filled her nostrils with the scent of flowers and sea.

"I bought it on sight. Come on in. I'll send Mo after your bags."

He led her around to the ocean side where they entered the living room through an opening in the glass wall. Tall, stained-wood shutters, which had been pulled open and stacked together, could be used to close off the glass to provide privacy or protection from the weather. Quarry-tile floors were polished to mirror perfection and dotted with oriental rugs.

The furniture emphasized comfort, not formality. The upholstered pieces were done in a nubby, oatmeal-colored fabric. Brightly colored pillows in varied prints and stripes provided splashes of color. Fresh flowers filled vases and bowls strategically placed around the room. An ebony grand piano stood in stately dignity in one corner; a stone fireplace filled another. Tables were of glass or wood and trimmed in brass. It was one of the most gorgeous rooms Arden had ever seen, and it set the tone for the entire house.

"Formal dining room, breakfast room and kitchen through

there," Drew said, pointing. "My office is on the other side.
Powder room behind the stairs."

The open staircase had solid-oak steps and a banister inlaid
with strips of brass. Drew led her up to the second floor.

"I'm going to put myself back in favor with my housekeeper and my son by bringing you home to them."

They went down a wide second-story hallway, and Drew
pushed open a door. Mrs Laani had somehow wriggled her
bulk into a rocking chair and was singing softly to a sleepy
Matt.

He sat up instantly when they entered the room. The
moment he saw his father and Arden, he flung himself out
of Mrs. Laani's arms and hurled himself across the room. He
all but tackled Arden, wrapping his chubby arms around her
calves. Drew, smiling, lent her support as she knelt down to
embrace the boy.

"Hello, Matt," she said, combing her fingers through
his halo of blond curls. "Have you been a good boy today?
Hmm?" Earlier today she'd planned to leave him. Now she
had been granted a few more precious hours. She gathered
him to her and hugged him hard. Her eyes grew cloudy with
tears when she felt his arms going around her neck and returning her hug.

Pushing her away, his stubby finger found a button on his
pajamas, and he declared proudly, "But-n."

"Oh, how clever you are," Arden cried, hugging him
again. She searched her own bodice, then realized that her
sundress didn't have any buttons. "Well, sometimes I have
buttons, too," she said, laughing.

"He's been a terror, so don't you dare compliment him,"
Mrs. Laani said. "Trying clothes on him is like trying to dress
an octopus." She was attempting to maintain a demeanor of
solid authority, but she was beaming at Drew and Arden.

"You two must be hungry. Mr. McCasslin wouldn't stop to eat before he had us pack up everything and hustled us out to the airport to catch the last flight for the evening. I swear I never saw him in such a hurry." Drew glared at her and cleared his throat threateningly, but she only smiled back, her round dark eyes flashing merrily.

"Don't you have something you could be doing?" he growled.

"As I was about to suggest," she said huffily as she squeezed herself out of the chair, "if the two of you will bed down Matt—and you're welcome to him—I'll fix you a light supper." She folded her arms over her massive bosom and eyed Drew. "I take it you offered the young lady dinner."

He caught her less-than-subtle rebuke. "Arden will be our houseguest for...as long as I can talk her into staying. Will you please ask Mo to get her bags out of the car?"

Mrs. Laani waddled to the door of the nursery. "And which room shall I tell him to put them in?" Her indifference was far too overdone to be authentic.

"In the guest room you think most appropriate," Drew said.

Arden hid her confusion and flaming cheeks by carrying Matt to the rocking chair and continuing where Mrs. Laani had left off. When the housekeeper had left the room, Drew squatted down in front of the chair and rested his hands on Arden's knees. Their eyes met, and an electrical spark arced between them.

"I think Mrs. Laani knows I have the hots for you."

"Drew!" Arden exclaimed.

"And I think she knows you have the hots for me."

"Hot," Matt said, wrinkling up his brows and blowing on his hands. The two adults laughed.

"I'm glad he can't interpret that in the context you said it," Arden said chastisingly.

"But you do, don't you?"

"Do what?" She pretended interest in the design on Matt's pajamas.

"Never mind," Drew said in a voice rife with promise. "We'll continue this discussion later." He slapped Matt lightly on the thigh. "Well, son, are you glad to have your favorite girl back?"

Unaware that he was answering his father's question, Matt laid his head against Arden's chest and yawned broadly.

"He's had quite a day," Arden said, feathering his cheek with the back of her finger.

"Don't spend all your sympathy on him. Save some for me. I've had a helluva day, too."

She looked at him and smiled gently, a Madonna's smile. "You certainly have. This is the first of many tremendous days for you, Drew. I'm sure of it. What happened after the match?"

"I was a captive of the press for about an hour. Everyone wanted to know the gory details of my life this past year— why I became a recluse. They wanted to know if I was on the wagon."

"And what did you tell them?"

"Yes. I told them that the drinking had been the result of my wife's death. That I had come to my senses about six months ago and since then had been working like hell until I felt ready for a day like today."

"You were more than ready. When will you play again?"

He outlined the schedule of tournaments Ham was lining up. "I'm still going to take it slow for a while. I can't catch up this year, but next year I think I can make an impressive showing."

"How many years did you win the Grand Slam?" The research she'd done before coming to Hawaii had taught her that the Grand Slam referred to winning the Australian Open, the U.S. Open, Wimbledon and the Paris Open.

"Twice. With two years in between. I'll never do that again, but it won't matter, Arden. As long as I know I'm playing the best that I can, the winning's not so important anymore. I've won the really important battle."

She reached out to touch his hard, sun-tanned cheek. She could almost feel the new strength and confidence he'd found within himself. Just as her fingers brushed the line of his jaw, she jumped in surprise and uttered a sharp cry.

Matt had curiously slipped his hand into the wrapped bodice of her sundress to investigate something he'd never seen before. He had found her breast and its coral nipple an intriguing formation. He was lightly pinching it between his fingers.

"But-n, but-n," he said in proud discovery.

"Matthew!" Arden gasped, taking his hand away from her and refolding her dress.

Drew fell backward on the floor laughing. "He hasn't been around very many women."

"He's been around Mrs. Laani," Arden said, not daring to meet Drew's dancing eyes.

"Come, now, Arden. You and Mrs. Laani are hardly built alike. Matt saw something new and wonderful and had to check it out."

"Well, perhaps before he does too many things like that, you ought to have a man-to-man talk with him."

Drew rolled to his feet and scooped the boy into his arms, carrying him toward the crib. "Yes. I believe I should." He placed his mouth directly over Matt's ear and said loud enough for Arden to hear, "Son, you've got excellent taste in women."

★ ★ ★

Mrs. Laani had set a table in the "casual" dining room. Drew looked at his housekeeper from under reproving brows when he noted the candlelit table. She bustled around busily, ignoring his glower.

"I thought this would be cozy and restful after such a long, tedious day. I hope you like salmon, Ms. Gentry."

"Yes. That sounds wonderful."

Indeed, the cold salmon with cucumber and dill sauce, the vegetable casserole that Mrs. Laani served with it and the rich custard dessert were delicious. But part of Arden's satisfaction over the meal didn't come from the food but from the man who stared at her as intently as she at him.

Drew's eyes sparkled in the candlelight as he discussed the match at her urging. He seemed reluctant to talk about it, self-conscious, humble, but she coaxed him to tell his impressions of it. He seemed pleased that she had watched so closely and knew each stroke he referred to.

"You didn't mind losing it?"

"I always mind losing, Arden. I told you once, I like to win. But if I must lose, I want to lose with dignity in a fair fight. Today was a victory in spite of the score."

"Yes, it was."

His eyes looked into hers across the candlelit table. "I was afraid you weren't going to be at the club after you sneaked out of the hotel."

"I didn't *sneak,*" she said evasively.

"I guess it was just a coincidence that I was in the shower when you returned to your room and an oversight that you didn't leave a message with either Mrs. Laani or the desk as to where you'd be."

She ran her thumb and forefinger up and down the slender taper in the candlestick. "That was inconsiderate of me,

I suppose, since I was your guest. Jerry Arnold told me you were angry before the match." There was an unspoken question dangling at the end of the statement.

"I was. When I got to the club and he didn't have a ticket for you, I raised hell. I told him he'd better find a choice seat or else. As you know, he got hospitable real quick." His grin was just short of devilish.

She leaned across the table. "You know something? I think you like to shake people up, throw your weight around, be a bully."

He chuckled. "I do. Especially when something means a great deal to me." He was all seriousness when he said, "Your being at that match meant more than you'll ever know. I could feel your support and encouragement."

Her eyes went round with disbelief. "But you didn't even look at me."

"I didn't have to, to know you were there," he said in a tone that stirred her blood.

Mrs. Laani interrupted the intimate mood. "If you don't mind, I'm going to bed, Mr. McCasslin," she said from the doorway. "I'll clear these dishes in the morning. Ms. Gentry is in the room next to yours. Will that be satisfactory?"

"That will be fine. Thank you, Mrs. Laani. Good night."

"Good night." Arden's voice sounded like corn husks shifting against each other.

"Let's walk on the beach," Drew said, helping her out of her chair. He dropped a light kiss on her shoulder. "But you'd better change into something warmer. The wind can get cool after sundown."

He was waiting for her at the bottom of the stairs when she descended five minutes later wearing an apricot-colored velour warm-up suit. The pants were banded at her ankles, and she was barefoot. She had beautiful feet, with wellpedicured toes. He noticed the tantalizingly free swaying of her breasts beneath the sweatshirt and knew she didn't have a bra on. He had a strong desire to close his hands over her breasts, to feel their full softness under the velvety cloth. The pulses inside his head began to pound and were echoed in the lower part of his body.

"Sure you won't be too cold?" he asked as evenly as his unstable senses would let him. She nodded. He settled his arm over her shoulders and led her out into a moon-bathed night.

It seemed that speaking had become difficult for her, too, and he appreciated the fact that she didn't force conversation. He could see the emotion, the anticipation of what was about to happen, in her eyes. Words would be superfluous to what their bodies were communicating to each other.

They walked in silence down the gradual slope of the well-kept lawn, stepped over a low brick wall and onto the sand that led to the shore. Drew's beach was in a small semi-circular cove. Waves rolled in to spend their force on the lava rocks before gently continuing forward to foam over the sand. The moon shone on the ocean in a silver band that stretched from the shore to the horizon. Its light shimmered in the curling crests of the waves. Wind soughed through the broad fronds of the palms. It was an enchanting setting.

As many times as he had sat on this beach alone and thought it a magical place, Drew now knew this scene would forever lack something if it didn't have Arden in it. She made the magic real, tangible, touchable. The moonlight paled her skin, but made her hair as dark as ebony. The stars had no brilliance compared to the emeralds of her eyes.

He seated himself on the firmly packed sand and pulled her down with him. He sat with one knee raised behind her, the other leg tucked firmly against her derriere, her back against his chest. For a moment, he didn't make any move to touch her or to speak. After all, he didn't know how she would respond when he told her what he felt compelled to say. If he'd known fear that day as he faced Gonzales across the net, he was terrified now. The outcome of the tennis match wasn't nearly as important to him as the result of the conversation to follow.

"I love you, Arden."

There. A simple confession. A bold truth plainly stated.

Her hair swept his face when she turned her head. The moist lips he wanted to claim forever were parted in surprise. "What did you say?"

"I love you."

He looked out at the ocean and felt a kinship with it. It seemed so placid on the surface, yet was roiling beneath, just as he was. "I never thought I'd say that to another woman. I loved Ellie very much. I didn't think I'd ever love that way again. And I don't. I love you more."

All the air left Arden's body. She could feel her chest contracting and it was painful. He was going to kill her with softly spoken words. She couldn't let him. "You have me in residence. You don't have to say that."

He ran his finger down to her cheek, smiling gently. "Don't say something ridiculous and get me mad all over again." His lips caressed her temple, but barely. "I'm not saying it for any reason except that it's true. I've given you ample reason not to trust me. I've behaved badly on occasion. But don't you see, Arden, that I was responding defensively? I felt guilty because I was coming to love you more than I ever loved Ellie. I couldn't cope with that. Today, when I thought you'd left me for good, I nearly went crazy."

"But during the match—"

"Not then, later. After the match, when you couldn't be

found anywhere." He laughed. "Actually, during the match, I was still angry over the scene this morning. I don't think I would have played with such energy if you hadn't made me so furious."

She ducked her head in embarrassment. His fingers threaded through her wind-tossed hair. He loved the satiny feel of it as it slipped coolly along his skin. "You played it just right. You didn't coddle me. Nor did you try to talk me into or out of playing. You realized the decision had to be mine even though you knew I had no choice but to play."

"That's right. I knew you had to play. I knew you wanted to. But I couldn't tell you that. You had to figure it out for yourself."

"That's my point, Arden. You didn't tell me what I wanted to hear. As Ellie used to do."

"Drew, please don't."

"I want you to know."

"But I don't need to know."

"Yes, you do. I agreed that when we made love, it would be with no ghosts, no secrets between us."

She looked away quickly, but not for the reason he thought. She still harbored a secret, a secret that might cost her his love.

"Ellie backed anything I said or did even when she must have known I was wrong. She wouldn't come to watch me play because she was afraid I might suffer a defeat and she couldn't stand to see me down."

Arden did look at him then, in amazement. "Strange, isn't it?" Drew asked, seeing her incredulous expression. "When she traveled with me, she stayed away from the courts. And she couldn't be objective when I lost. If she had been alive today, she'd have made excuses, apologies, and commiserated with me over the loss. I'm not sure she would have understood that it was a personal triumph. You did."

He cupped the back of Arden's head and pressed it down to the hollow between his throat and shoulder. "Ellie could share victory with me. But I don't think she could have ever shared defeat. Even after all we went through to get Matt, I worried about what she'd do if our bubble burst one day."

Arden closed her eyes at the mention of Matt. What would have happened had he not been born perfect and healthy? Would Ellie have rejected him? Ron would never have reared another man's child. He might have even had the infant terminated. The thought made Arden shiver, and Drew's arms tightened around her.

"I was almost more afraid of the future when I was playing well and living with Ellie than I have been recently. I don't think she could have faced a tragedy and survived." His lips found her ear, and his breath filled it warmly. "Arden, I feel that we could face anything together. You make me feel strong and confident, at peace with myself but always trying to be better. When someone thinks you are perfect, as Ellie did me, there isn't much to strive toward."

He captured her face between his hands and looked down into her swimming eyes. "Do you realize what I'm telling you?"

"Comparisons are unfair, Drew. To everyone."

"I know. I just wanted you to know that I wasn't substituting you for her in my life. You're different. Better for me."

"Drew," she whispered, and laid her forehead against his chin, rolling it back and forth. She wasn't prepared for this. God, the last thing she'd ever expected was to have him fall in love with her. It was even more unheard of than her loving him. It was too much. She couldn't take that much goodness in her life. It frightened her. What price would she have to pay for it?

But with his hands warm and soothing, his words of love drifting into her ear, his heart pounding in tempo with hers, she didn't want to think of the future. She only wanted to revel in the fact that he was loving her. She should tell him about Matt now, while the mood was mellow and he was being honest with her. But...

"Arden, Arden." He uttered her name, only a heartbeat before his tongue filled her mouth. It plundered sweetly, rediscovering her taste, a miracle that happened each time he kissed her.

His hand slipped under the velour top. Her skin was warm velvet; he could feel her heart pulsing against his hand as he held her breast.

She sighed his name and moved against him in unspoken but undeniable need. "I don't want to usurp anyone's place in your heart, Drew."

He kissed her throat as he continued to fondle her breast. "You aren't. You're too rare. You hold a place uniquely your own because no one else has ever been able to fill it." His hands spoke as eloquently as his words as they touched her reverently. Then he withdrew them from her sweatshirt and wrapped his arms around her with unquestionable possession. Her head fell back against his raised knee as he kissed her.

Tongues swirled together in an erotic ballet. His lips clung to hers as though they never intended to let go. "I love tasting you," he said as his mouth moved back and forth over hers. His tongue flicked at the corners of her mouth maddeningly, until her hands came up to imprison his head.

She arched upward, flattening her breasts against the wall of his chest. Bravely, her tongue pushed past his, and she kissed him in a way she'd never dared kiss anyone before.

Former inhibitions fell aside. Again and again, she kissed him, declaring her desire.

"My God," he rasped, when at last they fell apart, groping for oxygen. He clasped her head between his hands as he stared down into her eyes. "Inside?"

She nodded her consent, and they rose together. The house was quiet. Only night-lights along the hallways had been left on. At the door to her room, he settled his hands on her shoulders.

"I've crowded you, Arden. Ever since I first met you, I've had things my way. I won't bully you again. I've told you I love you, and I do. But it's unconditional. It doesn't require anything of you. If you come to me, I'll show you how much I love you. If not, I'll understand."

He faded into the shadows of the hall and disappeared into the room next to hers. Moving automatically and purposefully, she went into the room where her things had already been unpacked. She didn't even notice the blue, avocado and beige décor that was somehow both elegant and informal. The adjoining bathroom was equally well decorated.

She peeled off the sweat suit and turned on the taps of the shower until it was steamy. Meticulously, she showered and shampooed, still caught in that trance that would not let her think beyond her senses, beyond her instincts. Certainly it wouldn't let her conscience become involved in her thoughts.

She dried her hair, splashed herself with a perfume too expensive for such lavish usage and glossed her mouth with peachy gel. With an economy of movement, she wrapped herself in a silk kimono and left the room.

Her soft knock was answered immediately. He stood with a terry-cloth towel around his middle. His hair was only partially dry. The hair blanketing his chest curled damply. His eyes gleamed like sapphires in the dim light.

"Arden?" he questioned softly.

"I want you," she admitted huskily.

"In bed?"

"Yes."

"Naked?"

In answer, she stepped close to him and placed her hands flat on his chest. The springy hair teased her palms, her fingertips. She feathered it; she combed through it down the length of his torso. It became silky just above his navel and narrowed to a fine strip of gold. Her hands fumbled with the tuck he'd made in the towel; then it fell away.

The drumming of her heart drowned out every other sound, even that of her uneven breathing as her fingers drifted downward. They stirred in the thicker, coarser hair. Then courage deserted her, and she raised imploring eyes to him.

"I...can't...I'm..."

"Shh," he said, pulling her against him. "You've come more than halfway. That wasn't a test. You'll never have to do anything just because you think I want it or expect it. Let's learn to love each other together."

His lips were suppliant as they met hers. They moved over her mouth with gentle persuasion until her momentary shyness vanished and she responded with the true sensuality that had lain dormant all her life. Her mouth flowered open beneath his. His tongue dipped repeatedly into it, giving, taking, enriching, ravishing.

His hands trembled with eagerness as he slipped them inside the kimono. He curbed an impulse to tear it from her body and crush her against him. She wasn't one of his fleeting, meaningless nighttime toys. They were in the past.

Arden was his present and future. And she was precious, so precious. He wanted to go slow, to appreciate every nuance of her and their lovemaking. He let his hands rest at her waist, caressing softly. Only when he heard her soft whine of longing did his hands lift the garment from her body and let it float to the floor.

He stepped away from her and treated himself to the sight of her perfect nakedness. His hands touched her lightly, following the track of his eyes. Arden was dismayed to feel tears of gratitude flooding her eyes. Drew's slow savoring of her body endeared him to her.

"I've never been worshiped before. Only devoured," she whispered.

His face looked incredibly sad, then incredibly happy. "You're so beautiful," he said hoarsely. He swept her into his arms and carried her to the bed. The spread had already been folded down. He laid her on soft, fragrant linens and followed her down, nestling himself close to her. They smiled in pure enjoyment of the rough texture of his body against the satiny texture of hers.

He caught her wrists in one gentle fist and raised them above her head. His other hand massaged her breasts. "You don't look like you ever had a baby." She caught herself just in time from correcting him that she'd had two children, not one. "Your breasts are firm and round." He circled them with a talented finger. "Your nipples are light and delicate." He touched them in turn, and they responded. "You have no stretch marks."

She arched her back when his finger trailed down the straight column of her stomach and into the dark shadow at the top of her thighs. "You're perfect," he whispered a second before his mouth covered hers. When she had been thoroughly kissed, his lips trailed down her throat. His caresses had prepared her breasts for his mouth, and he suckled them with infinite care. His tongue rolled over her nipples, lubricating them deliciously.

"Let go of my hands." When he complied, she tangled her fingers in his hair and pressed his head closer. "Oh, God, Drew. I've never been loved like this."

"I hope not. I want to be the only man you ever remember having touched you."

"No one has. Not like this."

His mouth practiced merciless torture on her navel, deflowering it with a nimble tongue, loving it with sipping lips. She twisted and writhed beneath him, a stranger to herself. A shudder rippled through her when his mouth nuzzled the dark delta of her femininity. She called his name half in panic, half in joy, when she felt his lips nibbling the inside of her thighs. Then he parted them gently, and the artistry of his touch told her she'd known nothing of intimacy before.

"Please, please, Drew."

He honored her hoarse request and the urgent clawing of her hands and climbed her body until he was poised over her. His eyes locked with hers as he introduced himself into her body. He didn't pause or hesitate but pressed deeply and slowly until she knew all of him. Then he did something her husband had never done during lovemaking; he smiled down into her face. When he began to move, he was still watching her, cataloging her pleasure, memorizing her rapture, noting what movement made her eyes grow smoky with passion.

"You feel so good inside, Arden."

"I do?"

"Oh, God, yes," he ground out. "Move with me."

Conversation? Unheard of during lovemaking. The only sounds she'd ever heard in Ron's bed were meaningless grunts and groans.

"L-like that. Again," she stuttered when he stroked the portal, then sank into her completely. "Yes, yes, yes."

When the crisis came, it wrapped them both in a velvet glove of ecstasy, shook them, squeezed the breath from them and spun them about, lifted them, tossed them to the mercy of the heavens, then let them fall into a realm of glory to which each was alien.

Long minutes later, Drew raised his head from her shoulder and with his little finger lifted damp bangs from her eyes. When they opened in sleepy contentment, he dropped a kiss on her mouth and said, "Thank you, Arden, for making me new."

Chapter 9

The sheer drapes at the wall of windows overlooking the ocean billowed into the room. Arden's eyes opened languorously, and she sighed with the deepest pleasure she ever remembered feeling. The room, bathed with the ethereal lavender of dawn, encapsulated her like a sensuous cocoon of love. In it she had learned the meaning of life in its most splendored dimension.

Drew's breathing was deep and even. She could feel it on her naked back as he held her close to him, sharing the pillow, his arm lying along her thigh. She turned her head slightly, careful not to awaken him, as she looked about the room she had been too entranced to observe in detail the night before.

It was as tastefully decorated as the rest of the house. The walls were covered with grass cloth that contrasted in texture to the lambskin covering the bed. The thick carpet was ivory colored. Against that neutral background, there were accents of pumpkin and chocolate in two easy chairs arranged close to a small table near the windows, in numerous pillows that had been heedlessly tossed off the bed onto the floor, in subtle prints that hung in brass frames on the walls. The furniture had clean, uncluttered lines. The fireplace, in the wall opposite the windows, was a luxury that she found delicious in a tropical climate. It was bricked in the same ivory color and had a fan-shaped brass screen. She liked the room.

She loved the man.

A sliver of sunlight beamed across the carpet like a miniature spotlight. She ought to return to her room before anyone else began to stir. It was about time for Matt to wake up, and after that, no one slept, Arden thought, smiling.

She eased Drew's leaden arm off her thigh and inched to the edge of the bed. Gaining the floor, she pulled on her jade silk kimono and tiptoed over the carpet, which was lush and seductive against her bare feet. The doorknob was under her hand, and she was twisting it slowly when Drew's arms flattened against the door on either side of her.

She stifled a soft scream and collapsed against the wood.

"Where do you think you're going?" he growled into her neck. He pressed forward, trapping her against the door and his hard frame.

"To my room."

"Guess again." He kissed her neck, parting his lips and letting his tongue moisten a vulnerable spot. "You're not going anywhere except back to bed. With me."

She shivered as his mouth made a damp, treacherous path to the back of her ear. Playfully, his tongue batted at her earlobe. "Ah…Drew…don't…I have to go back to my own room."

His hands slid down the smooth surface of the door to her waist. With a tiny yank, the tie of her kimono, which she'd carelessly looped but hadn't bothered to knot, fell away beneath his deft fingers. "Give me one good reason why."

"Uh…" He separated the folds of her kimono and ran his fingertips over her ribs. Moving closer, he settled his middle against her derriere. She knew he had come to her as he had slept—naked. And she couldn't think of one good reason why she had to leave him at that moment.

His arms crisscrossed her chest, and he closed a hand over each breast. "Your breasts are so pretty," he murmured as his hands formed gentle cones around them. "I like that line that marks your tan about here," he said, letting his index finger trace it. "Of course, if you'd sunbathe on my beach, you wouldn't have a line. I could rub you with oil, and you could tan evenly all over while I watched."

His hands and provocative suggestions were lulling her into that same enchanted sphere she'd known the night before. Through no conscious thought, her body became malleable, conforming to the curves and bulges of his.

The tender caresses on her nipples had made them bead with desire. He whispered his praise of them in her ear, making her both exult and blush with the boldness of his language. "I love the feel of your skin against my tongue. You taste like all things maternal and all things erotic. Your taste epitomizes womanhood."

Drained of all energy and will to resist now, she laid her head against his shoulder. Moving slightly, she rubbed against him and felt his fierce passion nudging her hip.

His breath was like a storm in her ear as one hand surveyed the smooth plain of her stomach and abdomen. He paused not at all in finding his final destination. His palm settled over the gently swelling mound, while his fingers curved inward to seek the mysteries chastely hidden between her thighs. His thumb roved through the dusky nest.

"I love you here." Even as he spoke, he was moving his thumb in that lazy, hypnotic way that stole her breath, her reason. "Dark. And silky. So silky."

His exploring fingers discovered her dewy and ready for his love, but he prolonged the rapture. Tenderly and carefully, he adored her with his fingertips, giving her untold pleasure and asking nothing in return. He stroked her to unbearable, mindless passion, finding and kneading the magic key that unlocked all that made her woman.

She shuddered against him, soundlessly and breathlessly and incoherently chanting his name. He turned her, and with his hands beneath her hips, lifted her and let her find his accommodating maleness. She sank upon him fully.

She sobbed her love as again and again he arched his back, driving himself higher and higher. The world fell away in one swift, sudden explosion. Her thighs clamped his, and her arms closed around his neck. Her breasts muffled his own ecstatic cries.

When Arden's consciousness returned, modesty prevented her from lifting her head to look at him. Sensing her shyness and knowing the reason for it, Drew carried her back to the bed and laid her down like a child. Still, she wouldn't look at him. He smiled in faint amusement and love, stroking her back.

"Arden," he whispered. "Was it so terrible?"

She rolled over to look up at him. Shaking her head, she closed her eyes. "It was beautiful."

"Then why can't you look at me?" He brought her hand to his lips and kissed the backs of her fingers. There was a tentative smile on her delicious lips.

"I'm embarrassed." The words were spoken so softly, he could barely hear them.

"I didn't mean to embarrass you."

"No!" Her eyes flew wide. "Not you. You don't embarrass me. I embarrass myself. I've never…been like this before." Her eyes stared at the forest of golden hair on his muscular chest. She longed to touch it, but was still timid, half-afraid of the changes taking place in her personality. "I've never done…well, things like this. I don't know myself when I behave with so little self-control."

She rested her cheek against his arms, speaking aloud the thoughts that went through her mind. "It's like there's another woman inside me that I didn't know of before I met you. But that's not right, either, because it's not another woman—it's *me*. I didn't know that part of me existed. And I'm having a hard time getting acquainted with it."

"In other words," he said quietly, "you didn't know until you met me that you were a lusty wanton with an insatiable sex drive." Startled, she looked up at him, but laughed in relief when she saw the teasing light in his blue eyes. "Frankly, I'm delighted."

He clasped her to him, and they laughed softly, rolling together on the bed. His heart was soaring because they took such pleasure in each other and were able to laugh and love in the same minute. Since Ellie died, there had been no joy after sex for him, only a kind of frantic despair.

He couldn't stand the thought of that now, of how empty his life had been. He didn't want to even imagine a life without Arden in it. His arms held her prisoner as he kissed her, not with passion but with a telling need, a message of how vital she had become to him.

"Let's go wash," he said with a huskiness that came from a tangle of emotions.

The bathroom was hedonistically opulent. The sunken bath was enormous and had whirlpool jets placed at intervals along its deep sides. A picture window provided a view of the ocean. The oversize shower had a clear glass door. It was into this that Drew led Arden.

Whatever modesty she had left was swept down the shower drain, never to be regained. Drew's eyes and hands idolized every part of her. And instead of feeling sullied by his frank sexual interest, she felt purified because she knew it came not from lust but from love.

They kissed, licking droplets of water from each other's faces. Her hands slid down the muscled expanse of his back. The narrowness of his waist was briefly appreciated before her hands smoothed lower over his taut buttocks. Bravely, her eyes locked onto his as her hands familiarized themselves with each curve, each masculine line.

He watched with incredulous pleasure as she soaped her hands slowly, provocatively. His throat tightened, and he swallowed convulsively when she took his sex between her lathered hands. Her touch was timid at first but gained confidence and increased pressure as she watched his eyes grow dark and hot.

"Arden," he gasped, "do you know what you're doing to me?"

"I'm doing something wrong?" she asked in alarm, yanking her hands back.

"No, God, no." He caught her hand and replaced it and at the same time pulled her to him with his other arm. "You're perfect, and so sexually innocent despite having been a wife and mother."

"One had nothing to do with the other." She was thinking not only of her private life with Ron but also of the sterile precision with which she'd conceived Matt.

"I'm a selfish bastard to say this, but I'm glad."

They rinsed and went back into the bedroom. "Lie down on your stomach," he instructed gently. Without a qualm, she obliged him. He stretched out beside her. "We really must do something about these strap lines," he murmured. Her back was marked by several pale stripes, and her bottom was noticeably white against her tan back and legs.

"What do you suggest we do now?" she asked sleepily, her head resting on her folded arms.

"Umm, what do you think?" he said with a lascivious inflection.

"You're incorrigible."

"Where you're concerned, I am."

His hands were massaging her shoulders and rubbing her back with a gifted touch.

"What will we do if Matt comes barging in?" she asked.

His hands slid down her ribs and back up again, lifting the plump sides of her breasts on their ascent. She sighed blissfully. "He won't. I locked the door." He leaned over her back and spoke directly into her ear. "I didn't want to be disturbed, even by my son."

His hand seesawed in the curve of her waist, then coasted over the slope of her derriere. She uttered a responsive moan when she felt his teeth nipping at her waist. As lifeless as a rag doll, she obeyed the urging of his hands to turn over. His lips continued their trail of kisses over her stomach and then lower.

Agilely, he positioned himself between her thighs and laid his head on her abdomen. His breath stirred the dark down. Idly her fingers trailed through his thick, tousled hair. She was astounded at her own acceptance of this new intimacy, her explicit trust in him, the now-familiar way her body began to warm and liquefy and swell with renewed longing.

Her bones melted beneath the warmth of his mouth when he kissed her stomach. "I want to love you again, Arden."

His breath struck her skin in hot puffs that made her insides quiver.

"Then love me."

He levered himself up over her, nestling his sex against hers but not taking possession. "Your breasts are going to be sore," he said miserably, looking at their fullness and the tempting crowns. "Not to mention the rest of you."

She hooked a hand around the back of his head and pulled him down to her breast. "Kiss me here," she whispered. "Make them wet."

He groaned softly as he took her nipple into his mouth. He drew on it gently, ever mindful of hurting her. Lifting his head, he appraised his handiwork before painting the hardened tip again with delicate strokes of his tongue. He continued on each breast until they were glistening in the morning light. Arden writhed beneath him, loving the way he tugged on her so sweetly. She felt each contraction deep inside the heart of her femininity. She moved against his body, begging him to fill the void he had created.

With one sure thrust, he obliged her. He buried himself into her warmth, and she sheathed him tightly.

As before, it wasn't a culmination but a beginning. A rebirth. For as surely as Drew's life showered into her body, she filled him with her own essence. They lay together, breathing in the scent of their loving, feeling not depleted but filled with new life and energy.

"Arden," he said softly as he left her, only to gather her close to him.

"Hmm?"

"This illicit affair must come to an end."

She felt as though her heart plummeted to the floor and shattered into a million pieces. "End?"

"Yes," he said earnestly. "You must marry me."

★ ★ ★

"You haven't responded to my proposal, Arden."

It was hours since he'd made it. Arden knew no more now how she was going to respond than she had when he'd first astounded her with his proposal. They were on the beach, playing with Matt. The three of them comprised a family unit, and that as much as anything panicked Arden.

Lightly, she shrugged off his statement. "As I recall, it wasn't so much a proposal as an order."

"What else could you expect from a bully?" His retort was spoken lightheartedly, but she could see the underlying seriousness in his eyes.

He hadn't demanded an answer of her when he had first mentioned marriage. Instead, he had held her while he slept. She, however, couldn't go back to sleep. Her mind had been turbulent with thoughts of the night just past, the sensual discoveries of the new day and Drew's unheralded marriage proposal.

Her? Marry Drew McCasslin, world-famous tennis pro? Drew McCasslin marry Arden Gentry, a nobody, the hired surrogate mother of his child?

When Drew had awakened, they decided they'd been self-indulgent long enough. Matt was already at breakfast when they came down the stairs. He waved at them glee-fully and sputtered cornflakes all over his high-chair tray. Drew had dressed in tennis attire, Arden in a casual pair of shorts. He had tried to talk her into going with him while he practiced.

"Drew, my clothes have been packed in a suitcase in a musty closet for nearly a week. I need to sort them out for laundry and dry cleaning."

"I can do that for you," Mrs. Laani offered as she placed a

plate of fresh fruit in front of Arden and poured her a cup of coffee.

"I appreciate that," Arden said, smiling at her. "But I'd feel better putting things away myself so I'll know where everything is."

No one seemed to doubt that she was staying indefinitely. Only Arden herself.

Drew had left for his tennis practice alone. After her clothes had been pressed and hung in the closet of the guest bedroom, Arden helped Mrs. Laani sort through the new clothes that had been bought for Matt in Honolulu.

"Oh, this is precious," Arden exclaimed, holding up a playsuit with two tennis rackets appliquéd on the bib.

Mrs. Laani laughed. "I thought his daddy would appreciate that."

Matt was underfoot and in the way and meddlesome as they unwrapped his new clothes and put them either in the closet or the chest of drawers. Arden didn't mind even when he shredded tissue paper all over his bathroom floor. Periodically, she'd hug him to her, examining his face time and again and marveling over him.

How had Drew's seed, transfused into her body so clinically, without the loving emotion such a miracle warranted, produced this unblemished specimen? She thanked God she had had a part in bringing this life into the world.

Drew had returned just before lunch. He was crackling with excitement. "You should have seen the crowd watching Gary and me work out today. They gave me a standing ovation when I walked out on the court. UPI and the Associated Press picked up news of the match yesterday. The story's gone worldwide. Ham's beside himself. He called the resort while I was there and said phone calls have been pouring in, inviting me to play in tournaments both in the States and abroad. My sponsors called to congratulate him."

He referred to the companies whose clothes and shoes he wore, whose tennis racket he used, whose planes he flew when he traveled, whose toothpaste he hyped. These endorsements comprised as much—if not more—of his income as prize money. When his playing began to slide, so had the offers from these companies.

"I was scared that when my contracts came around for renewal, the sponsors would let them drop. Now they're talking bigger and better things. They're still wary, of course. It was only one match, and I didn't *win* it, but at least they haven't given me up for lost. I need to win one. Now I know I can."

His eyes sparkled as he clutched Arden's hand across the luncheon tabletop. "I only need one thing in my life to make me completely happy."

Arden knew what that something was. It had been haunting her all morning. Her heart was full to bursting with joy that Drew loved her enough to marry her. Why was she hesitating? Why hadn't she flung her arms around him the moment the words were out of his mouth and said, *Yes!* she'd marry him? Because she'd been immediately reminded of what had brought her to this man in the first place.

Matt.

What more could she ask for? She'd have her son, live with him, be his mother in every sense of the word, be able to watch him grow into boyhood, adolescence, manhood. She'd be there, witnessing it all, helping him through the tough spots, loving him. Why couldn't she tell Drew that she wanted to marry him more than anything in the world?

Because he had been honest with her and she hadn't been with him. She couldn't enter into a marriage with that lie of omission between them. She'd been in a marriage like that, and it had bred contempt. Ron had married her for self-serving reasons, and she'd never forgiven him. She'd hated him for it. And he'd come to scorn her for her constant, meek submission.

What would happen if Drew found out who she was and the role she'd played in his past? He would think she'd married him solely because she wanted to be with her son. Would he ever believe that she loved him now as much...no, more... than she did the son she'd conceived of his seed? Knowing his pride, she doubted it.

So tell him now, she commanded herself. *Don't risk his finding out later. You can't have this secret between you, so tell him now. Today.* She shivered with dread. No matter who Matt's mother was, Drew wouldn't be happy to meet her. Each time he mentioned the trouble he and Ellie had had "getting" Matt, his eyes betrayed an uneasiness about it. No, he wouldn't be glad to meet Matt's mother. He certainly wouldn't be glad to learn that she was a woman he'd come to trust, to love, who had kept the secret far too long already.

When they had walked down to the beach after lunch, her mind had still been swirling in ever-changing patterns of indecision.

Now Drew was pinning her down for an answer. But Matt chose that moment to launch himself into her chest, knocking her backward. "Oh, you!" she cried, catching him around the waist. "I think you need to go on a diet."

Matt crowed with laughter as she tossed him down on the beach blanket beside her, wrestling him and tickling his fat stomach. When he'd worn her out, he pushed himself up and went jogging toward the surf. "Be careful," Arden called after him. He stopped, turned and then spontaneously came running back. He flung his arms around her neck and kissed her wetly and enthusiastically on the mouth.

Tears blurred his image as he tripped back toward the tide.

"He loves you, too, Arden." Drew's quiet voice compelled her to look at him. When he saw her tears, he smiled. "You love him, don't you?"

The truth couldn't be withheld. "Yes."

"And me? Am I seeing something that really isn't there?"

The tears rolled down her cheeks. She reached out to caress the wind-tousled strands of hair above his rolled-bandanna sweatband. "I love you, too." Her fingers outlined his bottom lip. "I love you so much it hurts."

He caught her hand and pressed it to his cheek. "Then say you'll marry me. Ham wants me to go on tour in two weeks. I want you and Matt to go with me. I want you to go as my wife." The thought of going without her was too dismal to contemplate. On the other hand, he knew he had to go. The timing was right.

"Two weeks," she said mournfully.

"I know I'm not giving you much time. But why wait? If you love me—"

"I do."

"And you know I love you. Marry me now, Arden." He looked toward the boy who was chasing a shallow wave to shore. "I never thought I'd blackmail a woman into marrying me, but I'm going to play every ace." He sighed grimly and said, "Matt needs a mother, Arden."

"He has Mrs. Laani." It was a weak protest. Her heart seemed anchored to something in the bottom of her soul, and it was pulling her down, down, down, into a situation from which there was no easy escape. *Please don't use my son to talk me into doing something I know I shouldn't do.*

"I don't know what I would have done without her," Drew said of his housekeeper and friend. "She put up with my drunken abuse and my dark moods when a less charitable woman would have packed her bags and left. She's great with Matt. I consider her more family than employee, but she could never be a mother to him. She's too old, for one thing."

He took Arden's hand and pressed it between his. "Arden, in a few years I'll have to move from here. When Matt's older and I'm too old to play the circuit, we won't be able to live in this partial isolation. Matt will need a mother, you, when he goes to school and sees that every other kid has one."

He could still see the indecision in her eyes. He had one more shot. It was a mean one, but he was a desperate man. "Be to my son what you couldn't be to Joey."

Her head whipped around, and she jerked her hand from his. "You're being unkind, Drew."

"I know that, dammit, but I can see I might lose you, and I can't let that happen. I'm fighting for my life, and I'm going to use all the ammunition I've got." His eyes were fierce, his jaw hard and stubborn.

"I told you, you weren't merely a replacement for Ellie, and that's the God's truth. Matt can't be a replacement for the son you lost either, but you've said you've grown to love him. Give him what you didn't have a chance to give Joey." He touched her lips with his. "We could even have a child of our own."

"Oh, God," she cried, covering her face with her hands and slumping against him as he pulled her forward. He cradled her in the shelter of his arms, stroking her head and whispering endearments.

"I know I'm bullying you again, but, Arden, I want you in my life. More than tennis. More than anything. Still, I wouldn't ask you if I didn't think you needed Matt and me just as much."

Arden felt a clammy hand on her shoulder and raised her head to see Matt standing beside her. His lower lip was trembling, and his eyes, so like Drew's, were shimmering with silver tears. "Ah-den," he said on the brink of crying. "Ah-den."

"Oh, precious, no, don't cry." She wiped the tears from her eyes and forced a bright smile. "See, nothing's wrong." She remembered that Joey was never so upset as when he saw her crying. It shook a child's world to see an adult so visibly distressed. "I'm fine. See."

He looked doubtfully toward his father, but Drew's eyes remained on Arden. She pulled the boy to her and hugged him, distraught over causing him one moment of insecurity and pain.

"There, see, I'm happy," she said. "Where's your belly button? I see it, I see it," she said, poking it playfully. He giggled, and the tears began to recede.

Mrs. Laani called them from the wall separating the beach from the lawn. "Shame on you, letting that boy run naked like that," she scolded the two adults. "He'll grow up a pagan."

"This is the way God made him, Mrs. Laani," Drew said, casting a conspiratorial grin at Arden.

"Blasphemy," the older woman grumbled as she retrieved the boy and tried to pull bathing trunks up his thrashing, sandy legs. He squirmed and protested until she gave up with a resigned sigh. "See what I mean? He's half-heathen now."

She labored up the hill carrying the boy, who repeated, "No nap," until they were out of sight.

"I didn't know he saw me crying. I shouldn't have upset him."

"If I start crying, will you say you'll marry me?" Drew's expression was so boyishly winning and his eyes so sad that she broke out laughing.

"Oh, Drew," she said, leaning over to kiss him. "I love you, but there are reasons why I shouldn't marry you."

"And so many more why you should."

She rested her head against his breast, letting the crinkly hair tickle her nose. She loved the salty, musky scent of his skin. "There's one profound reason why I shouldn't marry you. Something about me...my past. Something I did that..."

He tilted her head back to peer into her eyes. "Arden, there couldn't have been anything that shameful in your past. And even if there were, when compared to me, you've lived like a saint. I don't *care* about anything in your past. I care only for our future." His fingertips skimmed her cheek. "For that matter, there is something that I've been wavering about telling you, but I honestly can't think of what difference it makes. It doesn't concern or affect the love I have for you."

He kissed the corner of her mouth. "Does this secret have anything to do with me? What you feel for me? Do you love me less because of it?"

She could answer him honestly. "No. It takes nothing away from the love I have for you."

"Then forget it. Our lives started when we met each other. Our pasts we'll keep sacred and private. We'll close the book on them and begin to collect our own sacred and private memories." He kissed her. It was a deep and probing kiss, as though he wanted to erase physically her objections with his mouth. "Marry me, Arden."

"Drew, Drew," she said, meeting his mouth for another long kiss that made everything but the love she had for him seem unimportant.

He ground their mouths together, folding his arms around her possessively and symbolically sealing them off from the rest of the world. "Take off your top," he mumbled against her mouth.

She wriggled free of him in mock exasperation. "Is that the only reason you asked me to marry you? For unlimited carnal use of my body?"

"One of the reasons," he drawled, letting his eyes descend in lecherous approval over the curves that the scant bikini did little to hide.

If he was going to keep Matt's origins from her, was her own secret so much worse? She suddenly felt free of shackles. She wanted to celebrate their love, to be happy, to shed the cloak of worry and guilt. "What if someone moseys by?" Her voice held a hint of mischievous promise.

"Mo and Mrs. Laani are the only ones allowed on the property without my prior approval. They both know that when I'm alone on my beach with a woman, they are to make themselves scarce."

"Oh? And just how many times have you been alone with a woman on your beach?"

"This is the first time. I circulated a memo this morning."

She bit her lip to keep from laughing. "What about boats? What if someone sails by and sees us…me…without any clothes on?"

"We'll see the boat first and duck for cover."

"I see you've thought of everything."

"Everything," he said, looking at her through a screen of thick, sun-gilded lashes. "By the way, did you ever say yes to my proposal? Or am I to assume by your kisses that the answer is yes?" His hands went around her. One untied the string at her neck; the other untied the one across her back.

"I didn't say yes…" The top of her bikini was caught by the wind. It fluttered against her body for a few seconds before being whisked away. "But since I'm going to be cavorting…" Drew stood up and peeled off his trunks. He was a modern rendition of Adam, perfect, golden and strong, a paragon of masculine beauty. The sweatband around his forehead lent him a savage aspect as he slowly lowered himself back to the blanket.

"…cavorting on the beach with you…" As his burning eyes watched, she peeled off her bikini panties. "…naked…" He came to her with sleek grace, and they reclined together on the blanket. "…I guess I'll have to become your wife."

His kisses were hot, almost as hot as the elements—sand, wind, sun—and just as primitive.

Chapter 10

"Helluva honeymoon," Drew muttered. He was driving toward the picturesque village of Lahaina.

"I think it's wonderful," Arden said, laughing and straightening Matt's shirt under his overalls for the umpteenth time.

"My idea of a honeymoon is having you naked in my bed engaging in all sorts of lewd physical acts."

"We'll get to that," she whispered. Drew's head swiveled around to look at her, branding her with a heated gaze. "But for now, please keep your eyes on the road."

Once she had consented, he'd wasted no time in making arrangements for their marriage, completing everything in a few days' time. The ceremony that morning had been private. They'd flown to Honolulu to be married by a minister Drew knew well. Only Mrs. Laani and the pastor's wife had been in attendance. And Matt. At Arden's request, Drew hadn't notified the press.

"Please, Drew," she had pleaded. "I don't want to be in the

limelight. I'll go on tour with you. I'll be there cheering you on at every match, but I don't want to be photographed or interviewed."

She remembered the photographers swarming around him and Ellie as they left the hospital. How had they managed to keep the secret that Ellie wasn't the child's real mother? Arden had her own secret to keep. At least for a while. She had resolved to tell Drew she was Matt's mother, but not until he was secure in her love for him. For now, the fewer people who knew about their marriage, the better. She wanted to maintain a low profile.

"But I'm proud of you," he had objected. "Why would you want to hide the fact that we're married?"

"I don't want to *hide* it. I just don't want it publicized." She groped for a plausible excuse. "Because...because of Ellie. She was so beautiful, so much a part of your life. Until I learn the ropes of the touring life, I don't want people comparing me to her."

"There is no comparison," he had said tenderly, rubbing strands of her dark hair between his fingers.

"Others might think so, and that would make me terribly uncomfortable."

He'd conceded grudgingly, and they'd returned to Maui in the middle of the afternoon to put a cranky Matt down for a nap.

"You need to call Gary for a practice set or two."

"On my wedding day?" Drew had complained.

"Do you want to win on tour or not?"

He'd turned to Mrs. Laani and spread his hands wide. "Married only a few hours and already she's nagging." Beneath his teasing, Arden could tell he was pleased that she understood how demanding his career was. "You'll go with me and watch, won't you?"

"I wouldn't miss it."

Arm in arm, they went upstairs to the master suite. Mrs. Laani had already moved many of Arden's clothes into the spare closet. Her toilet articles and makeup were neatly arranged in the bathroom dressing area. "How'd she manage this so soon?" Arden asked Drew in dismay.

"She was under strict orders to move you in here as soon as possible. You made that ridiculous rule about not sleeping with me again until we were married." He came to her and wrapped his arms around her waist, nuzzling her breasts through the silk blouse she'd worn under her wedding suit. The evidence of his impatience pressed hard against her middle. "I'm hungry for you, Arden," he rasped against her breast, and it swelled with her own desire. "From now on, expect me to be merciless."

Their mouths met urgently, moving together with suppressed longing finally given vent. Keeping his mouth on hers, his hands fumbled with her clothes until she stood in an ivory charmeuse slip. He fondled her breasts, and when her nipples tightened in response, he ducked his head to touch them with his tongue through the shiny, slinky cloth.

She rid him of his shirt and worked feverishly on his belt buckle until he could kick his way free of the trousers. She slid her hands into his tight briefs and over his buttocks. The muscles she kneaded were taut with his forced control.

He caressed her back, her derriere, her thighs, smoothing his hands over the silky slip and her pale panty hose. At the top of her thighs, his thumbs rotated arousingly over her hipbones. When he rubbed the triangular mound of her womanhood with his knuckles, she caught his hair in her fists and pulled his head away from hers.

"You've got to play tennis," she said with heaving breaths.

"To hell with it," he snarled, reaching for her again.

She was adamant. "That's exactly where your game will go if you don't practice."

He muttered a curse but stepped away from her to finish changing his clothes. She puttered with the things that had been left on her dressing table, placing them in drawers and trying not to be distracted by glimpses of Drew's body as he dressed. He wasn't in the least modest about his nakedness as he went back and forth from closet to bureau locating his tennis clothes. She'd never seen a man built finer than he.

He was stepping into a brief-style athletic supporter that he wore under his tennis shorts when he happened to catch her rapt gaze in the mirror. Insolently, he dragged the white stretchy garment up his thighs and adjusted himself within its tight confines. "See anything you like?" he asked, winking at her.

She blushed, rattling the contents of the drawer as she closed it. "I like everything I see," she admitted, risking another glance at him in the mirror. He came up behind her. "I'm glad." He lifted her hair to kiss the back of her neck.

When he had finished dressing and was stuffing a change of clothes into his tennis bag, she was still fiddling with things at the dressing table. "After spurning my romantic overtures for the sake of time, are you going to make me late by dawdling?"

She felt like a schoolgirl as she stood facing him in stocking feet and slip. "Why don't you wait for me downstairs? I... uh...I'll be ready in just a few minutes."

"What's the mat—" He caught himself. Walking to her, he placed understanding hands on her shoulders. "It's been a while since you've shared a room with a man, is that it?" She swallowed hard and nodded her head, feeling like a ninny, a fool. He kissed her cheek and squeezed her shoulders lightly. "I'll be downstairs. Take your time."

Before he was out the door, she halted him. "Drew?" When he turned around, she said, "Thank you."

He smiled and slapped the doorjamb with the palm of his hand. "I'll think of some way for you to repay me." After another hasty wink, he was gone.

Despite his objections to playing tennis on his wedding day, he played well. Another crowd had gathered to watch the practice match, and they applauded enthusiastically whenever Drew executed a particularly difficult return. He was in his element and loving every minute of it. He seemed oblivious to Arden, but she knew he was aware of her supportive presence.

He had planned to take her out for an elaborate celebration dinner, but Matt had set up a howl when they started to leave without him. "Couldn't we take him with us, Drew?" she had asked, clutching the tearful boy to her.

"Arden, since I kissed my bride this morning, I've been sharing her with other people. I want you to myself."

"And I want you, too. But I won't have a good time if we leave Matt crying this way."

Drew appealed to her intelligence. "He's only doing that to get your sympathy."

"I know. And I also know I'll have to start disciplining him. But not tonight."

Several colorful curses later, Drew gave in. "But don't get any ideas about him sleeping with us," he'd warned as he swung the car onto the highway.

"Where are you taking us tonight?" Arden asked now as the traffic on Lahaina's main thoroughfare slowed them down.

"Since you insisted on this family outing," Drew said dryly, "I'm going to let you cook my meal."

"What?" she asked, laughing in surprise.

"Just wait. You'll see."

He took them to the Pioneer Inn, an historic hotel that had accommodated seamen when Lahaina had been an important whaling port. The inn was built around an open-air central courtyard that was lit by lanterns and torches and filled with lush tropical plants.

"I love it," Arden exclaimed as the hostess led them to a table.

"I'm glad. But I wasn't kidding about cooking your own meal. See." He pointed to a large charcoal grill under a protective shed. A clock was mounted on the wall so one could monitor the cooking time according to preference. Condiments and bottled steak sauces lined the grill.

"I happen to be a terrific cook," she boasted. "When I was married and had Joey, I enjoyed planning meals and cooking. Then, after..." A spasm of sadness crossed her face. "I lost interest."

He squeezed her hand. "If you like to cook, you may cook for Matt and me whenever you want to. Starting tonight."

They gathered around the grill after they'd ordered Drew's New York steak, Matt's hamburger and Arden's *mahimahi*. The island fish was filleted and marinated, then wrapped in foil for broiling. There was much joking and advice giving as Arden wielded the long metal spatulas. Matt squealed every time a hissing flame shot up out of the charcoal pit. When the meat dishes were done, they carried them to their table and ate them with hefty salads and bowls of baked beans, the house specialty.

"Delicious," Drew said, rolling his eyes and smacking his lips over his steak. Matt comically imitated him.

Arden's heart was full to overflowing with love for the

two men in her life. She cautioned herself about feeling smug. So much happiness terrified her.

Making travel arrangements for them all was an awesome responsibility. Mrs. Laani and Matt would share one room, Drew and Arden another, while Ham occupied a third. Fortunately the manager handled most of the details. With Mrs. Laani's help, Arden learned to pack with economy of space in mind, yet the job seemed endless.

Arden was nervous about meeting Ham Davis. He was a grizzled man well under six feet tall. He chomped a cigar that was foul and fat. His belly poured over pants he was constantly hiking up with hairy, beefy hands. But his charm was undeniable. Arden liked his brusque, candid manner immediately.

He was there to meet them when their plane landed at Los Angeles International. Taking her hands between his, he pressed them hard. His dark eyes probed into hers and apparently liked what they saw. "Whatever you're doing for Drew, keep it up" was all he said, but Arden knew she had earned his unqualified approval.

He was a little put out with Drew for insisting on two things. First, that he honor Arden's request for no publicity about herself. And second, that he leave them a few free days to visit Drew's mother in Oregon.

That was another hurdle Arden dreaded, and she was fidgety and nervous on the flight to Portland. She needn't have worried. Mrs. McCasslin was gracious and warm. After the flurry at the airport and the good-natured confusion of getting them settled into her home for their two-night stay, she and Arden had their first moments alone. They were in her sunny, immaculate and homey kitchen, waiting for the teakettle to come to a boil.

"You're not what I expected," Rose McCasslin said as she reached into the pantry for a tin of flavored tea bags.

"What did you expect?" The blue eyes were a family trait. Rose's were as bright as her son's and grandson's.

"I don't know exactly. Someone stridently efficient. Someone who would have taken over Matt's upbringing and either whipped Drew into shape or browbeaten him into alcoholism. Someone not nearly as beautiful or as...soft."

"Thank you," Arden said, moved. "Drew had whipped himself into shape before he married me."

"That's why I know you're good for him. You let him do it." She cocked her head to one side. "He's very much in love with you, you know."

"I think he is, yes."

"I'm glad. And relieved. I thought when we buried Ellie and he moved to that tiny island, he'd rot there for the rest of his life. He's happy again. I have only one request to make of you."

"What?"

A familiar glint of humor lit the older woman's eyes. "Make him bring you and my grandson to see me more often."

They traveled first to Phoenix, then to Dallas, Houston, New Orleans, St. Petersburg. Drew was making an impressive showing, winning steadily in the qualifying rounds but losing in the finals. He wasn't discouraged, and neither was Ham. He was giving the best in the business a run for their money. Then he won in Memphis. And in Atlanta. And in Cincinnati. His ranking began to climb.

Arden was tired of traveling but radiant over Drew's success. Life on the tour was hard, especially with a child as energetic and inquisitive as Matt. She had written all the articles she'd been under contract to do before they left Hawaii. Through long-distance telephone calls, she had been pleased to learn they would all be printed without revisions. For the time being, she had declined requests to do more.

"What do you do all day while I'm working out?" Drew had asked her one night as they lay wrapped together in the aftermath of loving. "Are you getting bored?"

"Bored? With Matt to chase after? Hardly." She snuggled closer, loving the protective feel of him beside her. "I look forward to your matches, and…I daydream…about this." She swept her hand down his stomach to touch him intimately. He gasped softly as her fingers closed around him.

"Good God, Arden, are you trying to kill me for the insurance money? I've played a hard match of tennis today. Five of seven sets and…then made love…. Sweet heaven…"

"You don't feel as though you're on the verge of collapse to me. On the contrary…" she whispered, stroking his hard length.

"When you're not thinking of ways to drive your husband into an early grave, what do you do?" he panted.

"I write."

"Write…? No, don't stop… Yes, like that… Oh, damn… Write what?"

"Things. Notes for a novel. Poetry."

"Poetry? What you're doing to me now is poetry." Rolling her onto her back, he let her guide him into her receptive body. "Write a thousand verses of it."

They were glad to get home. Ham had been argumentative and badgering. He'd even tried to coerce Arden into lending him her support.

"He needs to play in every tournament he can," he said, punctuating each word with stabbing motions of his cigar.

"Drew wants to go home for a few weeks, Ham."

"You can convince him otherwise."

"Perhaps, but I won't."

"I figured that." He shoved the cigar in his mouth, cursed, and then said he'd drive them to the airport.

Mo had the house opened and aired and ready for them. They resumed a reasonably normal routine. Drew played every day with Gary at the club, working on the weak spots that he and Ham had discussed. Arden busied herself with Matt and made plans for their next tour, which would take them to Europe. Just thinking about it exhausted her. How could she convey to non-English-speaking waiters that Matt would prefer a peanut butter and jelly sandwich to anything on their overpriced menus? She hadn't been able to convince English-speaking ones.

One afternoon, she was relaxing in the master suite, curled in one of the chairs beside the wide windows, when Drew came in. He dropped his tennis bag just inside the door. They watched each other from across the room, silently telegraphing the love that had grown between them over the past few weeks.

"You look beautiful sitting there, Arden," he said quietly. "The setting sun's making your hair shine with red streaks."

"Thank you. I planned to be dressed by the time you got back, but I got busy on something." She closed a folder over a tablet and laid it on the table beside the chair.

He closed the door and locked it before proceeding into the room. She was wearing a dressing gown he was partial to. It fell on her shoulders in a wide scoop neckline. It was floor-length, loosely covering her body like a filmy blue cloud. "You've just bathed," he commented.

She smelled of flowery bubble bath and woman. The sheer femininity of her seemed to beckon to his maleness. He knelt beside her chair and placed his fingertips on either side of her neck. He liked to think he felt her pulse accelerate when he touched her.

She symbolized peacefulness, home, love, all the things he'd given up hope of ever having again. Each time he saw her after brief little absences, he was surprised again at how much he loved her, how from the beginning there had been a oneness between them that he couldn't understand or explain.

"What something were you busy on?"

"Nothing really," she said in that offhanded way that he'd learned meant just the opposite. Who had convinced her that her opinion wasn't valuable? The husband she spoke so little of? Almost daily, Drew condemned the man to hell. She had been hurt. Terribly. And by more than Joey's death. The traces of abuse still lingered, though she never talked about her past. If it took a lifetime, Drew planned to teach her how valuable she was.

"You've written something, haven't you?"

Her eyes fluttered away from his. "It's terrible, I know, but it's something I've wanted to put on paper for a long time."

"May I read it?"

"It's not good enough for anyone to read."

"I don't believe that."

She licked her lips. "It's very personal."

"I won't insist if you don't want me to read it."

"I'd like your opinion," she said hurriedly.

He took the initiative of picking up the folder and opening it to the first page of the tablet. "Joey" was written on the top line. He lifted his eyes to hers, but she evaded them. She left the chair and went to stand silhouetted against the window and the vermilion western sky.

Drew read the four-page poem, his throat constricting

tighter with each line. It was obvious that the words had seeped out of her soul and that it had been a painful process. They were poignant but not syrupy. They were spiritual but not pompous. They expressed the abysmal, impotent grief of a parent watching a child slowly die. But the last verses were a testimony to the blessings that had been drawn from that child. They expressed an enviable and rare joy.

Drew's eyes were wet when he stood, reverently replacing the folder on the table and going to her. His arms slid under her arms from behind and pulled her tightly against him, laying his forehead against her shoulder.

"It's beautiful, Arden."

"Do you truly think so, or are you just saying that?"

"It's beautiful. Is it too personal for you to share?"

"You mean submit for publication?"

"Yes."

"Is it good enough?"

"God, yes. I think parents, any parent, whether they've suffered the loss of a child or not, would empathize. I know I do. I think you should have it published. It may help someone who's going through what you did."

She turned to him and laid her head on his heart. She loved its steady, solid beat.

"I wish I'd been there when you needed someone. You were here for me to help me out of my crisis, but you had to go through your hell alone. I'm so sorry, my love." His fervently spoken words and the strong hands caressing her back told her of his sincerity. "Come here," he said, taking her hand and leading her to the bed.

He sat down on it and moved her to stand between his thighs. She looked into his loving face and smoothed the bushy slash of his eyebrows with her finger.

"I wish I could love away all that hurt inside you." He leaned forward and rested his head on her midriff.

"I wish I could love away yours, too. But it will always be a part of us. Maybe we love each other better because of past disappointments."

"I only know I love you more than I ever thought it possible to love." His breath, filtering through the gauzy gown onto her skin, was warm and moist. He nuzzled his nose against her breasts, loving their delicious weight on his face. "Arden, you're not using any contraceptives, are you?" He lifted his head and looked up at her.

She shook her head before answering in a strangled voice. "No."

"Good. Let's have a baby." His hands touched her breasts tenderly. He examined their shape, measured their fullness as though touching them for the first time. "Did you breast-feed Joey?"

"Until he got sick."

He nodded. His fingers caressed the nipples, and when they got hard, he rubbed his face against them, back and forth. "I want a baby with you." She clasped his head and pressed it into the softness of her abdomen. "A baby that's exclusively yours and mine. One we make together."

If only he knew what he was saying. She knew why he didn't feel that Matt had been exclusively his and Ellie's. Was this the time to tell him that they had a baby that was theirs, that they had made a beautiful baby together? Could she tell him now? Would his lips continue to ravish her gently? Or would he stop loving her, accuse her of manipulating him unforgivably?

Her lips opened to voice the confession, but she had waited too long. His mood had passed from poignancy to passion. He was kissing the delta between her thighs, paying tribute to her womanhood with his loving mouth and adoring words. His hands gathered up the airy fabric of her dressing gown, raising it up her legs, over her thighs, until it was bunched at her waist. He buried his face in the frothy material, breathing in her scent.

When his lips touched her bare skin, she shivered with anticipation and clutched his shoulders with anxious hands. He pressed ardent kisses into her dark, silky down. "Let me give you a baby, Arden," he whispered. "Let me give you that most wonderful of gifts." His hands went around her, cupped her hips and tilted her forward to meet his mouth.

"Drew," she gasped. "You can't do this." He could. He did. Her whole body was caught up in a conflagration of passion. His seeking mouth sent columns of fire shooting upward, through her loins, through her heart, into her soul.

She responded mindlessly to his directing hands as he laid her down on the bed. He placed her legs over his thighs and knelt before her. "I love you, Arden. Let me heal your pain."

His mouth was masterful. He kissed her again and again with lips that were sure and possessive, yet conversely meek. His tongue was a bold, thrusting, pleasure-giving imp that brought her again and again to crashing climax, then soothed her afterward.

Hovering on the brink of oblivion once again, she tangled his hair around her fingers and drew his head up. "Inside me. Please, now," she gasped as another convulsion shook her.

Somehow he worked free the fastening of his shorts and slipped them over his hips. He was a full, hard, warm pressure that filled her completely. He moved more adventurously than ever before, stroking the walls of her cleft, pausing, stroking again until she was senseless and knew only him and the rhythm of his loving. He plunged deeply time and again, touching her womb, making promises and then fulfilling them with one bursting rush of love so sublime that her fears flowed as freely.

When he withdrew, her body felt leaden, lethargic, yet seemed to defy gravity with a sensation of floating. He removed the rest of his clothing, pulled the twisted dressing gown from her perspiration-sheened body and lay down beside her.

Barely gathering the energy to form the words, she whispered, "Why did you do that?"

He let his finger trail down the center of her body to the dusky shadow of her sex. He followed with his eyes and then brought them back to marvel over her breasts. His eyes shone with the internal light of a fanatic worshiping his idol. "To show you there are no limits to how much I love you."

"I'm weak with love for you."

He smiled tenderly. "And you make me strong." Dipping his head, he plucked at her nipple lightly with his lips, then caressed it with his tongue. "And so very glad that I'm a man."

Her fingers wound through his blond hair. "Do you think we...made a baby?"

He chuckled softly. Laying his head next to hers on the pillow, he snuggled close. "We'll just keep doing it until it takes."

Then, wearing only the purple twilight for raiment, they slept.

"You two are bonkers," Arden called to the two tennis professionals.

Drew and Gary were batting the ball back and forth across the net, lobbing it as high as they could. They were clowning to entertain Matt, who was standing beside the court, clapping his hands. When Drew bent over and hit the ball through his legs, Matt yelled happily and jumped up and down.

"Okay, show-off," Arden said, "before you hurt yourself and I have to be the unlucky one to inform Ham you're out of commission, I'm taking your audience home. Maybe then you'll get in some real practice time."

"Party pooper," Gary called congenially before trotting over to confer with his latest conquest, who was waiting for him with a towel and a thermos of cold water.

"Ditto," Drew said, wrapping a towel around his neck. He draped one over Matt, who beamed up at him. "Your mother is a slave driver and a spoilsport," he told the boy before kissing him on the forehead. He straightened up and dropped his voice to a whisper. "Except in bed, and then she's a regular party girl."

"And you're the life of the party," Arden said with a suggestive drawl, rubbing noses with him. "I'd love to kiss you, but I can't find a dry spot."

"Isn't that Bette Davis's line?"

"No, she said, 'I'd love to kiss you, but I just washed my hair.'"

"Oh. I knew it was something like that. Well, owe me a kiss. Do you have to go?"

"You know Matt's a monster if he doesn't get his nap. When you get home, maybe we can take him down to the beach."

"And play *nekkid*."

"Don't you ever think of anything else?"

"Yes," he answered, acting offended. "Sometimes I think about making it with our clothes *on*."

"You're terrible!" she cried, throwing a towel in his face. "Play well and we'll see you at home."

She hoisted Matt onto her hip, and settling her shoulder bag on the other arm, headed toward the parking lot where she'd parked the Seville. She had more or less inherited it after Drew bought himself a Jeep.

They had been in Europe for three months, hopping from country to country, tournament to tournament, and had only returned the week before. Drew was now ranked number five in world tennis. He was hoping that by the same time next year he'd be the number-one seed again.

"Then I'd retire."

"And do what?"

"How does a chain of sporting-goods stores sound? The emphasis would be on family participation. You know, jogging shoes for father and son, matching tennis dresses for mothers and daughters, yard games for the entire family. Things like that."

"It sounds terrific. And I like the concept."

"So do I. We're going to lead the pack."

"We?"

"Ham will retire, too. He says he's too old to start all over again with a cub tennis bum. He wants to go into the business with me. And *you,*" he kissed her quickly, "of course."

Her poem "Joey" had been published by a ladies' magazine and then by *Reader's Digest.* The ladies' magazine had asked if she'd think about writing a short story or novelette. She was toying with several ideas.

"Did you enjoy watching daddy play?" she asked Matt, who had celebrated his second birthday in Paris. He was really too heavy for her to carry, but she never passed up an opportunity. He called her "mum," and each time she saw the name on his perpetually damp lips, she wanted to weep with happiness. "Isn't he terrific? But then you're biased in your opinion of him, just as I am."

Arden didn't see the man in the car parked next to hers until he got out. She glanced over her shoulder as she was unlocking the car door. And everything inside her froze. She felt as though the blood were damming up in her veins, her lungs shutting down operation, her heart thudding to a standstill.

He was heavier by twenty pounds. His hair was thinner, grayer and badly cut. His skin looked pallid and contrasted garishly with the capillaries in his nose, which had reddened with too much drink. The jowls on either side of his face looked like empty, oversize pockets. His clothes were less natty and seemed uncomfortably hot and tight. His shoes were scuffed.

But that conniving look still lurked in his eyes. He still wore that familiar smirking grin, the grin that said he had something on someone and couldn't wait to use it to his advantage.

Arden needed very badly to vomit. She swallowed the hot bile that gushed into her throat and instinctively, with the fierce protectiveness of motherhood, clutched Matt to her.

"Hello, Mrs. McCasslin."

He made the name sound like an obscene insult. Revulsion swamped her, and she had an overwhelming impulse to run as far and as fast as she could. Instead, she stared back at him with eyes turned icy with hatred. "Hello, Ron."

Chapter 11

The bleary eyes took a tour down her body that made her feel as though she needed a scalding bath. She didn't want him to know how much he frightened her. That was the only thing that kept her from screaming.

"You're looking well," he said when his thorough appraisal brought his eyes back to hers.

"You look like hell," she said flatly, wondering where her new-found courage came from. But she knew. It was an outgrowth of Drew's love and the happiness she'd found with him.

Ron Lowery blinked, momentarily disconcerted by her uncharacteristic flippancy. When he grinned, it was with an evil curl to his mouth. "True. But then I didn't land on my feet the way you did, Mrs. McCasslin."

She set a squirming Matt down on the parking-lot pavement. He had long since lost interest in the conversation and was much more interested in the yellow metal button that marked the parking space in front of the automobile. Arden saw to it that he was well out of Ron's reach.

"Don't blame me or anyone else for whatever misfortunes have befallen you, Ron. You had all the makings of success handed to you on a silver platter. Or should I say through a golden wedding ring? If you failed to take advantage of those opportunities, then you've no one to blame but yourself."

His fists balled at his sides, and he took a threatening step forward. "Don't get all high and mighty with me. I can topple your little world with one fell swoop, *Mrs. McCasslin*. How'd you find him?"

She decided that her only defense was to admit nothing, to brazen it out. She tilted her chin up haughtily. "I don't know what you're talking about."

Steely fingers bit into her upper arm as Ron hauled her closer to him. "How did you find McCasslin? And don't think I'm stupid enough to believe you're his blushing bride by some wild coincidence."

She swallowed a lump of fear and blinked against waves of pain. She was seeing a side of Ron's nature that she had always known was there but didn't want to acknowledge. He would be ruthless, cruel, violent, if he had to be to get what he wanted.

"Deductive reasoning," she said with relief when his fingers uncurled from around her arm. "I had seen him and his wife the morning they left the hospital."

"Well, congratulations. You pulled off a clever one, didn't you?" He looked down at Matt in a way that made Arden's blood run cold. "He's a cute kid. I did a good job fathering him."

An ocean of nausea washed over Arden, and she thought she might very well faint. It came as a surprise to her to find herself still standing several seconds later. "You?" she wheezed.

He laughed. It was an ugly sound. "What's the matter, Mrs. McCasslin? Do you think you went to all that trouble for nothing? Do you think you're married to the wrong man? Hmm?"

His taunts sickened her further. "Is Matt Drew's child?" she asked desperately.

Ron eyed her slyly, enjoying to the fullest the tidal wave of despair he'd inflicted on her. "He provided the semen, yes. But as you'll recall, I did all the work."

Her relief was so vast that she slumped against the hot metal body of the car. It was several moments before the vertigo passed and the world righted itself. But the brassy taste in her mouth and the sickness in her stomach remained. This man was diabolical, capable of anything.

"Actually, you've done me a great service by marrying McCasslin," he was saying, idly picking his fingernails of imaginary dirt. Or maybe it wasn't imaginary.

She wouldn't humor him by inquiring how that might be. Instead, she met his cunning eyes levelly.

"I've fallen onto hard times, Arden. I know you'll be devastated to learn that the practice your sainted father worked so diligently to establish is no more."

"I divorced myself from it when I divorced myself from you," she said. "It was no longer my father's work but only your plaything. And I wanted nothing of yours."

"Well—" he shrugged "—it's gone, anyway, which brings us to the point of this pleasant visit." He leaned forward and whispered conspiratorially, "You're going to help me recoup some of my losses."

"You're insane. I wouldn't spit on you if you were on fire. And this pleasant little visit, as you call it, has just come to an end. Don't bother me again." She knelt down and picked up Matt, absently dusting off his knees. Yanking open the car door, she shoved him inside, ignoring his protests.

"Just a minute, bitch," Ron said, grabbing her arm before she could climb into the car. "How would you like it if I paid a visit to that new husband of yours?" Arden stopped struggling and held her breath as she stared wordlessly into Ron's feral eyes. "You hold a low opinion of me. But remember he and that insipid wife of his regarded me as just short of the Almighty. He'd be pleased to see me. Shall I go have a chat with him?"

Her panic surged to the surface, and she could only hope it was invisible to her ex-husband. But by the victorious gleam in his eyes, she knew that he'd seen it. "That's what I thought," he crooned. "Mr. McCasslin doesn't know who your former husband was, does he? He doesn't know what a high-priced whore he's married to. Fifty thousand dollars' worth of whoring. He doesn't know all that, does he? Well, isn't that interesting?" He pushed her into the seat of the car, where she landed with a jolt that stunned her. "I'll be in touch."

It was a vow, a threat that left her arms and legs rubbery as she drove home.

"You don't like the veal scallopini?"

Arden stopped stirring the food around her plate and smiled across the table into her husband's concerned, questioning eyes. "I'm sorry. I guess I wasn't up for a crowd tonight." They were having dinner alone in one of Lahaina's favorite night spots.

"You should have said something. We could have gone somewhere else." He reached for her hand and squeezed it. His look was heart-meltingly intimate. "Or we could have stayed at home, had dinner in our room and had a *really* good time."

The insinuation behind his words, the recollection of just such evenings, the love so evident in his eyes, made Arden ache with the guilt she lived with.

All afternoon, she'd been as jumpy as a cat, afraid to look over her shoulder for fear of seeing Ron's leering, ominous presence. She loathed him. He was an odious person, and she despised his self-serving motives. Yet was she any better? Hadn't she manipulated Drew McCasslin in the most despicable way? Why hadn't she told him who she was in the beginning? And why was it so hard to tell him now?

The answer to both questions was the same. She loved him too much. The moment she had set eyes on Drew, her objectivity had flown. It had never returned. She could no more tell him now that she was Matt's mother than she could have that first day he'd walked up to her and said hello. But the guilt she lived with was becoming unbearable. It ate at her like a cancer. She didn't like to think of herself in league with someone like Ron Lowery.

"I'm sorry I'm ruining your evening." She sighed, wishing she could climb inside the security of his body and hide from all external dangers.

"No evening I've spent with you has been a ruin," he said softly. A grin slashed across his handsome face. "Well, maybe a few evenings before we married when I wanted to be in your bed and you did everything short of castration to keep me out of it."

She laughed in spite of her mood. "I was only being ladylike," she said with mock demureness.

"A curse on being ladylike. I'll bet you—"

His sentence hung unfinished as he spotted something across the room that rendered him speechless.

"Drew?"

It took a moment for his eyes to drift back to her, and then he seemed unable to focus. "I...what? Oh, I'm sorry. What were you saying?"

"You were saying something, not me." She laughed and turned to see what had captured his attention. Her laugh caught in her throat when she saw Ron Lowery sitting alone at a table across the room, casually studying a menu. His being there was no accident. Of that, Arden was positive.

She whipped her head back toward Drew to see if he had read her dismay, but he was still staring at Ron. "Do you know that man?" she asked hesitantly.

In that moment, she realized she'd chosen to perpetuate her lie. She had been presented with an ideal opportunity to say, "Drew, I believe you know my former husband. You and Ellie went to him about three years ago. He found a surrogate mother for your child. I was the woman." Instead, she had taken the path of least resistance. She couldn't gamble with Drew's love now. It was still too new and fragile. Matt was too precious to her. She couldn't take the risk.

"Uh, yes," Drew said. He was watching Ron as he laughed with a waitress over the wine list. Was there a trace of bitterness in Drew's voice? His lips had narrowed in a way that Arden knew indicated he was displeased with something. Apparently, he didn't hold Ron in the esteem Ron thought.

"He...he...Ellie and I knew him on the mainland. At one time, he was a special friend to us."

"I see," Arden said, gulping at her ice water.

"He's a doctor. He did us a special service for which he was very well paid. Then he tried to wheedle more money out of me."

Arden could feel what little food she'd eaten churning in her stomach. Once she'd borne Matt, Ron had pressed the

McCasslins for more money. Was the man totally without principles? "How could he expect you to pay more than he'd asked for?" She hoped the question sounded casual.

"He said he'd run into complications that he hadn't anticipated," Drew said absently, still staring piercingly in Ron's direction. Then, as though realizing he might have said more than he'd intended, he reverted his attention to Arden. His grin was forced. "We came to an understanding. I wonder what's brought him to Maui. Vacation, I suppose."

"No doubt." Arden wondered how her voice could sound so normal when she felt like screaming.

"If you're not going to mutilate that piece of veal anymore, we'll go."

"No. I'm done."

God, how was she going to live through this? she asked herself as she let Drew steer her through the maze of tables toward the door. They would have to pass Ron's table to reach the exit. She knew he'd followed them to the restaurant. It was his way of demonstrating to her just how serious his threats were. He wanted something from her, and he'd hang on with the tenacity of a bulldog until she capitulated. And she knew that to safeguard her life with Drew and Matt, she would.

He played the scene with the aplomb of a Barrymore. He actually let his eyes widen with surprised pleasure when he spotted Drew. Toward her, he exhibited not one sign of recognition. Her heart was hurling itself against her ribs like a caged animal gone mad as she heard him say, "Drew McCasslin! What a treat to see you after all this time."

Drew was coolly polite. "Hello, Dr. Lowery. How are you?"

They shook hands. "You're looking great, Drew," Ron said expansively. "Reports about you on the sports pages have been fantastic lately." His eyes clouded, and his voice lowered sympathetically. "I was sorry to hear about your wife. How is the little boy?"

Arden could feel Drew's muscles contracting with tension, but his voice was composed as he replied. "Thank you for your condolences. Matt is a strapping two-year-old now. He's terrific."

"Ah, that's good to hear."

"And—" Drew pulled her forward "—this is my wife, Arden. Darling, Dr. Ron Lowery."

It occurred to her that playwrights had often created comic scenes out of situations such as this, and she wondered how anyone could ever consider them funny. The irony was too cruel to be humorous. The hysteria that had threatened all day almost erupted. She didn't know if it would have taken the form of a high, deranged laugh or an imbecilic scream. She was able to stop it just in time. "Dr. Lowery," she said. Nothing could have compelled her to extend her hand.

"Mrs. McCasslin," Ron said kindly.

His sincere-looking smile infuriated her. She wanted nothing more than to expose him for the sham he was. But to expose him would be to expose herself.

The two men exchanged pleasantries, Ron saying that he was on the islands for several weeks' vacation and Drew wishing him a good time. Somehow she lived through it without going berserk. The smile on her lips was so brittle, she thought her face might crack like a china plate if she held it much longer.

"It was wonderful to see you again," Ron said silkily as Drew finally escorted her toward the door.

"Same here. Have a good trip," Drew said as they walked away.

Once in the car, he started the motor, but didn't engage

the gears. He stared sightlessly over the hood ornament. "Is something wrong?" she asked.

"No, not really. There's just something about…" Drew's voice faded to nothingness while Arden sat stiffly beside him, only her rigid physical control managing to keep her hysteria at bay. "Dr. Lowery was important to Ellie and me. I told you that she had trouble conceiving. He…well, he made Matt possible. I have him to thank for my son. But…hell, I can't explain it, Arden."

He shook his head, as though by doing so, his random thoughts would rearrange themselves logically. "It's more than his demand for additional money. There's something about his mannerisms that bugs me, makes me wary of trusting him too far. I don't know why exactly, but for some reason, it disturbed me to see him tonight. On my turf, so to speak. I haven't seen him since Matt was born, and I didn't plan on seeing him ever again."

He chuckled in self-derision and shifted the car into drive. "I guess you think I'm crazy."

"No," she said, staring entranced at the lighted dials on the dashboard. "I don't think you're crazy. I don't trust him, either."

"Now that the lights are out, will you tell me what's been troubling you all day?"

Arden had already been in bed for several minutes when Drew snapped off the bedside lamp and joined her. He was naked, as was she. She had dispensed with wearing nightclothes. "Saves time," Drew had said with a sexy grin the first week of their marriage. That night, Arden hadn't put on a nightgown, but she had wanted to. Her impulse had been to hide, to cover herself. She had curled up on her side of the bed, facing the edge, holding herself stiff.

"Nothing's troubling me," she mumbled into the pillow.

"Then you've undergone a personality change since you left the club this afternoon. You've been a bundle of nerves— you didn't eat your dinner, you were silent on the way home, and most unusual of all, you almost forgot to go into Matt's room to kiss him good-night. Now dammit, something's wrong."

All her anxiety surfaced, and she lashed out at the nearest object, Drew. "Just because I don't want to make love tonight, you think something's wrong. Maybe I'm just not in the mood, okay? My God, you expect me to turn on and off like a light bulb. Can't I have one night's peace?" She pulled the covers up higher.

Several seconds of silence elapsed before Drew flung the covers off himself and shot out of bed. "Your memory is playing you false. I don't recall asking you to make love tonight."

He was three lunging strides across the room before she implored him to come back. "Drew!" she cried, sitting up and extending her arms. "I'm sorry, I'm sorry. Please come back. Hold me."

The moonlight filtering through the wide windows revealed the silver streams of tears on her cheeks. He was there instantly, gathering her to him tightly, smoothing her hair with loving hands, pressing her face into the curve of his shoulder. "What is it, Arden? What's wrong? Something I've done? Not done?"

"No, no," she said mournfully, rolling her head from side to side. "I shouldn't have been cross with you. I didn't mean it. I…"

"What? Tell me."

She searched her soul, looking for the courage to tell him about Ron, about Matt. She couldn't find it. At that moment, bravery was as elusive as the moonbeam that glinted on his hair.

She sniffed back her tears. "It's nothing, really. Just...I haven't felt 'with it' today. That's all."

"Lie down," he instructed softly, and reclined with her onto the soft linens. It was warm enough for them to lie uncovered, with the ocean breeze whispering across their flesh. He lay behind her, drawing her to him and wrapping his arms around her protectively. His breath sifted through her hair to caress her ear as he whispered, "I love you, Arden."

"I love you, too," she vowed, nestling her hips against him, feeling his manhood proud and warm.

He moved his hands up and down her front, trailing his fingertips in the shallow valley that divided her torso into left and right. "Are you worried because you haven't become pregnant?"

She had been concerned but hadn't spoken of it. Ever since that day he'd read her poem, they had been hoping she'd become pregnant soon. "It will happen," she said quietly.

"I think so, too. But whether it does or not doesn't matter all that much to me. I love you. *You.* I don't want you to think that if we don't have a child of our own, I'll love you any less."

She brought his hand to her lips and kissed it. "I'm selfish. I want to be everything to you."

"You are. I already feel like you're Matt's mother. To see you two together, no one would guess otherwise."

She stifled a sob and snuggled closer. She didn't deserve this blind trust. This love.

"When I make love to you, Arden, making a baby is the last thing on my mind. You are on my mind. I'm loving you. Exclusively."

Her dwindling sobs mingled with a sigh as his hand closed

around her breast. His deep voice murmured a lullaby of love words in her ears.

"I think about your breasts, how perfectly they are shaped. I love their fullness. I like to caress them. Like this." His fingers grazed the dainty peaks and found them already aroused by his heated words. "You're so pretty," he whispered as his fingertips worked their magic on her flesh.

"Your skin is creamy and smooth." His hand stroked down her stomach. "I love kissing it. It feels so good against my face and lips. And this…" His fingers brushed through the tuft at the top of her thighs. "This is what woman should be." The sweet exploration intensified. "I love you here."

Arden moaned in ecstasy at his bold touch and the tender invasion of his fingers. "It feels so good when you hold me here, buried inside you."

"Drew." She turned her head to meet his mouth. He kissed her deeply.

"Nothing you do could make me love you less. You can't win my love, Arden. You already have it. Free and unqualified and unconditionally and eternally."

She twisted in his arms and turned to face him. "I've changed my mind. I want to make love very much."

He smiled in pleasure and surprise when she flattened her hands on his shoulders and pressed him onto his back. She positioned herself over him, and he groaned his ecstasy. Her breasts were a tantalizing display before his eyes. Not believing her own daring, she cupped one in each hand like an offering. "Can you…?"

He levered himself up to replace her hands with his, accepting her gift gladly. He laved her tight, aching nipples with his tongue, rolling it over the dusky beads until she felt the swirling motion deep inside her. He took one breast into his mouth just as she sank onto his sex.

Against her breasts, he ground out curses that might have been prayers as she rocked upon him, sending him deeper into the well of her love to find its very source. "Ah, sweet..." he moaned, collapsing backward onto the pillows.

She rotated her hips, raised them, lowered them, wanting to take all of him inside herself so there could be no doubt of their belonging together, no question of the rightness of their marriage.

His breath was uneven and harsh, but his touch was tender. He fondled her breasts, then let one hand slip into the deep shadow where their bodies were fused. An exquisite thrill rocketed through her body at his knowing touch.

"Oh, Drew. Please, please." Whether she was pleading for him to stop or never to stop, she didn't know. But he knew. He continued that divine torment until he felt her body quaking with the coming tumult. His hands gripped her hips and anchored her to him as they experienced the final sensual assault together.

Exhausted, she collapsed onto him, their stomachs moving in and out together, panting for air. Their bodies were dewy with perspiration, their muscles limp and useless, but their hearts were full.

At last, Drew rolled them to their sides. He brushed damp strands of dark hair from her face as he held her close. "Our love represents all that is pure and good and honest in the world, Arden."

"Yes," she said huskily, smiling up at him. It was after he fell asleep that she began again to weep quietly.

"Is this the lady of the house?"

Arden's fingers gripped the telephone receiver tighter. She recognized the oily voice immediately. For days, she had dreaded hearing it. She had known Ron would call, she just hadn't known when. Now that he had finally contacted her, she could almost feel relieved. At least the suspense was over. Now she only had to dread what he wanted of her. "Yes," she replied curtly.

"The Orchid Lounge. Three o'clock."

The phone went dead in her hand. She replaced it with the care of one who has gone through physical therapy and wants to make sure his actions are precise and correct. Ron hadn't given her much time. It was past two now. Matt was taking his nap. Drew was in his office talking to Ham long-distance on the other line. As soon as Matt awakened, they planned to go down to the beach.

"Mrs. Laani," Arden said, sticking her head around the corner of the kitchen door. "I don't want to disturb Drew while he's on the telephone. Would you tell him I've decided to do some shopping this afternoon. He and Matt should go to the beach without me. Maybe I can join them later."

"I'll be glad to do any household shopping for you tomorrow," the housekeeper offered.

"No, thank you. I need a few things for myself. I shouldn't be long."

She left the house a few minutes later, dressed in a poplin skirt and a polo shirt. She'd be damned before she'd dress up for Ron.

She knew the Orchid Lounge was in a ramshackle row of buildings on the outskirts of Lahaina. She had passed it many times on her way into the town. It was worse than she had expected. It was dim and smoky, the smell of stale beer permeating its gloomy atmosphere.

It took her several minutes to adjust her eyes to the darkness, and when she did, she noted she was the only female in the place. Pairs of leering eyes glowed at her from dark corners. Swallowing her trepidation, she walked straight to the nearest red vinyl booth and slid into the lumpy seat.

"Club soda, please," she said to the bartender, who came scurrying to the booth to serve her. His hair was thick with white grooming cream. The Hawaiian print shirt he wore was loud and baggy and none too clean.

"Yes, ma'am," he said in a lilting voice that made her flesh crawl. She trained her eyes on the neon clock on the opposite wall and left them there, even when the glass of soda was thumped down in front of her without benefit of napkin or coaster. She wouldn't have drunk out of it for all the gold in the world. She ignored the speculative glances thrown in her direction, the whispered comments followed by guffaws of laughter, the sinister stares.

Ron was over fifteen minutes late. *Damn him.* He was doing this on purpose to weaken her, frighten her, humiliate her. It was just the kind of psychological warfare he was capable of. Well, she wasn't going to stay in this sleazy tavern another moment.

Just as she was gathering up her purse to leave, Ron slid into the booth across from her. "Where are you going?" he asked belligerently.

"I don't like your choice of meeting places," she said tightly. The other patrons were smirking at her knowledgeably. She had been there to meet a lover. Or a client? She shivered in revulsion.

"You're not supposed to like it." Ron signaled to the bartender. "Double Scotch. Neat." Then he pinned her with those treacherous eyes that penetrated her wall of defenses like twin battering rams. "I need twenty thousand dollars."

The bartender asked if she wanted another drink when he set Ron's whiskey down on the greasy tabletop. It was a ludicrous question, since she hadn't touched the first. She shook her head, not deigning to look at him. He reminded her of a cockroach, the way he scuttled around in the dark.

Ron tossed down half the drink, winced, swallowed hard, then took a smaller sip. "You're going to get it for me."

"Go to hell. I'll do nothing of the sort."

His eyes slithered down her chest as a nasty curl deformed his heavy mouth. "Yes, you will." He took another pull on the drink. "I've got men after me, Arden. Hard men, butchers. I'm up to my ass in debt to them. They want their money."

"That's your problem, not mine."

"Oh, it's yours all right. I'm making it yours. You're married to a rich tennis player now. VIP. High roller. Big-timer. You wouldn't ever have met him if it weren't for me. You owe me."

She did something she never thought she'd do in Ron Lowery's presence. She laughed. "You fool," she said with unveiled contempt. "After all you did to hurt me, even asking me to have a child for another man, you say that *I* owe *you*."

He shrugged. "Whatever. You'll do as I say just as you always have. Because you're a spineless coward, Arden."

"I am not!" she retorted.

"No?" he asked with a sneer and another softly sinister laugh. He glanced over his shoulder at the dozen or so men watching them with keen interest. "Weren't you just a teeny-weeny bit afraid before I came in? You didn't like it in here, did you? All these guys were ogling you, thinking about what's under your skirt. Did that scare you a little? Huh? Weren't you just the least bit nervous? I'll bet there's a little river of sweat running between your breasts. Right? Are those nice big tits of yours damp with sweat?"

"Stop it."

"And there's probably a trickle of sweat between your

thighs, too. Hmm? One word from me and I'll bet these guys would check that out."

"Ron, please."

He feigned surprise. "What? Did I actually hear a tremor in your voice? A plea for mercy?" He crossed his arms on the table and leaned forward. "That's where I want you, Arden. Compliant." He sat back after taking another sip of whiskey and signaled for more. "Now, let's get down to business." When he had his fresh drink, he said, "I need five thousand immediately. The other fifteen, we can spread out over a few weeks."

"Ron," she exclaimed, struggling to hang on to her reason. "I don't have that kind of money."

"You have a goddam checking account, and I know it!" he shouted, his fist crashing down on the table.

She jumped in spite of her resolve not to show her fear. "Yes, I have a checking account," she said with forced composure. "But how am I supposed to account to Drew for that kind of spending?"

"That's up to you. If you're resourceful enough to con this guy into marrying you, you can think of a way to get that money."

"I didn't con him into marrying me," she said heatedly.

"But that's what he'd think, wouldn't he, if I went to him and told him who I had impregnated with his semen?" He shook his head pityingly. "No. I don't think he'd be quite the ardent groom if he found that out."

"I could deny it. I could admit that you were my husband, but that doesn't prove that I had Drew's child. I'd claim you were lying for the sake of blackmailing us."

He tsked. "Arden, Arden, are you still so naive? Remember the lawyer, sweetheart? He's a buddy of mine. He's got the records sealed in a safe. All I'd have to do is show them to McCasslin. Besides, I told you he thinks I hung the moon because I got him that boy."

It was her turn to look smug. "Don't count on that, Ron. He told me how you tried to get more money out of him because of the *complications* you ran into. He doesn't think nearly as well of you as you think."

One corner of his mouth tilted. "Be that as it may, he wouldn't want me to tell the press that I know about that kid. It would make him look like a fool, not to mention besmirching the reputation of his dear departed wife." He lowered one calculating eyelid. "Tell me. Isn't it crowded with the three of you in bed? You, your tennis player and his wife's ghost?"

He had intended to hurt her, and he had. Whether he knew it or not, he had touched her one vulnerable point. "It's not that way," she said desperately.

"No? He was crazy in love with that woman. Even some-one as jaded as I on the topic of love could see that. Do you expect me to believe you've replaced her? Remember, I was married to you, too, Arden. And you may be a helluva of a housekeeper, cook and mother, but as a lover, you're pathetic."

Hatred, undiluted and pure, coursed through her. She wanted to flaunt her sex life with Drew, to tell this buf-foon every glorious detail of their life together. Her fists were tightly clenched as she said, "He loves me. I love him. We want to have a baby. We—"

His rude laughter interrupted her. "Baby?" He laughed harder. "*You* have another baby? Where did you get the mis-taken idea you could still have children?"

Chapter 12

"Wha…what do you mean?" Her lungs were squeezing closed. She had no air. She was going to die in the Orchid Lounge.

"I mean, Mrs. McCasslin, that when you had your baby, you were fixed. Spayed. Sterilized."

"That's impossible," she whispered. "That's impossible."

"You were anesthetized, remember?"

"But…but there was no incision. For a tubal ligation—"

He waved off her arguments. "There are always new methods to try. Who is a better guinea pig than a gynecologist's wife? I was afraid you might regret giving up the baby later on, especially in light of Joey's health. Should your maternal instincts surface, I didn't want you to be able to have another child. I certainly didn't want another one. Joey cost me a fortune in medical expenses."

She uttered an anguished cry, as if he'd dealt her a mortal blow. How could he speak that way of Joey, his own son? And now all hope of her having another child was banished by the base cruelty of this man. Feeling utterly defeated, she groped blindly for her purse. "How much do you need? Five thousand?" She wanted him out of her life. If buying him off would achieve that, she would give him any amount.

"For starters, yes. I need it tomorrow."

"Tomorrow?" How could she come up with that kind of money in that length of time? "I don't think I can get it that soon, but I'll try," she said as she stood. Dizzily, she swayed.

He caught her arm. "You'll deliver it tomorrow, or I'll pay a visit to that good-looking husband of yours. He and I have a lot to chat about."

Arden, still feeling poleaxed, worked her arm free and stumbled toward the door. The sunlight blinded her. Or was it her tears?

"Tomorrow?" Arden repeated. Drew had dropped his bomb just as she was bringing a bite of food to her mouth. Her fork was held suspended in midair. She lowered it to her plate. "We're leaving for California tomorrow?" Tomorrow, tomorrow, tomorrow. The word rolled around inside her head like a roulette ball. It seemed that she had echoed that word all day.

"I know it's a nuisance, but I only found out myself a few minutes ago." He had joined them in the dining room late. He'd been talking on the telephone to Ham again. Matt, as usual, was restless and eager for his dinner, so Arden had begun to feed him. "Mrs. Laani can pack for Matt tonight. We're catching a one o'clock plane to Honolulu tomorrow afternoon, then an overnighter to L.A."

"But why the rush?" Arden was dismayed. How was she going to pay off Ron? Ever since she'd left him, she had been trying to come up with an excuse to give Drew when she asked him for the five thousand dollars.

"Use your napkin like daddy, Matt," Drew said, demonstrating for his son. He smiled when the child did as instructed. "There are several reasons. First, there are three tournaments that Ham thinks I should play in. Few of the top seeds are going to play, so I might be able to rack up some wins. One's in San Diego, one's in Vegas and the other is in San Francisco, so the travel won't be extensive. There are only a few days between them. And Ham and I have other business to take care of."

She stared into her plate. It had been increasingly difficult to meet Drew's eyes ever since she had returned from her meeting with Ron. Now she had two secrets to hide—that she was Matt's mother and that she was barren. Should he find out either one, he'd have more than ample reason to despise her. Now she was trying to come up with a way to con him out of money to pay off her blackmailer. God, what had she sunk to?

Contrary to what Ron believed, she didn't have a limitless bank account. Drew had opened up an account in her name and kept a generous reserve in it. Into that account, too, went her checks for the articles or stories she sold. "It's yours to do with as you see fit," Drew had said when he made the initial deposit. "Just don't spend it on the household. There's another account for that. This is yours to play with."

She had checked the balance of it that day, and it was a far cry from twenty thousand. Currently, it was even short of five thousand. She knew Ron wouldn't hesitate to tell Drew about her should she not come up with the money. By tomorrow. And tomorrow they were leaving for the mainland.

She only nodded absently when Mrs. Laani came in to carry Matt upstairs so she and Drew could finish their dinner alone. She kissed the boy's cheek but later didn't even remember it. She felt like a mummy, swathed tightly in her problem, restricted and immobile, separated from life.

"You see," Drew went on once they were alone, "Ham and I have a chance to buy into an existing chain of sporting-goods stores right now. It's a nationwide operation. We figure that in a few years we can buy out the other partners and then do with it as we want."

"That's wonderful, Drew."

"I've arranged a line of credit with a Honolulu bank. Cash may be tight for a few months until I chalk up a few wins and some of those renewed contracts start paying off. Can you stand living on a budget?"

His eyes were sparkling teasingly, but she could barely manufacture a smile. Even if she came up with a believable lie, Drew couldn't give her any money now. He would be using all the cash he had to buy into the sporting-goods business so that their future would be sure. Arden could feel her spirit suffocating, could see her dreams leaking out of her heart, to be swallowed up by a black oppression.

Drew was startled by Arden's anxiety over their imminent departure. But then he'd been worried sick about her for days. He didn't know what to think of her sudden reversal of temperament. She'd never been nervous or high-strung before, but lately the slightest provocation set off either a crying jag or a fit of temper.

If he wasn't talking to her directly, she was gazing into space, totally unaware of what was going on around her. Even when they were engaged in conversation, her eyes would often glaze, and he knew that though she made the proper responses, she wasn't really listening to him. Even Matt, for whom she always had unlimited patience, had felt the brunt of her temper.

At first, he'd thought it was her monthly cycle throwing

her off balance, but it had lasted too long. Then he'd thought with a surge of hope that she might be pregnant, but when he suggested that possibility with a teasing smile, she'd burst into tears and accused him of wanting her only as a brood mare. He'd stymied the impulse to curse and stamp from the room. Instead, he'd gone to her, taken her into his arms and comforted her with words that declared his boundless love. She'd cried all the harder.

Damned if he knew what was troubling her, but something was. Why wouldn't she open up to him, confide in him? He could help. He knew it. If only she'd tell him what was bothering her. He wanted his wife back, the one who laughed and loved as generously and as spontaneously as a young girl.

Her distress had been compounded by the news of their trip. Why? Was she dreading tour life? He had thought she'd adjusted to it so well. Nothing had seemed to ruffle her. *Dammit, what was wrong?* Was it him? Was she unhappy with their marriage? The thought brought an excruciating pain to his chest.

"I...I don't really have to go, do I?" He saw her tongue flash out to wet her lips nervously. "I mean, it sounds to me as though you'd get along better without me...without all of us tagging along after you. Meetings and all..."

He studied her for a moment, his dinner forgotten. "I never think of you and Matt as 'tagging along.' I want you with me. As for the other, I was hoping that you'd attend the business meetings, too. I want you to be a visible and integral partner in any endeavor of my life. Since this venture is vital to our future, I would have thought you'd want to get involved."

His eyes bored into hers incisively. "There's another reason why you must go. More important than all the others. I want you to see a doctor."

To keep her hands from trembling, she clasped the seat of her chair until her knuckles turned white. "B-but that's ridiculous. A doctor? Why?"

"Because I think you need a thorough checkup. You insist that nothing is wrong, but I want a professional opinion."

"What kind of doctor?" she asked testily. "A psychiatrist?"

"I think we'll start with a medical doctor." His gaze softened appreciably. "Arden, you're not Wonder Woman. You've taken on a new husband, child and climate. It's understandable if your psyche and your body are going through a period of readjustment. I think we'd both feel better once you see a doctor."

No doubt she'd feel very good when the doctor told her husband, "Your wife is in perfect health, but she's barren. I'm sorry, Mr. McCasslin. I hear you wanted another child."

What could she do? *What?* She really didn't have to do anything. Because when Ron didn't get his money the next day, he'd tell Drew about her, and then it would all be over, anyway. There would never be a doctor's appointment to worry about. For the time being, she wouldn't fight it. It was too energy consuming. The heartache and guilt plaguing her had depleted her strength. "All right, I'll see a doctor."

"Super. Ham's making an appointment for you."

Drew didn't make love to her that night. Instead, he showed his love by kissing her thoroughly and tucking her against his warmth. Even so, she shivered through the long hours of the night.

"What do you mean you can't get it?" Ron's voice was both threatening and desperate.

"Just what I told you," she whispered, fearing she'd wake

the rest of the household. It was just past dawn. She'd slipped out of Drew's arms, wrapped a robe around her and crept downstairs to call the number Ron had given her. She didn't know where the telephone was. She didn't want to know. But he answered on the second ring. "I can give you a little over three thousand today. That's all I've got, and I can't get any more."

"That's no good!" he shouted. "I've got to have five."

"I haven't got it," she snapped back.

"Get it."

"I can't. Ron, you gave me less than twenty-four hours. Be reasonable."

"The guys after me won't be reasonable."

"You should have thought of that before getting mixed up with them." She tried to push down the panic in her voice. "We're leaving for the mainland. Perhaps when we get back—"

"And when will that be?"

"About three weeks."

"Forget that, I'll be dead by then."

She couldn't say that that would be a relief, but that was what she was thinking. He sensed it. "Don't think my sudden demise would get you off the hook. Before I let them blow my brains out, I'd tell them where they could collect their money and give them the scoop on you and your new husband. If you think I'm a nuisance, honey, you haven't seen anything like these guys. You're far better off dealing with me."

"I'll get you the money," she said firmly. "You'll just have to put your creditors off for a while."

"No sale, Arden. You be at that bar at noon today with five thousand cash, or I'll make a lovely scene at the airport." He hung up.

She sat staring at the ocean for a long while before she climbed the stairs. It seemed as though she had a ball and chain around her ankles, making each step a dragging effort. Drew was right. Her mental anguish was like a physical ailment.

She heard sounds of laughter and scuffling coming from her bedroom the moment she reached the landing. Pushing the door open, she saw that Matt had joined his father in bed. They were wrestling, one as naked as the other. Matt was shrieking with laughter as Drew tickled him, making growling sounds.

Arden went to the bed and sat down on the edge. Love flooded her heart, as tears did her eyes. These two were all she had in the world. They loved her. Until that afternoon. Then she would be exposed to them as a fraud. But her love wasn't fraudulent. She should tell Drew now, but she feared his wrath and misunderstanding. She had waited too long. And there was an outside chance she might be able to put Ron off. Perhaps if she went to the bar with what cash she had in hand, she could buy time. Each day with Drew and her son was valuable. She would collect as many as she could.

Drew winked at her as he stood Matt on his flat, hard stomach. "He's quite a boy, isn't he?"

"Yes." Her voice was husky with emotion.

Matt was toasty brown, but against his father's bronzed body, he was several shades lighter. His little buttocks were round and dimpled. Rolls of baby fat scalloped his thighs. Stubby, fat toes dug into his father's flesh. With unabashed vanity, he submitted to their adoring inspection. Taking his small penis in his hand, he declared, "Pee-pee."

Drew hooted with laughter. "Yeah, you know all the terminology, you just haven't learned the practical applications."

He turned to Arden, smiling with paternal pride. When he saw her tear-clouded eyes, his smile faded. "Arden?"

She smiled a watery smile. "I love you both so much. So very much. You're my world, my life, everything."

Drew's own eyes became embarrassingly misty. "God, I've waited days for you to tell me that again. I was beginning to wonder if you felt you had made a bad bargain."

She reached out and touched his chest, combing her fingers through the luxuriant golden hair. "No. I got far more than I bargained for."

"More than two can join this orgy of the flesh," he suggested gruffly.

It wasn't fair to him for her to make love with lies weighing heavily on her heart, but it might be the last time she would ever know his touch, his kiss, his earth-moving lovemaking. Demurely, she lowered her lashes, drawing her fingernails over his flat brown nipples. "I've always thought more than two at an orgy was too many."

"You're absolutely right. One of us has to go." He sprung upright as though hinged at the waist and came nose to nose with his son. "Guess who, pal." He carried the boy to the door, set him on his feet, smacked him on the seat and said, "Go find Mrs. Laani. I think you're a fugitive from bathtime, anyway."

Matt took off down the hall shouting, "Yawni, Yawni."

Drew locked the door behind him and hastened back to the bed. He wasted no time. He fell upon Arden, feasting hungrily on her mouth while his hands rid her of her robe and daringly explored.

Her fingers wound through his thick hair, holding his head still as she twisted her mouth under his for a better vantage point. She arched and writhed against his body, touching him in the places she'd learned he loved being touched, stroked, scratched. Her nipples beaded against his chest in their own caress. Her thighs parted to cradle his, and she strained toward him. He was full and throbbing with his need.

"God, I've missed you," he said frantically, as though she'd been away and had just come home. "I've wanted you like this, unbound by whatever it was that was upsetting you. Don't ever withdraw from me that way again, Arden. It scares the hell out of me. I can't lose you. I can't."

He rubbed her neck with his mouth, letting his teeth nip the delicate flesh. She moaned her consent to this gentle abuse, and when his lips closed over one flushed nipple, she told him in panted, disjointed phrases what heaven that was.

Her fingers glided down the ridges of his ribs, over his lean pelvic bones and into the dark golden thatch at the juncture of his thighs. She brushed him timidly, examined him, then ringed him with massaging fingers. She let him know her readiness, rubbing him against her body, moistening him.

"Sweet, sweet Arden." His sighs were music, love songs composed exclusively for her.

With one surging thrust, she arched up to drive him home. Hearts and bodies pulsed together. He stroked her long and leisurely, then quick and furiously, and she matched the pace he set, answering with responsive movements.

Despair was vanquished. He exorcised all of her devils and gave her his blessing, his love. This was her celebration of life before death, her swan song, the last wish granted to one doomed. She chanted his name and cried it softly when she felt his life stream bathing her womb.

She clung to him long after it was over, folding her legs across his back. She filed every sensation away in her mind for the time when she'd be without him. Greedy for his touch on her damp skin, his intoxicating smell in her nostrils, his hard fullness within her, she trapped him tighter in her velvet warmth.

His groan was one of pure animal pleasure. "Guess what?"

"What?"

He began to move again. "We're not finished yet."

"But...Drew...ahh...the time...?"

"We'll make... Oh, my love, yes...we'll make time."

"I need to run a few errands," Arden said uneasily once she was showered and dressed and downstairs. Drew and Matt were eating a breakfast of Mrs. Laani's macadamia-nut muffins.

"Now?" Drew asked, brushing crumbs from Matt's mouth. "Don't you want to eat something?"

"No, no," she said hastily. "There are a few things I need to pick up before the trip."

"Well, don't get too carried away shopping. Remember our flight time. Are you already packed?"

"Yes, except for last-minute things."

She was almost out of the room when Drew called her back. "I almost forgot. You have mail." Drew got up and left the informal dining room.

Arden sat down beside Matt and ate the bite of muffin he offered her even though she didn't think she could swallow anything. Drew's lovemaking had been the sweetest, most fervent, most dear, she'd ever known. In her silent way, she'd said her goodbye to him. Now she scanned Matt's face, loving everything about him. Her fingers treasured each curl on his head. She touched him lovingly, wondering how she'd survive giving him up again.

"Here," Drew said, resuming his chair and pushing an envelope toward her. It was from the magazine that had published her first short story. Inside was a check for two thousand dollars.

"Oh!" she exclaimed, tears springing into her eyes. "I'd forgotten all about this." Unconsciously, she clutched the check to her breasts. Drew laughed.

"You sure look relieved to see it. Do you think I can't support you?"

"No, no," she stammered. Her heart was racing with exhilaration, but she couldn't let on too much. "Of course, I know you can support me. But last night you said…your business…"

His smile was the wide, brilliant one she loved. "Darling, just because I said we'd be on a budget for a while, that doesn't mean you have to start living the life of a pauper. Did I give you that impression?" He patted her hand. "You spend that money in whatever way you see fit. It's yours. I'll handle the family finances."

On a sudden inspiration, she sat down and called for Mrs. Laani to bring her a cup of coffee. "I think I'll wait and do my shopping in L.A. or maybe San Francisco. I want to have breakfast with my husband and son."

Matt clapped his hands when his father leaned across the table and wrapped his mother in a warm embrace, sealing her mouth with a blazing kiss.

Arden left the house long enough to cash the check and make a withdrawal from her account. She sealed the five thousand dollars in a manila envelope and stopped at a pay telephone to call the Orchid Lounge. She asked to speak to Ron Lowery, purposefully leaving off any form of address.

"Where the hell are you? You're thirty minutes late."

"I'm not coming." She let him digest that for a moment before she continued. "The money will be in our mailbox when we leave. It's on the road that fronts the house and is plainly marked."

"What are you trying to pull? I said—"

"If you want your money, that's where you can find it. We're leaving for the airport about two-thirty. Goodbye, Ron."

"Wait a minute!" he shouted. "When do I get the next installment?"

"When we get back from our trip." She hung up the phone before he could say anything more. She had no doubt that he'd be there to take the money out of the mailbox. He was more terrified of the loan sharks he owed money to than she was of him.

As she sped home, she was glad that she'd been able to pay him off with her own money instead of having to ask Drew for it under false pretenses. That would mean one less lie. How she'd get the next five thousand, she didn't know. But she had bought another month of happiness.

Drew watched from the bed as his wife fumbled with the clasp on her strand of pearls. The slender, well-manicured fingers, usually so deft, were trembling. The body that he loved, the lithe form that became so malleable to his loving touch in bed, was drawn as tight as a piano wire. It seemed that all one had to do was touch her and she'd snap in two.

Mrs. Laani had left their suite of rooms earlier with Matt. Drew had instructed her to keep him entertained for several hours. Now Drew came up off the bed where he'd been lounging with the morning newspaper and crossed to Arden.

He extricated the delicate gold clasp from her fingers and latched it easily. He watched her in the mirror. He saw that hated wariness, that fear, clouding her green eyes just as he had dreaded he would. It had bewildered him several weeks before. It bewildered him more so now. For the last few weeks, they had been happier than ever before.

He'd won all three tournaments. He was now seeded third in world tennis. Few remembered and even fewer remarked on the months he'd been off the circuit or the reasons for his temporary retirement. He'd proved he could come back. He was a champion again. And Arden had been there to celebrate each victory with him. Now he could feel her withdrawing into that shell he couldn't penetrate.

By God, he wasn't going to let her slip back into it without a fight!

He caught her shoulders so she couldn't evade him. "You're making far too much fuss over a medical examination, Arden."

"*You* are making too much of it," she snapped back.

"That's the prerogative of a worried husband. If the shoe were on the other foot, you'd feel the same."

"I wouldn't badger you."

"Yes, you would."

Yes, she would, Arden admitted. But there was nothing wrong with her! Nothing except that in a few hours Drew would learn they could never have another child.

She put on her earrings. "I'm fine, Drew. Have I seemed sick to you?"

"No," he answered honestly. Since the day they left Hawaii, she'd been all a man could hope for in a wife, a woman, a lover. Only in the last few days, when he'd insisted that she see the doctor—two appointments in Los Angeles had already been canceled—had she started behaving in that guarded way again. And each mention of home dropped a veil of discontent over her features. Drew felt a sudden wrenching in his gut. Did she suspect that something terrible was wrong with her? Lumps? Pains? *My God, no.* Was there something she hadn't told him to keep him from worrying?

"Arden," he said, turning her to face him. His blue eyes searched hers as though looking for signs of suffering. "You're not...I mean, you don't hurt anywhere or anything, do you? Darling, if you suspect something is wrong, it's better to have it seen to. It's what you don't—"

She covered his mouth with her fingertips. "Shh." Her heart turned over when she realized the unnecessary worry she had caused him. "No. No, darling, no. I'm in perfect health."

His relief was visible. One arm slid around her waist and pulled her close. The other hand smoothed the glossy length of her hair. "You like our home on Maui, don't you, Arden?"

"Of course," she said earnestly, seeing the concerned furrow between his thick brows and hating herself for etching it there.

"Because each time we mention going home, you seem upset by the idea. If you don't like it there, we can leave. I bought that place as a refuge. I don't need it anymore. All I need is you. And Matt. With the two of you, I can live anywhere. It's difficult for some people to live in so remote a place—"

"But I'm not one of them. I loved your home the first time you took me there, and now it's *my* home. I could live there forever with you and Matt."

He crushed her to him, loving the feel of her compact body against his. He knew each curve, each hollow, each dainty bone intimately. He loved them all. Every time he touched her, naked or clothed, he was filled with strength. She had made him happier than he'd had any right to expect, and he couldn't bear to think that she wasn't completely happy with him.

"I love you, Arden. Have I told you that today?"

"I can't remember," she mumbled into his shirtfront. *Oh, God, he would feel so betrayed if he ever found out about Matt. It would kill him.* "Just in case, tell me again."

His lips said it all as they came down on hers tenderly. His tongue roamed her mouth lazily as the pressure of his lips increased. The knuckles of his right hand lightly rubbed her nipple until he felt it flower beneath the ecru georgette blouse. The tip of his tongue touched hers suggestively, and he smiled when he heard her throaty purr. His other hand found the firm curve of her derriere and squeezed it gently, urging her forward and upward.

She pulled back in alarm. "Drew, you're getting—"

"Um-huh." He grinned wolfishly and started to pull her back.

"We can't. I'm not supposed to right before going to the doctor."

"Oh, hell," he ground out, burying his face in the fragrant hollow of her neck. "I forgot about that."

Then a brilliant idea occurred to her. She pressed close again and let her hand trail down his stomach to the fly of his trousers. "It probably wouldn't matter," she cooed, out-lining his shape with a bold caress.

"No, you don't," he said, pushing her away. "I know what you're thinking, and it won't work." He made an agonized face as he turned away from her to pick up his sport jacket. "Get your purse. Let's go before I change my mind. Or lose it."

"Are you sure?" Arden stared at the doctor with wide, disbelieving eyes. Thank God Drew had agreed to let her see this doctor in San Francisco. The one Ham had made an appointment with would have known her as the ex-Mrs. Ron Lowery. This doctor was a stranger to her, but after what he'd just told her, she thought she might forever think of him as a friend. "Are you absolutely positive?"

The doctor chuckled. "I'm absolutely positive that there's no medical or physical reason why you can't have another baby. If you're asking me for a guarantee that you'll get pregnant, I'm afraid that's something I can't give you." He noted Arden's astonishment. "Where did you ever get the idea that you'd been sterilized?"

She licked her lips, trying at one and the same time to absorb the fact that she wasn't sterile and to tamp down a killing rage at Ron Lowery. This had been just another of his psychopathically cruel tricks. "I...I...uh...had an infection, and the doctor I was seeing at the time thought it had made me infertile."

The doctor looked puzzled. "I saw no remnants of any infection. You're a wonderfully healthy woman with a normal set of reproductive organs." Linking his fingers together on his desktop, he leaned toward her. "Are you happy with your husband? Do you love him?"

"Yes," she said fervently. She could actually feel the burden she had carried with her for over a month being lifted from her shoulders. "Yes," she repeated, breaking out in laughter.

"Then let's go tell him that you're as fine as a fiddle." At the door, he caught her arm. "Relax, Mrs. McCasslin. You'll have that other baby."

Arden was as impulsive and playful as a child as they drove the rented Lincoln back to the hotel. She virtually sat in Drew's lap, her left arm around his neck. Every chance she got, she stole a kiss from his lips. While he negotiated the hilly streets of San Francisco, she contented herself with nibbling his neck, his ear.

"For God's sake, Arden, did that doctor give you a tonic, an aphrodisiac? You're driving me crazy."

"How crazy?" she breathed as her hand slid between his thighs. There she felt a good indication of how near he was to losing control.

"What did you and that doctor do to turn you on like this?"

"That's crude." She punished him with a gentle squeeze that almost made him swerve the car into another lane. "I'm turned on because I have the handsomest, smartest, sexiest..." She placed her lips against his ear. "And hardest husband in the whole world."

His curse testified to his agitation. "Okay, two can play this lusty game. Did you know that every time I look at your breasts, I'm ready to make love right then? Remember that cocktail party in San Diego after the tournament? You were wearing that yellow halter dress, and I knew you didn't have a bra under it. All the time I was making small talk to everyone, I was thinking about how I'd love to slide my hand inside your dress and touch your breasts."

"Drew," she groaned. Moving slightly closer, she pressed her breast against his arm. His sensual monologue was producing the desired effect.

"The other day when we met Ham for lunch on Fisherman's Wharf, you wore that peasant skirt with sandals and no stockings. I had watched you dress that morning. All you had on under your skirt was that pair of lilac panties with the lace panel in front. I couldn't think about anything else but the last time you'd worn them and I kissed you through that lace—"

"Stop," she cried, laying her head on his shoulder. "This is insane. We won't be able to walk through the lobby."

That was close to the truth. They were breathless with excitement by the time Drew latched the hotel door behind them with a *DO NOT DISTURB* sign dangling from the knob. He had already stripped off his coat and tie, his shoes and socks, before Arden stopped him.

"Wait. I want to." First, she eased out of her own clothes with the practiced, sinuous moves of a courtesan. The georgette blouse had an interminable number of tiny pearl buttons, and Drew's eyes were glazed with passion by the time she peeled it off her shoulders and down her arms. Her breasts thrust proudly beneath the lacy confinement of her brassiere. It came off with deliberate slowness. His eyes ravaged the warm mounds and coral nipples. She peeled off her half-slip and panty hose with one graceful movement, then stood before him wearing the panties he'd mentioned earlier.

His mouth curved with humor as he reached for his top shirt button. Staying his hand, she led him to the bed. She sat down on its edge and ran her fingers up his chest to the top button. Each one was released with meticulous precision. Her fingers took leisurely detours over the crinkly mat of hair, the firm bunched muscles, the smooth flesh, the masculine nipples.

"Arden, please," he begged on a shuddering breath. She took off his shirt, then met the fiery gaze he turned on her upraised face. "Let me love you."

"Let me love *you*." She worked free his belt buckle, the snap of his trousers, the zippered fly. Her eyes were still locked with his as she slid her hands beneath the tight briefs and cupped his taut buttocks. She smoothed her hands down,

Chapter 13

The Orchid Lounge was as murky, the clientele as unsavory, as before. A dozen or so men were grouped in pairs and trios. Their conversations were low and indistinct to the only woman in the place. The air was thick with the odor of beer and tobacco smoke.

Arden had never been more composed in her life.

The trip home from San Francisco had been nothing short of a party for them all. Drew was still euphoric over his success at the tournaments. He was no less glad over Arden's frame of mind since her visit to the doctor. Whatever had been worrying her seemed to have been resolved in that hour. His heart still flip-flopped, and his breath grew short each time he remembered the unselfish way she had loved him afterward. That whole afternoon had been given over to sexual indulgence. He would recommend such an afternoon to any married couple.

Arden, after having dreaded it, was now anxious to return home. She was basking in the glow of Drew's success and his love. During the long flight over the Pacific, she could barely keep her hands off him. She took advantage of every occasion to touch him and he responded in kind.

Matt sensed their lightheartedness and was at his most good-natured. He charmed all the flight attendants until Mrs. Laani pulled him into her lap and he fell asleep on her generous bosom. Arden could have been jealous, but Drew pulled her into his own arms for a little "nap." Numerous times, she had to covertly swat his hand when it crept into compromising territory.

The morning after their return, Ron telephoned.

"It's about time you answered. The first two times I called, I got your housekeeper and had to hang up."

"I'm sorry to have inconvenienced you."

"Cocky all of a sudden, aren't you?" He chuckled unpleasantly. "Don't forget your bills are due."

"Where and when?"

"The same place. Two o'clock."

She had hung up without another word. Now she was sitting in the same booth, and he was as late as before. She had disdained the bartender's ingratiating invitation to have a drink on the house. Instead, she sat with her back straight, her hands folded in her lap. And rather than ignore the stares this time, she met them with enough condescension to turn them away.

"Glad to be back?" Ron asked as he slid into the booth opposite her. "Good trip?"

"Yes, on both accounts."

"Your husband's making a name for himself. Does it make you proud to have such a famous hubby?"

"I'd be proud of him whether he was famous or not."

He placed his hand over his heart. "Such wifely devotion makes me thirsty." He called his order to the bartender, then turned back to her. "Wonder how proud he'd be of you if he knew you'd sold your body for fifty thousand dollars?"

"I don't know. But I intend to find out. I'm going to tell him everything."

Ron's eyes glittered in reptilian fashion as he stared at her. Even when his drink was set before him, he didn't move.

"You bastard," Arden said in a calm, emotionless voice. That tone conveyed her contempt more than shouting at him would have. He wasn't worth wasting the energy shouting would require. "I didn't know that any man, even one as low as you, could play a trick as dirty as the one you played on me."

His grin was insolent and obnoxious. "You found out I'd lied about sterilizing you." He began to laugh a low, rumbling laugh that could have passed for the devil's. "Scared you, didn't I?"

"Why did you tell me that?"

"Because you were getting too self-assured. You seemed to think you could shake me off like a bad dream. I wanted you to know that I meant business. I still do."

"Well, I'm terribly sorry to disappoint you, Ron, but our *business* dealings are over. Your threats are empty ones. If they weren't, you wouldn't be skulking around in dives like this and hanging up when I don't answer the telephone. You accused me of being a coward, but you are the coward. It takes a man to make it in the real world. And you never could. Even when you had all the advantages handed to you, you couldn't hack it as a doctor, as a husband, as a father, as a man."

She stood up with proud dignity. "You don't frighten me anymore. You've browbeaten and used me for the last time. There's nothing you can do to hurt me any longer. Go to hell."

She turned on her heel and walked out. Her knees were weak and her mouth dry by the time she reached the car. But she had done it! She had rid herself of Dr. Ron Lowery forever. That night, she'd tell Drew the entire story. She was no longer afraid that their love couldn't withstand the truth. Their lives were grafted together too securely to be torn apart now. She would make the setting perfect. She'd tell him everything. And then, at last, she'd be free.

The bottle of wine almost slipped from under her arm as she maneuvered her way through the wide front door. "Mrs. Laani," she called, laughing. She clutched the bouquet of flowers, trying to keep them from being crushed against the box that contained her new negligee.

Mrs. Laani came rushing out from the back of the house, but the moment Arden saw her, she knew it wasn't her call that had brought the housekeeper running. "Mrs. McCasslin, I'm so glad you're home."

"Is something wrong?"

The housekeeper darted her eyes toward Drew's office. The door was closed. "Mr. McCasslin wants to see you right away. He said the moment you got back." The normally self-contained woman was wringing her hands.

"Why? What's—" Arden gripped Mrs. Laani's arm. "Matt? Has something happened to Matt?"

"No, he's with me in the kitchen. You'd better go to your husband." She wouldn't meet Arden's questioning eyes.

Arden's reflexes took over. She operated mechanically, acting as though nothing were wrong when indeed she knew something was terribly wrong. Mrs. Laani wasn't the kind to panic. "Chill the wine and arrange the flowers in a vase for our bedroom, please. We'll eat the steaks tonight. Please see that Matt's dinner is ready beforehand. And put this box in my closet."

"Yes, Mrs. McCasslin," Mrs. Laani said, relieving Arden of her packages and backing away from her. Arden was alarmed by the commiserating look on the woman's face.

She smoothed her hands over her skirt and was amazed to note that the palms were damp. Stifling her panic, she turned the knob and pushed her way through the door into Drew's office.

"Darling, I'm—" The first thing that caught her eye was the bottle of Scotch on the polished surface of Drew's desk. She stared at it for several seconds before her eyes wandered to the highball glass next to it. A white-knuckled hand was wrapped around the glass. Drew's hand. It wasn't until then that the incongruity of that struck her.

Her eyes flew up to meet his, and she flinched at the hatred she saw smoldering there. His hair was a wild blond tangle, and it wasn't simply windblown. It had been torn at with maniacal hands. The muscles of his jaw were working as he ground his teeth, and in his temple beat a furious pulse.

"Come in, Mrs. McCasslin," he said in a voice Arden had never heard. It dripped with sarcasm and repugnance. "I believe you know our guest."

For the first time, Arden noticed the man ensconced in the deep easy chair facing Drew's desk. He turned, and she met Ronald Lowery's mocking face. Her knees collapsing, she slumped against the door, clutching at it for support.

Drew laughed harshly. "You act surprised to see your ex-husband when in fact Ron's told me that the two of you have been seeing a great deal of each other."

Bile rose into her throat, but she forced it back down. She must make Drew see the true situation. "Drew," she said, reaching out a beseeching hand. "Drew, what has he told you?"

"Quite a tale, quite a tale," he said with that same sneering laugh. "I thought I was the king of sinners. I certainly didn't think any form of human treachery would surprise me. I congratulate you on your ingeniousness."

"Drew, please," Arden said, advancing into the room. "Listen to me. I don't know what he's told you, but—"

"*Did* you let your husband impregnate you with my sperm, and *did* you carry my child for nine months, and then *did* you give him...or should I say *sell* him...for half the one hundred thousand dollars your husband charged me? *Did* you do all that?"

Tears streamed down her face. "Yes, but—"

"And then *did* you have a change of heart and come to Hawaii to worm your way into my confidence, into my life? *Did* you?"

"It wasn't—"

"Godammit, what a fool I've been." The chair went flying backward when he lunged out of it. He drained the glass of Scotch and then slammed it back onto the desktop. He turned his back on them as if they were too disgusting to look at.

"It wasn't like that," Arden said. "It *wasn't*."

Ignoring her pleas for understanding, he whirled around. "How much were you planning to bleed me for, huh?"

He was demanding that of her, not Ron. "Nothing."

"Nothing! Nothing? My money, my son? When was it going to be enough? You already had my life sewn up with your deceit."

She swallowed, trying to capture the thoughts that were darting through her head. She couldn't think with Drew scowling at her, his eyes as hard and cold as diamonds. "He contacted me several weeks ago. He said he'd tell you who I was if…" She quailed at his snarl but doggedly continued. "If I didn't give him twenty thousand dollars. He's a gambler and indebted to loan sharks. That's why he needed the money before, the money you paid him for Matt. I needed that money too, for Joey. And I wanted to be free of Ron." Distressed, she rubbed her forehead when Drew righted the chair and dropped down into it. His whole being reflected indifference to her dilemma. She must make him understand!

"I paid him five thousand dollars before we went to the mainland. It was my money, Drew, not yours. Mine. And I would have given him twice that to spare you this scene."

"So you would have gone on giving this scum money indefinitely to keep me from finding out what a deceitful bitch I'm married to. Your concern for my welfare overwhelms me."

She sobbed and shook her head. "No, Drew, no. I was going to tell you myself."

"When? When, Arden? I'd be interested to know. When Matt went off to grade school? When he graduated from college? Or when he was marching down the aisle with his bride, were you planning to tap me on the arm and say, 'Oh, by the way, I'm the woman who gave him birth.' Is that when you planned to tell me?"

The scornful words pounded against her skull like tiny mallets. "I couldn't live with the secret any longer. I love you and Matt. I was going to tell you…tonight."

He bellowed with laughter then, ugly, ridiculing laughter. "*Tonight!* Isn't that touching?" He stared up at her from under glowering brows. "Do you really think I'll believe that now, when you've lied to me from the very beginning?"

"I didn't lie!"

"This whole goddamned affair has been a lie!" he roared. Once again, he came out of the chair like a bullet. "When I think of how you duped me." He shook his head, laughing mirthlessly. "So prim and proper, so polite, so sympathetic, so—" He waved a hand toward her and then dropped it at his side in a gesture that stated how pathetic a creature he found her.

His attention returned to Ron, who was sitting like a vulture anticipating the bleeding carcass that would be left for him to finish off. "Get out," Drew said succinctly. The gloating smirk on Ron's face disappeared.

"Wait a minute. We haven't talked about how we're going to handle this."

"If you think I'll give you one goddamn cent, you're crazy as well as criminal. And if you don't get out of here now, I'm going to beat the bloody hell out of you, and then I'm going to turn you over to the police."

Ron stood, trembling with rage. "You'll sing a different tune when I tell the newspapers my titillating story about you and your pale wife and how you came to me asking to find a mother for your baby. That would make the son you hold so dear little more than a freak in a sideshow. To top that off, you're now married to the natural mother. Maybe I won't tell them that I artificially inseminated Arden. Maybe I'll let them think Matt came about in the natural way. That would make the kid a bastard."

Arden shivered, but Drew shrugged theatrically. "Who do you think is going to believe such a farfetched story? Especially from a doctor who has lost his practice, the respect of his peers, who is in debt to everyone in the world, including the Mafia, and is now living the life of a bum. Who do you think they'll believe? Me or you? Celebrities of my status are constantly the victims of crackpots out to make a quick buck, and the press knows that. They'll laugh in your face, Lowery."

Arden could see the confidence leaking out of Ron as freely as his sweat. "That lawyer. He's got papers. He'll back me up."

"Will he? If you were him, who would you back up? A world-famous tennis player who's on the rise or a derelict out for revenge on the wife who left him? Even your caliber of friend wouldn't be that stupid. If he were, I could pay him more to keep quiet than you could to talk."

Ron's face had gone the color of putty. Drew came around the desk. "I say once again, get out. And if you so much as show your face to any member of my family or household again, I'll have you locked up so tight that only your Mafia buddies can get to you. And you know what they'll do when they find you."

"You can't get rid of me so easy, McCasslin."

"Yes, I can, and you know it. That's why you stink of fear."

Ron looked at Arden, his gaze filled with hate. "At least I ruined you, too. He despises you, just as I always did." He left the room. Moments later, she heard the front door opening and closing.

Minutes passed. There was no movement in the study. A deathlike pall hung over them. Drew stared out the window at the incessant motion of the ocean. Arden stared at his back, wondering how she could ever make him understand enough to forgive her. Why hadn't she told him? *Why?* If only she had it all to live over, she would tell him everything. She could imagine him taking her in his arms and whispering his understanding. "You did what you had to do at the time," he would say. "I can't fault you for that. I know you married me because you love me, not because you wanted to be with Matt. I know. I understand."

Instead, he was brittle with fury and wounded pride. She didn't recognize the face that turned to her now. "Are you still here? I thought maybe you would leave with your first husband to see what new adventure the two of you could embark upon."

She bowed her head. "It was never an adventure. I did it for Joey."

"So there really was a Joey? I was beginning to wonder."

Her head snapped up a moment before she lurched toward him angrily. "I did it to prolong his life. I did it because it was the only way I had to get out of an intolerable marriage with a man I loathed more every day. When you stop feeling sorry for yourself, maybe you can see your way clear to understand what it was like for me."

"Feeling sorry for myself!" he shouted. "I feel nothing but contempt for my blind stupidity. Every time I think about the callow way I watched you, how I carefully planned my approach like a jerk asking for his first dance, how I sat there talking to you with my pants near to bursting, I could retch. How did you manage to keep a straight face? I don't know why you didn't collapse with laughter."

"It wasn't like that, Drew," she protested urgently. "Initially, yes, I wanted to meet you because of Matt. *I wanted to see my son!*" she shouted. "Was that so wrong? But once I met you, I wanted you, too. Even more than I wanted Matt." That admission cost her dearly, but she knew it to be the truth.

"You wanted nothing but to seduce me."

"Seduce…" she began incredulously. "Have you lost your memory as well as your reason? If that's all it had taken, I'd have done that the first night."

"Oh, no, not you. You're too smart a schemer. If you'd taken me to bed right away, I might never have come back. No, you baited me with all that well-thought-out resistance. To a man who has women clustered around him all the time, that's the strongest turn-on of all."

"Yes, you could have had your pick of girls. They follow you in packs. So don't make me out as a temptress who snared you into a trap with the promise of sex that couldn't be had anywhere else." Her impatience with his bullhead-edness was increasing and with it her volume. "You were a bonus I hadn't counted on. My objective was to become a trusted friend, not a lover. Then I fell in love with you and couldn't find the courage to tell you who I was for fear you'd act exactly as you're acting. Your pride, your fierce temper, makes you unreasonable, Drew."

Her breasts heaved with agitation beneath her silk sweater. He found himself staring at them and tore his eyes away, sending blistering curses toward the ceiling.

Even now, knowing what he did about her, she appealed to him as no other women ever had. She was so damned beautiful. He still wanted her. Vivid in his memory was the first time he'd seen her sitting under the umbrella of that patio table. Her serenity seemed to lure him. He'd wanted to be near her, to absorb that peace she seemed to exude. How could she have fooled him? Why hadn't he been able to see the calculation in her eyes? It must have been there no matter how much she denied it now. She'd plotted the whole thing long before he'd ever seen her. All right, yes, part of his anger was out of pride. But what man likes to find out that he's been manipulated like a puppet into loving and marrying a woman? What man with any pride could tolerate that?

He kept telling himself he hated her. Why then did he want to kiss her mindless, to empty his frustration, which was only a hair away from being desire, into her? Why did he still crave the succor of her body and the joy of her laugh and the balm of her love? He hated her most for the weakness she induced in him.

"I tried to tell you once," she said barely above a whisper. "And you said that any secrets about our pasts were better kept to ourselves. That if they didn't affect the way we loved each other, they were better left unspoken."

"I didn't know your little secret was of such magnitude, Arden." It was his superior tone, that arrogant drawl, that went down her spine like fingernails on a blackboard and brought her own temper to the surface.

"And what about *your* secret, Drew? You never told me that Matt was born not of Ellie, your beloved wife, but of a woman you wouldn't recognize if you met her on the street. You were willing to let me marry you without knowing that, weren't you?"

"What difference did it make?"

"None!" she yelled. "That's my point. I would love you and Matt just the same if I weren't his mother."

"Would you, Arden?"

The question had the impact of an explosion in the room. For seconds after it had been detonated, there was an intense silence.

"Yes, Drew," she said with soft intensity. "Yes."

He impaled her with his startling blue gaze. "But I'll never know for sure, will I? You sold your body to me once for the sake of a son. Isn't that what you've done again?"

She watched in helpless desperation as he went to the desk and picked up the bottle of Scotch. Going to the open window, he leaned forward and shattered the bottle on the outside wall of the house. He tossed the jagged bottle neck into the shrubbery.

"I sure as hell won't let you drive me back to *that,*" he said. "I'm a winner again, and I won't let you or anyone take that away from me."

"You're making a mistake."

Arden turned from folding a blouse into her suitcase to see Mrs. Laani standing in the door of the master suite. She looked comfortingly domestic and normal with a dish towel slung over her shoulder. Arden longed to go to her, to lay her head on that maternal breast and let loose the tears that she thought should have been spent by now. She'd been crying for a week, ever since Drew left.

Without a word of goodbye to her, he'd left his office and packed quietly. The next thing she knew, he was striding across the lawn calling to Mo. "Drive me to the airport, please." He'd called three times since to check on Matt. He spoke with Mrs. Laani, never to her. He was in Los Angeles, ostensibly working with Ham on his serve and closing the final negotiations of their business deal.

"I don't think it's a mistake," Arden now said quietly, and turned back to the suitcase that lay opened on the bed.

She heard Mrs. Laani's shuffling footsteps as she came into the room. "He's a stubborn man, Mrs. McCasslin. Proud. I would have had to be deaf not to hear the argument the two of you had after that horrible man left. You're Matt's mother. I should have guessed."

Arden smiled. "It was easy to slip into the active role. Sometimes I thought my love would be so transparent that you...or Drew...would guess, but..." Her voice trailed off on a tremulous sigh.

"It was a shock to Mr. McCasslin, but when he thinks about it, he'll realize how irrational he's been."

"He's had a week to think about it. I don't know what he

plans to do about us, but I can't just sit here like a convict awaiting execution. I'm the intruder. He was already playing competitive tennis before he met me. He and Matt have a close relationship. They don't need me interfering in their lives any more than I already have."

Mrs. Laani pulled herself erect and crossed her arms over her stomach. "So you're going to play the martyr and sneak away like a coward."

Arden sat down on the bed and looked up at the woman's reproachful expression. "Try to understand this, Mrs. Laani. All my life I've been a coward. I did what my husband wanted me to do even when I knew it was wrong. Before that, my father took care of me, made my decisions for me."

She sighed and fiddled with the lacy hem of a slip she'd been folding. Drew liked its peachy color. He'd remarked on it every time she wore it. Once, jokingly, he'd pretended to take a bite out of her breast, chewing lustily. "The ripest fruit on the tree," he'd said, and they'd laughed together at his clowning. Would memories like that haunt her in the lonely years to come?

"The cowardly thing to do would be to stay and submit to Drew's scorn, to live with it, just like I lived with my former husband's. He actually hated me for the doormat I became. I can see that now. He contrived ways to humiliate me, perhaps in the hope that I'd show some backbone and say no to him just once."

"But Mr. McCasslin would never be like that," Mrs. Laani protested vehemently.

"No, he wouldn't be cruel. But year after year, I'd see his respect dwindling. Because I'd be so afraid of offending him again, I'd want to do everything he asked. I'd be tempted to cater to him for fear he'd throw my one major mistake in my face again and again. I'd feel forced to prove my love by never disagreeing with him. And very soon, he'd hate me. And I'd hate myself worse."

She looked back up at the housekeeper, whom she considered a friend. "I can't live like that again. If Drew doesn't know by now how much I love him, then no amount of demonstration will convince him. I won't spend my life trying."

"But Matt." Mrs. Laani's eyes were filled with tears.

"Yes, Matt." Arden smiled gently with remembrance of the week they'd had together. She'd spent every waking hour with him. At night, she'd go into his room, sit in the bentwood rocker beside his baby bed and watch him as he slept. Her heart ached for what she must do. "Hopefully, Drew will let me see him periodically. I wouldn't be so unreasonable as to fight him for custody. This is the only life Matt knows. I couldn't uproot him from it." A tear rolled down her cheek. "It's just that he changes every day. Months will go by, and I won't see him, and I'll miss so many of those wonderful changes."

"Please change your mind." Mrs. Laani was weeping unashamedly now. Arden envied her the freedom to do so. "You love them both too much to leave."

"I love them too much not to," Arden responded quietly.

She explained the same thing to Matt later that night. He had long since fallen into the innocent sleep of a child.

"I don't know what your daddy will tell you about me. I hope someday you'll know who I am and that you'll forgive me for giving you up. I was trying to save your brother's life, Matt." A poignant smile flickered over her lips. "I wish you had known Joey. You would have liked each other." She wiped her cheeks of flowing tears.

"Your father is a competitor, Matt. He can't bear to lose without having fought an honest fight." She remembered the match against Gonzales. It had been a defeat, but a defeat Drew hadn't minded because he'd played hard and fair. Arden hadn't allowed him to play fair. She'd cheated him of an honest game, because the victory had been certain. He'd been a pawn and not a participant. That was what he couldn't forgive.

"I love your father, Matt. And I don't want to leave either of you. But it would be an unhealthy family environment for you to grow up in with him holding me in contempt and me hating him for his intolerance. Someday you may learn that love can't exist if one's self-esteem is sacrificed to it. I can't be an object for any man again, something that goes with the house, something with no will, no opinion worth considering. Please understand why I must leave."

She fingered the soft, butter-colored curls. She traced his pudgy cheek to the drooling mouth. She touched the dimpled knuckles of his fist.

"I had to give you up before, Matt. Then as now, it wasn't because I didn't love you." She stood, groped her way to the door and fumbled for the light switch. She didn't look back before she plunged the room into darkness, a darkness not nearly as absolute as the one in her soul.

Chapter 14

The motel room was like an efficiency apartment. It was on the wrong side of Kalakaua Avenue if one wanted a view of Waikiki. The complex had seen better days. Now it was only an insignificant, inexpensive motel dwarfed and humbled by progress and modern architecture. It suited Arden's budget and needs, as good a place as any to idle away the long, lonely days.

She wasn't completely without occupation. She took long walks along the beach. She thought about Matt, wondered what he was doing, if he was missing her. And she thought about Drew, what he was doing, if he was missing her. She wrote. Thoughts and impressions that had no form filled tablet after tablet. She was seized by a compulsion to put her feelings on paper.

She was doing just that on the fourth day after leaving Maui. The muses had taken leave, for she had stared at the blank page for fifteen minutes. A shadow crossed the sheet of paper, and she looked up at the window to see Drew standing there.

For a small eternity, they stared at each other through the smudged window screen. Her mental faculties failed her. Stunned fingers let go of the pen. It dropped to the tabletop and rolled onto the cheaply carpeted floor. He didn't speak before he moved toward the door.

She had to persuade her muscles to move. Wobbly knees brought her to her feet. Self-consciously, she smoothed her hair and ran her palms over the old jeans covering her thighs. It was ridiculous, but she wished she had put on a bra that morning under the T-shirt she wore. Unreasonably, she felt vulnerable, unprotected; she would have felt more confident behind the lacy armor. She stepped to the door. He hadn't knocked, but she pulled it open.

His face looked so ravaged that at first she feared he'd been drinking abusively again. But despite the lines around them, his eyes were clear, and his marvelous athletic body was agile and lithe as he walked into the room. His hair was longer and shaggier than usual. He had on a pair of white shorts and a yellow polo shirt. To her, he'd never looked better. She ached with the need to touch him.

After one cursory glance around the stark room, he turned to her. "Hi."

"Hi."

"Are you all right?"

She looked down at the floor, then as quickly back up into his eyes, unable to keep from looking at him. "Yes." She could sense a tension about him as powerful as that which gripped her. He seemed to radiate a heat that her body responded to. Her breast filled with emotion. "You? Are you well? Matt?"

"I only returned to Maui this morning."

"Oh."

"I wasn't home long, but Matt seemed fine. Healthwise,

that is. Mrs. Laani said he's been crying a lot lately." He seemed to find the palm tree outside the screened window captivating. He stared at it as he said, "He misses you."

She ducked her head. "I miss him, too." A pain like a laser beam shot through her heart. *And I miss you!*

"I...uh...I didn't know you had left until I got home." He coughed unnecessarily and cleared his throat. It sounded loud in the cramped room. "I flew back to Honolulu immediately."

She turned toward the window and gazed out. Her pulse was pounding so hard she could count each beat, and her hand trembled as she toyed with the draw cord of the tacky drapes. "How did you find me?"

"With a bag of quarters."

She turned her head. "Pardon?"

"I got a bag of quarters from the bank, found a pay phone and started dialing."

"Oh." She turned back to the window before allowing herself to smile. "I decided to stay in Hawaii until arrangements were made in Los Angeles. Since...since my trip over here was left deliberately open-ended, I gave up my apartment before I left. I'm waiting to hear from a friend. She's looking for a place for me."

"You're going back, then? Back to L.A., I mean?"

Was there anxiety underlying the question? She didn't dare look at him. What if that tremor in his voice indicated relief? "I suppose so, yes," she mumbled.

She heard him coming nearer. He stood in front of the table where she'd been working. The sheets of paper she'd discarded rustled under his hand. "You're writing?"

"Yes," she said huskily. He wasn't going to argue with her about the separation. He was going to let her go. He was condemning her to a sterile existence without color, without life. "I write when the mood strikes me," she said with forced casualness.

She heard more paper crackling in the brief pause that followed. "What mood were you in when you wrote this?"

In her peripheral vision, she saw a wrinkled piece of paper floating to the tabletop. Turning slowly, puzzled, she looked first at Drew. His eyes seared into hers, and she rapidly shifted her gaze to the sheet of paper he referred to.

She recognized her handwriting instantly. After reading the first line, she realized it was a poem she'd penned more than a month before. Like everything she wrote, she had dated it at the top of the page. They'd been in San Francisco. Mrs. Laani had taken Matt downstairs to the hotel's restaurant for his breakfast. They'd ordered theirs up from room service. After a leisurely breakfast in bed, they'd made even more leisurely love. When Drew left for his practice session, Arden had reached for a tablet and pen and, still languorous from their sweet lovemaking, she'd composed the poem.

It was a tribute to him, to what he meant to her. The last two lines were, "Where once your life transformed my body, / Your love now shapes my soul."

Tears blinded her and made the edited lines bleed together. "I think the mood is self-explanatory." She hazarded a glance up at him to find his own eyes shiny and wet.

"I found it crumpled in the corner of the suitcase yesterday."

"I'd forgotten what I did with it."

"I had decided days ago that I was the biggest heel in history. You had every right to hate me for the things I'd said, not to mention my goddamned stubborn pride and short temper. I was going to beg you for your forgiveness, promise that I'd never consider you an opponent again. Finding this gave me the courage to come home and face you. I figured that if you felt this for me once, you might find it in your heart to feel it again."

"*You* were going to ask *my* forgiveness?"

"Yes. For behaving like a moron, a sore loser, a spoiled brat."

"But darling, your anger was justified. I tricked you into marrying me."

They had been inclining toward each other. Now he pulled her into his arms and crushed her against his body. He buried his face in the glossy mass of her hair. "You did no such thing. I married you because I love you. I wanted you for my wife. I still do. God, I almost died when Mrs. Laani told me you had left. Don't leave me, Arden."

"I didn't want to," she cried. "I only left because I thought you couldn't bear the sight of me." She pushed him away and peered up into his eyes. "But I can't live with judgment every day. I have to know you understand why I did what I did. Given the same set of circumstances, I'd make the same choice, Drew. I won't live the rest of my life being censured for it."

"Come here," he said gently, leading her to the bed. They sat down on the faded spread, and he took both her hands in his. "What you did wasn't wrong, Arden. Unorthodox, maybe, but not wrong. When Lowery told Ellie and me he had found a healthy young woman who was willing to have our child, in our minds, we placed her on a pedestal. The day Matt was born, we thought she was the most wonderful woman on the face of the earth."

Lovingly, he touched her face, her hair, as he talked. "Why I acted the way I did when I learned you were that woman, I can't explain. I guess I felt betrayed because you hadn't told me in the beginning that you were Matt's mother. It hurt that you hadn't trusted my love enough to tell me. What I should have done when I found out was what I'd felt like doing the first time I saw my son. I should have dropped to my knees and thanked you from the bottom of my heart."

"You don't think less of me because I sold my baby?"

He lifted tears from her cheeks with his fingertip. "I didn't think badly of you before I knew who you were. Why would I now? I know you did it to try to save Joey's life. If I thought I could save Matt such a fate, I'd make a bargain with the devil."

"I did."

He smiled wryly. "Having come to know your former husband better, I couldn't agree with you more. I can't believe that at one time I actually considered him a miracle worker."

"You're not afraid he'll make more trouble?"

"I don't think he will. He's a gutless bastard running scared."

"I should have realized that the first time he approached me on Maui. I was so afraid of what he might do. Kidnap Matt. Anything was possible."

"He's got more than us to worry about. But if he does bring on a crisis, I know I can face anything as long as I have you and Matt with me." He planted a tender kiss in her palm. "You will come home with me, won't you? And never leave?"

"Is that what you want?"

"It's what I wanted from the first time I saw you, touched you, kissed you." His mouth blended with hers as they fell back onto the bed. It was a sweet kiss, but rife with hunger. He sampled the texture and taste of her lips before breaching them with his tongue. He reclaimed her mouth with the gentle thrusts and lazy strokes that characterized his kisses. They sent desire curling around her breasts and weaving between her thighs. But the time wasn't right for them to give way to their physical needs, and Arden was gratified that Drew was sensitive enough to realize it, too.

Pushing her away gently, he sat up. His eyes darted around the room. "God, this is a depressing place. Let's go home."

Matt was elated over having such an appreciative audience. His parents sat on the living-room floor on the oriental rug and applauded his playful antics, which became wilder by the minute. He somersaulted and jigged and ran in circles until he toppled over backward and bumped his head on the leg of the grand piano and set up a howl.

"You'd better put him to bed before he gets any more wound up," Mrs. Laani cautioned. She'd been dabbing copious tears of happiness out of her eyes ever since Drew and Arden came through the front door, arm in arm, looking grubby but radiant.

"Okay, Bozo, you heard the voice of authority." To quell Matt's tears, Drew lifted him up to straddle his neck. His hands caught in his father's thick blond hair. Arden placed her arm around Drew's waist as they ascended the stairs.

Arden decided that they had waited too late to calm Matt down. He was uncontrollable, bucking their attempts to snap him into pajamas. "Pee-pee," he kept repeating.

"Maybe it's not a false alarm," she said. Drew looked highly skeptical. He was wondering how many more delays were going to keep Arden and him from their own bed. His body was raging. He made his decision quickly.

Off came the pajamas, off came the bulky overnight diaper. Matt was carried into his bathroom and placed in front of the training potty. He did the deed, to his mother's overwhelming praise and his father's astonishment. Matt beamed up at them and submitted to their hugs and kisses of congratulations. Even Mrs. Laani was summoned to join the celebration. Such adoration was tiring. As soon as he was redressed for bed, Matt curled up into a ball and fell asleep, one chubby arm strangling Pooh Bear.

"We made a great kid," Drew whispered, his arm keeping Arden close.

"We certainly did," she concurred, snuggling against him. "Before I gave Ron the five thousand dollars, he told me he had sterilized me after I had Matt."

Drew's curse was vivid. "No wonder you walked around here like a zombie during those weeks."

She shivered, and he placed his other arm around her, as well. "That's why I protested so much over seeing a doctor. I didn't want you to find that out. I was already keeping one secret from you."

"It doesn't matter, Arden. We don't need any other child—"

"No," she cried softly, not wanting to disturb their sleeping son. "He was lying. He only told me that to terrorize me."

"That son of a bitch," he said viciously.

"That's why I was so relieved and happy after we left the doctor's office. Remember?"

His hand found her breast and fondled it lovingly. "I remember," he rasped.

"The doctor said there was no reason why I couldn't have as many children as we want."

He branded a kiss on her forehead. "I'll love them if we do. But it won't bother me if we don't. I'm going to be the top-seeded professional tennis player next year." She squeezed his waist to show him she fully agreed. "Then I can gracefully retire. I have a wonderful son. And I have a wife whom I love with all that I am. What more could I ask for?"

They gave the sleeping boy one final good-night kiss and left the room. The hallway yawned before them, and they were both suddenly self-conscious and nervous.

Drew looked down at her. "I can't help wanting to rush you into my bed again, but I know you like to be courted."

Her eyes took on a dreamy glow. "That was before I was married."

"And now?"

"Now I want to make love with my husband."

"I need to clean up."

"So do I."

"I'll use the bathroom downstairs. Fifteen minutes?"

She smiled, glad that he was going to leave her alone to prepare for him. "Or less."

She bathed and shampooed quickly, blew her hair dry, scented herself with perfume and moisturized her skin with lotion. The negligee she had brought home the day her world fell apart was still in its long, flat box. She shook out the transparent violet folds and slipped into it. Its sheer covering only enhanced her nakedness beneath.

She was reclining against the pillows when he came in, wearing only a terry-cloth wrapper around his loins. It rode low, just below his navel with its whorl of dark golden hair. She tracked the intriguing pattern of hair up a silky narrow strip to the spot where it fanned out over the broad expanse of his chest.

Locking his eyes with hers, he walked to the bed, un-snapped the wrapper and let it fall. Unashamed, she looked at him.

"That's pretty," he said of the new nightgown. His eyes traveled down the slender column of her throat to the curves of her breasts. Beneath the gossamer fabric, he could see her nipples. The material clung to her thighs and legs, outlining their shape. Her slender, high-arched feet were chastely crossed.

"Thank you," she answered.

"I like you in that color."

"I'll remember that. I like you in that color, too."

He flashed her a wide grin. "I need to work on my tan. It has paled in the last week." Leaning down, he slipped one finger into the V at her bosom and peeped inside. "Yours needs work, too."

The tantalizing touch of his finger near her nipple made her breath falter. Her breasts rose and fell against his finger, and her eyes took on that slumberous quality that made desire concentrate in his loins.

"Arden," he whispered. He lay down beside her facing the opposite way, resting his head on her thigh. "I love you. I've hated being separated from you. Let's never be apart again."

"Never," she vowed, running her fingers through his hair.

He parted the folds of her nightgown and laid his hard cheek against her silky skin. "You smell so good," he murmured. His kissed her navel, consummating his love for it with his tongue. "You had my son. Carried him…here." His lips glided over her abdomen as he flicked the responsive flesh with his tongue.

"Yes," she breathed. She turned her head into his warmth, pulled his scent into her body by taking deep breaths of it. His body hair felt good against her face, her lips. Her mouth encountered the deep dimple of his navel and explored it inquisitively.

"Oh, God, Arden." His fingers dug into her hair, pressing her head nearer.

"Each time I felt the baby move, I'd think about you." Her arm slid around his hip. "I wondered what you looked like, prayed that you'd be a good father to my child, imagined what I'd say to you if we ever met."

"I thought about you, too. I knew you were healthy, so I couldn't see you as overweight or too thin. But I was curious about what you looked like, your personality, your motivation for having a stranger's child. I wondered if you ever thought about me."

She smiled against the golden nest that surrounded his manhood. "Yes. I did." His whole body convulsed when first her lips, then the tip of her tongue, touched him. "Drew," she murmured, "when you…collected the…the…" She couldn't bring herself to ask, and she didn't want to speak of Ellie now. Not now. Not when his hand was closing over the curve of her derriere and drawing her toward his mouth.

"I was alone," he said, divining her thought. His breath stirred the dark down that sheltered her feminine mystery. "And had I met you before then, seen you, thoughts of you might have conflicted with thoughts of my wife." He planted an ardent, intimate kiss at the point of the triangle, using all his mouth.

The love play went on and on until desire was flowing through them like warm, thick honey. He turned to her, kneeling between her thighs and parting them lovingly and slowly. Just as tenderly, he draped her thighs over his and slid his hands under her hips, lifting her to him. His gaze fused with hers just as he sheathed himself in her.

Working his hands up her back in a sensuous massage, he brought her upward to face him. He sealed her mouth with his in a kiss that declared his eternal need for her. His hands stroked up her rib cage to her breasts. Touching them, he marveled over their lushness, their womanly heaviness. Then his thumbs lightly circled the love-swollen nipples.

"Drew, do what I never felt Matt do."

He understood. Lowering his head, he lifted her breast to his mouth. Her nipple was drawn between his lips with sweet tugging pressure. He suckled her gently, but with an urgency that continued to build. Responding to it, her body milked him, contracting and releasing him until their passions reached a summit. When the crisis was imminent, he gently lowered her to her back and followed her down. With one final surge, he imbedded himself deep within her and gave her all his love.

The earth swirled around them, timelessly, directionless, in uncharted chaos. They didn't mind. They had created their own private universe in each other. Jealously, they guarded it. It was a long time before they returned to a world more mundane and less splendored.

"Arden, I love you." He braced himself above her and gazed down at her replete body with unqualified love.

"I love you. From the first. Irrevocably."

"Tell me everything. From the beginning. Fill me in on all the details I don't know, no matter how insignificant. I want to know how you felt when you learned you had conceived. What did you think and feel when you discovered I was the man who had fathered your child? How did you find out about me? Let me experience it all with you."

Painstakingly, she began, leaving out nothing, neither the heartache nor the joy. Her quiet voice drifted on the cool ocean breeze that wafted through the open windows and caressed their entwined naked bodies.

Loving lips frequently got in the way and promised that the best chapters of their life together were yet to unfold.

★ ★ ★ ★ ★

Above & Beyond

Chapter 1

"You're doing fine, Kyla. Take quick, light breaths. That's right. Good, good. How do you feel?"

"Tired."

"I know, but hang in there. Go with the pains now and push. That's it. A little harder."

The young woman on the delivery table ground her teeth while the labor pain held her in its fierce grip. When it subsided, she forced her body to relax. Her face, though flushed and mottled, was radiant. "Can you see him yet?"

No sooner were the words out of her mouth than another pain seized her. She pushed with all her might.

"Now I can," the doctor said. "Give me one more push… there…here we are. All right!" he exclaimed when the new life slipped into his waiting hands.

"What is it?"

"A boy. Beautiful. Heavy son of a gun, too."

"And he's got great lungs," the obstetric nurse said, beaming down on Kyla.

"A boy," she murmured, pleased. She let the blessed lethargy steal over her and sank back onto the table. "Let me see him. Is he all right?"

"He's perfect," the doctor reassured her as he held up the squirming, crying baby boy where his mother could see him.

Tears stung Kyla's eyes when she saw her son for the first time. "Aaron. That's what we're naming him. Aaron Powers Stroud." For a moment she was allowed the privilege of holding him on her chest. Emotion welled inside her.

"He's a boy his daddy can be proud of," the nurse said. She lifted the baby from Kyla's weak arms, wrapped him in a soft blanket and carried him across the room to be weighed. The doctor was attending Kyla, though it had been an easy, routine birth.

"How soon before you can notify your husband?" the doctor asked.

"My parents are standing by outside. Dad's promised to send Richard a telegram."

"He's nine pounds three ounces," the nurse called out from across the room.

The obstetrician peeled off his gloves and took Kyla's limp hand. "I'll go out now and break the news so he can get that telegram on its way. Where did you say Richard was stationed?"

"Cairo," Kyla replied absently. She was watching Aaron kick angrily as he was footprinted. He was beautiful. Richard would be so proud of him.

Considering that Aaron had been born at dusk, she spent a reasonably peaceful night. They brought him to her twice during the night, though her milk hadn't started and he wasn't hungry yet. The pleasure of holding his warm little body against hers was immense. They communicated on a level that was unlike any other she had experienced.

She studied him, turning over his tiny hands and examining his palms when she could pry open the fingers he stubbornly kept clenched in a fist. Each toe, each fine strand of hair on his head, his ears, were investigated and found to be perfect.

"Your daddy and I love you very much," she whispered drowsily as she relinquished him to a nurse.

Hospital sounds—squeaky laundry carts, rattling breakfast trays, clanking equipment dollies—roused her early. She was in the middle of a huge yawn and a luxuriant stretch when her parents entered her private room.

"Good morning," she said happily. "I'm surprised you're here instead of at the nursery window with your noses pressed against the glass. But then they don't open the curtain—" She broke off when she noted their haggard expressions. "Is something wrong?"

Clif and Meg Powers glanced at each other. Meg gripped the handle of her purse so tightly that her knuckles turned white. Clif looked as though he'd just swallowed bad-tasting medicine.

"Mom? Dad? What's happened? Oh, my God! The baby? Aaron? There's something wrong with Aaron?" Kyla threw off the covers with flailing arms and pumping legs, unmindful of the pinching soreness between her thighs, intent only on racing down the hospital corridor to the nursery.

Meg Powers rushed to her daughter's bedside and restrained her. "No. The baby's fine. He's fine. I promise."

Kyla's eyes wildly searched those of her parents. "Then what's wrong?" She was on the verge of panic and her voice was shrill. Her parents rarely got ruffled. For them to be so obviously upset was cause for alarm.

"Sweetheart," Clif Powers said softly, laying a hand on her arm, "there's some distressing news this morning." He silently consulted his wife once more before saying, "The American embassy in Cairo was bombed early this morning."

A violent shudder shimmied up through Kyla's stomach and chest. Her mouth went dry. Her eyes forgot how to blink. Her heart thudded to a halt before sluggishly beginning to beat again. Then, gradually gaining momentum as she assimilated what her father had said, it accelerated to a frightening pace.

"Richard?" she asked on a hoarse croak.

"We don't know."

"Tell me!"

"We don't know," her father insisted. "Everything is in chaos, just like the time this happened in Beirut. There's been no official word."

"Turn on the television."

"Kyla, I don't think you should—"

Heedless of her father's warning, she snatched the remote control from the bedside table and switched on the television set that was mounted on the wall opposite the bed.

"…extent of the destruction at this point is undetermined. The President is calling this terrorist bombing an outrage, an insult to the peacekeeping nations of the world. Prime Minister—"

She changed channels, frantically punching the buttons on the remote control with trembling fingers.

"…costly, though it will probably be hours, even days before the death toll is officially released. Marine units have been mobilized and, along with Egyptian troops, are clearing the rubble looking for survivors."

The camera work on the videotape was substandard and testified to the pandemonium surrounding the ruins of what had been the building that housed the American embassy. The shots were jerky and out of focus, random and unedited. "Taking credit for this abomination is a terrorist group calling itself—"

Kyla changed channels again. It was more of the same. When the video camera swept the area and she saw the bodies that had already been recovered neatly lined up on the ground, she threw down the remote control device and covered her face with her hands.

"Richard, Richard!"

"Darling, don't give up hope. They think there are survivors." But Meg's soothing words fell on deaf ears. She clutched her weeping daughter's body hard against hers.

"It happened at dawn Cairo time," Clif said. "We were notified just as we were getting up this morning. There's nothing we can do at this point but wait. Sooner or later, we're bound to get word of Richard."

It came three days later, delivered by a Marine officer who rang the doorbell of the Powers's house. Kyla realized the moment she saw the official car pull up to the curb that subconsciously she had been waiting for it. She waved off her father and went to answer the door alone.

"Mrs. Stroud?"

"Yes."

"I'm Captain Hawkins and it is my duty to inform you…"

"But, darling, that's wonderful!" Kyla had exclaimed. "Why are you so downcast? I thought you'd be jubilant."

"Well, hell, Kyla, I don't want to go off to Egypt while you're pregnant," Richard had said.

She touched his hair. "I'll admit I don't like it for that reason. But this is an honor. Not every Marine is selected for guard duty at an embassy. They chose you because you're the best. I'm very proud."

"But I don't have to do it. I could apply—"

"This is a chance of a lifetime, Richard. Do you think I could live with myself if you turned down this honor on account of me?"

"But nothing's more important than you and the baby."

"And we'll always be here." She hugged him. "This will be your last tour and it's a fabulous opportunity that will only come around once. Now you're going and that's final."

"I can't leave you alone."

"I'll live with Mom and Dad while you're away. This is their first grandbaby and they'll drive me crazy calling and checking on me. I might just as well make it easy on us all and move in with them."

He framed her face between his hands. "You're terrific, you know that?"

"Does that mean I don't have to worry about you with those mysterious Eastern women?"

He had pretended to ponder it. "Do you know how to belly dance?"

She had socked him in the tummy. "That would be a sight to see, with the belly I'm going to have soon."

"Kyla." His voice was tender as he threaded his fingers through her hair. "Are you positive you want me to do this?"

"Positive."

That conversation, which had taken place seven months earlier, played through Kyla's mind as she stared at the flag-draped casket. The soulful notes of taps were snatched from the lone trumpet by an unkind winter wind and scattered over the cemetery. The pallbearers, all Marines, stood rigidly at attention, resplendent in their dress uniforms.

Richard was being interred beside his parents, who had died within a year of each other before Kyla ever met him. "I was all alone in the world before I met you," he had told her once.

"So was I."

"You have your parents," he had reminded her, perplexed.

"But I've never belonged to anyone, really *belonged,* the way I do to you."

Because they had loved each other so much, he had then understood.

His body had been shipped home in a sealed casket that she had been advised not to open. She didn't have to ask why. All that was left of the building in Cairo was a dusty pile of twisted stone and steel. Since the bomb had exploded early in the morning, most of the diplomatic corps and clerks had yet to arrive for work. Those who, like Richard and the other military personnel, had had apartments in the attached building, had been the victims.

A friend of Clif Powers had offered to fly the family to Kansas for the burial. Kyla could only be away from Aaron for several hours at a time because of his feeding schedule.

She flinched when she was handed the American flag, which had been removed from the coffin and ceremonially folded. The casket looked naked without it. Irrationally she wondered if Richard were cold.

Oh, God! she thought, her mind silently screaming. *I have to leave him here.* How would she be able to? How could she turn and walk away and leave that fresh grave like an obscene, open wound in the ground? How could she get into that private plane and be whisked back to Texas as though she were deserting Richard in this stark, barren landscape that she suddenly hated with a passion?

The wind whistled with a keening sound.

She would and she could because she had no choice. This part of Richard was dead. But a living part of him was waiting for her at home. Aaron.

As the minister recited the closing prayer, Kyla offered one of her own. "I'll keep you alive, Richard. I swear it. You'll always be alive in my heart. I love you. I love you. You'll always be alive for Aaron and me because I'll keep you alive."

He was cocooned inside a cotton ball. Once in a while the world would intrude on his cloudlike confinement and these were unwelcome interruptions. All sounds were clamorous. The slightest movement was like an earthquake to his system. Light from any source was painful. He wanted no part of anything outside the peacefulness of oblivion.

But the intrusions became more frequent. Compelled by a force he didn't understand, finding handholds and footholds in sound and feeling, clinging precariously to every sensation that hinted he was still alive, he slowly climbed upward, out of that safe white mist to greet the terrifying unknown.

He was lying on his back. He was breathing. His heart was beating. He wasn't certain of anything else.

"Can you hear me?"

He tried to turn his head in the direction of the soft voice, but splinters of pain crisscrossed inside his skull like ricocheting bullets.

"Are you awake? Can you answer me? Are you in pain?"

It took some doing, but he managed to coax his tongue to breach his lips. He tried to wet them, but the inside of his mouth was as dry and furry as wool. His face felt odd and he didn't think he could move his head even if the pain hadn't been severe. Tentatively he tried to raise his right hand.

"No, no, just lie still. You have an IV in this arm."

He struggled valiantly and finally managed to pry his eyes open to slits. His lashes, forming a screen across his field of vision, were magnified. He could almost count them individually. Finally they lifted a trifle more. An image wavered in front of him like a hovering angel. A white uniform. A woman. A cap. A nurse?

"Hello. How do you feel?"

Stupid question, lady.

"Where…" He didn't recognize the croaking sound as his own voice.

"You're in a military hospital in West Germany."

West Germany? West Germany? He must have been drunker than he thought last night. This was a helluva dream.

"We've been worried about you. You've been in a coma for three weeks."

A coma? For three weeks? Impossible. Last night he'd gone out with that colonel's daughter and they'd hit every night spot in Cairo. Why the hell was this dream angel telling him he'd been in a coma in where?…West Germany?

He tried to take in more of his surroundings. The room looked strange. His vision was blurred. Something—

"Don't become distressed if your vision is fuzzy. Your left eye is bandaged," the nurse said kindly. "Lie still now while I go get the doctor. He'll want to know that you're awake."

He didn't hear her leave. One instant she was there, the next she had vanished. Maybe he had imagined her. Dreams can be bizarre.

The walls seemed to sway sickeningly. The ceiling swelled and then receded. It was never still. The light from the single lamp hurt his eyes…eye.

She had said his left eye was bandaged. Why? Disregarding

her caution, he raised his right hand again. It was a Herculean effort. The tape holding the IV needles in place pulled against the hairs on his arm. It seemed to take forever for his hand to reach his head and when it did, he knew the first stirrings of panic.

My whole damn head is covered with bandages! He raised his head off the pillow as far as he could, which was only an inch or two, and glanced down at his body.

The scream that echoed through the hall seconds later came straight out of the bowels of Hell and set the nurse and doctor flying down the corridor and into the room.

"I'll hold him down while you give him a shot," the doctor barked. "He'll tear up everything we've done so far if he keeps thrashing that way."

The patient felt the sting of a needle in his right thigh and cried out in indignation and frustration over his inability to speak, to move, to fight.

Then darkness closed in around him again. Soothing hands lowered him back to the pillow. By the time he reached it, velvet oblivion had claimed him again.

He drifted in and out for days...weeks? He had no point of reference with which to measure time. He began to know when IV bottles were changed, when his blood pressure was being taken, when the tubes and catheters entering or exiting his body were monitored. Once he recognized the nurse. Once he recognized the doctor's voice. But they moved around him like ghosts, solicitous specters in a soft misty dream.

Gradually he began to stay awake for longer periods of time. He came to know the room, to know the machines that blipped and beeped out his vital signs. He was increasingly aware of his physical condition. And he knew it was serious.

He was awake when the doctor came through the door, studying a chart in a metal file. "Well, hello," the doctor said when he saw his patient staring up at him. He went through a routine checkup, then leaned against the side of the bed. "Are you aware that you're in a hospital and pretty banged up?"

"Was...I...in an accident?"

"No, Sergeant Rule. The American embassy in Cairo was bombed over a month ago. You were one of the few who survived the blast. After you were dug out of the rubble you were flown here. When you're well enough, you'll be shipped home."

"What's...wrong with me?"

A flicker of a smile touched the doctor's mouth. "It would be easier to say what's right." He rubbed his chin. "Want it straight?"

An almost imperceptible nod encouraged him to proceed in a blunt, no-nonsense manner. "The left side of your body was crushed by a falling concrete wall. Nearly every damn bone you've got on that side was broken, if not mangled. We've set what we could. The rest," he paused to draw in a deep breath, "well that will take some doing by the specialists back home. You're in for a long haul, my friend. I would say eight months at least, though twice that long would be a more accurate guess. Several operations. Months of physical therapy."

The misery reflected on the bandaged face was almost too poignant to witness, even for the doctor who had earned his stripes on the battlefields of Vietnam.

"Will I...be...?"

"Your prognosis at this point is anybody's guess. A lot of

it will be up to you. Sheer gut determination. How badly do you want to walk again?"

"I want to run," the Marine said grimly.

The doctor came close to laughing. "Good. But for right now, your job is to get stronger so we can begin patching you up."

The doctor patted him lightly on the right shoulder and turned to go. "Doc?" The medical man turned at the hoarse sound. "My eye?"

The doctor looked down at his patient sympathetically. "I'm sorry, Sergeant Rule. We couldn't save it."

The doctor's stride was brisk and businesslike as he strode from the room, and belied the tight lump in his throat. The most eloquent sign of despair he'd ever seen was that single tear trickling down a gaunt, darkly bewhiskered cheek.

George Rule was allowed to see his son the next day. He came to the bedside and clasped Trevor's right hand. Slowly he lowered himself into a nearby chair. Trevor never remembered seeing his father cry, not even when his mother had died several years earlier. Now, the attorney from Philadelphia, who struck terror in the heart of any lying witness, wept bitterly.

"I must look worse than I thought," Trevor said with a trace of wry humor. "Shocked?"

The elder Rule pulled himself together. He'd been cautioned by the medical staff to appear optimistic. "No, I'm not shocked. I beat you here by several hours and saw you when you first arrived. It might not feel like it, but you've come a long way since then."

"Then I must have been bad because I feel like hell now."

"They would only let me see you once a day while you were in the coma. Then since you came out of it, they wouldn't let me see you at all. You're going to be fine, son, fine. I've already been talking to doctors in the States, orthopedic surgeons who—"

"Do something for me, Dad."

"Anything, anything."

The last time Trevor had seen his father they hadn't been on very good terms. If Trevor hadn't been so preoccupied with other thoughts now, he would have noted his father's drastic change of attitude toward him.

"Check the casualty list. See if Sergeant Richard Stroud made it."

"Son, you shouldn't be worrying—"

"Will you do it?" Trevor groaned, already physically taxed by his father's visit.

"Yes, of course I will," George rushed to say when he saw his son's anxiety. "Stroud, you say?"

"Yes. Richard Stroud."

"Friend of yours?"

"Yes. And I hope to God he didn't die. If he died, it's my fault."

"How could it be your fault, Trevor?"

"Because the last thing I remember is falling asleep in his bunk."

"Psst! Stroud? You awake, buddy?"

"I am now," came the grumbled reply. "Jeez, Smooch, it's three o'clock. Are you drunk?"

"How 'bout a drink?"

Richard Stroud sat up in his bunk and shook off sleep. "Must have been a helluva weekend pass."

"'s wonderful. Ever had an orgasm?"

Stroud laughed. "You're drunk all right. Here, let me help you with your pants."

"An orgasm, an orgasm. I think I had three las' night. Or was it four?"

"Four? That's a record even for you, isn't it?"

A wobbly finger was pointed at the end of Stroud's nose. "Now shee, Schtroud. You're always thinkin' the worscht of me. I was talking about the *drink*. An Orgasm. Has vodka and liqueur and... Are my pants off yet?"

"They will be if you'll lift your feet up."

"Oops!" Trevor Rule fell over onto Stroud's bunk, dragging the other man with him. "Do you know Becky?" he asked with a goosey smile.

"I thought her name was Brenda," Stroud said, disentangling their limbs.

"Oh, yeah. Come to think of it, I think it is Brenda, I think. Great legs." He winked lewdly as Stroud helped him with his shirt. "Strong thighs. Know what I mean?"

Stroud chuckled and shook his head. "Yeah, I know what you mean. And I don't think Colonel Daniels would appreciate you talking about his daughter's strong thighs."

"I think I love her." Trevor said the words with the seriousness only a drunk can conjure. The avowal was punctuated with a moist belch.

"Sure you do. Last week you loved the brunette secretary on the third floor. And the week before that it was the blond AP reporter. Now come on, Smooch, let's get you to your own bunk."

He put his arms under Trevor's and tried to heave him up, but the other man was deadweight and only grinned up at him sappily. "I've got a better idea," Stroud said when Trevor couldn't be budged. "Why don't you just stay in my bunk tonight?"

For an answer, Trevor fell backward onto the pillow.

Stroud felt his way across the dark room to Trevor's bunk. He settled down to go back to sleep.

"Nighty-night."

He raised his head to see Trevor waggling his fingers at him like a dimwit. Laughing, Stroud said, "Nighty-night."

Before either of them woke up, the terrorists struck.

Trevor's recovery was harder than he anticipated—and he had anticipated that it would be a living hell.

He was in the hospital in West Germany for another month before he was transported home. The expert doctors who examined him went away grimly shaking their heads. The left side of his body was a mess.

"Fix it," Trevor said tersely. "Do what you can. I'll do the rest. But you can bank on this. I'll walk out of here."

He had had nurses read him newspaper accounts of the embassy bombing. He went through stages of disbelief, then despair, then anger. The anger was healthy. It gave him the strength he needed to fight the pain, to overcome the trauma of one operation after another, to withstand the grueling hours of physical therapy.

Once his medical discharge was official, he let his Marine haircut grow out long. He had told the nurse who came in to shave him every morning to leave his mustache. He refused to be fitted with a prosthesis for his eye.

"I think it looks...dashing," was the opinion of one nurse. There were several clustered around his bed as a doctor fitted him with a black eye patch. Half the nursing staff was in love with him. His extensive injuries hadn't detracted from his brawny build. Greatly admired and discussed at the nurses' station were his ruggedly handsome face, long limbs, wide chest and narrow hips.

"It goes with your wavy black hair."

"When you leave here, you'll have to fight the women off with a stick."

"With my cane, you mean," Trevor remarked, studying the eye patch in the hand mirror someone had passed to him.

"Don't give up yet," the doctor said encouragingly. "We've only just started."

He knew of seasonal changes only by the landscape through his hospital room window. The days bled into each other. He kept track of time by keeping a calendar on his bedside table and jotting down at least one entry on it each day.

One afternoon an orderly, who occasionally came in to play poker with him after his shift, dumped a duffel bag onto the chair near the bed.

"What's that?"

"All the stuff they could salvage from your room in Cairo," the orderly told him. "Your dad thought you might want to sift through it and see if there was anything worth saving."

There wasn't. But one thing caught his attention. "Hand me that metal box please."

It was an unremarkable green square box with a hinged top. The combination lock had only one number. Miraculously he remembered it. He turned the lock and, when it came open, raised the lid.

"What's all that?" The orderly was peering at the contents over Trevor's shoulder. "Looks like a pile of letters."

Trevor felt a constriction in his chest. It squeezed his throat as well, so much that he could barely say, "That's exactly what it is."

He hadn't remembered them till now, but suddenly he recalled that afternoon with stark clarity.

"Hey, Smooch?"

"Hiya, Stroud. What can I do for you?"

"You know that metal box you keep your poker stakes in?"

"What about it?"

"Would you mind if I put these in there for safekeeping?" Embarrassed, Stroud held up a stack of letters, bound with a rubber band.

"Hmm. Are those from that wife who keeps you as chaste as a monk?"

"Yeah," he admitted bashfully.

"I didn't think she could write."

"Huh?"

"I didn't know angels did such mundane things," Trevor teased, poking his friend in the ribs.

"Not you, too, please. The guys are ribbing me about saving her letters, but I like to read them several times."

"Mushy?" Trevor's green eyes twinkled mischievously.

"Not really. Just personal. What about the box?"

"Okay, sure, lock them away. All you have to do to open it is turn the lock to four."

"Four? Thanks, Smooch."

He caught Stroud's arm as he turned away. "Sure they're not mushy?"

Stroud grinned. "Well, a little mushy."

They had gone out for a beer and that was the last Trevor had thought of Stroud's letters from his wife. Until now.

He slammed the lid down, feeling as guilty as if he had watched them making love through their bedroom window. "Throw the rest of that junk away," he said irritably.

"You keepin' the box with the letters?" the orderly asked.

"Yeah, I'm keeping it."

He didn't know why he did. It probably had something

to do with his guilt over being alive when Stroud had died while sleeping in his bunk. He told himself a million times through that afternoon's hand and arm exercises that he wasn't going to violate a dead man's privacy by reading letters from his wife.

But when night fell, when the hall was emptied of visitors, when the last of the medication had been dispensed, when the nurses had taken up their posts at their station, Trevor lifted the box from the bedside table and set it on his chest.

He was lonely. It was dark. He had slept alone for more nights than he cared to count. It had come as a tremendous relief to him to feel his body respond every time the orderly sneaked him the monthly issues of *Playboy* and *Penthouse*. That part of him wasn't impaired.

He needed a woman.

It wasn't that he couldn't have one. He knew that if he gave any of several nurses a certain look, they would have been more than willing to accommodate him.

But he had had about all the melodrama in his life that he could handle. Hospital gossip being what it was, it would be foolhardy to become romantically entangled, especially when what he wanted and needed had little or nothing to do with romance.

Yet he yearned for a woman's touch. A woman's voice. There was no satisfaction to be derived from looking through the magazines on this night like so many others. Those women, with their voluptuous bodies and abundant hair and affected smiles were as two-dimensional as the slick pages they were printed on.

The composer of the letters was real.

The lid to the metal box opened without a sound, but the paper rustled when he touched the letters. He yanked his hand back. Then, cursing himself for a fool, he picked up the letter on the top of the stack.

There were twenty-seven in all. He sorted them and put them in chronological order. When all the busywork—designed to delay the commission of what he supposed was a grievous sin—was finished, he opened the first envelope, took out the plain pastel sheet, and began to read.

Chapter 2

Sept. 7

My darling Richard,

It's only been weeks, but it seems like years since you left. Missing you has become a sickness. Instead of getting better each day, I grow worse. My imagination plays cruel tricks. I often think I see you, especially in a crowd. My heart begins to beat fast with excitement. Then I go through the wrenching realization that someone only reminded me of you....

Sept. 15

Dearest Richard,

I dreamed about you last night and woke up crying....

Sept. 16

My darling,

Forgive me yesterday's letter. I was blue....

Oct. 2

Dearest Richard,

I felt the baby move today! Oh, darling, I can't tell you what a thrilling experience that was. At first it was only a fluttering. I held my breath, standing very still. Then he (I know it's a boy) moved again, much stronger. I laughed. I cried. Mom and Dad came running. They couldn't feel the movements because they are slight, but somehow I know you could. If you were here, touching me, I know you could. I love you. So much.

Oct. 25

...and your excursion to the pyramids sounds wonderful. I'm jealous. Mom and I went to NorthPark yesterday and did some shopping. If anything, the traffic in Dallas is getting worse. I was so tired by the time we got home, I could barely climb the stairs and Dad brought me supper on a tray. But we had a productive day. I won't have to buy clothes for the baby until he's six!

We all laughed over your story about the consul's wife. Does she really dress that way? And about your friend Smooch, STAY AWAY FROM HIM! He doesn't sound like a very good influence on a married man with a pregnant wife....

Thanksgiving Day

...and I want you here so badly. I went to a movie with Babs last night. I should have know better. It was sexy, steamy actually. And now I want you! I'm climbing the walls. For shame! Nice pregnant ladies aren't supposed to feel like sex kittens, are they? But it's cold and rainy and I think, given the chance, I could even lure you away from the football games on television today.

Dec. 21
My love,
I got your letter yesterday and laughed out loud. So you want me to stay away from Babs? You've got a deal if you'll end your friendship with Smooch. He sounds like the kind of man I detest. Thinks he's God's gift to women, doesn't he? Even though you say he's as handsome as the devil, I know I wouldn't like him....

Dec. 24
My dearest,
The days are short, but they seem endless. My spirits are down. I wish I could have slept through Christmas. Everywhere I look people are celebrating, smiling, sharing the season with those they love. I feel like an alien in a world made up of couples only. Where are you? I can tell Mom and Dad are worried about me because I've been so depressed. They've done their best to cheer me, but I miss you so terribly that nothing they do works. The packages you sent are under the tree. Dad splurged and got a Noble fir this year, my favorite. I hope you received your presents in time. I would trade all the presents I've ever gotten and will get on future Christmases for one of your kisses. One of those long, slow kisses that fulfills and tantalizes. Oh, Richard, I love you. Merry Christmas, darling.

Jan. 11
...but I'm much better now that the holidays are over and we've passed the halfway point of your year away.

It grows increasingly uncomfortable to sleep. The baby is going to be a fullback, you'll be glad to know. Or maybe a placekicker. But in any event, in about twenty-two years the Cowboys will be recuiting him for sure! By the way, what do you think of Aaron as a name? If it's a boy, of course. Which it had better be since I've come up empty on girls' names so far.

You would go wild for my breasts. They're huge! Unfortunately the rest of me matches them. I didn't realize the baby would make such a drastic change in them. Even the nipples have grown larger. I'm preparing them to breast-feed. (That naughty Babs says she wishes she had that good an excuse. She's so bad!) I wish you were here to help out on the project. (Come to think of it, I'm pretty bad myself.)

But I can't think of anything more wonderful than nursing our baby...Aaron....

Jan. 25

...and it was the most horrible dream I've ever had. I woke up sweating. I won't eat any more chili before the baby comes!

Was Smooch along on that weekend trip to Alexandria you wrote me about? You didn't mention him and I think that was an intentional oversight. If you have done something indiscreet, if you have a real lech for a belly dancer, don't confess it to me. I feel like a water buffalo and cried yesterday because I was so fat...at the same time I was stuffing down a banana split that Babs assured me would cheer me up. (Three scoops of chocolate almond!) Sometimes I despair that I'll never see you again, Richard. Will you ever hold me? Will I ever feel you inside me again? Sometimes I think you aren't

real, that you're someone wonderful that I dreamed up.
I need you, darling. I need to know that you love me.
As I love you…with all my heart….

"You're being released next week?"

Trevor turned away from the window. "Yeah. Finally."

"That's great, son," George Rule said earnestly. "You look as good as new."

"Not quite."

There was no bitterness in Trevor's tone. Over the past thirteen months, he had come to realize how fortunate he'd been. His strolls through the wards of the hospital had convinced him of that. He could have been confined to a wheelchair for the rest of his life, like so many he saw in physical therapy.

He could walk, with a slight limp, but he could walk. He had even gotten accustomed to the eye patch, so that he wasn't bumping into furniture any longer. It was true what was said about the body's ability to compensate for the loss of one of its members. He could barely remember what it was like to have both eyes.

"They want me to come back every week on an outpatient basis for physical therapy, but I said no," he told his father. "I think this is as good as I'll get. I can do the exercises myself."

"What do you plan to do now?" George Rule asked his son hesitantly.

Trevor's choice of career had been a bone of contention since his graduation from Harvard. His joining the Marines had been an act of rebellion against his father, who had wanted Trevor to become a lawyer like himself and had refused to listen to his son's own plans.

"What I always planned to do, Dad. Be a builder."

"I see." Rule's disappointment was apparent, but he squelched it. He had almost lost his son. Trevor's close brush with death had scared the indomitable George Rule. He didn't want to lose Trevor in another way now. He had no doubt that he would if he tried to direct Trevor's future. "Where? How do you plan to start?"

"Texas."

"*Texas!*" It might just as well have been another planet.

Trevor laughed. "You've heard of the building boom in the Sunbelt states. That's where the action is now. There's still land waiting to be developed. I've chosen a small town near Dallas. Chandler. It's a booming community and I intend to capitalize on its growth."

"You'll need a bankroll."

"I've got back pay from the Marines coming."

"That's hardly enough to go into business."

Trevor looked at his father steadily. "How much would a law degree from Harvard have cost you, Dad?"

George Rule nodded. "You've got it." He stuck out his hand and Trevor gripped it firmly and shook it.

"Thanks."

For the first time in Trevor's memory, he was embraced by his father and hugged tight.

Later that night, after he had packed his things, Trevor stretched out on the hospital bed for the last time. But he was too excited to sleep. He had been given a second chance at life. His first shot at it hadn't amounted to much. But this new one, which would start tomorrow, would. No more angry wasted years. Now he had a mission.

He reached for the green metal box. It was never far from his hand. The letters were worn at the creases, frayed around the edges. He knew all twenty-seven letters by heart. But he derived pleasure from looking at the swirls and curves of her feminine handwriting. He selected one, and it wasn't a random choice.

...end your friendship with Smooch. He sounds like the kind of man I detest. Thinks he's God's gift to women, doesn't he? Even though you say he's as handsome as the devil, I know I wouldn't like him....

Trevor folded the letter carefully and replaced it in its envelope. He didn't go to sleep for a long time.

She was beautiful.

He had seen her many times in the past few weeks. But never this close. Never for this long. It was a luxury to be able to study her.

In a thousand years he would never be able to describe the color of her hair. "Blond" wasn't sufficient because of those burnished streaks threaded through it. But she wasn't a true redhead. "Strawberry blond" connoted sweetness to the point of insipidity. And there was nothing insipid about Kyla Stroud. She radiated energy and light like a sunbeam.

That indescribable hair was pulled back into a casual ponytail. The ends of it were curly, as were the strands that had escaped it to frame her face.

And what a face. Heart-shaped. With a dainty chin. Brows that arched over wide-set eyes. A smooth, high, intelligent forehead. A complexion that made his mouth water for a taste. Cheeks naturally tinted the color of ripe peaches.

She had on casual tan slacks, a striped cotton shirt with the sleeves rolled up to her elbows and a cardigan tied around her neck. Her figure was neat and trim. Perfectly proportioned.

She was...well...perfect.

He liked the way she talked to the child, as though he was understanding every word she said. And perhaps he was, because when she smiled, so did the robust toddler. They

seemed impervious to the heavy foot traffic in the mall, un-
affected by the Saturday afternoon crowd that was patron-
izing the shops and food stands.

It was at one of those concessions that she had bought
the ice-cream cone. With miraculous agility she had held
the ice-cream cone in one hand while she pushed the baby
stroller through the crowd to a bench. She had assisted the
little boy, though he hadn't needed much encouragement to
climb out.

Now, they were seated on a bench and the child was de-
stroying the ice-cream cone while his mother alternately
laughed with delight and admonished him for making such a
pig of himself. Her right hand governed the cone, while her
left deftly wielded a napkin.

When the cone and napkin had both been mutilated to a
soggy mess, she spoke sternly to the child, then left the bench
to throw the refuse away in the nearest trash can.

The instant her back was turned, the toddler slid off the
bench and hit the floor of the mall running. As fast as his
short, sturdy legs could carry him, he headed for the sparkling fountain that gushed toward the skylit ceiling. Surrounding the fountain was a pool about two feet deep.

Reflexively Trevor pushed himself away from the wall
where he had been indolently propped on one shoulder while
he watched them. He risked taking his eyes off the child for
a few seconds to see Kyla turn away from the trash can and
notice that the boy was gone. Even from that distance he
read in her expression the instantaneous panic only a mother
whose child is missing can register.

Without thinking, Trevor began weaving his way through
the crowd toward the fountain. The boy was now climbing
onto the low wall surrounding it and reaching toward the
bubbling water.

"Oh, God," Trevor murmured as he pushed aside a man with a pipe. He increased the length of his stride and picked up his pace. But he wasn't fast enough. He watched the child go over the wall and into the water.

Several bystanders noticed, but Trevor was the first to reach the fountain. He swung his right leg over the wall, stepped into the pool, caught the boy under the arms and scooped him out of the water.

"Aaron!" Kyla was frantically pushing her way through the crowd.

Aaron, sputtering water, looked curiously at the man holding him. With apparent approval of his rescuer, the boy smiled, revealing two neat rows of baby teeth, and said something that could have been "water."

Sloshing water, Trevor stepped out of the fountain. The bystanders fanned out to give him room.

"Is he all right?"

"What happened?"

"Where's his mother?"

"Wasn't anybody watching him?"

"Some parents just let their kids run wild."

"Excuse me, excuse me." Kyla finally elbowed her way through the gathering onlookers. "Aaron, Aaron!" She lifted her son out of Trevor's arms and clutched him to her chest, squeezing hard, regardless of his wet clothes. "Oh, my baby. Are you okay? You scared Mommy. Oh, God."

The moment Aaron sensed his mother's distress, his adventure turned into a trauma. His lower lip began to tremble, his eyes filled with tears and his face crumpled. Opening his mouth wide, he began to wail.

"He's hurt! Is he hurt?" Kyla said frantically.

"Come on, let's move over here. Please, folks, let us through. He's okay, just scared."

Kyla was vaguely aware of a large man beside her. She felt his hand between her shoulder blades, propelling her through the crowd toward an out-of-the-way bench. She was so busy examining Aaron for possible injuries that the man went unnoticed until she was seated on the bench. Finally, hugging a crying Aaron to her, she looked up at him.

It took a long time for her eyes to reach his face, so her first impression of him was that he was very tall. She wasn't quite prepared for the curving mustache, much less the black patch over his left eye, and caught her gasp just in time. "Thank you."

The large man sat down next to her. "I think he's all right. Your reaction frightened him."

She whipped her head around, showing him that her chin wasn't only dainty. It could be stubborn when she was challenged. When she saw that he wasn't being critical, she smiled with chagrin. "I guess you're right. I overreacted."

Aaron's crying was beginning to subside. She held him away from her and wiped the tears off his ruddy, round cheeks. "You scared me half to death, Aaron Stroud," she scolded. Then looking at the man again, she said, "One minute he was there, the next he wasn't."

She had brown eyes. Velvety, dark-brown eyes that he felt himself sinking into.

"He moved like greased lightning." When she tilted her head, obviously puzzled, he explained. "I had been watching him eat his ice-cream cone."

"Oh." It didn't occur to her to ask why they had attracted his attention in the first place. She was wondering what had happened to his eye. It was a shame he had lost it because the one that looked back at her was green, deeply green, beautifully green, surrounded by spiky black lashes.

It gazed back at her like a steady emerald flame. Self-conscious at having been caught staring, she looked away. It was then that she noticed his wet jeans and boots. "You went into the fountain?"

He laughed, glancing down at his legs. His jeans were wet from his knees down. He rolled his foot back on the heel of his wet boot. "I guess I did. I don't remember it. I was thinking about Aaron."

"How did you know his name?"

Trevor's heart did a somersault. "Uh, I heard you call him that when you reached for him."

She nodded. "I'm sorry you got wet."

"It'll dry."

"But those look like expensive boots."

"They're not as valuable as Aaron." He chucked the boy under the chin. Aaron had the sleeve of his mother's cardigan in his mouth, gnawing away. Mechanically, she lifted it away from him and smoothed it back down over her chest.

"Oh, my gosh!" she exclaimed. As though to reinforce what she'd just realized—that they were both soaking wet—Aaron sneezed.

"You're wet," Trevor said.

He was staring down at her front in a way that made Kyla feel hot rather than chilled. She surged to her feet. "Thank you again. Goodbye." Holding Aaron in front of her like a shield, she rushed toward the nearest exit.

"Wait!"

"Why?"

"Aren't you forgetting something?"

"What?"

"Your purse for one thing. And Aaron's stroller. They're still over there by the ice-cream stand."

Feeling like a colossal fool, she shook her head, laughing shakily. "I'm still—"

"Upset. I can imagine. Let me get them for you."

"You've done enough."

"No problem."

He was walking away from her before she could offer another protest. Surreptitiously she glanced down at her chest
to see if she was indecently exposing herself and was only
slightly relieved to see that her exposure wouldn't get her
arrested.

Hastily she glanced back up at the man's retreating figure.
It was then that she noticed his limp. It was almost undetect-
able, but he definitely favored his left side. He must have
been in a terrible accident to have lost his eye and partially
crippled his entire left side.

But even the limp didn't hamper the lithe way he moved.
For such a large man, he was graceful and had the oiled gait
of an athlete. And the build. Broad shoulders and narrow
hips. His hair was midnight-black, wavy and long enough
to cover the tops of his ears and curl over his collar. Kyla
noticed that the women he passed took a second look. None
seemed put off by the eye patch. In fact, it contributed to his
appeal, which was rakish and a tad disreputable.

Yet, masculine as he was, he seemed indifferent to slinging
the strap of her purse over his shoulder and pushing the baby
stroller through the mall back toward where she stood waiting with Aaron.

"Thank you again," she said, avoiding Aaron's swinging
fist, which was aimed for her earring. She reached for her
purse. Trevor slid the strap down his arm, up hers, and patted
it into place on her shoulder.

She's so dainty, he thought.

He's so tall, she thought.

She leaned down and tried to seat Aaron in the stroller, but
he was having none of it. His stout little body went as stiff as

a board and she couldn't forcibly bend his legs. He began to protest strenuously.

"He's getting tired," she said by way of explanation, embarrassed that her child was behaving in such an undisciplined way. They were attracting attention again, and those passersby new on the scene were staring curiously at the sodden child, damp mother and the man with the wet jeans.

"Why don't you carry Aaron and let me push the stroller out to your car?"

She straightened, lifting Aaron with her. "I can't let you do that. I've inconvenienced you enough."

He smiled. His teeth were very straight and very white behind his very sexy mustache. "It's no inconvenience."

"Well…" she hedged.

The man made Kyla nervous. Why, she couldn't exactly say. He had behaved with enough courtesy to earn him a Boy Scout badge. He hadn't looked at her suggestively. More than likely he thought she had a husband out playing golf or at home working in the yard.

Still, *she* was aware that *he* was aware of her wet blouse, and even though he couldn't actually *see* anything the suggestion was there, and that made her jittery.

"Come on. Let's go before Aaron becomes more than the two of us can handle."

The boy was becoming heavier in her arms with every passing second and his fractiousness was increasing. He was squirming discontentedly, because he was no doubt as uncomfortable as she in his wet clothes. "All right," she said, pushing back a wayward strand of hair that had met with the flying fist she had tried to dodge. "I would appreciate that."

"Out this way?" Trevor asked, nodding toward the exit.

She looked uneasy. "No, actually, I'm parked on the other side of Penney's."

He could have asked why, if she was parked on the other side of Penney's, she had headed toward this exit as though the devil were after her just a few minutes ago, but in true gentlemanly fashion he said nothing and, after waiting for her to precede him, steered the empty stroller toward the department store at the other end of the mall.

"My name is Trevor, by the way. Trevor Rule." Holding his breath, he watched her face for signs of recognition and when none were forthcoming, he felt a tightness in his chest relax.

"I'm Kyla Stroud."

"Pleased to meet you." He cocked his head toward Aaron, who had stopped crying now that he was in motion again. "And Aaron, of course."

Smiles like his should be outlawed, Kyla thought. It was hazardous to the female population. His appeal crossed generational barriers. She saw a gaggle of teens openly flirt with him as they walked past. Plenty of grandmothers turned their heads. It didn't matter whether a woman was accompanied by another man or not, they all noticed Trevor Rule.

He wasn't classically handsome. There was nothing pretty about his face. It was lined. Twin grooves extended from the edges of his nostrils down to bracket his mouth and wide mustache. Kyla wondered how they could be so deeply engraved there. Pain from his debilitating accident? He couldn't be any older than his early thirties. Not much older than Richard would be.

Richard. At the thought of him that familiar pang shot through her. If he were alive, he would be walking by her side. She wouldn't need the assistance of a stranger. The first anniversary of his death had passed.

According to all the books on the subject, that was a landmark and she should be getting over the loss by now. But not a day went by that she didn't think of Richard, usually at a moment when she least expected it. Like now. And she was glad. She had vowed to keep her husband alive both for her sake and for Aaron's. Nursing memories of Richard day by day kept him a vital part of her life.

"How old is Aaron?" Trevor asked suddenly.

"Just over fifteen months."

"He's hefty, isn't he? I don't know much about babies."

"Yes, he's hefty," Kyla said, laughing and shifting him from one arm to the other. "But his daddy was muscular."

"Was?"

Why had she left that gate open? She hadn't intended to. "He died," she said without elaboration.

"I'm sorry."

And he meant it. Or did he?

Trevor had waited for this day for months. After he left the hospital, he had marked time, waiting until the time was right. He was anxious to get his business started, but even with his father's unabashed string-pulling, there had been a million and one tedious details to see to. The hours he had spent cooped up in offices seemed endless to a man who had months of his life to catch up on. There had also been hours spent outdoors shirtless, so he would lose his sickly hospital pallor.

During it all, he had imagined his first meeting with Kyla a hundred times, asking himself where it would happen, what she would look like, what he would say.

He hadn't set out to meet her that day. But it was happening! He was living it. And having seen her, he honestly couldn't say whether he regretted sleeping in Richard Stroud's bunk that fateful night or not. Out of sheer selfishness, he was extremely glad to be alive at the moment.

"I'm afraid we still have quite a walk," Kyla said apologetically as he held the door open for her.

"I don't mind."

The parking lot was a good indicator of the crowd inside the mall. Motorists just arriving were fighting over parking spaces as they became available.

"Are you from around here, Mr. Rule?" Kyla asked conversationally as they entered the melee.

"Call me Trevor. No, I'm not. I moved here about a month ago."

"What brought you to Chandler?"

You.

"Greed."

Startled by his answer, she looked up at him. "Pardon?"

A strand of hair blew across her lips. His heart skipped a beat, just thinking about moving aside that strand of spun gold and kissing her lips. She had the most kissable mouth he'd ever seen. "I'm a builder," he said a trifle too loudly after clearing his throat. "I want to be a part of the expansion going on around here."

Maybe he should have bought a few nights with a woman before meeting Kyla. Maybe he should have cultivated some casual relationships based solely on sex. Maybe he shouldn't have subjected himself to abstention.

"Oh, I see. Well, that's my car." She pointed out a pale blue station wagon.

"Petal Pushers?" he asked, reading the stenciled logo on the side panel.

"My friend and I have a flower shop."

Fifty-two ninety-eight Ballard Parkway. He knew exactly where it was, the colors in the striped awnings over the paned windows, and what the hours of operation were. "A flower shop, hey? Sounds interesting."

He waited while she secured Aaron in his car seat and helped her put the collapsible stroller into the backseat. "I can't thank you enough, Mr. uh, Trevor. You've been awfully kind."

"Don't thank me. I enjoyed it. Everything but seeing Aaron go over that wall into the water."

Kyla shuddered. "I don't even want to think about that." She looked at him for a long moment. There seemed to be no graceful way to leave. How did she say thank you and goodbye to a stranger who had saved her child's life? "Well, goodbye," she said, feeling awkward and having absolutely nothing to do with her hands.

"Goodbye."

She slid behind the steering wheel and closed the door. He stepped back, waved and walked away. Kyla turned the key. The car made a hateful grinding sound, but the engine didn't catch. She pumped the gas pedal and tried again. Wrrra, wrrra, wrrra. Again and again. But the car didn't start. She muttered something her mother would be horrified to hear coming from her daughter's mouth. Or, more likely, her mother didn't even know that word.

"Problem?" Trevor Rule had spoken through the window on the driver's side. His hands were braced on his bent knees.

She rolled down the window. "It doesn't want to start."

"Sounds like your battery has gone dead."

Stubbornly she tried again, several times. Finally admitting defeat, she twisted the key off and flopped back against the seat. Aaron was fussing in his car seat, flailing all four limbs against the confinement. This was turning out to be a heck of a Saturday.

"Can I help?" Trevor asked after a moment.

"I'll just go back into the mall and call my dad. He'll come pick us up and send someone out to look at the car."

"I have a better idea. Why don't I drive the two of you home?"

She stared at him mutely, then looked away. A prickle of fear chased up her spine. She didn't know this man. He could be anybody. How did she know he hadn't rigged her car not to start, then befriended her in the mall and...

Stop it, Kyla. That's crazy. He couldn't have orchestrated Aaron's fall into the fountain. Still, she had better sense than to get into a car and go anywhere with a total stranger.

"No thank you, Mr. Rule, I'll manage."

The refusal came out sounding brusquer than she had intended, but she couldn't let herself feel charitable toward a possible abductor. She reversed the energy-draining process she had gone through only minutes before, unbuckling Aaron and lifting him out of the car, picking up her purse, rolling up the window and locking the car door. She struck out in the direction from which they had just come.

"I don't want to detain you, Mr. Rule," she said as he fell into step beside her.

"It will be no trouble for me to take you anywhere you want to go."

"No thanks."

"Are you sure? It would be much—"

"No thank you!"

"Is it this damn thing?" He flung his hand up toward his left eye. "I know it automatically makes me suspect, but I swear I'm not someone you need to be frightened of."

Kyla came to a sudden halt and turned to face him. *Oh, Lord.* Now he probably thought she had a prejudice against handicapped citizens. "I'm not afraid of you."

The tension in his face was gradually replaced by an

engaging grin. "Well, you should be. You can't trust strangers these days." They laughed softly. Unmindful of the traffic they were blocking, he took a step closer and looked down at her earnestly. "I'm only trying to help by offering you a ride."

She felt like an idiot. Any man who would ruin a four-hundred-dollar pair of boots to fish a little boy out of a fountain wouldn't be inclined to kidnap, kill or maim. "All right," she conceded softly.

"Good."

The patience of the driver waiting to pull out of the parking space finally gave out and he honked his horn. They started walking.

"Where's your car?"

Trevor indicated the direction with a hitch of his chin. "About an acre and a half from here," he said, laughing. "Why don't you let me carry Aaron?"

With only a trace of reluctance, Kyla handed her son over to him. Aaron smacked him on the cheek with the palm of his chubby hand. He seemed to be not at all wary of the tall, dark, handsome man with the patch over his left eye, the charm of a medicine show barker and a smile that could do an iceberg serious damage.

Chapter 3

He apologized for the pickup truck.

"I didn't know I'd be driving you this afternoon, or I would have left the truck at home and brought my car."

He unlocked and opened the door with his right hand while still holding Aaron in his left arm. As soon as Kyla was situated in the cab of the truck, he passed Aaron to her, setting him in her lap.

Trevor's arm brushed against her breasts. She pretended not to notice. So did he. At least he closed the door quickly. They pretended it hadn't happened, but she knew he must be thinking about that fleeting touch just as she was.

"It's warm in here," he remarked as he slid behind the steering wheel and started the motor. "The sun's been shining in."

"It feels good. We're still damp."

She could have bitten her tongue for mentioning that. He glanced down at her chest, swiftly and guiltily. She was glad that Aaron still provided her with a shield.

They fell into an awkward silence as he negotiated the traffic through the parking lot. Once he looked toward her and smiled apologetically for the delay. She smiled back and wondered if the tepid grin looked as sickly as it felt. Why couldn't she think of anything to say?

When he pulled up to the exit ramp, he turned his head. She could feel him looking at her, but she concentrated on smoothing down Aaron's soft brown hair.

Why was he staring at her like that? And maybe she should have asked that he please turn on the air conditioner. It was becoming uncomfortably warm inside the truck. Or was it her own temperature that was rising?

"I have to ask you something," he said softly.

Her heart lurched.

Are you game?

What should we do with the kid?

Are you protected?

Your place or mine?

The possibilities marched through her head. She dreaded hearing any of them. Up until now he had been so nice. She should have known it wouldn't be that easy. No man picks up a woman, gets her into his car, does her a favor and expects nothing in return.

Keeping her eyes trained on the cowlick on the crown of Aaron's head she said, "What?"

"Which way?"

A nervous laugh of relief escaped her lips on a gust of breath. "Oh, I'm sorry. To the right."

He smiled disarmingly and followed the directions she now supplied without being prompted. *He must think I'm a real ninny,* Kyla thought. He's just a nice man who is playing the Good Samaritan to a widow with a baby. Nothing more.

He might have suited the role better if he hadn't been

quite so handsome, quite so…manly. His hands for instance. Large, strong, tan. When he reached for the dial on the radio she saw that his nails were bluntly trimmed. The back of his hand and knuckles were sprinkled with dark hair, sun-bleached on the tips.

He moved his right foot from accelerator to brake. Kyla noticed the supple contraction and stretching of long thigh muscles.

His lap, too, attracted her attention.

"Hot?"

"What?"

"Are you hot?"

Her face was flaming. Her insides were afire. Had he caught her staring at…that? "Yes, a little." He adjusted the thermostat and cool air began to whisper through the cab. But from that moment, she kept her eyes away from him.

Clif and Meg Powers had lived in the same house since Kyla was born. When they purchased it, it had been in a fashionable part of town. But the town's industrial expansion and its increased importance as a commuter's alternative to living in Dallas had changed their neighborhood. It was no longer fashionable.

The houses, once attractive and well maintained, now belonged to owners who didn't take much pride in them. Like frumpy matrons who had resigned themselves to middle age, the houses looked unkempt, the yards ungroomed.

The only exception on the block was the Powers's property. The deep front porch was bordered by a white wrought-iron railing, which Clif had painstakingly repainted the previous summer. The shrubbery had been pruned to make room for new growth. Flowers bloomed in well-tended beds.

As Trevor's truck turned onto the street, a sprinkler was vigorously watering one half of the yard. The grass on the other side of the center sidewalk leading up to the front porch was glistening in the late afternoon sunlight, having already been watered.

"That's it," Kyla said, pointing out the house for him.

Trevor's foot was already on the brake. He knew which house she lived in. In the past month he'd driven by it often enough to know what days their garbage was collected.

Kyla hadn't noticed his familiarity with the neighborhood because she was inwardly groaning. A familiar car was parked in the driveway. Babs. As if making explanations to her parents wasn't going to be difficult enough, she would have Babs and her vivid imagination to contend with. Maybe she could just hop out and thank Trevor without further ado. Maybe he would drive off before anyone saw him.

No such luck.

Trever had no sooner pulled the pickup to a stop at the curb than the front door opened and her father came out. He looked at the truck curiously as he bent down to turn off the water faucet and cut off the sprinkler. He looked even more curious when he recognized Kyla and Aaron sitting on the far side of the cab.

"That's my dad," Kyla said, as Clif Powers came ambling down the front walk. For reasons she couldn't explain she felt nervous and shy.

Trevor pushed open his door. "Hi," he said with a friendly air as he stepped out of the truck. "I've got some passengers who say they belong here." Clif Powers appeared dumbstruck.

Kyla already had her door open by the time Trevor came around to her side. "Better hand Aaron to me. It's a long step down for you." Reluctantly she let him lift Aaron off her lap.

As though he'd been doing it for years, he caught Aaron

under the bottom and anchored the boy against his chest. With his free hand, he helped Kyla down. He kept his hand beneath her elbow as they rounded the truck to face her puzzled father.

"Hi, Dad."

"Where's your car? Is something wrong?"

"No, nothing's wrong, but it wasn't the most uneventful trip to the mall I've ever had," she said ruefully. She wondered how she could take her son out of Trevor's arms without creating an awkward situation. She didn't want to risk touching him again. Which was ridiculous because he was perfectly harmless.

"What's going on? Clif? Kyla?"

The voice belonged to Meg Powers, who was just then pushing her way through the front screen door. Her pleasant face wore an expression of concern. Behind her was Babs. Kyla didn't even want to contemplate what Bab's speculative expression conveyed.

Meg rushed down the front steps and took the sidewalk at a trot. Her eyes were moving back and forth between Kyla and the tall, dark-haired stranger who was holding her grandson.

"Mom, Dad, this is Mr. Rule. Trevor Rule."

"Sir, ma'am," Trevor responded politely and shifted Aaron to his left arm to shake hands with Clif Powers.

"And that's my friend and business partner, Babs Logan," Kyla added.

"Hello, Ms. Logan."

Babs's eyes danced over Trevor appreciatively. "Hi. Where did she find you?"

Babs wasn't acquainted with tact. She didn't know how to exercise restraint. She blurted out precisely what the Powerses were thinking, but didn't have the gumption or lack of manners to ask.

"He sort of found us," Kyla said.

"Where's your car?" Clif repeated.

"Still at the mall."

"I think the battery has run down, sir," Trevor added politely for Clif's benefit.

"Mr. Rule offered us a ride home."

"How chivalrous," Babs said. Her eyes were still busy with their inspection of Trevor. "What did Mrs. Rule think about that?"

Kyla was going to kill her! As soon as she had an opportunity, she was going to kill her with her bare hands!

Trevor only smiled as he bent down to set Aaron on the ground. Normally Aaron would have taken off at a run. But as soon as his feet made contact with the sidewalk, he began to whine. His chubby hands clutched at Trevor's damp pant legs. Bending down again, Trevor lifted him back into his arms and patted his bottom. Contentedly Aaron snuggled against him.

"I'm sorry," Kyla murmured, embarrassed that her son had formed such an attachment so quickly. "I'll take him now so you can get on your way."

"It's all right," Trevor assured her with a soft smile.

For an instant, as their gazes locked, it was as though they were alone. They momentarily forgot that they had an avid audience of three.

"The baby's clothes are wet," Meg ventured meekly.

"Oh, yes," Kyla said, shaking herself out of the brief trance. "He fell into the fountain."

The Powerses were immediately alarmed. Babs was merely more curious. "Was this before or after the battery ran down?" she asked, amused.

"Before. Trevor reached in and pulled him out. Don't worry, Mom, Aaron was okay. Just wet."

"How did it happen?"

"I was feeding him an ice cream." Kyla gave them a condensed rundown of the sequence of events. "When I looked around, Aaron was gone, but a crowd had encircled the fountain. Mr. Rule was standing there with a dripping Aaron in his arms."

"You jumped in the fountain and fished Aaron out?" Babs asked Trevor, nodding toward the denim that was obviously still damp below the knees.

"Yeah."

"Hmm," Babs purred, looking at Kyla in a knowing way that made Kyla want to slap her.

Clif and Meg were busy thanking Trevor for his quick action and commending him for his kindness to Kyla and Aaron. None of them saw the mouthed conversation going on between the two friends.

"He's yummy."

"Shut up."

"Your blouse is wet."

Kyla immediately ducked her head and saw that indeed the damp material of her shirt was still clinging to her breasts and outlining the lacy brassiere.

Her eyes swung up in time to catch Trevor looking at her. His gaze had followed hers down. It immediately sprang back up to her face. All this happened just as Meg, who had been expounding on how quickly a toddler could get out of sight and into mischief, concluded with, "Why don't you come in and have a cup of coffee with us, Mr. Rule?"

"No!"

Kyla's cheeks turned a warm pink when she realized she had voiced aloud the word that had shot through her mind.

She wet her lips. "I mean, we've kept Mr. Rule too long as it is." She reached for Aaron and virtually yanked the boy out of Trevor's arms. "Thank you again. You've been very helpful, and I appreciate the ride home." Now please leave! she finished silently.

"It was my pleasure." He pinched Aaron's chin. "Bye, Scout. Nice to meet you," he said, nodding his head toward the others. With a lean-hipped saunter, only slightly hindered by his limp, he turned and walked back to his truck. With a final wave, he drove off.

Self-consciously, Kyla faced her parents and Babs, who were staring at her expectantly. "I've got to get Aaron out of these wet clothes." She wedged past them, but they trooped after her and were surrounding her by the time she reached the wide, spacious entrance hall.

"Tell us!" Babs demanded.

She had been Kyla's best friend since grade school. Her mother had died when they were in junior high. Since then her father often worked double shifts at a manufacturing plant in Dallas. Through the secondary school years, Babs had spent as much time under the Powerses' roof as she had under her own. She considered herself part of the family and so did they.

"Tell you what?"

"About him! What gives?"

"Nothing." Kyla headed for the kitchen, ostensibly to get Aaron a drink of juice. She placed him in his high chair and opened the refrigerator. Her parents and Babs crowded around her.

"Did he really jump into the fountain to rescue Aaron?" Meg asked, moving aside only when Kyla reached around her for a glass.

"Don't make it sound so heroic, Mom. He didn't dive

into shark-infested waters. It's a shallow fountain, and Aaron couldn't have been in the water for more than a few seconds."

She couldn't believe she was making light of the incident now. Only an hour ago, she was thinking that Aaron could have drowned had it not been for Trevor Rule's quick reflexes.

"What about the car?" her father asked. "How did he know about the car?"

"Well, he, uh, had walked out with me."

"All the way to your car?"

"Yes. Because Aaron was crying and I was still shaken."

"He volunteered to do that?" Babs asked.

"Yes," Kyla said tightly.

"Hmm."

"Will you stop saying, 'Hmm'? You're not making a diagnosis. And I wish all three of you would stop looking at me like I've got the lowdown on a juicy piece of gossip. He's just a man, all right? A male person who was kind enough to offer his help. Honestly," she said with exasperation, "you're acting like hungry cats who've trapped the last mouse in town."

"He didn't have to drive you home," Meg said.

"He was being nice."

"He limps. Wonder what happened to him," Clif mused.

"It's none of our business. We'll never see him again. And, Dad, you'd better call someone at the garage and have my car taken care of. Do you need any help with supper, Mom?"

They recognized her tone. It was the clipped, terse one she had started using several months ago to let them know that she was officially out of mourning for Richard. With that brusque inflection she had indicated to them that they didn't need to walk on eggshells around her anymore or speak in hushed tones as though they were still at the funeral. It clearly stated that she would brook no more coddling. They knew by that tone when to back off, and now was the time.

"No, dear, thank you," Meg said, declining her offer. "You take Aaron upstairs and change him. We're only having sandwiches and I can manage. Are you staying, Babs?"

"Not tonight, thanks. I have a date."

Kyla left the kitchen and carried Aaron upstairs. Babs followed her. "I thought you had a date," Kyla said crossly as she carried Aaron into the spare bedroom that had been converted into a nursery for him.

"I've got time."

"Anybody I know? Or is this a new one?"

"Won't work, Ky," Babs said, plopping down in the rocking chair and crossing her legs Indian fashion.

"What won't work?" Kyla asked nonchalantly as she unsnapped Aaron's suspenders and took his shorts off.

"Trying to avoid the subject of your tall, dark and handsome hunk."

"He's not *my*...anything."

"Do you think he's married?"

"How should I know? Besides what difference does it make?"

"You mean you'd get involved with a married man?"

"Babs!" Kyla exclaimed, whirling around. "I'm not getting 'involved' with anybody. He offered me a ride home, for Pete's sake. What kind of day did we have at the shop?"

"Fair to middling. I don't think he's married," Babs went on doggedly. "He wasn't wearing a wedding band."

"That doesn't mean anything."

"I know. But he didn't have that married *look,* you know?"

"No. I don't know. I didn't look at him that closely."

"Well *I* did. All six feet three or so inches of him. And speaking of inches, did you notice the way he filled out the front of those jeans?"

"Stop it!" Babs had touched a nerve and Kyla kept her back to her friend because she didn't want her to see the telltale stain on her cheeks. "You're terrible."

"What did you think of the eye patch?"

"I didn't think anything of it."

Babs shivered. "I think it's wildly sexy. With that positively wicked mustache it makes him look like a highwayman or something."

"Wildly, wicked? You've been reading too many historical romances."

"And that single blue eye."

"It's green." The moment the words left her mouth, she knew she had incriminated herself. Hoping that Babs had missed the slip, she cautiously glanced over her shoulder.

Babs's smile was angelic, but there was pure devilry in her eyes. "Thought you said you didn't look at him that closely," she taunted.

"Will you go home?" Kyla pulled Aaron, now naked, into her arms. "I'm going to give Aaron a bath because he's going to bed as soon as he's had his dinner. You've got a date. And…" She drew in a deep breath. "I don't want to talk about Mr. Rule anymore. I don't even want to think about him."

"Bet he's thinking about you," Babs said, unfolding her legs and coming to her feet. She wasn't perturbed by Kyla's crankiness.

"Don't be ridiculous. Why should he give me a second thought?"

"Because he seemed damned reluctant to leave. If you hadn't acted like you'd just sat on a tack when your mother offered him a cup of coffee, I'll bet he would have accepted her invitation as an excuse to stay. *And* he noticed your wet blouse just like I did."

"He did not!" Kyla cried indignantly.

"Oh, yes, he did. Bye."

Before Kyla could offer another protest Babs was on her way downstairs. Through dinner the Powerses were just as curious about the man who had "rescued"—as Meg seemed determined to call it—Kyla and Aaron. Their questions weren't as explicit as Babs's, nor as sexually oriented, but they were just as pointed.

When she could stand their subtle quizzing no longer, Kyla stood up and said, "I wish I had just called a cab. I didn't know one man could cause such a commotion. We'll never see him again. Now good night!"

She carried Aaron upstairs and put him to bed. In her own bedroom, she tried to read, but she kept thinking about Trevor Rule. "No wonder, with everybody talking about him all evening," she grumbled, slamming her book closed.

"No matter what Babs says, he wasn't looking at my wet blouse," she averred as she pulled it off. "He wasn't!" she muttered again as she took off her brassiere.

But the thought that he *might* have been kept her awake for a long time.

"I don't believe it," Babs said suddenly, making the front-porch swing rock erratically as she sat up from her lounging position.

"Don't believe what?" Kyla asked around a yawn. She was stretched out in one of the chairs on the porch. Her head was resting on the back and her eyes were closed. It was a warm, sunny Sunday afternoon and she was feeling lazy and luxuriously indolent.

"It's *him*."

Kyla opened one eye and saw whom Babs was referring to, then her other eye popped open, as well. Trevor Rule was braking a car in front of her house.

"What'd I tell you?" Babs said. "He's come back for another look."

"If you say anything to embarrass me, I'll murder you," Kyla threatened her friend. She smiled wanly at Trevor as he made his way up the sidewalk to the front porch.

"Hi."

"Hi," the women chorused.

He gave Babs a cursory glance before his gaze homed in on Kyla. She became shyly aware of her shorts and bare feet. Her sandals had been kicked aside, but to retrieve them now would have called more attention to how casually and comfortably she was dressed.

"I was worried about your car, but I see you got it back all right." He indicated the station wagon parked in the driveway.

"Yes. Dad called the garage he patronizes. He met the mechanic on the mall parking lot and they charged my battery. The car started, but I'll probably have to get a new battery."

"That would be a good idea. Did you go with him?"

"No."

"How did he locate it in the sea of cars that was out there yesterday?"

She laughed. "It was the only one with Petal Pushers painted on the side."

His rich laughter echoed softly off the porch's covering. "Well I'm glad you got it back okay."

"Me, too."

Nervously Kyla hooked a strand of hair behind her

ear, wondering if it looked like it had been styled with an eggbeater.

Trevor's own nervous reaction to the cessation of conversation was to slide his hands into the back pockets of his jeans, stretching the cloth tight across his narrow hips. Kyla wished she couldn't remember what Babs had said about his build. But she did remember and it left her mind wide open for unladylike speculation.

For her own part, Babs could have throttled Kyla for acting like such a simp. She took matters into her own hands. "Won't you sit down, Trevor? Would you like something to drink?"

"Uh, no," he said, swiftly removing his hands from his pockets. "In fact, I came by hoping I could talk Kyla and Aaron into going for an ice cream with me. I know he likes ice cream."

Kyla opened her mouth to refuse his invitation, but Babs piped up, "Now isn't that a shame? Aaron's taking his nap." Then her blue eyes opened wide with sudden inspiration. "But *you* could go, Kyla."

Flustered, Kyla stammered, "I don't—"

"Am I interrupting anything?" Trevor looked at Babs inquiringly.

"Oh, don't worry about me," Babs said, laughing. "I don't live here, but I'm not company who has to be entertained. Kyla and I are old friends. Why, her folks practically raised me. We've been working on our tans this afternoon. You see, there's this part of their roof just outside Kyla's bedroom where we can sunbathe in total privacy." She winked audaciously. "If you get my meaning."

He did. He wasn't stupid. And when it came to playing these kinds of word games, he could make even the flirtatious Babs look like an amateur. Hell, he had invented some of the games. He could have leaned down, included them both in a suggestive smile and glibly delivered a dozen witty, leading innuendos on the subject of nude sunbathing. But the smile on Kyla's face was so strained that he didn't pursue the subject.

"But it got too hot," Babs went on. "So we came in and showered and now we're just relaxing here in the shade. In fact, I was about to drop off to sleep, so there's no reason for Kyla not to go."

Trevor met her gaze and smiled. "Would you like to?"

"No, I—"

"Kyla, who's… Oh, Mr. Rule," her father said from behind the screen door. He pushed it open and came out in stocking feet, wearing only his old-fashioned undershirt over his trousers.

"Hello, sir." Trevor shook his hand politely. "I hope I didn't disturb a nap."

"No, no," Clif lied. "I wasn't finished with the Sunday paper yet. I think I'll bring it out here on the porch."

"Trevor came by to take Kyla out for an ice cream. Wasn't that nice of him?" Babs made the announcement with a broad smile, as though some monumental decision had been reached and signed into law.

"Yes, it was," Clif agreed.

"But I don't think I'd better go because Aaron—"

"He'll be fine. He and your mother are still asleep. I just checked on him. Go on. It would do you good to get away for a spell."

Kyla couldn't remember when she had last been allowed to complete a sentence. She could have gladly strangled all three of them, her father for being so accommodating, Blabbermouth Babs, and Trevor Rule for putting her in this compromising position in the first place. "All right, I'll just go in and change." She bounded out of her chair and headed for the front door.

"You don't need to change." Babs spoke with the authority of a drill sergeant. She knew what Kyla would do. She would go upstairs and wake up Aaron and use him as an excuse not to go.

Well she wasn't going to get by with that trick. She was a widow, granted. But she was a young, vibrant widow, and Babs intended to see that Kyla didn't retreat any further into her shell.

Trevor Rule was the first man brave enough to pursue Kyla despite the cold shoulder she had given him. Whether Kyla wanted her to or not, Babs was making it her business to see that he didn't get discouraged, take his losses and go away. Her inflection softened as she asked, "Does she need to change, Trevor? You're not going anyplace where she would need to dress up, are you?"

"Hardly. Kyla?"

There was such a compelling tone to the way he spoke her name that she couldn't find a polite means of turning him down. "I guess I could go," she said, nervously tugging on the hem of her shorts. "If we're not gone too long." She returned to her chair and put on her sandals. After shooting Babs a venomous look, she came to her feet again. "I guess I'm ready."

Trevor placed his hand under her elbow and they left the porch. "Don't rush back. Take your time," Clif called after them. "We'll watch the baby."

"Have fun," Babs said, waving gaily.

Mortified, Kyla slid into the front seat. She fought a compulsion to hide her face behind her hand as Trevor got in and started the car. As soon as they turned the corner at the end of the block, he surprised her by pulling the car to the curb.

He put the automatic gear into "Park" and, laying his right arm on the back of the front seat, turned to face her.

"Look, I know they embarrassed you back there, but I don't want you to be. Okay?"

There was a hint of a smile at the corners of his mouth. She ducked her head and let go of a short, small laugh. "I was embarrassed."

"I know. I'm sorry."

"It was nothing you did. They acted like they wanted to hog-tie you before you ran away."

"I take it you haven't dated much since your husband's death."

"I haven't dated at all. And I don't want to."

Trevor took the news like a surprise right hook under his chin. He turned forward and contemplated the hood of the car through the windshield. On the one hand he was thrilled to know that she hadn't been seeing other men. On the other hand, she was spelling out the ground rules right off the bat and seemed in no rush to alter them. But she was in his car, right? He had gotten this far, right?

Kyla was thinking that perhaps she had been blunt to the point of rudeness and was just on the verge of offering an apology when he turned his head and said, "Not even to go for ice cream?" He took her spontaneous laugh as consent and engaged the gears of the car again. "Besides, eating ice cream is kind of like drinking."

"How's that?"

"It's no fun if you do it alone."

He drove through Chandler's streets, which should have been familiar to her, but which he seemed to know more about than she did. "I bought this tract of land."

"That's where the post office used to be before it moved into that new shopping center."

"That's what I hear. Anyway, I'm building a small office complex on this lot. Very nice. There'll be a central courtyard with plants and fountains. I hope it'll attract the professionals—doctors, lawyers—you know."

"I've bid on that piece of land but I don't think I'll get it," he said of other property as they cruised past. "There'll be a new supermarket over there."

"But it's a cow pasture!"

He laughed. "Give it a year. I understand there will be a movie theater complex, too."

He seemed to have inside information on what was going on in a town she had lived in all her life. What's more he seemed to be one of the movers and shakers who were making it all happen.

"Maybe Babs and I should consider moving Petal Pushers to a new location."

"No, you're fine where you are."

She looked at him quickly. "How do you know where we are?"

"I drove past your shop today before I picked you up," he said easily after a slight pause. "I was curious about any store called Petal Pushers. How long have you been in business?"

"Almost a year. Six months after Richard died...that was my husband." Idly she pleated the hem of her shorts between her fingers. "Anyway, when Babs and I were growing up, we loved the movie *My Fair Lady* and had always said we were going to work in a flower shop like Eliza Doolittle wanted to. So, when I found myself at loose ends, Babs started hounding me about it. She was unhappy with her job at the time. My parents thought it was a good idea. I needed something to do with my life and an investment for Aaron's future. So..." she said, drawing out the word, "we pooled our resources and before I knew it, I was co-owner of a flower shop."

"And has it been good for you?"

"So far, very good. The other florist in town has dated ideas and no imagination. We're closing in on him," she said with a mischievous smile that Trevor would have given heaven and earth at that moment to taste. He had been aware of every pleat she had pressed into the cotton shorts against her smooth, lotion-creamy, flower-scented, suntanned thigh.

But to his supreme irritation he had to devote his attention to his driving. He had driven off the main highway into a lane that hadn't yet been paved. It was rough.

"Do you know about an ice-cream parlor I don't?" Kyla asked.

He smiled broadly and winked. "Maybe I'm just carrying you off into the woods." Her smile faltered and he laughed. Reaching over, he patted her knee. "Relax." *I'm touching her knee. My skin against hers. God! But don't press your luck. Remove your hand. Now, Rule, now.* "I'm building this house on spec. Some of the carpenters are working today for overtime wages and I want to make sure I'm getting my money's worth out of them. Do you mind stopping for a few minutes?"

No, she didn't mind. But "relax"? Impossible. Not when she could still feel the imprint of his hand burning into the skin of her bare knee.

Chapter 4

The lane wound through a forest of pine, oak and pecan. At the end of it stood a house currently under construction. Even at this stage of completion Kyla could see that the structure would be contemporary and impressive. The lot sloped through the woods to a shallow creek.

"This is beautiful, Trevor," she exclaimed, not even noticing how easily his name had come to her lips.

But he noticed and smiled at her as he brought the car to a stop. "Do you like it?"

"The lot is beautiful."

"Come on, let me show you around."

"I don't think I should get out." She was self-conscious of her skimpy outfit and the curious workmen, who, without exception, had suspended their labors when the car drove into the clearing.

"I'm the boss around here," Trevor said, shoving open his door. "If I say you should get out, you should get out."

The sun spread heat over her bare legs. A warm breeze

caressed them. But she wasn't nearly as conscious of the elements as she was of the stares directed toward her as Trevor prodded her forward over the rough ground and around piles of building materials toward the house. They picked their way carefully. After one dark frown from Trevor, the building activity was resumed. Hammers rang out. A buzz saw shrilled. A drill whirred.

"Careful of nails," he cautioned. One of his hands was curled around her elbow. The other was riding the small of her back. When they had cleared most of the obstacles, he regretfully removed his hands. "The front door will be here. I was thinking of something with etched glass."

"How lovely."

"You'll step into an entry with a tall ceiling. Skylighted."

"I like skylights."

"Yeah?" One of her letters had told him so.

...and went in. It was just the kind of house I've always dreamed about. Contemporary. It was surrounded by trees and had a skylight.

"I saw a house like this once and loved it."

"Watch your step." Taking her hand chivalrously, Trevor led her down to the next level. "This is the living room. Very informal. A fireplace on that wall. The dining room is through there. Kitchen is that way." He pointed out the floor plan and Kyla tried to imagine what it would be like when the walls were up. Concentrating on the house kept her mind off how small her hand felt in his.

"Can you step through here?"

"Sure," she said, grateful for the opportunity to remove her hand from his.

But it didn't turn out that way, because he kept holding her hand firmly tucked into his as they squeezed through a maze of two-by-fours. "This is the master bedroom. Of course, before too long you won't be able to walk through the walls. You'll have to use the hallways."

"It seems a shame to enclose it."

The rooms were so open and airy, you could get the feeling that you lived outside.

"Exactly what I thought. Nearly every hallway has one wall of floor-to-ceiling windows so you won't get that closed-in feeling."

Dappled sunlight angled in through the overhead beams to shadow and highlight his face. The light found each iridescent streak in his black hair. His dark mustache spread wide over a lower lip so sensual that it bordered on being pouty.

Kyla withdrew her hand from his and just barely resisted the urge to wring it with her other. Casual as his touch had seemed, she didn't think it was casual at all. It just wasn't possible for a man to have a face and body like Trevor Rule's and not be a lady-killer. She could well imagine any number of female hearts dangling from his belt like trophies. The sooner he knew she wasn't in the chase, the better.

"What goes there?" she asked, putting space between them.

"Another fireplace."

"You're kidding!"

"No, why?"

She had always pictured her dream house as having a fireplace in the master bedroom, but something cautioned her about telling that to Trevor. "Nothing. I think having a fireplace in here sounds wonderful."

"And romantic."

She glanced away. "I suppose so."

"Mr. Rule?" One of the carpenters had joined them, but up until that instant had gone unnoticed. "Excuse me, but as long as you're here, could I ask you a question? It's about that breakfast nook."

"Sure. We'll be right with you." They retraced their footsteps through the framework of the house into the area of the kitchen.

"Over here in this informal dining area, you said you wanted a window. Which wall did you want the window on?" the carpenter asked.

Crossing his arms over his chest, Trevor pivoted on his boot heels to face Kyla. "Since you seem to have an instinct for these things, which wall should we put the window on?"

"I don't know anything about building."

"I'm merely asking for your opinion."

"Well," she said hesitantly, "let's see. That's south, right? And that's east?"

"Yep," the carpenter confirmed.

She contemplated the layout for a moment then said, "Why not both?" At their puzzled expressions she rushed on, "Could they meet in the corner? Maybe have one of those angled roofs that are made of glass? Then it would be like eating outdoors surrounded by trees."

The carpenter was scratching his head skeptically. "I've seen those prefab sunrooms. I reckon one might work."

Trevor, sold on the idea, clapped the carpenter on the back. "Consult with the architect tomorrow and let me know. I love the idea." He turned to Kyla. "Thanks!"

She felt her cheeks growing warm beneath his praise. "I'm sure the architect won't be too happy with me for spoiling his house plans."

"The architect has to worry about pleasing me."

They stepped out into the open again and began making their way to the parked car. "I think the house is going to be spectacular," Kyla said honestly. "I wonder who'll end up living in it."

"Never can tell. Maybe you and Aaron."

At his surprising words she stumbled over a discarded sack of concrete mix. Trevor's arm shot out, encircled her waist and secured her against his chest before she could blink.

"Careful there. Are you all right?"

She was fine except for a sudden breathlessness, a tingling sensation along her exposed skin and a curling warmth in her middle. She had forgotten how wonderful it felt to be held in a man's arms. The scents associated with masculinity—shaving soap, cologne, sweat—filled her head. She had missed those distinctive smells. He was hard and lean and strong. His breath was warm as it fanned against her cheek when he bent over her solicitously.

"I'm f-fine," she stammered and pushed herself away.

"Sure?"

"Yes. Clumsy, that's all."

The near fall had caused a strap on her sandal to become loose. She bent down to readjust it and when she did, one of the workers whistled. She sprang back up and whipped her head around. All of them were bent industriously over their tasks. And all of them looked too innocent not to be guilty.

She glanced up at Trevor, who smiled sheepishly and said with a shrug, "So they've got terrific taste. Ready?"

By all means she was ready to get away from there. She had gone on this outing to appease Babs and her father. It shouldn't have lasted longer than half an hour. How long did it take to drive to the ice-cream parlor and buy two cones?

But they had driven all over town before coming here. She had no business being on a work site with him, offering him her opinions on the house he was building. What had she been thinking of?

"You'd better take me home," she said as soon as he guided the car into the bumpy lane. "Aaron will be waking up soon."

"I promised you an ice cream."

"That doesn't matter."

"It does to me."

And that, it seemed, was that. At least if the rigid way he held his jaw was any indication. Kyla got a glimpse of another Trevor Rule then. He might be affable enough to jump into a fountain and lift a little boy out. He might be good-natured enough to push a baby stroller through a crowded mall on a Saturday afternoon. He might be kind enough to see that a stranded woman got home safely. But he also had a purely male stubborn streak. That sheer male dominance was slightly intimidating and vaguely unsettling to the woman sitting next to him in the air-conditioned car.

The car was another contradiction. She would have expected him to drive something powerful, mean, low, sleek and probably imported. Instead he was driving an all-American, conservative, middle-class family car with a full-size backseat that would accommodate Aaron's car seat.

Good Lord! What had made her think that?

"What's your favorite?"

She jumped, startled by his sudden question and her last thought. "My favorite what?"

"Ice cream. Mine's chocolate almond."

"Mine, too!"

He grinned at her. "Seriously?"

"When it comes to my chocolate almond ice cream, I'm dead serious."

On this first summery Sunday afternoon of the season, the ice-cream parlor was packed with people. Trevor seated Kyla on a high stool near the windows, then patiently stood in line. She had asked for a single dip; he brought her a double. "I'll never eat all this," she said, licking at the sinfully rich ice cream.

"Give it your best shot. Let's go outside to the gazebo. You're cold."

The air-conditioning in the ice-cream store had been turned up high and Kyla had goose bumps on her bare arms and legs. She didn't know whether to be impressed by his attentiveness or disconcerted that he was so aware of her body as to notice her chills.

As they went through the door on their way outside, a family of five came in. A little girl about six said, "Daddy, what's that thing on that man's eye?"

The mortified parents hustled the children inside and in frantic whispers admonished them not to stare.

"I'm sorry," Trevor mumbled.

Kyla was at a loss for words. She was embarrassed for him and for the parents. She certainly didn't blame the children who were naturally curious and didn't mean to be cruel.

"Does it bother you to be seen with me?" His voice was self-defensively harsh.

"No," she cried, turning to face him.

"I know the patch puts some people off."

"And attracts others." He looked at her in surprise. She explained. "Babs said it makes you look like a highwayman."

He shook his head, laughing. "A highwayman, huh?" Then his smile faded. "One who frightens children."

"Aaron wasn't frightened," she pointed out quietly.

"No, he wasn't, was he?" His tense posture began to relax. "I'm sorry if you were embarrassed by what the little girl said."

"I wasn't. It's just that I know situations like that must be awkward for you."

"I'm getting used to them." He licked at his cone, then ran his tongue along his upper lip beneath his mustache. Kyla couldn't help but wonder what that felt like. Silky or scratchy? "Sometimes I even forget what I look like to other people. Like today. I pulled on a pair of shorts, then changed my mind and put on these jeans."

"Why?"

He laughed. "If you think this damn thing is scary, you ought to see my left leg. I didn't want to repulse you."

"Don't be silly. Wear shorts around me anytime you want to."

His smile became reflective as he gazed deeply into her eyes. "I'll remember that," he said in a low, stirring voice.

Damn! Did he think she was hinting that they would be seeing each other again? To alter the course of the conversation she asked, "Were you in an accident?"

"Sort of."

Another blunder. Obviously talking about the cause of his disabilities made him uncomfortable and that topic was closed. She searched for something they could talk about and came up empty. What did they have in common but a hectic half hour at a shopping mall?

Trevor didn't seem to notice their lack of common ground as he led her into a latticed gazebo that provided shade from the new summer sun. They sat down on the bench ringing it and fell to eating their ice-cream cones.

"Better?" he asked after a long silence, nodding down toward her arm. "Your goose bumps are gone."

"Much better." If she broke out in goose bumps now it would be because his thigh was resting very near hers on the bench. Occasionally she could feel the brush of soft denim against her leg.

"You're wearing another pair of boots," she remarked. Her teeth crunched into her sugar cone.

He glanced down at his feet, which were indeed shod with another pair of lizard boots. Having grown up in Texas, Kyla knew they hadn't come cheap. "I've never owned a pair of cowboy boots until recently. Now I'm convinced I may never wear anything else."

The ice-cream parlor was situated in a row of shops and boutiques. The developer of the shopping center, who, as Trevor had told Kyla earlier, was one of the cleverest around, had created a parklike setting in the open-air mall. Willow trees bowed toward a man-made, rock-lined brook as though paying homage to the waterfowl that swam there. Halved whiskey barrels overflowed with blooming flowers. It was a pastoral place for sitting in the grass, wading in the water, walking hand in hand with someone special.

Kyla noticed that another couple had come to stand near the gazebo. Obviously the two young people were so absorbed with each other that they didn't see Trevor and herself sitting in the shadows of the interior. Speaking in soft whispers, his arms around her waist, hers locked behind his head, their middles nudging playfully, they nuzzled in the universal manner of all lovers.

"You obviously didn't grow up in this part of the country." Kyla cleared her throat uneasily, wondering if Trevor had seen the other couple. When he took a long time responding to her leading statement, she glanced up at him. He was staring at the young man and woman through the slats of the gazebo.

Feeling her eyes on him, he swiveled his head around guiltily. "Uh, no. Philadelphia. I went to school in the Northeast."

The man's hand was now strumming the woman's arm,

sliding the backs of his fingers from her elbow to her shoulder. Then he loosely closed his hand around her neck.

"That's why you don't have an accent," Kyla said.

The young man kissed the woman lightly, a soft pecking kiss.

"I guess so."

The woman angled her head back and said something that made her lover laugh softly.

"Do you have a family?" Kyla's voice was light and breathy, as though it was her neck that hungry male lips were nibbling.

"Family?" Trevor repeated dully. "Oh, family. Yes, my dad. He's a lawyer."

The man's mouth nudged aside the woman's collar and disappeared between the folds of fabric. Reflexively Trevor raked his mustache with the tip of his tongue.

"That's all? Just your dad?"

The woman made a soft sound and moved one of her hands to the man's chest. Her thumb languidly stroked the vicinity of his nipple.

Squirming on the bench, Trevor coughed. "That's all. My mother died several years ago. No brothers or sisters."

The lovers kissed. In earnest this time. There was a tilting of heads. A caressing of tongues. Arms and legs moved simultaneously to bring two yearning bodies together. Thighs adjusted themselves to interlock. Groans of pleasure and murmurs of arousal were carried on the whimsical wind that danced in and out and around the gazebo.

The muscled thigh that was now pressed tightly against Kyla's on the bench, bunched and went hard. "Lick it."

At the raspy command, Kyla's eyes flew up to meet a fierce green stare. "What?"

"Lick it. Quick. Before it drips." Lips parted, eyes glazed, she stared back at him mutely. "Your ice cream."

That roused her and she immediately jumped back. "Oh!" The melting ice cream was running over her fingers.

Trevor stood up abruptly, a pained expression on his face. "Are you finished with it?"

She glanced down at the remains of the ice-cream cone and was amazed to find that she had squeezed it to a pulp. As though it were a murder weapon she'd been caught holding, she practically threw it at him. "Yes, I'm done."

No matter how hard her mind willed it, her heart would not slow down. Her mouth was dry. Lord, what she would give for one good deep breath. Oxygen, that's what she needed to ward off this vertigo that had first hit her when he mentioned her and Aaron's living in the house he was building.

Trevor carried their trash to the receptacle near the doorway of the gazebo. Kyla stood, though her knees were wobbly, and followed him. He was stunned by how lovely she looked framed in the opening.

Sunlight struck her hair and set it aflame as it swirled around her face. Her parted lips were red and moist. She squinted against the sun, and long curly lashes crinkled around velvety brown eyes.

"Trevor? Is something wrong?"

"No," he replied huskily. "I was just thinking about you sunbathing on the roof." Color, hot and vivid, rose out of Kyla's halter and spread up over her throat and onto her cheeks. She said nothing. But his face seemed to have magnetized her eyes. She couldn't look away. "That must be a sight worth seeing."

She swallowed. "Yes. Babs has a terrific figure."

He waited an interminable amount of time before he said softly, "I wasn't thinking about Babs."

When they pulled up in front of the house, Kyla knew there was a pair of eyes at each window. She wished she could bolt from the car and race for the front door, but she knew that a gentleman like Trevor wouldn't allow that. He came around to her side and held the door for her, offering her his hand as she climbed out. She pretended not to see it. She couldn't bring herself to touch him.

On the porch, she faced him awkwardly. She hadn't been able to meet his gaze since he had mentioned what she looked like sunbathing. "Thank you, Trevor. I had a nice time."

How insipid can you get, Kyla? He probably can't wait to get away, she was thinking.

I had to go and get horny and make that comment about her sunbathing. That probably ruined everything, he was thinking.

"So did I." The new boots suddenly felt too tight for his feet and he shifted from one to the other. "Well, goodbye, Kyla."

"Goodbye."

She turned toward the front door and nearly collided with her mother, who was stumbling over her own feet in her haste to get to the porch. "Oh, my goodness," Meg said, flustered. "Mr. Rule, how nice to see you again."

Her surprise over catching them together was as phony as a three-dollar bill. Trevor knew it and Kyla knew he knew it, and she wanted to sink into a deep hole and never have to come out again.

"Hello, Mrs. Powers," he said.

"I just made some sandwiches and lemonade. We thought

we'd eat in the backyard on the picnic table. Why don't you join us?"

Tempted, Trevor glanced at Kyla. Her smile was strained. No, better not, he thought. He'd pushed just about as far as he could for one day. If he hadn't said what he had about the sunbathing.... But he had. Well, damn it, she had looked good enough to eat standing there in the sunshine, and he had had to endure watching while she made eating a damned ice-cream cone look like an erotic exercise. Oh, hell, the damage was already done.

Hating the necessity of it, he declined Meg's invitation. "That sounds great, but I've got some work waiting for me."

Meg's anxious smile collapsed. "What a shame. Well, another time."

"I'd be delighted." He smiled at them both, then loped down the front porch steps and down the sidewalk to his car. As soon as he had driven out of sight, the front door disgorged Babs and Clif.

"Well, how was it?" Babs asked. "Did he ask you out?"

"Will you see him again?"

"Did he ask permission to call?"

"Oh, for heaven's sake!" Kyla exclaimed cantankerously. "I wish all of you would grow up and leave me alone." She stormed past them and went through the front door in a huff.

But who was she mad at? Trevor? Her well-meaning parents? Babs? Or herself?

Because she was just the slightest bit sorry Trevor hadn't accepted her mother's invitation.

"No, no, Aaron," Kyla repeated for the hundredth time. "Don't touch the flowers."

They were in the back room of Petal Pushers. Meg, who sat with Aaron when Kyla worked, had needed to go to the dentist. Clif hadn't returned from an errand in time, so she had dropped Aaron off at the flower shop saying she wouldn't be long.

Kyla was keeping an eye on him while she did the month's accounting. When they had divided the labor of running the shop, Babs had volunteered to keep it open and actually deal with the customers if Kyla would do all the ordering, billing and accounting. Babs loved people but was a disaster at figures. The bookkeeping tasks kept Kyla's hours flexible, which was essential since she had a child to care for.

As she ran another tape through the adding machine, Kyla was vaguely aware of the tinkling sound of the bell over their front door. She didn't pay any attention to it until Babs called out, "Oh, Kyla?"

"Hmm?" she responded absently, jotting down the sum of her tally.

"You have a customer."

"A cus—"

The question died on her lips as Trevor Rule stepped through the swinging louvered door that separated the shop proper from its back room.

"Hi."

Babs was standing behind him, grinning like a Cheshire cat. "I thought you might want to deal with this customer personally."

Kyla's eyes threatened her friend with annihilation. Sunday evening had been torture. They had eaten supper in the backyard on the picnic table under the trees. The old table's paint was blistered and peeling because it had been in the backyard for as long as Kyla could remember. She and Babs used to drape it with blankets and play "tent" under it.

"Aren't you going to tell us *anything?*" Babs had asked around a mouthful of Meg's famous baked beans.

"There's nothing to tell," Kyla had said. "And would the three of you stop staring at me? My nose is not going to start growing like Pinocchio's."

"You can lie by omission," Babs intoned. "I don't think it's very sporting of you to keep us in the dark."

Kyla laid her fork on her plate, stared down at it while she slowly counted to ten, then raised her head. "All right. He drove me into the woods, parked, tore off all my clothes and we made wild, passionate love in the backseat of his car. We were both like wild beasts, consumed by spontaneous lust and licentiousness."

Kyla was the only one smiling when she finished her tale. "That's not very funny," Meg said stiffly. "For months we've been telling you you're too young and pretty to seal yourself off from life. We've encouraged you to start seeing men. Mr. Rule is the first one you haven't run from. We're only excited for you."

Kyla sighed wearily. "That's my point, Mom. There's nothing to be excited about. I had a husband. His name was Richard Stroud. He'll remain my husband until I die. I'll never fall in love again, never love anyone but Richard, and am not looking for someone to love that way again."

"Love, love, love," Babs cried in exasperation. "Do you always have to bring *love* into it? Why not just go out for kicks? Have some fun. You don't have to love a guy to enjoy him."

"Maybe you don't, but I do. And you know damn good and well, Babs, that men don't take out women 'for kicks' without expecting them to jump into bed with them for a payoff. I'm sorry, Mom, Dad," she said to them when their faces paled, "but that's the way it is these days. Now, I don't want to hear another word about Trevor Rule or any other man. I'm not in the market for one. Is that clear?"

They had honored her request and changed the subject, though she could tell that Trevor Rule was far from being a dead issue. All day Monday her parents had leaped toward the telephone each time it rang. It was the same at work with Babs. Kyla was relieved that none of the callers had been the one they obviously expected.

Relieved, but a trifle disappointed, too. He could have at least *tried* to reach her and given her the satisfaction of saying she didn't want to see him again. Despite her best intentions, her thoughts often strayed back to him.

Now, seeing him filling the doorway to the back room made her insides turn to mush. A dull roaring sound, not unlike the ocean, was rushing through her head.

"Hello, Trevor."

Some smart advertising executive should hire him to model jeans, she thought. He wore them so well. His chest and upper arms filled out the cotton shirt to perfection. His hair was agreeably mussed by the wind. The patch over his eye gave him the dangerous air of a mercenary, a man who lived just beyond the pale, a man to be wary of. Extremely wary of.

Belying his macho image, Trevor crouched down to speak to Aaron, who was standing in front of the large refrigerated cabinet that stored the flowers they used in their arrangements. "Hiya, Scout." The boy was happily slapping his hands against the cold glass. Trevor patted him on the bottom and Aaron gurgled a happy sound by way of greeting. He flashed their unexpected visitor a slobbery, toothy grin.

"I've got work to do. Excuse me," Babs said and disappeared.

For no good reason Kyla stood up behind her desk. Then, when Trevor also stood up, she sat back down. If she could have found it within herself to see the humor in their seesawing, she would have laughed.

"You look nice," he said.

She glanced down at her simple dress. It was the color of champagne, a color she knew she wore well. But it was nothing special and she wondered why he had even commented on it. Then she remembered that he'd never seen her dressed up. "Thank you." Was she supposed to tell him he looked nice, too? But he didn't look nice. He looked…sexy. She certainly wasn't going to tell him that because she had an idea he already knew.

"It smells good in here."

She forced her hands, which were gripping her ballpoint pen, to relax. "That's one of the benefits of working in a flower shop. It always smells good."

"I thought it might be you. Your perfume."

The ballpoint pen was strangled again. She tore her eyes away from Trevor's face and happened to catch sight of Aaron. "No, Aaron." She came out of her chair and rounded the desk hurriedly in an attempt to save the carnations. They were standing in a bucket of water, waiting to be used in an arrangement that had been ordered that morning. Kneeling down, she turned her meddlesome son away from the allure of the flowers and tried to distract him with his toys. "Here, play with Pooh Bear."

When she stood up again, she found herself as close to Trevor as his shadow. She stepped back quickly. "He's into everything." A nervous hand fluttered up to the gold chain around her neck, which seemed to have captured Trevor's interest. Count Dracula had never studied a neck so intently.

"Do you always keep Aaron here while you're working?"

"No." She explained about her mother's dental appointment. At that moment she couldn't have said whether she wished her mother would return and save her from being alone with Trevor. (Babs certainly was no help.) Or whether she would rather her mother never know about his visit to the shop.

But why was she herself making such a big deal of it? He was just another customer. "Can I help you with anything?"

"Oh, yeah," he said, jerking his attention back to the business at hand. "I need to order a corsage."

"I see."

Several thoughts tumbled through her head. Uppermost was whom the corsage was for. Then: If that's all he wanted, why hadn't he placed the order with Babs out front? Then: Oh, Lord, maybe he hadn't wanted to see her at all. Had Babs ushered him back here to see her when all he had intended to do was give Petal Pushers his business?

"I'll, uh, let's see, yes, here's an order pad." She yanked up the tablet and held her pen over it. She filled in his name at the top. "What did you have in mind?"

"I'm not sure. What do you suggest?" He moved up behind her as she bent over the desk. She felt his legs brush against her skirt and madly thought about a French movie Babs had dragged her to a few months ago. She closed her eyes for a moment until the pornographic image was banished.

Drawing a ragged breath, she asked, "What's the occasion?"

"A banquet. Semiformal."

What banquet? Where? Whom was the corsage for? "A banquet. All right."

"I like orchids," he said.

"Orchids?"

"Yeah. Those big, fluffy ones. White ones."

You'll never guess what I found in a keepsake box the other day. That first orchid corsage you gave me for the Chi Omega spring dance. Remember? That's when I fell in love both with you and Bow Bells.

Kyla looked at Trevor with surprise. "Bow Bells?"

"Pardon?"

"Bow Bells. That's what you described. It's a cattleya hybrid." When he said nothing, she elaborated. "They're very pretty. They have large white ruffled petals and a deep golden throat." He was watching her lips as they formed each word. Kyla wondered how, in only a matter of seconds, "throat" had become the most provocative word in the English language.

"That's exactly what I had in mind."

"I...I have to order them from Dallas. When did you need the corsage?" Why was he looking at her as though he were about to make her his lunch and why was she allowing it?

"Saturday night." He took a step closer.

"No problem," she said briskly, alarmed by how quiet it had become in the shrinking room and how close they were standing. She could delineate each hair in his thick mustache.

She bent back over the desk. "One flower or two?"

"Two."

"They're expensive."

"That's okay. Don't scrimp on it."

"What time do you want to pick it up?"

"Do you deliver?"

"Yes."

"Then please deliver it Saturday afternoon."

"The address?"

"Two twenty-three East Stratton."

The ballpoint pen fell from fingers suddenly gone bone-less. It rolled across the desk and dropped off the edge. Kyla turned around and gazed up into the dark, handsome face bending over hers. "That's my address."

"Will you go to the banquet with me?"

Speechless, she stared at him and began shaking her head even before she found her voice. "No, no I can't."

"It wouldn't be a date," he said in a rush. "It's a banquet for bankers and other potential lenders. A group of us developers have put together a videotape presentation on business opportunities in the community."

"What does that have to do with me?"

"You've lived here all your life. I'm still a stranger in town. I'd like having you there to introduce me around."

If Kyla was ever certain of one thing, it was that Trevor Rule didn't need anyone to introduce him around. One smile like the one he was bestowing on her now and people, especially women, would flock to him. His grin was of the stuff that sold everything from toothpaste to brandy. When sex appeal had been doled out, Trevor Rule had gone through the line at least twice. He had charisma. He was the kind of man who attracted men and women alike. Everyone would want to be his friend.

"No, Trevor, I'm sorry, but I can't."

If he had posed no threat, then maybe she would have accepted. But he was too attractive. All she needed to do to start rumors flying was to be seen in the company of the newest eligible bachelor in Chandler. By Sunday morning her mother's friends would be talking wedding.

He made a small regretful sound and rubbed the back of his neck. "I never thought I'd have to resort to this to get a date with a beautiful woman, but I'm desperate."

"Resort to what?"

He looked at her cajolingly from beneath his brows. The green eye was twinkling. "You owe me a favor."

"Do either of you claim this little hoodlum?"

As one, they turned toward the door to see a vexed Babs holding Aaron in her arms. He had three drooping carnations clutched in one tight, moist fist. He had left a trail of wilted flowers from the back room into the shop. The stems had dripped water onto the floor. Aaron was waving at them with another battered blossom.

"Oh, gosh, Babs, I'm sorry." Kyla rushed forward and took Aaron out of Bab's arms.

"That's all right. He only destroyed about ten dollars worth of carnations, not to mention the vase he was stuffing his Pooh Bear into. You must have been awfully busy in here." Her blue eyes were teasing as they bounced between Trevor and Kyla.

"We were, uh…Mr. Rule was ordering a, uh, some flowers."

Babs gave them both a knowing glance before smiling benignly and leaving them alone again.

"Well?" Trevor said. "About Saturday night."

"I don't know." Kyla and Aaron were battling over possession of the carnations because she was afraid he was going to eat them and she didn't know if they were poisonous or not. When he finally lost that skirmish, he reached for her earring.

How could she wrestle with him and make a decision like this? She should coolly refuse Trevor's invitation, no matter how charmingly it had been extended. She had never written up an order for flowers she was to receive before. And that much charm coming from a man she hardly knew was disturbing.

But, she did owe him a favor, and if he considered this a business occasion…

"It wouldn't be a date?" she asked tentatively.

"No."

"Because I wouldn't want you to get the wrong idea."

"I understand."

"I mean, I'm a widow and I don't date."

"You've already told me that."

She had, hadn't she? So why was she babbling on about it? If she made too much out of it, he would think she was protesting too much. "All right, I'll go."

"Great. I'll see you Saturday about seven. And don't forget the corsage."

"You still want me to make it?"

"Sure. Goodbye, Aaron." He cuffed the boy under the chin. "See you Saturday night, Kyla."

Seconds after he had gone through the swinging door, Babs pushed it open. "'See you Saturday night, Kyla.' Is that what he said?"

"Yes. I'm going to a banquet with him."

"That's wonderful," Babs said, clapping her hands together. "What'll you wear?"

"I won't wear anything." When Babs's mouth formed a small *o,* Kyla sighed resignedly. "I mean, it doesn't matter what I wear because it's not really a date."

"Oh, sure."

"It's not. It's a business affair and he asked me to go with him to introduce him around."

"Uh—huh."

"He did!"

"Uh-huh."

"It's not a date."

"Uh-huh."

"He said so himself. It's not a date."

Chapter 5

It certainly felt like a date.

Kyla didn't remember being this jittery getting dressed for her first car date, her senior prom or her wedding. She didn't want to think about her wedding or Richard. But *not* thinking about them only implied that this "date" with Trevor Rule meant something, which she vowed repeatedly that it didn't.

Still, she was clumsy as she tried to apply her makeup. Nothing went right. She had to do one eyelid three times. Aaron, who seemed to have grown an extra pair of hands, was into everything. Her mother and father kept popping into her room, apprising her of the time, the current weather conditions, asking questions, offering assistance and generally making pests of themselves.

Thankfully, Babs had a "heavy date," so Kyla was spared her interference. Babs had insisted that Kyla buy a new dress for the occasion when all the while Kyla had insisted that it wasn't an "occasion."

Kyla's eventual capitulation only resulted in another argument, over which dress she should buy. Babs had gone on the shopping expedition without invitation.

"I like this yellow dress," Kyla said. Babs had mimed gagging herself by poking her index finger into her open mouth. "Very eloquent," Kyla had said sarcastically.

Placing her hands on her shapely hips, Babs asked, "Would you rather look like Mata Hari or Little Mary Sunshine?"

"I'd rather look like me."

"Try on the black one again."

"It's too...too..."

"Exactly," Babs had said, shoving the garment at Kyla impatiently. "It's terrific and it *is* you. Right?" she demanded of the intimidated sales clerk who was cowering against the dressing room wall.

"Right."

Kyla had left the store with the black dress, knowing instinctively that she was making a mistake. The yellow would have been much more suited to her. The black dress was too sophisticated. Trevor would think...God knows what he would think.

Her previous worries were compounded as she zipped up the back of the cocktail dress and caught her reflection in the mirror. The silk clung and swirled just where it was required to. Black complemented her complexion, especially since she had already enhanced it with pastel blushers and frosted eye shadows, and lip gloss the color of peach sorbet. Her hair was soft and shiny and had about it a look of artful disarray. She had left it to curl softly on her shoulders, sweeping one side back and holding it above her ear with a decorative comb. At the base of her throat lay a single strand of pearls. Pearl studs adorned her ears.

Hearing the doorbell downstairs, she reached for the

orchid corsage and hastily pinned it to her dress. She pricked herself with the pins and was glad that Aaron, who parroted everything these days, wasn't in the room to hear her soft curses.

The corsage had brought on another argument between herself and Babs as recently as that afternoon. "It's four-thirty and you haven't made that corsage Trevor ordered."

"I'm not going to," Kyla had replied.

"The hell you're not. I've already sent him a bill."

"You what?"

"He's a customer, Kyla. He ordered a corsage and I billed him for it. Now we owe him an orchid corsage."

Casting her smiling friend a stormy look, Kyla made up the corsage.

"Won't do," Babs said, surpervising over Kyla's shoulder. "He asked for two flowers."

"How do you know?"

"I overheard. And he said not to scrimp either, so put some more of that lacy stuff behind it."

"Did you eavesdrop on the entire conversation?"

"Sure. At least I think I did. Did either of you say anything you're ashamed of?"

"Of course not," Kyla said heatedly.

"Then why are you getting so bent out of shape?"

Now, as Kyla made one last inspection of herself in the mirror, she had to admit that it all went together well: the black silk dress, the pearls, the hothouse flowers.

And that was just what she felt like, a hothouse flower who had been cultured and protected and was about to be thrust into the elements for the first time.

Such qualms were juvenile. She knew they were. But knowing they were juvenile and shaking them off were two different things. She had been married. She was a mother.

But she felt like an old-world, convent-bred ingenue about to meet her first man.

"This is ridiculous," she told herself in exasperation as she yanked up the small black beaded evening bag and switched out the light. "This isn't even a date." She repeated that to herself, in cadence to her trepid footsteps down the stairs.

Trevor was standing in the entrance hall holding Aaron in his arms. He was bouncing the boy up and down as he conversed with Meg and Clif.

"...should be finished in about two weeks." He swung his dark head around when he realized that something on the staircase had captured the Powerses' attention.

Only an act of will kept Kyla's feet from faltering on the next step as Trevor looked up at her. She forced herself to descend calmly. Unfortunately she had no such control over her heartbeat.

"Hello, Trevor."

"Hi."

Aaron was plucking at Trevor's mustache, but he seemed not to notice. His gaze was fixed on Kyla. She was having just as hard a time keeping her eyes off him. He was gorgeous.

His suit was charcoal-gray, so dark that it almost looked black. The crisp white shirt only intensified the color of his hair and the depth of his tan. The correct silver and black striped tie would have looked ordinary on any other man, but Kyla realized then that Trevor was by no means ordinary. He was never going to be. Perhaps his distinction lay in the ever-present eye patch, which was so familiar now, so much a part of his face, that she didn't see it as something apart.

"The orchids are beautiful."

"Yes," she said breathlessly. She touched the corsage lightly, self-consciously, where it reposed on her breast. "Thank you. Do you like them?"

"Do you?"

"Very much."

"Good."

Think of something else to say, you idiot, she ordered herself.

Aaron came to her rescue. He chose that moment to take one of those unpredictable dives that toddlers often take from one pair of arms to another. Without warning, he lunged toward her and she barely had time to get her arms up before he landed against her with a solid thud.

But Trevor, whose relaxed arms tensed around the child immediately, hadn't quite let go of Aaron yet. So his right arm became trapped between Aaron and Kyla's breasts. As she gradually got a better grip on Aaron, Trevor withdrew his arm. There ensued a few moments of awkwardness, which everyone tried to cover with loud chatter.

"Here, give me the baby," Meg said.

"You two had better be going or you'll be late," Clif said.

"Are you ready?" Trevor asked.

"Yes. I think I have everything. Good night, Aaron."

"We'll get Aaron to bed, so there's no rush about coming home early," Meg said.

"Drive carefully. You've got plenty of time," Clif called to them as they went down the walk.

Kyla was grinding her teeth. Anyone would think this was her first date. She wouldn't have been surprised if Clif had posed them in the hall while Meg went searching for the camera.

Trevor stepped around her to open the car door. He didn't touch her and she was grateful. All too well she was remembering the feel of his hard arm moving across her breasts. It had left a tide of heat in its wake.

Once he was behind the wheel, he said, "I know this isn't a date, but am I allowed to tell you how pretty you look?"

His attempt at humor put her at ease somewhat and she glanced over at him. "Yes, and thank you."

"You're welcome."

He reached for the dials of the radio and turned to an easy-listening music station. His suit coat sleeve slid up. His shirt cuff was starched and stiff and had been skewered with a cuff link that had a smooth square of ebony fixed in a trim gold setting.

He had impeccable taste.

"I haven't talked to you since Tuesday. How was your week?"

"Busy," she said, silently thanking him for opening up an avenue of conversation. She seemed to have lost all talent for making small talk. Trevor hadn't, though, and before she knew it they had arrived at their destination.

The Chandler Country Club was only two years old. The landscaping was still immature, but the modern building of native stone couldn't be faulted. Sprinklers out on the dark golf greens were swishing as Trevor escorted her up the footpath that connected the parking lot to the front door.

She had almost, *almost,* gotten accustomed to having his hand wrapped around her elbow. But she wasn't prepared for him to slow his stride, lean down close to her and come near to pressing his face against her neck before standing straight again.

"This time I know that fragrance isn't flowers. It's you. And you smell wonderful."

"Thank you."

The words had been difficult to speak for the constriction in her throat. He overwhelmed her. He was so tall, so purely masculine. Around her, he had never acted like anything but a gentleman. Nonetheless she felt threatened by him. Not afraid, just threatened.

Every time he smiled down at her, as he was doing now, she remembered the discussions she and Babs used to have about kissing and how it would feel to kiss a man with a mustache.

Trevor's dark mustache was thick, but well groomed. It virtually obliterated his upper lip, while emphasizing the shape of the lower. It curved over the corners of his mouth as though caressing it. His teeth shone beneath it, startlingly white. The overall effect was disturbingly sensual.

Kyla tried convincing herself that her interest in it was purely casual, a holdover from youthful curiosity. But her powers of persuasion seemed to be taking the night off.

The cocktail party preceding the banquet had already started by the time they entered the room overlooking the golf course and swimming pool. The laughter-spiked din almost drowned out the music being provided by the combo playing a popular hit from a dais in the corner.

"Would you like something to drink?" Trevor had to bend down and place his lips close to her ear to be heard over the racket.

She turned, stretched up and spoke directly into his ear. "Club soda and lime, please." He nodded, smiled and elbowed his way through the crowd toward the bar, leaving behind him the scent of his cologne. Kyla liked it very much. It was clean and brisk, with an air of citrus. She couldn't help but notice how well the tailored coat fit his broad shoulders and—

"Why, Kyla Stroud! I told Herbie it was you. It's so good to see you out, dear."

"Hello, Mrs. Baker, Mr. Baker."

"How are your folks?"

"They're fine, thanks."

"And your little boy?"

"Aaron's a typical toddler." She laughed softly. "Almost more than I can keep up with."

"Kyla, your drink." She turned and accepted the glass of soda from Trevor. The surprised expressions on the older couple's faces were just what she had expected and dreaded.

"Thank you, Trevor. I'd like you to meet Mr. and Mrs. Herb Baker. Mrs. Baker taught me seventh-grade English grammar and literature. Mr. Baker has an insurance company. Trevor Rule," she said, presenting Trevor to them.

"Rule, Rule," Mr. Baker repeated as he pumped Trevor's hand. "Sure, Rule Enterprises! I've seen your signs everywhere. Contractor, aren't you?"

"Yes, sir. I've just formed my own company."

"Couldn't have picked a better place to start," Baker said. "Chandler used to be a sleepy little town. Nothing but a cotton gin here for decades. We're gradually changing all that. You joined the Chamber of Commerce last week, didn't you?"

"Yes, sir, I did."

"Glad to hear it. I'm on the membership committee."

While this conversation had been going on, Mrs. Baker's eyes had been busily bouncing between the two of them. She couldn't have been more obviously greedy for information if she had had a radar detector growing out of her forehead. "Did the two of you know each other *before?*"

Before exactly what, Kyla was never to know because Trevor intervened. "Please excuse us. Someone across the room is waiting to meet Kyla. Mrs. Baker, Mr. Baker."

Trevor nodded politely; Kyla smiled vapidly and let him usher her away. "I know that makes you uncomfortable."

"What?"

"Being seen with me."

"It's not that. It's what everyone is thinking that bothers me," she admitted.

"What do you think they're thinking?"

"You know, things like, 'It's about time the little widow got out in circulation again.' Or, 'It's too soon for her to be out in circulation again.' My parents acted like they had to foist off the eldest daughter before they could marry off the other six."

Trevor laughed. "It wasn't as bad as all that."

"Wasn't it?"

"No. You're far more self-conscious about that than I am."

"I wouldn't have blamed you if you had turned and run."

"But I didn't. I'm still here."

He spoke with such intensity, that Kyla's uneasiness was far from relieved. To avoid looking at him, she gazed out over the crowded room. "Now I feel like people I've known all my life have become spies and gossips."

"You can waste a lot of time and energy worrying about what people are thinking and saying behind your back."

She sighed. "I know. But this can't be much fun for you, either. Don't you get the feeling that you're a window dressing and everyone's staring at you?"

He drew a serious face. "Don't worry about me. What people think doesn't really bother me. I don't want *you* to be uncomfortable. That's the only reason I mind it."

"We know this isn't actually a date. I just wish everyone else did."

"Short of announcing it over the microphone, what can I do to let them know this is not a date?"

For starters he could remove his hand from the small of her back. Because they had reached the other side of the room after maneuvering through the crowd—and his hand was still there, a firm, warm pressure against the arch of her back.

Then they could dispel more rumors by engaging other people in conversation. As it was, with the two of them silhouetted against the sunset beyond the plate glass windows, with Trevor's face bending close to hers in serious conversation, they must surely be giving everyone the impression that what they were saying was private and personal. It *felt* private and personal.

She moved, ostensibly to take a sip of her drink. Actually it was to put a few safe inches between them. Trevor sipped at his own drink, a pale whiskey.

"Would it make you feel better if I told you that you look sensational?" he asked.

She traced the rim of her glass with her finger. "No, I don't think so."

"Okay. Then maybe I'd better not mention that your dress is a real knockout."

Her eyes slid up to his face and caught his teasing smile. Her own stiff, plastic, party-manners smile became genuine. "Thank you for not mentioning that."

"Maybe we should migrate toward the dining room," he said. "Some are already moving in that direction to locate their table."

On their way into the dining room they were joined by a young banker and his wife. Lynn and Ted Haskell were new to town and therefore didn't know Kyla and her past. Trevor introduced her merely as his "friend." She enjoyed their lively conversation through the filet mignon dinner.

Trevor was attentive to her every need, always making certain she had salt, pepper, butter, fresh bread, water, coffee. She found herself basking in his attention. Mealtimes with Aaron were more like battles. Attack and retreat. Sometimes when she finished, she couldn't remember having eaten because she had snatched bites between mopping up spilled milk and wiping Aaron's dodging mouth.

"Didn't you like the food?" Trevor asked as the waiter whisked away her embarrassingly empty plate.

She blushed at his teasing and laughed self-deprecatingly. "I loved it, mainly because I got to eat it in peace. Having dinner with Aaron isn't quite so relaxing. It was all I could do to keep myself from cutting your meat for you. If I start patting your napkin back into your lap, try not to notice."

He blinked, startled. Then a slow grin spread across his rugged face. Leaning closer he said, "Kyla, if you start patting my lap for any reason, I'm going to find it damn near to impossible not to notice."

She could easily have died at that moment. In fact she even prayed for a sudden death. Her cheeks were scalding. Her fingertips and toes were throbbing with an influx of blood. Never had she been so embarrassed.

"I...I meant—"

"I know what you meant." Trevor, sensing her mortification, squeezed her hand. "More coffee?"

She made no more verbal blunders and they settled back in their hard chairs for the program. After the videotape presentation, the speakers droned on endlessly, extolling the attributes of Chandler in particular and north central Texas in general.

"Bored?" Trevor whispered, leaning close.

She had unsuccessfully tried to hide a delicate yawn with her hand. "No. It's all very interesting."

"You're a terrible liar," he growled close to her ear. She laughed, ducking her head. "Do you want to leave?"

"No!" she exclaimed, knowing this evening was important to him. He was here to see and be seen.

"We can sneak out."

"No. I'm fine. Really."

"Sure?"

She nodded her head.

"Positive?"

She nodded again.

"You're lovely, Kyla."

Her head snapped up and she met his gaze, which was compelling and hot. "I just threw that in to see if you were paying attention."

Slowly he pulled away and sat back in his chair. Kyla swallowed hard and removed her gaze from his. She glanced around anxiously, wondering if anyone had noticed their whispered exchange. She caught sight of Mrs. Baker's expectant face and looked away quickly.

Her eyes landed on the banker and his wife. Lynn's hand was lying on Ted's thigh. He was idly stroking the back of her hand. Kyla smiled at such a sweet display of marital intimacy. The subconscious kind. The kind that came automatically. Those demonstrations that said so much, but that wouldn't even be remembered later.

Richard and I used to do things like that all the time.

Mentally she sprang erect. That was the first time she had thought of Richard in hours. Guilt pierced her to the core. What was wrong with her?

She concentrated on him, on his face, his smile, his funny laugh, until the final speaker concluded his speech. Trevor and she said their good-nights and were among the first to leave. They barely made it to the car before it began to rain.

Once under way Trevor asked, "Would you like to go somewhere for dessert?"

"Remember the cherry cheesecake?"

"Oh, yeah." After a pause he said, "Coffee?"

"I don't think so."

"A drink?"

"No thank you, Trevor. I should be getting home."

"Right."

He sounded disappointed. Surely she was mistaken. He must be as glad as she that this evening was almost over.

They said little, which only made the tapping of the rain on the roof of the car and the rhythmic clacking of the windshield wipers seem louder.

Apparently he wasn't accustomed to driving with both hands on the wheel because he kept his right one in constant motion while he steered the car with his left. At first he fiddled with the radio, turning the volume up, then seconds later turning it back down.

He reached for the thermostat. "Comfortable?"

"Yes, fine."

His hand was withdrawn, but was no less restless. With that fidgeting right hand he worked loose the knot of his necktie. He raked back his hair. He adjusted the volume on the radio one more time. Finally he let that hand rest.

On the seat.

Halfway between them.

From the corner of her eye, Kyla watched that hand as though it posed some grave threat.

What if it inched toward her? Would she say something?

What if it reached out and grabbed her? Would she scream?

What if it reached for her own? Would she allow her hand to be held?

What if it caressed her thigh? Would she slap it away?

Her heart was thudding and she felt her palms grow slick with moisture. Never had the house where she lived safely with her parents and baby been such a welcome sight.

The hand didn't do anything but turn off the key in the ignition after the car had rolled to a slow stop. "Sit tight," he said, when she reached for the door handle. "I have an umbrella." Turning, he stretched his arm over the seat and reached behind him for the umbrella. His coat gaped open and Kyla saw the hard muscles of his chest straining against his shirt.

He got out and popped the umbrella open. He was holding it over his head when he opened her door and reached inside to take her hand and lift her out.

How it happened, she was never quite sure. Maybe they were crowding beneath the umbrella in an effort not to get wet. But somehow, *somehow,* when she stood up on the sidewalk, she was very close to him. So close that their clothes were brushing against each other.

Instinctively, her head tilted back. His face loomed close. He was holding the umbrella with his left hand. With his right, he loosely enfolded her neck.

She felt the tickling brush of his mustache first, then his lips, warm and firm, rubbing against hers.

Oh, God, that feels good.

She pulled back quickly and lowered her head. He removed his hand from her neck. She could still feel the imprint of each finger, though he had barely touched her and his clasp could hardly be classified as such.

The rain pecked against the silk umbrella and rolled down its slick surface to drip off the edge. Beneath that meager shelter they stood still and silent...and close.

"I'm sorry," Trevor said after a long moment. "No kisses allowed on the first date?"

"This isn't a date."

"Oh, yeah. Damn. I keep forgetting that."

He turned them toward the front door. Carefully they

made their way up the walkway, made treacherous by the rainfall. No outside light had been left on to aid them in reaching the safety of the porch.

Trevor swung the umbrella down and shook it hard.

"Thank you for the evening, Trevor," Kyla said, edging toward the door.

"I know we said this wasn't a date." The umbrella was dropped onto the porch. It made a lazy spin on the axis of its handle before coming to rest.

"Yes. That's what we said."

"Right. We agreed that it wasn't a date, only—"

"What?"

"I'm not pushing. I don't want you to think I'm pushing."

"I don't."

"But…" He took a step toward her. Another. "Say this *was* a date."

"Yes?"

"Would you—"

"Would I what?"

His hands came up to frame her face tenderly. Her eyes slid closed. His lips met hers again. But they stayed this time. And pressed. And angled until hers parted. The tip of his tongue dared to penetrate, to make fleeting contact with hers, to sweep her mouth once, to sink deeply. Then it withdrew. He lifted his mouth away from hers. His hands fell to his sides.

"Good night, Kyla."

"Good night."

How the words found their way out of her mouth, she couldn't fathom. After watching him retrieve his umbrella and walk to his car, she automatically unlocked the front door and let herself in.

She drifted upstairs, telling herself every step of the way

that since it hadn't really been a date, that hadn't really been a kiss, either.

But her alter ego was saying, "Oh, it was a kiss all right. It was a dilly of a kiss. Babs, at her wildest, couldn't have imagined such a kiss. If you looked up the word *kiss* in the dictionary, a description of what you just experienced beneath Trevor's mouth would be the definition."

She unpinned the orchid corsage and laid it on the dresser. She carelessly dropped her pearls amidst her perfume decanters, when normally she would have stored them in their velvet box. The black silk dress was left heedlessly lying on a chair with her underclothes piled atop it.

She floated toward the bed, naked—for the first time in a long time.

When she reached to turn out the lamp on the bedside table, she noticed Richard's picture.

Then she burst into tears.

Chapter 6

"You're a damn fool."

He spoke softly. His breath fogged the window because the glass had been cooled by the rain. The room behind him was dark, so he was spared having to look at his reflection in the windowpane.

He sipped his drink. "A fool, a coward," he sighed, then added, "a liar."

Every time he saw her, he was lying by not telling her who he was. He knew what he was doing was wrong, but he couldn't bring himself to say, "I'm Smooch. Remember me? The guy your husband wrote to you about. The kind of man you said you detested. Egotistical. Thinks he's God's gift to women. Despoiler of reputations. Smooch." She had ridiculed him in her letters and he had deserved every reproachful word. In his place her beloved husband had died.

Clenching his teeth and closing his eyes, Trevor pressed his forehead against the window. What he was doing was manipulative and downright deceitful. There was no way he could excuse himself.

Actually there was an excuse, but who would believe it? Who would believe that he had fallen in love with a woman he'd never seen merely by reading her letters? He barely believed it himself. Certainly she would never believe it.

Sooner or later he would have to tell her who he was. But when? How? When she found out, what would her reaction be?

Impatiently he turned away from the rain-streaked window and slammed his highball glass down on the tacky table. It came with the drab, furnished apartment he hoped he was living in only temporarily.

He knew what her reaction would be when he told her. Fury. Contempt. Hate. Those weren't the emotions he wanted to see burning in her brown eyes when she looked at him.

Going into the bedroom, he stripped. The purple scars that meandered and crisscrossed down his left side were no more than he deserved, he thought with self-loathing. He deserved to be placed on the rack for not having identified himself to her when they had met.

But would he tell her the next time he saw her?

No. What good was making promises in the dark that he knew he wouldn't keep? He wasn't going to tell her. Not yet. Not until…

Lying in bed alone, he watched the rain splatter silver patterns on the windows. He thought about her. About the kiss.

"Oh, God, the kiss," he groaned.

She had such a delectable mouth. Warm and wet and silky. Beyond the restraint she had exercised, he knew there lurked a simmering passion.

You know how I've always loved rain. It's raining today, one of those relentless, steady downpours when it looks like the sun has deserted and forgotten us. I'm not enjoying it. I'm depressed. The raindrops aren't happy, sparkling drops that dance as they splash in puddles. But leaden, ominous things that would weigh me down like chain mail if they fell on me.

I've figured out the difference. Rain is something that must be shared. There's nothing cozier than seeking shelter from the rain with someone you love. But there's nothing lonelier than having to endure it alone.

As Trevor recalled that particular letter, he laid his hand on his body and moaned softly. Still tasting the kiss, he whispered to the shadows, "If you were here with me, Kyla, I'd share the rain with you. I'd share everything."

"But that's crazy!"

"I don't want to discuss it, Babs."

"Because you know you're wrong. Because you know you're just being pigheaded."

"It's not pigheadedness," Kyla averred. "It's common sense."

They were washing the breakfast dishes. Kyla's friend was as transparent as the plastic wrap covering the leftover biscuits. Her early appearance for Sunday morning breakfast was unprecedented. As soon as she had cleared the back door she had begun grilling Kyla about her date with Trevor.

"I can't believe you won't go out with him again."

"Believe it."

"Why won't you?"

"That's my business."

"And you're my best friend, so I'm making it mine."

Kyla draped the dish towel over the rack and turned to face Babs. "Leave it, Babs. Don't you have enough drama in your own life to keep you occupied? Must you meddle in mine?" She left the kitchen and headed for the stairs. Babs was right behind her.

"My love life doesn't need help. Yours is at a crisis point."

Kyla halted on the step and whirled around. "We're not talking about a 'love life.' I don't have one."

"Precisely my point."

"And," Kyla stressed, "I don't want one."

"All right. Delete 'love' and insert 'sex.' Let's talk about your sex life."

Kyla resumed her trip upstairs. "That's disgusting."

Babs grabbed her arm to detain her. "Disgusting? *Disgusting?* Since when is a healthy sex life disgusting? You used to have one."

"That's right," Kyla said, yanking her arm free. "With a man I loved, my husband, who loved and respected me. That's as it should be." Tears stung her eyes and she dashed up the remaining stairs before Babs could see them fall.

The Powerses had already left for Sunday school. Kyla was to join them in time for the worship service. They had taken Aaron with them.

When Babs entered Kyla's bedroom, the latter was shrugging off her robe. She took a dress from her closet and stepped into it. Somewhat subdued, Babs sat down on the edge of the bed.

"Ideally that's the way it should be," she acknowledged sulkily. "But we're not all that lucky, Ky. We take what we can get."

"I don't. What I had was perfect. I don't want anything less."

"Well, hell, look at him! Trevor Rule is just about as perfect as you can get."

Just the sound of his name caused Kyla's hand to tremble

as she tried to secure an earring in her ear. It wasn't taking much to rattle her today, not after the tearful night she had spent. Seeing Richard's picture on her bedside table had reminded her of her betrayal. She had vowed to keep him alive in her heart. Spending time with Trevor Rule, she had discovered, jeopardized her resolve to hold to that pledge.

To counter Babs's argument she said, "How do I know he's so perfect? I don't know anything about him. I only met him a week ago."

"You know how good he looks. You know that he's considerate, that he drives a nice—if rather boring—car, that he's ambitious, that he's kind to senior citizens and children, that he—"

"All right, I get the point. Besides the fact that he's good-looking, you could be describing thirty other men. I don't want to marry any of them, either."

"Who said anything about marriage?" Babs cried. "I'm talking about having fun. Going out." She glanced up at Kyla slyly, "Going to bed."

The kiss, the kiss, the kiss. Damn that intimate and evocative kiss. Why had she permitted it? Why couldn't she forget it? Why had it been so good?

"Don't be silly." Shakily she stuffed tissues into her handbag. Aaron invariably came out of the church nursery with sticky hands. "I don't even think about that anymore."

"Liar." Kyla's head swiveled around. "You might not consciously think about it, dear heart, but you think about it. Ky, you can't just cast off your own sexuality because somebody else dies. You don't dispose of it like a pair of socks that don't fit anymore. It's a part of you and you're going to have to come to terms with it."

"I already have."

"I don't think so."

"What makes you say that?"

"Because you've put on earrings that don't match."

Incredulous, Kyla checked the mirror. Babs was right. Aggravated, she began making the switch. "That doesn't prove anything."

Babs came off the bed and approached her friend. "I know you loved Richard. I'm not trying to talk you into forgetting him."

"I never will."

"I know that," Babs conceded with her kindest tone of the morning. "But he's dead, Ky. You're alive. And being alive is not a sin."

As though refuting her friend's words, Kyla said, "I'm going to be late for church."

At the front door Babs caught up with her. "Will you or not?"

"Will I what?" Kyla asked as she checked her hair one last time in the foyer mirror.

"Go out with him again?"

"No. End of discussion."

Babs pointed her finger at Kyla and glared at her with narrowed eyes. "You had a good time," she accused. "Damn it, I *know* you did."

Too good a time, Kyle thought. "I did him a favor to pay back one. Now we're even. Besides," she added as she pushed open the screen door, "he probably won't even ask me out again."

He did. On Thursday of that week. She hadn't seen or heard from him until the telephone rang in Petal Pushers. Since Babs was busy with a customer, Kyla answered.

"Petal Pushers."

"Kyla? Hi."

"Hello."

"This is Trevor."

As if he needed to identify himself. She had recognized his voice immediately. At the sound of it, a delicious weakness had spilled through her.

"How are you?" she asked, wishing her voice didn't sound so breathless.

"I'm all right. You?"

"Fine. Busy. I've hardly had time to think this week. The days have flown by." She didn't want him to think she had been sitting by the telephone waiting for a call from him. Why she felt it was necessary to play these courtship games, she didn't know.

"How's Aaron?"

"Cranky. I thinks he's cutting another tooth."

A deep rich laugh filled her ear before he said, "Then he has a right to be cranky."

She twisted the telephone cord through nervous fingers. Should she thank him again for Saturday night? No, that would remind him of their date. And of the kiss.

"The reason I'm calling..."

"Yes?"

"It's short notice, I know, but the Haskells... You remember Ted and Lynn?"

"Sure."

"Well, they asked me over for dinner tomorrow night. Steaks out on the patio. Would you like to go with me?"

"I don't think I can."

"Lynn suggested it," he rushed to say. "What I mean is, she asked if I'd like to bring someone and when I mentioned your name, she was glad. Seems you two hit it off."

"Yes, we did. I liked her very much. But Friday night is a problem. Aaron—"

"He's invited, too. Lynn said they have a wading pool. She thought all the kids—they have two, you know—could play in the pool." He laughed again and Kyla realized how much she was coming to like that rumbling bass sound. "We know how much Aaron likes water."

"I don't know, Trevor."

"Please."

Kyla gnawed the inside of her jaw in indecision. Should she accept? No. Because she didn't want to give him the wrong impression. On the other hand, how could he jump to the wrong conclusion if her baby was invited along? It didn't sound like an evening that would lend itself to romance. And wouldn't it be ungracious not to accept the Haskells' invitation? She really had liked the friendly couple. One could never cultivate enough friendships with bankers. As a businesswoman, having this contact might prove to be helpful later on. She and Babs might want to expand some day and need a business loan.

Good Lord, whom was she trying to convince?

The fact was that she wanted to go if only to prove that last Saturday night, and especially the kiss, had meant nothing. Trevor was new in town and didn't know many people. He wanted her company. That was all it amounted to.

Blame all her magnified erotic memories of the kiss on Babs, who had recently been taking her to movies redolent with skin, sweat and steam. Blame it on the fact that she hadn't felt the touch of a man's mouth on hers in almost two years.

It hadn't meant *anything*. So why make a big deal of it? Why not just go out and enjoy the Haskells' hospitality?

"That sounds like fun, Trevor. Thank you for inviting me…us. Aaron and I will be glad to go. What time?"

★ ★ ★

"Seven o'clock on the dot."

"Actually the digital clock says six fifty-eight, but we're ready."

Kyla stepped aside and Trevor walked through the screened front door. Between the times she saw him, she forgot just how tall he was. Or did he only seem so because he was so muscular? Impressive biceps bunched beneath the short sleeves of his white polo shirt. The casual tan slacks would have elicited a comment about his buns from Babs, had she been there to see him.

"Are your folks around?"

"No. They said to tell you hello. On most Friday nights they meet with friends for catfish and dominoes. They alternate houses."

"Is that the reason you hesitated to accept my invitation tonight?"

One of them, Kyla thought. A minor reason. "Yes. Baby-sitters are hard to come by. By the time they're old enough to trust, they're thinking of nothing but boys."

"Did you?"

"What? Think of boys? Of course," she said, throwing her head back and laughing softly. He liked the way her hair swirled around her shoulders. "With a friend like Babs I had no choice. All through high school we were degenerately boy crazy."

"I see you two degenerates have been working on your tans."

The white sundress showed it off. She had hesitated to wear it because it left her shoulders and most of her back bare, save for a network of straps. After her shower, she had smoothed on a lotion that gave her tanned skin a glowing patina. She had added to the luster by dusting her shoulders with a body powder that had a sheen to it. Her nose and cheekbones had been dabbed with the puff, too. With her sun-lightened hair, she looked summery and golden.

"In the afternoons," she answered, self-consciously aware of Trevor's green gaze moving over her. "There's enough sun left when I get home to get in a half hour's worth."

"It looks great." His voice sounded a bit hoarse. Just the way he had sounded before he kissed her.

She moved away quickly. "Aaron is upstairs."

"Let me help you bring him down."

"Don't bother."

"Four hands are better than two," he said as he followed her up the stairs. "Where Aaron's concerned, I'm not even sure that's enough."

When they came into the nursery, Aaron was standing up in his crib. At his first sight of Trevor, he pointed his index finger, began to bounce up and down against the rails of his baby bed and babbled something that only he could understand.

"I think he recognizes me," Trevor said, pleased. He lifted the boy out of the bed and swung him high over his head. "Hiya, Scout. Have you been a positive terror this week? Eaten any more carnations?"

It was while he was holding the baby over his head that Kyla noticed the scar on Trevor's left arm. It started at his wrist, twisted around his elbow and disappeared into the sleeve of his shirt. When Trevor turned, laughing, to address something to her, he saw where she was looking.

He sobered instantly. "I told you it was ugly."

Her eyes swung up to his face. "You must have suffered terribly."

He shrugged. "Not so much. Ready?"

He carried Aaron while she toted the diaper bag. He had

looked at it dubiously when she hoisted it onto her shoulder. "I know. It looks like we're moving," she said, laughing, "but I've learned to go prepared and I'm sure Lynn will understand."

He helped her secure the house. "We'll have to transfer Aaron's car seat from your car to mine," Trevor remarked as they stepped off the porch.

"How far are we going? He can sit in my lap."

"Uh-uh. Let's do this right."

"Will you at least compromise and take my car?"

"Will you let me drive?"

She smiled up at him and dropped the keys into his free hand. "How's the house coming?" she asked him once Aaron had been secured in his car seat and they were driving through the twilit streets.

Trevor had had to push the front seat back to accommodate his long legs. He drove as he had before, with his left wrist draped idly over the steering wheel. Only this time he stretched his right arm across the back of the front seat. His fingers were close to, but not quite touching, her left shoulder.

"Great. Your idea about the dining area in the kitchen was terrific. Even the architect liked it and was miffed that he hadn't thought of it himself."

"It's such a lovely lot. It would be a shame not to enjoy those trees to the utmost."

"That's why I chose to build there."

...that a house without a tree is nothing. I'd rather live in a tree house like the Swiss Family Robinson, than in a palace that was surrounded by nothing but concrete.

Ted and Lynn Haskell had equally effervescent personalities. Kyla and Aaron, over whom they made much ado, were welcomed into the noisy chaos of a happy home. Not that their house wasn't lovely. It was. Kyla even felt a mild envy for the gracious rooms that Lynn led her through on the tour that Kyla had requested.

The couple had produced two children as handsome and congenial as themselves. The eldest, a girl of seven, bossily took Aaron under her wing and kept him entertained while the men supervised the grilling of the steaks out on the patio. Lynn was unself-conscious enough to accept Kyla's offer to help in the kitchen.

"Trevor told us that you're a widow."

Kyla's hands paused as she tore at the iceberg lettuce. Had he been talking about her? Apparently Lynn sensed her tension. "I'm no gossip, Kyla. Neither is Trevor. I asked. He told me, but he didn't elaborate. If it makes you uncomfortable, we can talk about something else."

Trevor couldn't have elaborated because he didn't know the facts about Richard's death. Curious, that he had never asked. She glanced at Lynn. "Richard died the day after Aaron was born."

"My God," Lynn said, setting down the bowl of potato salad she'd just taken from the refrigerator. "What happened?"

Kyla related the story. "It hasn't been quite two years yet."

Lynn looked out over the patio where the men were sipping at beers while they tended both the steaks and the children who were splashing in the wading pool. As she watched, Aaron bent at the waist and ducked his head into the water. Apparently he got more than he bargained for. He came up sputtering. Instantly Trevor was kneeling beside the pool, wiping the boy's face with a towel and thumping him on the back. "Trevor and Aaron seemed to have formed quite an attachment. When did you start seeing him?"

"Only a week or so ago. We're only friends. What dressing do you want on the salad?" When Kyla turned around, Lynn was looking at her with an amused expression. "What is it?"

Lynn laughed. "Only that if everything Ted says about Trevor Rule is true, you'd better be careful."

"Why? What does Ted say?"

"That Trevor is ambitious, that he knows no fear, that he's daring in business ventures and that so far they have all paid off. In other words, he usually gets what he goes after." She smiled and sent a wicked grin in Kyla's direction. "If the attention he paid you the other night at the banquet is any indication, I'd say the man's after you. Unless you want to be caught, you'd better run fast." After taking two cans of beer from the refrigerator, she passed one to Kyla. "Come on. I think they can use another."

Trevor had lifted Aaron out of the pool, then had crouched down and placed him between his knees. He was drying the child briskly with a towel, as though it were something he did every day. Kyla popped the top off the beer and handed it down to him.

"I'll take over when you want me to."

Trevor looked up at her with a heart-stopping smile. He sipped the beer and licked the foam off his mustache. "We're doing fine, but thanks for the beer."

"You're welcome." Flustered, she turned away in time to see Ted accepting his fresh beer from his wife. He said, "Thanks, hon," and swatted her bottom. His hand stayed and squeezed her playfully before falling away. Lynn bent down and planted a soft kiss on the crown of Ted's thinning hair.

Kyla felt a loneliness more encompassing than any she had experienced before.

★ ★ ★

"The house is dark," Trevor commented as he drove Kyla's car into the driveway.

"I guess Mom and Dad are still out." It was odd that they were out this late. Usually the domino parties didn't last much past eleven and it was almost midnight. She strongly suspected that their delay in coming home was calculated.

"Ted and I should have challenged you and Lynn to a rematch."

"Men will never beat women at word games."

"How's that?"

"Women are more intuitive than men."

"Well, my intuition is that Aaron's become deadweight on your shoulder."

"This time your intuition is right."

Aaron, who had fallen asleep on the Haskells' living room sofa, hadn't taken kindly to being roused for the ride home. To prevent a tantrum to rival any recorded in history, Trevor had broken his own safety rule and let him ride in Kyla's lap rather than being strapped into his car seat.

Trevor got out of the car and came around to assist Kyla. "Is your key in your purse?" he asked.

"The side pocket."

He had found the key by the time they reached the front door. Juggling the key, her handbag and the heavy diaper bag, he barely managed to unlock the door and swing it open.

"Thank you, Trevor. I had a good time."

"I'll see you in. I wouldn't let you and Aaron go into an empty house alone this late at night."

There seemed no point in arguing, though it made her distinctly uncomfortable to have him precede her through the dark house and upstairs. He had already switched on the soft lamp on top of the bureau by the time Kyla reached Aaron's room. She lowered the sleeping toddler into the baby bed.

"Can you undress him without waking him up?"

"I think I'll let him sleep in his shirt. I'm afraid if he wakes up fully, he'll think it's time for breakfast."

Trevor chuckled as he set the diaper bag in the rocker near the bed. He watched, fascinated, as her capable fingers moved swiftly to remove Aaron's shoes and socks.

Without waking him, she peeled down his shorts and plastic pants. Automatically she reached for the adhesive tabs that held on his disposable diaper. There her hands stilled.

She became acutely aware of the man standing beside her. The room seemed to shrink, leaving barely enough room for the two of them beside the baby bed. The atmosphere became thick with tension. The air was heavy and uncomfortably warm, almost sultry. The house grew more silent.

It was silly. Ridiculous. Aaron was a baby, sexually undeveloped. But the man standing next to her *was* developed and she was embarrassed to remove Aaron's diaper with Trevor hovering so close. Looking at a naked male child would be an intimacy between them, an intimacy Kyla couldn't engage in.

Apparently he noticed that her deft fingers had suddenly become clumsy and inefficient, because he cleared his throat loudly and moved away.

Faster than she'd ever done it in her life, she changed Aaron's wet diaper. Miraculously, he didn't wake up. Trevor was standing framed in the doorway of the nursery when she turned around after covering Aaron with a light blanket and switching out the light.

"All tucked in?"

"Yes. He had a big night. I think I'll get him one of those wading pools."

She led the way downstairs. There was a tightness in her chest she couldn't account for. Her stomach was fluttering. She felt an insane impulse to talk loudly so that the encroaching silence in the dark house wouldn't smother them.

One of the stairs took Trevor's weight and groaned in protest. He laughed softly and spoke in a hushed tone. "You've got a squeaky step."

"Several, I'm afraid." She sighed as she was reminded of a problem that was never too far from her mind. "It was my parents' dream to sell this house when Dad retired. They wanted to buy one of those fancy motor homes and travel all over the country."

"Why didn't they?"

"Richard was killed." Trevor said nothing, though she sensed a hesitation in his stride before he took the next step down. "I became a liability to them all over again."

"I'm sure they don't see it that way."

"But I do." He had stopped following. She stopped leading and turned around to face him. He was poised several steps above her.

"Why don't they sell it now?"

"They don't want Aaron and me to live alone. Besides, the market for houses in this part of town isn't as good as it once was. Unless the neighborhood is rezoned, I'm afraid they wouldn't make much by selling."

"This worries you, doesn't it? You don't want them to feel responsible for you."

She smiled ruefully. "I'm just sorry they aren't able to realize their dream because of me."

They looked at each other. Silence fell like a final curtain. Even though Trevor had turned on a light in the foyer, the remainder of the house was shadowed and dark.

One side of his face was lit, the right side. She could sense the leashed tension in his body, though they weren't touching. His wavy black hair cast errant shadows over his face. Lean and dark and intense, he looked like the brooding hero of a Gothic novel. He posed no physical threat, but was dangerous just the same. What should have been sinister was scintillating.

He made her tremble.

"I'll let you out," she said hastily, breathlessly, and turned away.

She took only one more step down the stairs before she felt his fingers in her hair, reaching, closing into a fist that caught and captured. A small whimpering sound issued from her throat, but she was helpless. The fist closed tighter around the handful of hair. It rotated once, making his hold more tenacious. Then a steady, unrelenting pull gradually drew her head back, back, until she turned on the step.

With his other arm he lifted her up even as his head descended. He stamped his mouth over hers, hard and unyielding. He didn't step down to bring them together, but hauled her up instead and drew her against him.

Her hands made futile attempts to push him away, but his chest was like a brick wall. Her heart thrummed, echoing loudly in her head. Or was that his heart? She knew nothing but the prickle of his mustache and the firm pressure of his lips against hers.

When he angrily lifted his head, she gasped, "No, Trevor, please."

"Open your mouth."

"No."

"Kiss me."

"I can't."

"Yes you can."

"No, please."

"What are you afraid of?"

"I'm not afraid."

"Then kiss me. You know you want to."

His mouth claimed hers once again. This time it brooked no resistance. It slanted and moved. His lips parted. Hers, obeying a will more powerful then her own, responded. Then his tongue was there, seeking and finding hers as it had once before. He tasted her thoroughly, until they fell apart gasping for breath.

Hotly, he pressed his open mouth against the arch of her throat.

"No, no," she said, not even recognizing that panting voice as her own.

"I can't believe I'm kissing you."

"Please don't."

"And that you're kissing me back."

"No, I'm not."

"Oh, but you are, love."

His mouth brushed the skin of her throat with light airy kisses, pausing to plant heated ones at its sensitive base. "Your skin, oh, God, your skin." His hand was caressing her bare back. His fingers slipped between the straps of her dress and pressed her closer to him. Against her stomach she could feel what she told herself was his belt buckle.

Nonetheless she clung to him. At that moment he was the only reality left in the world. Not even remembering how they had gotten there, she discovered her fingers embedded in the thick strands of his hair. Again, her mouth was behaving wantonly beneath his.

"Is it even possible that you could want me?"

"Trevor."

"Because I want you."

Alarmed, she tore her mouth free of his scalding kisses. "No, don't even think—"

He cupped her face between his hands. "Not just sex, Kyla. I want more than sex. I know this is sudden, but I've fallen in love with you."

Huntsville, Alabama

They had bought a house for their fifth wedding anniversary, and it was moving day. The house was a mess. Boxes were stacked everywhere.

"How could we have accumulated so much junk? Did you finish cleaning out the attic?"

When the accountant's wife got no answer to either question, she turned her head to see what had her husband so preoccupied. He was looking through a stack of snapshots, studying each one intently. "What's that, honey?"

"Hmm? Oh, some pictures I took in Cairo."

She shivered and moved toward him. Closing her arms around his shoulders from behind, she leaned down and looked at the pictures over his shoulder. "Every time I think about how close I came to losing you, I shudder. How many days between the time you went on leave and the terrorist bombing?"

"Three," he said grimly.

"Who's that with you?" she asked softly, looking down at the picture he now held. She knew he often thought about the men who had served on guard duty with him at the embassy, especially those who had died.

"The one on the left was Richard Stroud."

"Was?"

"He didn't make it."

"And the other one?"

Her husband smiled. "That handsome devil is Trevor

Rule. A Harvard man. Distinguished Philadelphia family. He was a hell-raiser though. We called him Smooch."

She laughed. "No need to ask why. I can see where he might come by his reputation."

"He had a harem a sultan would envy."

"Did he survive?"

"He was rescued, but was severely injured. I don't know if he survived it or not."

"Will you save the picture?"

"Think I should?"

"Was Stroud married?"

"Yes. Why?"

"If the picture isn't that important to you, why don't you send it to his widow? She'd probably like to have it. You all look so happy, like you're having a good time."

"Smooch had just told one of his famous dirty jokes." He leaned back and kissed her. "Good idea. I'll send it to Stroud's widow. If I can track her down."

He tossed the picture into the box of keepsakes they would move to their new house.

Chapter 7

Sudden?

Sudden? Is that what he had said? "I know this is sudden, but I've fallen in love with you." "Sudden" hardly captured the earth-shattering essence of the statement. The following morning, as Kyla thought back on the scene, she still couldn't believe he had said that.

She had thanked heaven that her parents had walked through the front door only heartbeats later. Having been struck mute and paralyzed by what Trevor had just said, she had made a valiant effort at conversation, explaining that they had just gotten in and put Aaron to bed, and no, her parents weren't interrupting anything.

Trevor, while being polite to her parents, had stared down at her with that single green eye that more than compensated for the lost one. Avoiding his stare as best she could, she had escorted him to the front door and said a perfunctory goodnight before Clif and Meg could go upstairs and leave her alone with him again. Even as she closed the door on him, he had stood his ground, staring down at her. It was then that she had vowed never to see him again.

Now, in the light of day, now, with the memory of last night's kiss still burning in her brain, she repeated that promise to herself. "I can't, I won't, see him again."

But it wasn't going to be that easy. He called during breakfast.

"Kyla," he said as soon as she answered the phone, "I'm sorry it's so early, but I have to talk to you. Last night—"

"I can't talk right now, Trevor. I'm in the middle of feeding Aaron his breakfast and he's making a mess of it."

"Will the two of you have lunch with me? You and Aaron?"

"Thank you anyway, but we can't. Dad and I are going to paint my old swing set today."

"When? I'll come by and help."

"No, no, don't do that," she said hastily. "I don't know exactly when we'll be working on it and I can't let you tie up your entire day."

"I don't mind. I want—"

"I've got to go, Trevor. Goodbye."

He came by anyway late that afternoon. She feigned a headache and didn't even come downstairs to say hello. Her parents looked at her disapprovingly once Trevor had left, but they said nothing.

Babs had no such qualms about offering her opinion. Kyla had ignored her less than subtle disparaging looks and grunts. By the end of the week she had become considerably more vocal. The two friends squared off during a lull in business. "The guy has called here several times a day for the past five days."

"That's his problem."

"It's my problem, too. I've run out of excuses as to why you can't come to the telephone."

"With your imagination, Babs, I'm sure you'll invent others. *If* he calls again."

"He will. He's not nearly the coward you are."

Kyla rounded on her. "I am not a coward."

"No? Then why are you going to so much trouble to avoid him? What did he do, something despicable like try to hold your hand?"

"I can do without your sarcasm."

"Want to know what I think?"

"No."

"I think that it was more than hand-holding."

Kyla turned away so that Babs wouldn't see the color flaring in her cheeks. "As I said, you have a vivid imagination."

"Otherwise you wouldn't be running so fast and so hard. If Trevor Rule hadn't gotten to you in some way, you'd be laughing off his attempts to see you."

"They're not funny."

"That's my point. This is damned serious."

"It is not!"

Into that scene, already crackling with tension, stepped the subject of their dispute. The bell over the door of Petal Pushers jangled musically as Trevor came in. Simultaneously the two women turned their heads in that direction. He was looking at only one, the one whose face suddenly lost its high color, the one who nervously ran her tongue over her lower lip, the one who clasped her hands together at her waist in order to keep from flying apart.

"Excuse me," Babs said. She sashayed through the swinging louvered doors into the back room, mumbling something about Mohammed and mountains under her breath.

Kyla stared at the floor that spanned the distance between

them. Maybe he had come to order flowers. Maybe he had come to discuss the weather. Maybe he had come for any reason but the one she dreaded most.

His opening line instantly dispelled her hopes.

"Why are you avoiding me?"

All right, he wanted to play rough. She'd be rough. Her head snapped up proudly and she met his gaze. "Why do you think?"

"Because of what I said last Friday night?"

"Good guess."

"Did it offend you?"

"Tossing the word *love* around like that is offensive."

"I wasn't tossing the word around. I meant it."

"I find that impossible to believe."

"Why?"

She stared at him, aghast. "*Why?* Because we had seen each other exactly four times before you told me you loved me."

"You were keeping count?" Teasingly, his mustache curved above those sparkling white teeth into a lazy smile.

"Only because what you said was so outlandish." Damn his smile and damn his mustache and damn her stomach for doing cartwheels at the sight of them.

"It happens that way sometimes."

"Not to me."

"But to me. I'm in love with you, Kyla."

She turned her back on him and braced herself against the countertop with stiff arms. "Stop saying that. Please."

He moved up behind her. She felt him there even before he placed his hands on her shoulders. His warmth crept over her back the way the sun glides over the beach at dawn.

"What are you afraid of, Kyla?"

"Nothing."

"Me?"

"No."

"Are you afraid of what you're feeling?"

"I'm not feeling anything."

"You're feeling something." He moved her hair aside and trailed his fingers from one side of her nape to the other. "You kissed me back."

Her head fell forward until her chin was almost touching her chest. "It didn't mean anything."

"Didn't it?"

"Only that I hadn't been kissed in a long time."

"And it felt good?"

"Yes… No… Please. I can't talk about this with you."

"It felt good to me, Kyla. So damn good. And right."

She turned to face him, wedging herself between him and the counter. "But it wasn't right, Trevor," she said with emphasis.

"Tell me why."

"Because I love my husband."

"But he's dead!"

"In here he isn't!" she cried angrily, laying a hand over her heart. "He's alive inside me. And I intend to keep him alive."

"That's crazy. It's unnatural."

"And also no business of yours, Mr. Rule!"

She shoved him aside and moved away. When she faced him again, her breasts rose and fell in agitation. Breathing didn't come easily. "I haven't led you on. I've been fair. I told you the second day we met that I wasn't looking for a romance. I had one. A wonderful love affair that will last me the rest of my life. Nothing could top it and I would never settle for anything less."

Impatiently she dashed the tears out of her eyes with the

back of her hand. "In spite of my making that clear to you, you came on to me. I'm sorry if you fancy yourself in love with me, but that's something you'll have to come to grips with. I don't want to see you again, Trevor. Now just please leave me alone."

His jaw was rigid. The muscles along it were flexing with anger. Beneath his mustache his lips had narrowed into a tight, thin line. His hands were balled into fists and tapped his thighs. Kyla couldn't tell if he wanted to strike her or kiss her, and didn't know which to fear most.

Finally, he pivoted on his boot heels and strode out the door, letting it slam closed behind him. The bell over the door made a terrible racket.

Kyla slumped against the counter, not realizing until then just how physically taxing the encounter had been. Every muscle in her body felt as though it had been wrung out like a dishcloth. There was an excruciating piercing pain between her eyes.

When she had regained a modicum of composure, she pushed herself away from the counter and turned to find Babs standing in the doorway, her arms folded over her breasts, a sour expression on her face.

"Don't say a word," Kyla warned, meaning it.

"I wouldn't think of it," Babs said airly. "You said all that need be said and quite brilliantly, I thought. Any other man would probably turn tail and flee. But not our Mr. Rule. Not by a long shot."

"Damn it!"

His foot punished the brake of his pickup truck as he whipped it off the road onto the gravel shoulder. Rocks sprayed out from beneath the wheels and clouds of dust engulfed the truck before it came to a complete stop. Trevor shoved it into Park and folded his arms over the steering wheel. He laid his forehead on his hands.

"Well, what did you expect?"

Had he really thought that he could waltz into her life and, without too much time and effort, have her fall into his arms? Into his bed?

Yes, he admitted now. That's what he had subconsciously expected. Because to George Rule's son things had always come easy.

Sports. Leadership. Studies. Popularity. Women.

To Trevor, life had been a banquet spread out on silver platters. He had even successfully thwarted his father's plans for his life. He was doing what he had always wanted to do. Except for that setback in Cairo, he had led a charmed life. Even then his good fortune had not deserted him. The bombing had left him impaired, but not totally incapacitated as it could have.

Raising his head, Trevor propped his chin on his hands and stared through the dusty windshield. The north Texas plains extended to the horizon in every direction. A barbed wire fence stretched endlessly.

Was that where his life was going? Nowhere?

Kyla's rejection was a bitter pill to swallow. Was this gnawing emptiness inside his gut only the reaction of a spoiled man to whom life had been abundantly sweet until now? Was he to be denied the only thing that was truly important? Were the gods mocking him, laughing at him because he had made one honorable gesture in his life and was to be denied the privilege of carrying it through?

But it was more than that. Honor and duty had little or nothing to do with his behavior toward Kyla now.

He loved the woman.

No longer was she just words written on sheets of inexpensive stationery, words that had filled lonely hours, and alleviated pain, and given him an anchor to hold on to when things had looked their bleakest.

She was a personality. A voice. A scent. A smile.

"And she still loves her husband," he reminded himself grimly.

Richard Stroud had been a terrific guy. Now he was a terrific ghost. And ghosts had a way of making themselves more terrific than the person they had been. One forgot the faults of those departed and remembered only their finer qualities.

But Richard Stroud wasn't his enemy and he mustn't think of him in those terms. Maybe he should give up this whole crazy idea. She loved her husband's memory. She had made her feelings known in plain, understandable English.

Give up while you're ahead, ol' boy. She doesn't want you.

Then he remembered the passion of her kiss, the taste of her mouth, the scent of her hair, the feel of her skin beneath his hands, and knew he wasn't about to give up.

"Not yet." Each precise motion indicated his resolve as he engaged the gears of his pickup and pulled it back onto the country road.

He would give her space, breathing room, time. She was entitled to it.

In the meantime, his days would be busy. He had a lot to do. And at night, in his bed, when his body ached for the appeasement hers promised, he would content himself by reading her letters. They were like her voice whispering her innermost secrets to him in the dark.

"What's all that, Dad?" Kyla asked as she entered the kitchen.

"This, oh, this is nothing," Clif Powers said quickly and began gathering up the papers scattered over the table.

"It's *something*." She hadn't missed her father's haste in removing the documents from her sight, nor the covert glance that passed between her parents. Their expressions were as guilty as Aaron's when she had caught him uprooting her favorite ivy.

Placing her hands on her hips, she said, "All right, you two, confess. What gives?"

"Sit down and have a cold drink, why don't you, dear?" Meg suggested.

"I don't want a cold drink. I want to know what it is the two of you are trying so hard to hide."

Clif sighed. "We might as well tell her, Meg."

Kyla sat down in a chair across the table from her father and folded her arms over the laminated tablecloth. "I'm listening."

"The city council was petitioned for this street to be rezoned as commercial property. We, your mother and I, contested it, but none of the other home owners did. The petition passed in a vote of the council last night."

Kyla assimilated that, for the moment thinking only of what this would mean to her parents' future. "Why did you contest it? Won't that escalate the value of your property?"

"Well, yes, dear, but we don't want to leave this house," Meg said. "Not that they're rushing us. We have a while, but…"

"You don't want to leave because of Aaron and me," Kyla said softly, realizing the reason for their secrecy. "We'll manage. I've always told you that."

"We know, but we never wanted to sell the place out from under you."

"Well it seems that the city council has taken the decision from you. I'm glad. This is what you wanted, to sell the house, buy a motor home and travel."

"But you and Aaron—"

"I'm a grown woman, Mom. Aaron is a well-adjusted child. We'll get a home of our own. It will be good for both of us."

"But we promised you when Richard died that we would never leave you alone," Clif argued.

Kyla reached out to cover his hand. "I appreciate your concern, Dad. You've been wonderful. But you and Mom have your own lives. You've earned these years together. You shouldn't spend your retirement shackled to me." She glanced down at the folded documents. "You've already had an offer to buy the property, haven't you?"

"Well, yes," Clif finally admitted. "But we've got eighteen months to vacate. We don't have to take the first offer that comes along."

"But who knows what will happen in eighteen months?" Kyla said. "Opportunities like this don't come along every day. If this is a fair offer, accept it."

"No," Meg said, shaking her head stubbornly. "We promised you that we wouldn't desert you."

"But, Mom—"

"Until you and Aaron are settled someplace, we won't even think about selling this house. And that's final, young lady." Meg stood up. The discussion was closed. "Do you want that cold drink or not?"

Several hours later Kyla lay in bed and stared at the changing patterns of shadow the moonlight cast on the ceiling of her room.

She was worried about her parents' reluctance to sell the house. The sale would insure them financial security for the rest of their lives. She didn't want them to put it off until they were too old and feeble to enjoy their retirement.

It was for her sake that they hesitated to jump at this

chance. Didn't they realize how guilty their sacrifice made her feel? They had already postponed fulfilling their dream for almost two years, as a result of Richard's death. Granted, she would miss them. She would be sad to see the old house razed to make way for office complexes and filling stations. But growing pains always hurt.

It was time she experienced some of her own. Whether her parents sold the house or not, wasn't it time she made a home for Aaron and herself? How to convince Clif and Meg of that was the problem.

With a tired sigh, she forced her eyes to close.

And it happened again.

Trevor Rule's image was projected onto her eyelids. For hours each night, until she finally fell into a frustrated, exhausted sleep, he haunted her. It was as though he were communicating with her on some spiritual plane that she had no understanding of. Her obsession with him was irritating and unnerving.

It had been a month since their showdown in Petal Pushers. She wished she could forget how angry he had looked then. She wished even harder she could forget how he had looked last week when she had accidentally crossed paths with him.

It had been during the heat of the day. She and Babs were making a delivery in downtown Chandler. It had been an order large enough to require both of them, so Clif had volunteered to watch the shop while they were gone.

"Look at that," Babs had said.

"What?" The potted mums had leaked water on Kyla's hands and she was busy shaking them dry.

"Across the street. Yum-*my!*"

Using one damp hand to shade her eyes from the glaring sun, she followed Babs's gaze to the hardware store across the street. Trevor was stepping off the curb into the street where his pickup was parked. He was carrying a bag of concrete mix on his shoulder. As they watched, he swung it down into the bed of the pickup. From that distance, one would never guess he'd been in a terrible accident and had the scars to prove it. He had executed the chore with the strength and grace of an Olympic discus thrower.

Babs smacked her lips. "May the good Lord strike me blind if he's not gorgeous."

"Don't—"

"Hello, Trevor!" Babs sang out.

Gasping in outrage and mortification, Kyla turned her back and opened the car door. She scrambled in and slammed the door behind her. "I'm going to murder you," she whispered to Babs through the open window.

"If you act like an idiot, I'm going to murder *you*," Babs retorted.

Trevor had spotted them instantly and waved. While he was waiting for a car to pass, he took off the slouchy, straw cowboy hat that was shading his head and wiped his perspiring forehead on his rolled-up sleeve. He started toward them before the oncoming car had completely passed, even going so far as to step around its rear. He jogged the remainder of the distance across the street.

"Hi."

God was cruel. No man should have that much sex appeal and be left to run around loose, making a hapless victim of any woman he met.

He combed his fingers through his thick, black hair, pushing back the sweat-waved strands before pulling the cowboy hat back on. With the eye patch, he looked rakish and daring and piratical.

His throat was darkly tanned. At its base lay a rolled and

knotted white bandanna. His sleeves had been rolled up so far and so tight that they looked like ropes encircling the teak biceps. The blue work shirt had been left unbuttoned. Kyla envisioned him working shirtless until it was time to drive into town and then pulling on the shirt in haste. Because of the heat, he hadn't felt inclined to button it.

In any event, the long shirttails flapped against his thighs, and his chest was left bare, save for the carpet of dark, damp curly hair that covered it. And covered it beautifully, from the fan-shaped cloud that blanketed the curving muscles of his breasts and swirled around the flat nipples, to that slender, silky line that divided his corrugated stomach and eventually flared around his navel. His chest was magnificent, marred only by an arcing scar that curved under his left breast from beneath his arm.

His jeans had that snug fit and softly faded look that no less than a thousand washings can give them. He wasn't wearing a pair of shiny lizard boots this time, but a pair that had been abused by seas of mud. A pair of worn leather work gloves covered his hands and curled back over his wrist bones.

Most stirring of all was the wide leather carpenter's belt that was strapped across his lean hips. It rested there like a gunslinger's holster and symbolized masculinity just as flagrantly. The building tools dangled against his trim thighs, rubbing against the muscles with every supple movement they made.

He was a living, breathing fantasy, masculinity incarnate.

"What brings you out? It's hot as the dickens."

Babs laughed. "You're even beginning to sound like a Texan. Isn't he, Ky?"

Kyla, inside the sweltering car, sat as rigid and wooden as a mannequin. "Yes, he is."

He braced one forearm on the top of the car. The shirt

gaped open wider. Some of the springy hairs on his chest were beaded with sweat. He ducked his head to speak to her directly. "How are you?"

"Fine. You?"

"Fine. Aaron?"

"He's fine, too."

"Good."

"You seem to be working hard, Trevor," Babs said.

Kyla could tell by her strained tone of voice that Babs was irritated with the way the conversation was being conducted. Well, let her be! She was the one who had hailed him over like a streetwalker hollering, "Hey, sailor!" Let her chat with him.

She had thought she would be relieved when he straightened up to talk to Babs. But his doing so had left her with an unrestricted view of his torso. It fascinated her.

She watched a single bead of sweat form on the low curve of his right breast. It gathered itself there until it was a full, liquid pearl. Heavily, it detached itself. Slowly it began to roll downward. Kyla's eyes followed its undulating descent over each rib. It could have gotten lost in the soft hair that dappled his stomach, but it had too much momentum now and continued to slide over the bronzed skin. At last, it angled inward toward his navel and funneled straight into that hair-whorled dimple as though it were a chalice fashioned for such a treasure.

"Won't we, Ky?"

Kyla jumped. "What?" Babs had asked her something, but she was helpless to say what.

"I told Trevor that we'd come out to see the house he's building as soon as it was finished."

"Oh, yes, I'd like that," she said vaguely. *Don't look at him anymore. Keep your eyes on the horizon or the parking meter or anything but him.*

Right now her own body was pouring perspiration, and the midsummer heat was only partially responsible. She willed Babs to get in the car and leave.

But it was Trevor who said goodbye first. "I've got to be going. The concrete man is waiting on me. It was great seeing you."

"Bye-bye, Trevor," Babs said.

"Goodbye, Babs. Kyla."

"Bye," she answered in a thin voice.

Only when she knew he had turned his back and was almost at his truck, did she raise her eyes. Then she wished she hadn't. His shirt was plastered to his skin, stuck there by the healthy, virile sweat of a working man. The clinging cloth emphasized the breadth of his shoulders. And the jeans were as flattering to his behind as they were to his front.

Now, struggling to go to sleep more than a week later, she still saw him that way. His slight limp only accentuated the swaggering walk that never failed to make her mouth go dry.

Sighing resignedly, she turned onto her side and, surrendering to temptation, mentally followed that salty drop of perspiration down his chest again. This time her tongue followed it straight into his navel.

She woke up cranky.

Her mood didn't improve when she reached across the coffeepot on the breakfast table to answer the phone.

"Hi, it's Trevor."

She glanced quickly at her parents. The one time they had ventured to ask why Trevor didn't come around anymore, she had cut them short by saying, "I told you we were just friends. He's probably found a girlfriend." Unwilling to reveal the identity of the caller now, she simply said, "Hello."

"I got it finished."

"Finished?"

"The house."

"Oh! Congratulations."

"Thanks. Will you come see it?"

Her parents were looking at her curiously. Meg mouthed, "Who is it?" Kyla pretended not to understand the exaggerated pantomime.

"I don't know if I can," she hedged.

"You said you would," he reminded her.

"I know, but I've been awfully busy."

"Before I put it on the market, I'd like your advice on decorating."

"I'm not qualified to give you that kind of advice."

"You're a woman, aren't you?"

Yes, she was a woman. Otherwise her heart wouldn't be throwing itself against her ribs as though looking for a means of escape. Otherwise her thighs wouldn't feel like melting wax and her palms wouldn't be slippery and she wouldn't be thinking about his mouth and her breasts.

"I don't know anything about decorating a house like that."

She saw Meg's eyes slice to Clif, saw Clif's brows bob up once then slowly lower.

"Will you come anyway?"

"When?"

"This afternoon."

"This is my Saturday to work." She and Babs swapped off Saturdays.

"After work. I'll pick you up when the shop closes."

Kyla twirled the telephone cord, wondering if she dare use

Aaron as her excuse. Trevor would only tell her to bring him along. And her parents were digesting every word she said right along with their crunchy granola, so she couldn't use something involving them as a reason not to go.

What did she care how flimsy her excuse was? She had told him in no uncertain terms that she never wanted to see him again. He had a nerve even to call and ask.

But wouldn't it be rude to turn down this particular invitation? She had seen the house under construction. It was obviously important to Trevor to get it just right. His career could be riding on the success of this house. Perhaps he *did* want her opinion on suitable decor and that was the extent of it. He needed a sounding board, someone whose taste he trusted.

"All right. I'll see you at six o'clock."

"Great."

She was busy in the shop all day, but the hours seemed to crawl by. And she stayed hungry. Or was that sinking feeling inside her dread at the thought of seeing him? Or expectancy? She didn't want to know.

At exactly six o'clock, he entered the shop, looking devastating in a sport shirt and slacks. He smelled as though he had recently showered and shaved. His hair was still damp. It curled around his ears and fell over the eye patch with breath-stealing appeal.

"Got any flowers left to sell?"

She laughed, relieved that he was being friendly and treating this date with the lightness it deserved. "A few."

"Ready?"

"Let me get my purse and turn off the lights in back."

In less than a minute she was back. He escorted her out and waited for her to secure the front door. His hand was beneath her elbow as he helped her into his car, but his touch was impersonal. So far, so good.

They made light, inconsequential conversation as he drove through the streets of town, then out into the countryside toward the wooded lot and the new house. He inquired about her parents and she told him they were well. He asked about Aaron and she filled him in on his latest antics. They didn't speak of the argument that had taken place over a month ago.

"Oh, my heavens!" she exclaimed, when the house came into view. "I can't believe it."

He braked the car in the curved driveway that was lined with boxwoods. "Like it?"

"What's not to like?" Without waiting for him to assist her, she opened her door and stepped out, staring appreciatively at the house. "You didn't tell me it was going to have stained-glass windows on either side of the front door."

"You didn't ask," he replied teasingly. "Come on inside."

It was like stepping into the pages of *Architectural Digest*. The style overall was casual. The house had been designed for comfort and convenience, but no amenity had been spared. The rooms were spacious, but had a feeling of warm coziness about them.

Kyla gave a glad cry when she entered the dining area of the kitchen and saw how well her idea of the sun room had worked. "And look, a boiling water tap in the sink," Trevor said proudly, demonstrating it. "And a built-in refrigerator and freezer."

"It's perfect, perfect," Kyla said, smiling.

"You really like it?"

"It's wonderful!"

"Come outside. I want to show you the backyard."

Redwood decking extended for several yards beyond

the house to the lawn, which had already been landscaped. Clusters of azalea bushes encircled the trees, which had been shaped and pruned. Flowers of every variety bloomed in tubs placed strategically on the deck. A fern-bedecked gazebo housed a bubbling spa. In the distance, the creek shone like a silver ribbon threading itself through the leafy trees.

"I can't believe it, Trevor," she said in awe. "You've done wonders. It's beautiful. What decorating you've already done is perfect. You won't have any trouble selling this house."

He took both her hands in his and turned her to face him. Kyla was surprised. Up until that moment he had hardly touched her. He'd been jocular and funny as he had led her through the rooms of the house, showing it off with the enthusiasm of a ten-year-old with a new bike. Now he was staring at her with an intensity that set her pulse to racing.

"I've stayed away from you, as you asked me to."

"It was for the best."

He shook his head. "I stayed away, but that doesn't mean that I liked it or that I didn't think about you." Kyla swallowed. "Quite the contrary. I think about you all the time."

"Trevor, please, let's not argue."

"I don't intend to."

"Then don't say any more."

"Let me finish." When he saw that she would grant him that, he went on. "You know how I feel about you. Don't you?"

"You…You said…"

"That I love you. And I meant it, Kyla."

"Please, don't pressure me about it. I can't."

"Can't what?"

"I can't be involved in an affair."

"I know. That's why I'm asking you to marry me."

Chapter 8

"May I sit down, please?"

His mustache twitched with a smile. "That shocking, huh?" He led her to an old-fashioned porch swing similar to the one on the Powers's porch. It had been attached to the rafters over the deck.

Kyla was too stunned by his proposal to comment on the swing. She'd always had a fondness for porch swings. Any other time she would have remarked on it. Now she could barely command her limbs to move.

Trevor sat down beside her, but didn't touch her. For a few minutes the only sound between them was the faint squeak of the chain as the swing rocked gently. Crickets chirped from their hideouts. Cicadas had begun their nightly concerts from the dense branches of the trees. Words and phrases flitted through Kyla's head like fireflies, but they blinked and burned out before she could vocalize them.

"I don't know what to say."

"Say yes."

She looked at him through the gathering dusk. "Trevor, where did you get the idea that I wanted to marry you? To marry anybody?"

"I got no such idea. You've made it clear on several occasions that you aren't in the market for a husband."

"Then why did you ask me to marry you?"

"Because I love you and want to be your husband. I want to take care of you and Aaron, be a father to him."

"But that's crazy!"

"Why?"

"Because you know that I don't love you."

He stared down at his hands, turning them over and studying them as though seeing them for the first time. "Yes, I know that," he said finally. "You're still in love with Richard."

She felt compelled to touch him and shyly laid her hand on his knee. "Are you hoping that I'll change, that love will come in time?"

"Will it?"

She removed her hand. "I'll never love any man the way I did Richard."

"I still want you."

"How can you even consider wasting your life that way? Why would you want to marry a woman you know doesn't love you and never will?"

"Let me worry about the whys and wherefores. Will you marry me?"

"You're a very attractive man, Trevor."

He smiled broadly. "Thanks."

Her exasperation showed. "What I mean is, six months from now, or next week, or tomorrow, you might meet another woman, one who loves you."

"I won't be looking."

"But you should be."

"Look," he said patiently, "this fictitious woman could come up and pinch me on the ass, and it wouldn't matter. I've found the woman I want to give my name to."

"But you barely know me."

I know you inside out, he thought. *I know that you love porch swings and sky lights and stained-glass windows and houses surrounded by trees. I know that in the tenth grade you went with a boy named David Taylor and the bastard broke your heart. You have a patch of freckles under your right arm that you consider your birthmark. And you're self-conscious about your breasts because you think they're too small. But I think they're lovely and I can't wait to see them, touch them with my fingertips and tongue, make love to them with my mouth.*

Trevor cleared his throat and shifted uncomfortably on the swing. "I didn't believe in love at first sight either until I saw you in the mall that day. I thought you were beautiful, but you were more than just a pretty woman who caught my eye. I liked the way you talked to Aaron. I liked the way your hands moved as you tended to him." He grinned lopsidedly. "If he hadn't taken a mind to jump in the fountain, I would have devised a way to meet you." He inched closer to her. "Marry me, Kyla. Live with me in this house."

"This house!" she exclaimed softly. "You built this house with the intention of *our* living in it?"

Pleased that he had surprised her, he asked, "Why do you think I paid such close attention to detail?"

Behind her, beyond the walls of glass that opened onto the deck, Kyla could see the well-arranged rooms, rooms that, had she designed them herself, couldn't be more to her liking. "We have an uncanny similarity in taste. It is a lovely house, Trevor, but that hardly constitutes a good reason to marry."

"Right now, it's just a house. I want to make it a home. For Aaron. For you. For us."

She studied him for a moment, shaking her head. "It just doesn't make any sense."

"It makes perfect sense. I want us to be a family. I want to assume responsibility for you and Aaron."

The idea came from nowhere, but struck her with the impact of a speeding freight train. He wanted a wife and child. Now why would a man with Trevor's looks and Trevor's charm, a man who could have any woman he wanted, be proposing marriage to a widow with a child? Unless he couldn't come by them any other way.

Of course! All of Trevor's disabilities weren't visible. Was her main attraction that she didn't and couldn't return his love? Did he need a wife who would make no physical demands on him? To have a child, did he have to marry a woman who already had one? In a quaint fashion, was this to be no more than a marriage of convenience?

"Trevor," she said hesitantly, "your... When you were hurt...?"

"Yes?"

"Did...?"

"Did what?"

"What I mean is... Are you...?"

"Am I...? What?"

She took a deep breath. "Are you capable of intimacy?" She felt small and the world closed in. It had a stranglehold on her throat. Garnering all her courage, she raised her eyes to look at him.

"You've kissed me, haven't you?" he asked in a deep, throbbing voice.

"Yes."

"I've held you."

"Yes."

"Close."

"Yes."

Her eyes fell away and when she didn't say anything for an interminable time, he prodded, "Well then?"

She fiddled with the fringed sash at her waist. "I thought maybe since I was a widow with a child, and if...that...had happened to you, then..."

He tilted her head up with his hand beneath her chin. "I'm not only capable of, but eager for intimacy with you." Each word sent a vibrating current through her body that continued to hum, like harp strings long after deft fingers had plucked them. "And just so there's no misunderstanding later, I'll tell you right now that this marriage would carry with it all that the relationship implies. I want to be your husband in every sense of the word. I want you in my bed, Kyla. I want to make love to you. Frequently. Do you understand?"

She nodded her head with no more willpower of her own than one hypnotized. Neither of them ever remembered how his fingers had come to be loosely caging her neck, but both became conscious of it at the same time. They sat very still. His single green eye held hers in thrall as his face moved closer. The instant she felt the brush of his mustache against her lips, her eyelids closed.

What a waste, Kyla thought as his fingers threaded up through her hair to settle against her scalp. What a shame that a kiss like this had to be wasted on a woman who didn't and couldn't love him. How regrettable that the lips that were both fiercely possessive and gently persuasive, enough to cause hers to part as though they were hungry, couldn't be kissing a woman who could return such passion.

Lightly she rested her hands on his shoulders in order to

keep from tottering off the rocking swing and the rocking universe.

Trevor's other arm encircled her waist and drew her against his chest. A low masculine growl purred in his throat as his tongue penetrated her lips and tasted her mouth at will.

Kyla had a difficult time restraining her own low moans. The silky lash of his tongue made her think how lamentable it was that this kiss wasn't being bestowed on a woman who could appreciate it.

Then it occurred to her that she was giving every semblance of appreciation. Her back was arched, pressing her breasts against his chest. Her hands had wadded the fabric of his shirt in death grips. Her tongue was responding to the love play of his.

She broke away, experiencing an alarming scarcity of breath. Standing quickly, she wondered what ailment had befallen her knees. They were trembling so badly that they could hardly support her. "I've got to go."

Trevor was having a difficult time breathing too, if that rasping sound filtering through his lips was any indication. "All right," he agreed without argument. It took him a long time to stand up. One swift, forbidden glance down his body made a mockery of her earlier speculation.

Virtually at a run, she went back through the house and waited for him at the front door. Gratefully she sank into the front seat of the car when he held the door for her, not sure when her legs would collapse beneath her.

Trevor didn't attempt conversation as he drove her home. Kyla was relieved. Midsummer madness might have been responsible for his proposal. Maybe he'd only been joking. He could already be regretting that he'd asked her to marry him.

But she knew such was not the case when he cut the car's

engine at the curb in front of the Powers's house, turned, and laid his arm on the back of the seat and said, "Kyla?" in a blood-stirring tone she couldn't mistake.

It was shocking to discover his taste lingering on her lips when she nervously swept them with her tongue. "I don't think it even warrants further discussion. You can't be serious about this."

"Kyla." He waited until she cautiously turned her head and looked at him. "I'm serious. Do you think I could have kissed you like that if I hadn't been serious?"

"I don't know," she said with a trace of desperation.

He chuckled softly, finding that amusing. "I've kissed many women, but I've never proposed to one. At least I've never proposed marriage. Rest assured that I'm serious." Taking her hand he raised it to his mouth and kissed the palm. "I know I've taken you by surprise. I didn't expect an answer tonight. But promise me you'll think about it. Think about what our getting married could mean to you and Aaron. To your parents. Sleep on it."

Trevor Rule was a dirty fighter, Kyla thought angrily as she checked the digital read-out on her bedside clock for the umpteenth time. She had charted each hour of the long night, and he was to blame for her sleeplessness.

For one thing her body refused to relax. It was restless, alert to every sensual stimulant. Hadn't her bare legs ever felt bed linens against them before? If so, why were they sliding against the sheets as though that were a new indulgence? And why was this old cotton nightgown irritating her breasts? Why, tonight, were her nipples supersensitive to every brush of the fabric against them? Why did they need soothing? And why, every time she thought of them being soothed, did she imagine Trevor's lips against them?

Repeatedly she swore that these physical manifestations had nothing to do with his kiss. Was she about to have her period? That could be the cause for the achy pressure between her thighs. Could she have gotten into poison ivy? Was that the reason her skin felt itchy and in need of caressing?

"I'm *not* aroused."

Her body argued with her, saying otherwise.

Damn him for using such sneaky tactics. He knew the right button to push. He had subtly suggested that if she didn't marry him, she was being selfish.

All right, she'd play devil's advocate.

It *would* be good for her parents. They would feel free to make their own plans, knowing that she and Aaron would be under Trevor's protection.

And it would be good for Aaron. A growing boy needed a father. Clif Powers had filled that role in Aaron's life so far, but how long could he keep pace with his grandson? Would he be healthy and energetic enough to participate in sports with him in a few years, take him fishing and camping, and do all the myriad, physically taxing things a father does with his son?

But Aaron had a father! Kyla argued. Richard Stroud was Aaron's father. She had sworn to keep Richard alive for his son and she was determined to hold to that vow. It would take more than Trevor's smooth manner and glib tongue to sway her from that.

Besides, a woman didn't commit herself to a marriage because it would be beneficial to the people around her, no matter how attractive the man was. Granted, Trevor Rule was attractive and good husband material. She was aware of the strides he was taking in the community. He was constantly being quoted in the business pages of the newspaper. Obviously he was a man of integrity, honest in his business

dealings and respected for his innovative ideas for commercial growth. Physically—

No. It would be better not to think about his physical
attributes. Her burst of inspiration that he could have been
emasculated as a result of his accident had been disproved
only moments later.

No, leave his physical attraction out of this. Thinking
about that tended to cloud her mind and color her judgment.
The only way to approach this problem was pragmatically.

That was what she did until dawn, when she finally
reached a decision. She would find a place for Aaron and
herself to live. She would move from this house so that her
parents could sell it and carry on with their plans.

Marriage to Trevor wouldn't be necessary. Financially she
was holding her own. When he was old enough she would
see that Aaron had a close association with other boys his age
and their fathers. She didn't need a man in her life.

However, she supposed she should thank Trevor for his
proposal and for goading her into making decisions that she
had postponed since Richard's death. The sooner she turned
him down, the better.

While her parents were dressing for church the next morning, she made the telephone call. He answered in the middle
of the first ring. "Hello, Trevor. I hope I didn't wake you."

"Hardly."

"I've come to a decision. I—"

"I'll be right over."

He hung up before she could say another word. Disgrun-
tled, she replaced the receiver. It would have been easier to
turn him down over the phone and spare them both the awkwardness of meeting face-to-face.

Since she and Aaron were already dressed, she carried him
and his plastic beach ball outside. If she met Trevor on the

front lawn, this could be over and done with before her parents knew about it.

Trevor must have been standing by the telephone with his car keys in his hand because he got there in a matter of minutes. Kyla was surprised to see him emerge from his car wearing a dark suit. His hair gleamed darkly in the sunlight. He gave the large plastic ball a tap with his foot and Aaron toddled off to chase it.

"Good morning," he said.

"Good morning."

She was nervous. This was going to be more difficult than she had thought. While she was trying to concentrate on how ridiculous the idea of marrying him was, her mind ventured onto how good-looking he was. She was remembering the feel of his mustache against the palm of her hand, the way he had of kissing her throat and touching her neck with fingers that seemed to know just the right amount of pressure to apply.

"Trevor," she began, licking her lips quickly and clasping her hands damply together. "I—"

The dog seemed to drop out of the sky. Suddenly it was just there, dancing around Aaron and yapping loudly. The white poodle's movements were frenzied, quick and, to the fifteen-month-old, terrifying. What to the poodle were playful thrusts and parries, to the child must have seemed like vicious attacks.

Aaron screamed, but his screams only seemed to excite the dog more. It bounded around the child like a fluffy white dot, its barking as sharp and rapid as the rat-a-tat of a machine gun.

Aaron took several stumbling steps forward, seeking escape. The dog reared up on its hind legs. Aaron toppled over backward. Then, as agilely as he could, he scrambled to regain his footing and ran blindly toward safety.

Or rather not so blindly. He had a clear choice of whom to run to. But he didn't choose his mother. The child ran toward the large, strong man, who bent down to scoop him up just as Aaron's solid little body barreled into his shins.

The stout little arms wrapped around Trevor's neck. Aaron buried his tear-streaked face in the crook between Trevor's neck and shoulder. Trevor lowered his head over the child's and rubbed his back soothingly. "There now, Scout. It's all right. You're okay. I've got you and I'm not about to let anything hurt you. That puppy just wanted to play with you. Come on now, you're okay."

The animal's owner, a heavyset middle-aged woman, came huffing down the sidewalk. She grabbed up the poodle and swatted him on the rump. "You naughty thing, you. Why did you scare that little boy like that?" Tucking the poodle under her arm, she came rushing toward them. "Is your son all right?" she asked Trevor.

"He's fine. Just frightened." Trevor continued to rub Aaron's back. The boy hadn't moved. His face was still pressed against Trevor, but he had stopped crying.

"I'm sorry. I let go of his leash and he shot off like a rocket. He wouldn't bite. He only wanted to play."

"I think Aaron was overwhelmed." Trevor's large hand covered the back of Aaron's head and held it securely against his neck.

"I'm so sorry." The woman continued on her way down the sidewalk, still admonishing the dog.

Trevor patted Aaron's back. He nuzzled his cheek with his mustache and kissed his temple. "He'll be okay. I think he just—"

His words faltered when he noticed Kyla's face. She was

standing close, looking up at him with an expression that arrested his gaze and halted his speech. Tears were standing in her eyes. Her lips were tremulous and slightly parted. She was looking at him as though seeing him, really seeing him, for the first time.

For long moments, they stared at each other, not even aware that the Powerses had rushed out onto the front porch to see what the commotion was about. Meg started down the steps, but Clif caught her arm and held her back.

Trevor, still holding Aaron, reached out his left hand and folded it around Kyla's chin. He made a pass across her lower lip with his thumb. "You were interrupted. What were you about to tell me?"

In that instant, she knew what her answer would be. Aaron needed a father. A living father. Richard's memory would be kept alive, but he wasn't there as a safeguard against the day-to-day terrors of the world, like energetic puppies.

Trevor obviously cared a great deal for her son. Aaron had instinctively sought him out for protection. He was tender and loving and kind and generous. Where else would she find a man willing to take over the responsibilities of rearing another man's child, a man willing to marry her knowing she didn't love him?

"I was about to tell you that I'd be pleased to marry you. If...if you still want me to."

"If I still want you to?" he repeated gruffly. "God, yes, I still want you to."

He closed the space between them and with the arm that wasn't holding her son, embraced her. She didn't know what she had expected. A handshake to seal the bargain? A pre-marital document to sign? Certainly not the kiss she got. It was a Sunday morning. They were standing in broad day-

light, in full view of any neighbor who might venture outside or any motorist who happened to drive by.

But Trevor exercised no decorum in kissing her. He tilted
his head to one side, aligned his mouth with hers and kissed
her in a greedy, manly way.

Kyla felt a blow to her middle, as though a velvet fist had
socked her. It sent ripples of pleasure throughout her body.
Vaguely, in the back of her mind, she was disappointed that
he was still holding Aaron and therefore unable to pull her
against him and complete the circuits of sensation that were
popping and sizzling. Everything feminine inside her was
craving to be pressed against that hard, virile frame. She
wanted to be filled with him.

When he finally raised his mouth from hers, she reeled
slightly. His strong arm was there to steady her. It turned her
around and guided her toward the house, where she saw her
parents hovering on the front porch. Aaron was happily tugging on a fistful of Trevor's black hair. Trevor was smiling
broadly and every few steps he laughed out loud.

"Mrs. Powers, Mr. Powers, Kyla has done me the honor of
saying yes to my marriage proposal."

Meg immediately burst into tears of gladness. Clif hurried down the steps to pump Trevor's hand. "That's wonderful. We're very happy. We're…well, we're happy. When?" he
asked his daughter.

"When?" Trevor echoed.

"I, uh, I don't know." Now that she had made the decision, she felt as if she was being swept along by a tidal wave.
"I haven't had time to think about it."

"How about next Saturday?" Trevor suggested. "I came
dressed to go to church with you. We can check it out with
the minister after the service."

"I think that's a lovely idea," Meg said enthusiastically. "Here at the house, of course."

"Yes, why wait?" Clif added.

Yes, why? Kyla was asking herself. Why did she feel like applying the brakes? Accepting Trevor's marriage proposal had seemed like the thing to do just moments ago, but now she was realizing the enormity of her decision. This was for real. She was about to become Mrs. Trevor Rule. What would everyone think?

Babs left no doubt as to how she took the news. As was her habit she came over for Sunday dinner. Trevor answered the door when she knocked. Clif was cranking the freezer of homemade ice cream Meg had insisted on making for dessert in celebration of the occasion. Kyla was feeding Aaron so he could be put down for his nap before they ate. Meg was spooning up fresh green beans. Trevor was the only one available.

Babs stared at him in wordless awe as he pushed the screen door open and stepped aside. "Come on in. Everyone is in the kitchen."

Kyla hadn't told Babs that she was going to see Trevor. Babs hadn't seen him since that afternoon in town over a week ago when Kyla had acted like such a ninny. Now, where his carpenter's belt had been strapped, a blue and white gingham apron was tied in a bow. He had insisted on helping Meg get lunch ready.

Babs padded into the kitchen behind him. No sooner was she through the door than she demanded of Kyla, "What's going on here?"

Kyla's eyes swept across the other expectant faces, but when no one seemed inclined to answer Babs, the chore fell to her. "Trevor and I are getting married."

Babs's wide china-blue eyes found Trevor. He grinned engagingly. "Surprise!"

"You're getting married!" Babs exclaimed. When he nodded, she clasped his face between her hands and smacked a hearty kiss directly on his mouth. "Since you're marrying my best friend I think I'm entitled to that."

Laughing, Trevor hugged her around the waist and laid another sound kiss on her mouth. When he released her, he said, "I think so, too."

Everyone laughed, including Aaron, who didn't understand anything but the gaiety going on around him. He pounded his spoon on the tray of his high chair.

Lunch was a joyous affair. There was a lot of teasing and talk about the wedding and matrimony in general. Kyla couldn't get accustomed to the idea that in less than a week she would be a bride. Nor could she get accustomed to the affectionate way Trevor treated her.

He sat close. He took advantage of innumerable opportunities to touch her. His arm was often resting across her shoulders. Caresses seemed to come as naturally to his fingertips as kisses came to his lips.

Kyla wasn't annoyed by these demonstrations of affection. Quite the contrary. She found that she was beginning to look forward to them. That anticipation turned to guilt. As far as she was concerned, this marriage *was* a marriage of convenience. Wasn't it?

Trevor spent the afternoon with them. He acquainted them with his background. "I grew up in Philadelphia. Went to prep school, then to Harvard."

"Your mother is dead?" Meg asked him.

"Yes, she died several years ago. I'll notify my father about the wedding, but I doubt he'll be able to make the trip on such short notice."

"He's a lawyer?" Clif asked.

"A very successful one. It was a disappointment to him that I didn't want to follow in his footsteps and make the name of the firm Alexander, Rule and Rule."

"But surely he's proud of your success in your own field," Clif said.

Trevor became reflective. "I hope so."

By that evening everyone in town seemed to know about their forthcoming marriage. "Mrs. Baker has offered to give you a shower."

Horrified, Kyla turned away from the countertop in the kitchen where she was preparing a tray of sandwiches to take out to the men, who were sitting on the porch. "Oh, no, Mom. I don't want any of that folderol. Please thank anyone who calls to offer, but kindly refuse."

"But, Kyla, everyone's so happy for you."

She shook her head adamantly. "I don't want any parties. Nothing. Please. I had all that once and it was lovely. This... this marriage isn't like that."

Meg looked at her with undisguised disappointment. "Very well, dear."

Her parents, whose heads were in a cloud of romanticism, would never understand her motives for marrying Trevor. She wasn't certain Trevor understood them, either.

She escorted him outside after he had bidden her parents good-night. As soon as they stepped through the screen door and into the deep violet shadows of the porch, he gathered her in his arms and lowered his mouth to hers.

The kiss was intimate and evocative, a mating of their mouths. His tongue stroked hers. His hands slid from her back to the front of her waist. They glided up over her ribs and pressed her breasts. He moaned.

"God, I don't know how I'll make it till Saturday night."

His hands fell away. "Do you know how much I want to touch you? But I can't touch you now. If I touch you now, I won't be able to stop until there's no cloth between us and I'm holding you, kissing you, your mouth, breasts, stomach, everywhere."

The last word was sighed into her ear. Then his open mouth slid from just beneath her jaw to the base of her neck. His mustache was a pleasure-giving, conscience-ridding, memory-banishing instrument that left her tingling and warm and moist. If he had strengthened the embrace, she would have allowed it. He didn't.

"Good night, love."

The darkness swallowed him up. Long after she watched the taillights of his car disappear, Kyla stood there on the porch, trembling at the thought of their wedding night. She tried convincing herself that the shivers plaguing her were caused by dread.

But she didn't really think they were.

Everyone's mood the following week was festive. Her parents were more animated than she had seen them since Richard's death. It was plain to see that they adored Trevor and trusted him to make their daughter and grandson happy. Babs's enthusiasm was uncontainable and by midweek was wearing thin.

"But I don't need anything like this," Kyla said of the sexy negligee Babs was holding up to her.

"Every bride needs something like this. Not that they last very long," she said with a naughty wink. The implication made Kyla's stomach feel queasy.

"I've got plenty of nightgowns," Kyla objected in a muffled voice.

"I've seen them. They're wretched. At least for a honeymoon."

"We're not taking a honeymoon. Not right away. We're moving directly into Trevor's house."

"*Your* house and you know what I mean about a honeymoon. You don't have to leave town to have one. Or for that matter, you don't have to leave the bedroom to have one." She laughed gaily. "I've had several myself. So which is it going to be, the peach or the blue?"

"I don't care," Kyla said petulantly, plopping down on the chaise in the boutique's dressing room. "You're the one who insisted I needed a new negligee, you pick it out."

"Boy!" Babs said in exasperation. "What's the matter with you?"

Babs wouldn't believe her if she told her, and she wasn't going to tell her. When you were insane, you rarely went around announcing it to your friends. "Nothing."

"Well, you're sure grouchy. I can't think of a better way to improve your mood than to spend a few days in the sack with Trevor Rule."

She turned to call the salesclerk and missed Kyla's stark expression. She wanted to get caught up in the spirit of the occasion but couldn't allow herself to. Getting excited about the wedding would be disloyal to Richard. No one had mentioned his name in days. It seemed that he had been blotted from everyone's mind but hers.

She clung to his memory more tenaciously than ever, but inevitably it seemed to be slipping from her grasp. She noted these lapses of memory the most when she was with Trevor, who was playing the role of bridegroom to the hilt.

Every evening they went shopping for household items. He wanted her input on everything from blenders to bolsters. He could have read her mind and not picked out furniture she liked better. Their taste in everything coincided. Often she felt like Cinderella having all her wishes granted at once. He spared no expense. As the interior of the house began to take shape, she felt like pinching herself to make sure this wasn't some bizarre dream.

That was how she felt the evening he led her into the master suite to show her the final product of their combined efforts. "They delivered the chairs and bed today," he said, switching on the lamp with the lotus-shaped silk lampshade. "I think everything came together real well."

The room was lovely, out of her dreams. Her eyes surveyed it slowly, and when they came back full circle to the man, he was staring at her intently. Her hair was limned by the lamplight and her body was cast into silhouette through her soft voile dress.

"What is it?" she asked on a soft breath.

"Let's try out the bed."

She reacted with a sudden intake of breath, a lurch of her heart, a blinking of her eyes. He reached for her and within a heartbeat, she found herself lying on the bed with him bending over her. Holding her eyes captive with his gaze, his hand drifted down the side of her neck until it came to rest on her breast and the first button of her bodice. He unbuttoned it. The second. The third.

Still she couldn't move. Not even when he slipped his hand inside her bodice. Her breathing accelerated. Involuntarily her eyes closed.

He wedged his fingers beneath her bra strap and pushed it down over her shoulder. Down, down, until the top curve of her breast swelled over the lacy cup.

"God, you're lovely." He laid his hand on her and rubbed the gentle curve of her breast, then moved lower to graze the responsive crest.

He sighed her name an instant before his mouth claimed hers. His kiss wasn't tempestuous as she had expected. But infinitely sweet and tender and loving. As loving as the hand that continued to fan lightly over her nipple.

He pressed his mouth to her ear. "I want to be inside you, Kyla. I want to feel you coming."

He trapped her gasp behind another deep kiss. His fingertips soothed the flesh that shrank even tighter in response to his bold words.

"Please, love, don't make that sexy sound. Please don't feel this good," he groaned, as his fingers caressed her breast. "Or I won't be able to stop. And I want to be your husband the first time I take you."

Exercising tremendous control, he refrained from other caresses. He restored her clothing and drew her up to stand beside the rumpled bed. She sagged against him weakly.

Smiling into her hair, he returned his hand to cover her heart. "I'll make you happy, Kyla. I swear it."

She buried her face in his neck, not out of passion, but despair. He made her body sing. But she couldn't reciprocate his promise of happiness or love. Because keeping that one would jeopardize the one she had made long before she ever met Trevor Rule, the one she had made to Richard the day he died.

Chapter 9

Babs filled the house with flowers. Meg laid out a sumptuous buffet. The bakery delivered a multitiered cake. What Kyla had hoped would amount to no more than a small family gathering with their pastor, began to look very much like a wedding.

She fretted over it in her bedroom upstairs. "Everyone is making too much of this." She reached for the buttons on the back of her bodice.

"Everyone should. This is a wedding, for heaven's sake." Babs turned her around to do up the unreachable buttons.

"A *second* wedding."

"So what are you bitching about? Some of us have yet to see one."

Kyla stared at Babs in surprise. "I didn't think you ever wanted to get married."

Babs looked chagrined at having said something she wished she could recall. "Not to anybody I've met so far. But if one Richard Stroud or Trevor Rule came into my life I'd rope him and drag him to the altar."

Properly chastised, Kyla stepped into her skirt. "I'm sorry, Babs. I know how lucky I've been."

"Oh, hell, don't pay any attention to me. I'd hardly call it lucky to have a husband killed by a terrorists' bomb. I'm just jealous because not one wonderful man has loved me and you've had two groveling at your feet."

She laughed at the mental picture Babs's words painted. "I doubt Trevor would ever grovel."

Babs laughed, too. "Come to think of it, so do I." She sighed. "Jeez, Kyla, he's such a stud. But a nice stud and those two qualities rarely go hand in glove."

Kyla didn't want to think about the man who was waiting downstairs for her. Every time she thought of Trevor and the night to come, she began to quake.

"Are you sure this dress is appropriate?" she asked, changing the subject. "I feel like I should wear something simpler."

"It's perfect."

The two-piece silk design had detailed stitching at the shoulders and on the waistband of the dirndl skirt. The pale yellow color and the fabric's icy sheen made it look like lemon sherbet. The only jewelry she wore was a pair of pearl earrings.

"Don't you think you should take that off?"

Kyla followed the direction of Babs's gaze down to her left hand. "My wedding ring." She hadn't even thought of it because it was as much a part of her hand as her fingerprints. Tears welled in her eyes at the thought of removing it. It hadn't been off her hand since the day Richard had slipped it onto her finger with a solemn vow to love her until death.

Slowly, with a twist and a wrenching tug, she removed the

ring. Reverently she laid it on the velvet lining of her jewelry box and closed the lid.

"Are you ready?" Babs asked.

"I suppose so," Kyla answered shakily. Parting with the wedding ring had been an emotional upheaval as violent as that of leaving Richard in his grave. All week she had been making light of this occasion. But she couldn't any longer. She was about to marry another man. In a matter of minutes he, not Richard, would be her husband. "Has Dad already taken Aaron downstairs?"

"You're a bride! Stop worrying about Aaron. Surely your parents and I can handle him." Babs reached into a large square box she had carried into the room earlier. "Trevor asked me to give this to you before you came down."

It was a bouquet of white orchids, the Bow Bells that she loved, garnished with white rosebuds and clumps of baby's breath. "My Lord," Kyla breathed, taking the lavish bouquet from Babs's outstretched hands. "There must be—"

"A dozen orchids in all. He was very specific." Her blue eyes were twinkling. "I'm telling you, Kyla, the man is a jewel, and if you make a mess of this marriage, I'll snatch him up without an apology or a smidgen of conscience."

"I'll do my best to make it work," Kyla murmured as she walked dazedly toward the door.

Downstairs, Babs preceded her into the living room. Kyla heard the hushed conversation cease. She took a deep, hopefully steadying, breath. Everyone was looking at her when she entered.

Meg had a damp lace handkerchief pressed to her cheek, but she was smiling. Clif swallowed a lump of emotion that made his Adam's apple slide up and down. Babs was grinning with the romantic mischievousness of a wood nymph. The

Haskells, Ted and Lynn, were standing together, unusually solemn.

Finally Kyla looked at Trevor, who was so handsome that she went mushy on the inside. He was wearing the same dark charcoal suit he had worn to the banquet. This time his shirt was ivory. An ivory tie with black pinstripes matched the silk handkerchief folded into his left breast pocket.

Trevor moved toward her, but Aaron, who could move like a streak of lightning when one least expected him to, darted forward and reached her first. Meg and Babs took simultaneous steps forward to prevent him from tearing her stockings or wrinkling her skirt.

But Trevor reached down and picked the boy up into his arms. "Your mom looks beautiful, doesn't she, Scout?" he asked on a husky whisper when he straightened up.

Aaron babbled something that sounded like "Mama" repeated several times, then stretched forward to smear a rough, wet kiss on Kyla's cheek. He seemed content to remain in Trevor's arms, which was just as well since Kyla didn't know how she could hold her son and the bouquet of orchids at the same time.

"It seems like I'm always thanking you for flowers."

"Do you like them?"

"They're beautiful. Of course, I love them. You were too extravagant."

He shook his head. "This is my wedding day. You are my bride. Today nothing is too good for us, love."

They stared at each other for ponderous moments until Aaron began to wiggle within the grasp of Trevor's arms. Trevor shook himself out of the trance Kyla's appearance had induced and took her arm. Together they moved farther into the room where the others were grouped around the minister.

"Kyla, Trevor, this is a happy day," the minister began.

Though it was the middle of the afternoon and sunshine streamed in through Meg's polished windows, Babs had insisted on having candles. They flickered like winking eyes from every nook and cranny of the room, filling it with the heady scent of vanilla. Someone had thought to put an album of romantic instrumentals on the turntable of the stereo. Surely Babs had depleted the inventory at Petal Pushers because flowers, not limited to white but covering the spectrum of the rainbow, filled vases and baskets scattered throughout the room.

The service was by necessity informal. During the recitation of vows, Aaron sneezed, spraying Trevor's shoulders. Automatically Kyla reached for her mother's hanky, blotted the damp spots on Trevor's coat and dabbed at Aaron's nose. Trevor smiled on, fondly. Once that housekeeping chore had been attended to, the pastor continued. When he called for the bride's ring, Trevor shifted Aaron in his arm and reached inside his right coat pocket. Kyla stared down at her hand as he slid the circlet of diamonds onto her finger.

Trevor noticed the pale band of skin around the base of her finger and, realizing what had caused it, swiftly lifted his gaze to her face. Her soft look carried with it an apology. An expression she couldn't decipher flashed across his features, but was instantly gone. He pushed the dazzling ring into place on her finger and clasped her hand tightly. The awkward moment passed with only the two of them knowing it had occurred at all.

Several minutes later, the minister said, "Trevor, you may kiss your bride now."

They faced each other. Kyla's eyes came to rest on the knot of his necktie and seemed disinclined to move away. Finally they shyly climbed up his chin, along the sensual mouth beneath the thick brush of his mustache, over the chiseled perfection of his nose to meet that brilliant green gaze. She swallowed timidly.

Trevor angled his head and lowered his lips to hers. His were parted, damp and warm as they pressed her mouth with a tender, yet possessive kiss. When he withdrew, he smiled down into her face, then kissed Aaron's cheek.

"I love you both." He spoke softly to Kyla's ears alone and she felt a sudden urge to cry.

Before she could, she was spun around and embraced by her parents. Babs made a beeline for Trevor, taking advantage of the opportunity to kiss him again. Ted and Lynn joined in the exchange of kisses.

To record the day, Clif got out his camera. Kyla smiled for the lens, but she couldn't help but think about the white padded satin album upstairs in her closet that was filled with pictures of another wedding.

As Kyla filled her plate with food from the buffet, Trevor moved up beside her. "If you don't like the ring, I'll get you something else."

"I didn't expect it," she said, looking down at the unfamiliar ring. "But I like it very much." And she did. It was simple and elegant.

"The diamonds are from my mother's wedding ring. Dad sent it to me last week. The mounting was gaudy and didn't look like something you would choose, so I had the stones reset."

"You took your mother's diamonds and had a ring made for me?" she asked, flabbergasted.

"She told me before she died to give her ring to my wife."

"But Trevor, you should have saved it for—" She broke off

when she realized that she was about to say, "For a woman who loves you."

"For whom?" The back of his hand made a resting place for her chin and he tilted her head back slightly. "You are my one and *only* wife, Kyla." He bent down and kissed her lightly before dropping his hand.

"I'm sorry I didn't have a ring for you." She couldn't admit to him that it had never occurred to her. Indeed she hadn't thought of wedding rings at all until Babs—God bless her—had reminded her to remove hers only minutes before the ceremony. "I wasn't sure you would want to wear one. Some men don't."

"Well, I've been giving that some thought." He popped an olive into his mouth and chewed it slowly and exaggeratedly as though pondering a tremendously important decision. "I thought I might want something different. Untraditional."

"Like what?"

"Like maybe a gold ring in my ear."

Her mouth fell open and she stared up at him. Then she realized that he was teasing her and she burst out laughing.

"What's the matter?" he asked, pretending to be offended by her laughter. "Don't you think a pierced ear would go well with my eye patch?"

"Yes, I do," she said honestly. "Pierced ears for men is the 'in' thing and I think you would wear an earring with panache."

"Well then, why the levity?"

"I was just wondering what the guys on your construction sites would have to say about it?"

"Hmm, you're right. Maybe I should reconsider."

They laughed together and when it subsided, he said, "That's a start."

"What is?"

"I finally managed to remove that guarded, tense expression from your face and replace it with a genuine, relaxed smile. You actually laughed."

"I laugh all the time."

"Not with me. I want to see you laugh often." He leaned down and added on a whisper, "Except when I take off my clothes."

The thought of that rid her mind of all laughter. "I promise not to laugh then."

She could have kissed her father for interrupting them at that point to take another picture. They were photographed. They ate; they drank numerous glasses of Meg's punch; they said goodbye to the Haskells with a promise to get together soon.

Babs left for a date. "Poor guy," she told Trevor and Kyla at the door. "He doesn't know what he's in for tonight. All this wedding sentiment has put me in a very romantic mood." With a seductive wink and a jaunty wave, she left.

"Mom, let me help you clean up this mess."

"No, no, no," Meg said, shooing Kyla out of the kitchen. "You and Trevor get on your way."

"But not all of Aaron's things are packed yet. I thought I'd change and—" She fell silent when she realized the other three were staring back at her as though she'd taken leave of her senses. Only Trevor seemed faintly amused. She had come to know that the twitch of his mustache usually heralded a grin. "What's the matter?"

"Well, we, your mother and I, just assumed that you'd leave Aaron here for tonight at least," Clif said uneasily.

Kyla opened her mouth to speak, only to find that she had nothing to say. She closed her mouth without uttering a word.

"Thank you, Clif, Meg," Trevor said to fill an awkward

silence. "We appreciate the offer. If Aaron won't be any trouble we'll leave him here tonight. Tomorrow when we come for him we'll bring the pickup. Kyla still has some things to move, don't you, love?"

"Yes," she croaked. "I'll finish packing and get it all out of your way by tomorrow evening."

Since the announcement of her marriage to Trevor, the Powerses had officially sold their house. Kyla knew that the sooner she moved all her possessions out, the sooner the sale could be closed.

However, she wasn't thinking about that now. She was thinking about the night to come when she wouldn't have Aaron to act as a buffer between her and her bridegroom. She dragged out their leave-taking as long as she could without it being obvious.

"Meg knows how to throw a great party," Trevor said once they were alone and on their way home.

"She's always been a gracious hostess."

"I appreciate her efforts."

"She loved doing it."

"I like your dress."

"Thank you."

"Silk?"

"Yes."

"I like the sound it makes when you move."

"Sound?"

"That secretive rustling sound that makes me wonder what your body is doing underneath it."

Her eyes swung quickly to the horizon. "I didn't know it made a sound."

"It does. Each time you move. I find it terribly sexy." He reached across the seat for her hand and laid it high on his thigh. "And exciting."

Her heart slammed against her ribs. Breathing was difficult. She tried to concentrate on how the fabric of his tailored slacks felt against the palm of her hand, but her brain seemed determined to dwell on his excitement, the extent of which she could measure should she move her hand up a scant few inches.

The headlights swept across the front of the house as he braked the car to a stop. "Do you need the bag tonight?" He had carried a small suitcase to the car for her.

"Yes, please. It has makeup and...stuff...in it."

"Oh, I see. Stuff." His grin did nothing for her heart or her lungs, both of which seemed to have shut down operations for the night. "Well you can't do without your stuff, can you?"

On the porch, he set the suitcase down and unlocked the front door, pushing it wide. Before Kyla could prepare herself, he swept her up into his arms and against his chest. "Welcome home, Kyla."

He carried her inside. As soon as he crossed the threshold, he lowered his head and kissed her. And kissed her again. And again. Until soon it was hard to tell where one kiss stopped and another began.

Both of his hands were occupied. Kyla could have turned her head away and ended the kisses, but she lacked the will to do so. His mouth was incredibly sweet and warm. She felt an irresistible compulsion to see just how nimble his tongue could be. It thrust again and again into her mouth with a greediness tempered only by tenderness.

He relaxed the arm beneath her knees but kept her anchored to him as she slid down against his body. Finally she was standing toe to toe with him. And still the kiss went on uninterrupted.

With his arms now free, his hands explored. They slid up

and down her back. She felt the pressure of his palms on her bottom, urging her closer to his hard middle. Once she was secured there, he made vees of his thumbs and index fingers and bracketed her breasts in the notches. The vees closed and opened rhythmically, gently, causing his thumbs lightly to brush the peaks of her breasts.

She caught her breath. Trevor's hands fell away immediately, but he didn't retreat. He folded his arms around her protectively and pressed her head against his chest.

"I'm about to get carried away," he whispered into her hair. "Making love standing up in the entrance hall isn't the way I planned our wedding night." Chuckling, he put space between them and looked down into her face. "Not without closing the front door first."

When he turned to do that, Kyla moved as far away from him as possible without making it look like an escape. "Are you hungry?" she asked hopefully. "I'll fix you something."

"After that spread Meg had prepared?" he asked incredulously. "One more marinated artichoke and I'd have burst. But I do have some champagne chilling. Would you like to change first?"

First. First. He kept dropping in that one-syllable word that implied so much to Kyla. She knew what was at the culmination of all those "firsts."

"Champagne sounds good." Could he detect the tremors in the corners of her mouth when she tried to smile?

As he walked into the kitchen, he shrugged off his suit jacket and worked at the knot of his necktie. Casually he tossed both of them into one of the chairs at the kitchen dining table as he went by. He unbuttoned the top three buttons of his shirt and, after unclipping his cuff links, rolled the cuffs of his sleeves up to his elbows.

He seemed perfectly at ease. Kyla envied him that nonchalance. She would dearly love to slip out of the new shoes, which had made her toes numb, but she didn't even feel comfortable enough with their privacy to do that.

"Ah, good and cold," he said, swinging the bottle of champagne out of the industrial-size refrigerator. Kyla noticed that the shelves inside it had already been stocked with food, including Aaron's favorites. Didn't Trevor ever forget anything? "Would you get down the wineglasses, sweetheart? They're in that cabinet there," he said nodding toward one. "I put everything up, but you can rearrange it all if something's not convenient for you."

"I'm sure everything is fine," she said woodenly.

She found the champagne glasses and brought him two. She jumped when the cork popped out of the bottle. Laughing, he poured the foaming wine into the glass. Some of it washed over Kyla's hands. She began laughing, too. The icy effervescent wine tingled on her skin as the tiny bubbles burst one by one.

Having set the glasses on the countertop, she was shaking the moisture from her hands when Trevor captured one and lifted it to his mouth. "Allow me."

She watched it. She watched her finger disappear between his mustache and lower lip, but she didn't really believe that it was actually happening until she felt his tongue laving the pad of her finger.

Stunned, Kyla was powerless to do anything but watch as he finished with that finger and sucked the next one into the silky heat of his mouth. He slid his tongue between the next two fingers, gathering up all traces of the spilled wine. It curled around the beautiful wedding ring he had placed on her finger earlier.

Delicious sensations wound through her. His tongue's deft caresses never ventured beyond her fingertips, but seemed to touch her everywhere, in forbidden places. They coaxed responses from her body she had thought were buried with that flag-draped casket in Kansas.

That melting sensation in her middle. That aching in her breasts that made her want to feel Trevor's tongue there, doing what he was doing to her fingertips. That quickened respiration. That pounding of her heart.

Finally he turned her hand over and kissed the palm, whisking it with his mustache before relinquishing it. She had the impulse to tuck her hand under her arm as one does when one has been stung or has pricked a finger with a pin. Or did she want to hide that hand in shame because it had been guilty of such erotic responses?

"Here's your champagne." Trevor handed her a glass. "To us." He clinked their glasses together and they each took a sip. Then he lowered his head and kissed her softly. "Know what?" he asked while his lips were still resting against hers.

"What?" What cologne does he wear? her mind was asking distractedly. It was as intoxicating as the champagne.

"You taste better than champagne." His tongue swept her lower lip. "In fact you taste better than anything. I could make a glutton of myself on you. I could indulge until I was sated and drunk on you. And I still wouldn't have enough. I'd want... one...more...taste." Between the words, he pecked soft kisses. After the last word, his mouth stayed and he sent his tongue deep into her mouth.

Unmindful of the sloshing, he removed the wineglass from her hand. None too steadily, he set hers and his on the countertop without ever having released her from his kiss.

Slowly he raised her arms to his shoulders. Involuntarily they bent at the elbows to enclose his neck. His hands met at the small of her back. The kiss deepened. He inched forward until she was sandwiched between him and the counter. He rocked his hips from side to side, massaging her softness.

"Oh, God." She sighed when he left her mouth to plant one of those treacherous kisses on her vulnerable throat. Her head fell back. Her eyes drifted open and she gazed at the ceiling hazily as his open mouth touched her skin.

Why was God doing this to her? Why had he sent such a temptation into her life? The marriage itself had been a betrayal of Richard. She didn't love this man, yet she wanted him in a purely carnal way. It was wrong! How could she withstand such an inundation of sexual provocation and not submit to it?

"Would you like some privacy in the bedroom before I join you?" he asked roughly.

Witlessly, she nodded her head and he released her. Like a sleepwalker she turned and wended her way to the other side of the house and into the bedroom. Trevor, having followed her, set her suitcase just inside the door. "I'll be back shortly." The door closed softly behind him.

She carried the suitcase into the bathroom and opened it. As though programmed to do so, she automatically unpacked her cosmetics and toiletries and arranged them on the dressing table. When she chanced to catch her image in the mirror covering the wall, she froze.

Her eyes! What had happened to her eyes? They were aglow, lambent, limpid. They hadn't looked like that since the night she had discovered she was in love with Richard Stroud.

In love! Good Lord, yes. That's what she looked like, a woman in love.

The thought extinguished the light in her eyes immediately, extinguished it so quickly that she could almost convince herself that it hadn't been there at all, that it had been a trick of the lighting, a product of her imagination.

In love with Trevor Rule? Impossible. She hadn't known him long enough. She loved Richard. Solely. Exclusively. There was no room in her heart for any other man.

Even if she allowed Trevor the use of her body that night, she wouldn't be betraying Richard. It was, after all, just a body, material and impermanent. Her body had nothing to do with the personality inside it, the heart and soul and mind of Kyla Stroud.

Kyla *Rule,* a malicious imp reminded her.

Kyla *Stroud,* she insisted.

She would sleep with Trevor because she had made a bargain and she intended to uphold her end of it. She would swap him bedroom privileges for the parenting he would extend to Aaron. He would have access to her body, but never, never to her heart. She had promised her heart and love to Richard. Trevor Rule would never be allowed to violate that covenant.

She and Babs had moved her clothes the night before. Her entire wardrobe, all seasons included, filled only a fraction of the closet space Trevor had built into the master bedroom. After a quick shower, she slipped into the negligee she had bought under duress and brushed her teeth and hair. Almost as an afterthought, she applied perfume to the backs of her ears and the base of her throat.

In the bedroom she turned down the bed. She left only one lamp burning. When the soft knock sounded on the door, she whirled around, clasping her hands together. "Come in, Trevor."

He stepped through the door. When the soft lamplight fell on him, Kyla momentarily regretted that she didn't love him. The black pajama bottoms hung low on his hips, held there by a black cord. His chest was most impressive, shadowed by that cloud of dark hair that arrowed down past his navel. She didn't even want to think of what that stripe of hair pointed to. The scar that arced beneath his left breast intrigued her as it had before. She wanted to touch it, soothe it somehow. His feet were bare. There was a network of scars on his left foot.

Only after she had cataloged his body did she raise her eyes to his face. He was staring at her, a hint of a smile hiking up one corner of his mustache.

"You're beautiful, Kyla." He moved into the room until he was standing an arm's length away.

She couldn't have guessed how appealing she was to him at that moment. This was the woman of the letters, the woman who had spoken to his heart before he even met her. Now, she stood before him, naked, save for a few scraps of peach-colored silk and satin. His most erotic fantasy was close enough to touch. She was breathing, stirring the hair on his chest with each light exhalation.

The golden glow of the lamp enhanced her spectacular coloring. It made her hair shine like copper and her skin take on the richness of old satin. He wanted to wrap himself up in her. Her eyes were velvety dark, unusually wide, incredibly bright.

The nightgown was sheer and curtained her body like a veil. A ribbon was tied beneath her breasts, making their fullness more pronounced. Her nipples were dusky temptations beneath the filmy fabric. Above the brief bodice, the small mounds of her breasts swelled creamy and full.

Her body was cast in shadow against the lamplight. As his eyes moved down it, his manhood grew thick with desire for her. Her waist was incredibly narrow, especially for someone who had carried a child. He was transfixed by the shadowy cleft between her slender thighs, the heart of all that made her a woman. He wanted to honor it, cherish it with his caresses and his mouth.

Unable to stop himself, he extended his hand and cupped it over that soft delta. Shifting the material of her gown so that only one layer was between her and his hand, he pressed. "You're so warm," he whispered fiercely. "Standing here with you like this, I feel weaker than I did after my accident when I couldn't even move." His hand drifted up over her belly to her breast. "I want you so much it's painful."

His finger moved over her nipple and, when it responded beautifully, he made a hissing sound and crushed her against him. His mouth covered hers and he kissed her with all the fervency burning inside him. He fondled her breast lovingly as his other arm closed around her waist.

Kyla tried to keep herself indifferent. She wanted to step outside herself and observe the embrace from that viewpoint. But it was difficult to remain passive when the heat of his body was seeping into hers, when she throbbed where his fingers had just stroked her. The passion he transmitted delivered with it a lassitude that threatened her resolve not to participate with her mind.

Through the sheer nightgown, she could feel the crisp texture of his chest hair, the erection of his nipples. His thighs were hard and straining against hers. His maleness nestled in the cove her body offered it. He was hard and she wanted him.

Her body and her mind waged war. She struggled to keep her emotions intact. But in doing so, her body unwittingly went as unyielding as her heart.

Suddenly, Trevor withdrew his mouth from hers. The movement was so abrupt that her head snapped back and she fell victim to a cold green gaze.

He gripped her upper arms and shoved her away from him,

holding her at the end of stiff, strong arms fully extended. "No thank you, Kyla."

She looked at him fearfully. He was furious and it showed. His dark brows were pulled down low over his eyes. His nostrils flared slightly with each breath.

"No thank you?" she repeated in a thin voice. "I don't understand."

"Let me explain it then." He spoke in a tight voice she knew he must be having a hard time keeping below a shout. "I don't want a sacrificial lamb beneath me going through the motions of making love."

The hasty lowering of her eyes was as good as a signed confession. "You're my husband. You can demand—"

He laughed harshly. "If only you knew how laughable that was. Demanding isn't quite my style, Kyla. I certainly don't intend to exercise caveman tactics on my wife!"

He released her so abruptly that she reeled against the bedside table. "You may relax," he said scathingly. "You're safe from me. I won't impose my lust on you tonight. Nor will I ever."

Her eyes snapped up. "That's right, Kyla," he said silkily, reading her surprise. "I still love you, but it's not conditional on whether you go to bed with me or not. But I warn you," he said, pointing a finger at her, "that loving you as I do, it will be impossible for you not to love me back."

In a heartbeat, he was towering over her, his left hand knotted in her hair. With his right arm he hauled her high against him and positioned them so there could be no doubt of his readiness to take her if he chose to. He pulled her head back until she was forced to look up into his glowering face.

"I promise you this," he said with soft emphasis, "no one has ever loved you as much as I do. No one has ever made love to you as well as I can. I'll bury myself so deep inside you that when I'm not actually there, you'll feel like a vital part of your body is missing." He lowered his head and branded her breast with his mouth. "Now when you exorcise those ghosts that haunt you, come to me and I'll be more than glad to demonstrate what I'm talking about."

Releasing her, he spun on his heel and stalked to the door. "Sleep well," he tossed over his shoulder, a second before the door slammed behind him.

Chapter 10

"Good morning."

It wasn't the tone of voice she had expected, nor that, she secretly admitted, she probably deserved.

Surly, peevish, snide, cruel. Kyla would have expected him to be any of those, but not congenial and seemingly in a good mood.

"Good morning."

She skirted the table where he sat reading the newspaper and made a beeline for the coffee maker on the countertop. There was an empty mug waiting for her. She poured the fragrant, steaming coffee from the pot.

"I hope I didn't make it too strong for you."

She sipped. "It's fine. I like it strong."

"So do I."

She didn't realize he had come up behind her until his breath stirred her hair. She turned around quickly to face him. His arms slid around her waist and pulled her close. Ducking his head, he kissed her surprised mouth. It wasn't a passionate kiss, but a tender one that was almost as unsettling. "How was your night?" he asked solicitously.

Her night had been wretched. After Trevor had slammed out of the picture-perfect master bedroom suite he had created for his bride, Kyla had collapsed onto the wide bed and wept for what seemed like hours. She longed for familiar surroundings, her own bedroom, Aaron, the comforting presence of her parents. She longed to roll back the clock. She longed for Richard.

And she longed for Trevor.

That particular longing had brought on another wave of weeping.

She had finally fallen asleep shortly before dawn, and had awakened with a dull headache and puffy eyes. When she left the bedroom wrapped in an old robe that she had managed to sneak past Babs's eagle eye, she hadn't known what to expect from her husband of less than twenty-four hours, a husband to whom she had denied a wedding night, if not by deed then by attitude. Sullen fury at best.

She wasn't prepared for the cherishing embrace with which he enfolded her now. Nor for the soft kisses that he employed to trace her hairline. Nor for the gentle, tension-ridding massage his hands were giving her back.

Kyla felt anxiety slowly leaking out of her. She rested her cheek against the muscles of his chest, which were delineated by the tight white T-shirt he was wearing over a pair of ragged cutoffs.

"Can you cook?"

"What?" she mumbled sleepily.

"I asked if you could cook."

She raised her head and took a step backward. "Of course I can cook," she said with some asperity.

His mustache curved over a grin. "Then how about some breakfast?"

"What would you like?"

"What can you cook?"

"Anything," she boasted with a coquettish toss of her reddish-blond hair. "If you'll get out of my way, I'll prove to you what a good cook I am."

He bowed deeply from the waist, sweeping his hand wide. "The kitchen's all yours, milady. I'll just return to my newspaper if that's all right with you."

A few minutes later she set a frosty glass of orange juice in front of him. He tipped the corner of his newspaper down. "Thanks."

She smiled at him. "You're welcome."

"It smells good."

"It's almost ready."

He folded up the scattered newspapers and pushed them aside so she could set the table. Apparently she had found everything where he had had it stored. She laid out place mats and used the casual stoneware and silverware for their place settings. He watched her hands as she expertly folded linen napkins and arranged them in rings in the centers of the plates. Before she could turn away, he reached for her hand and drew it to his mouth. He kissed the back of it.

"It doesn't take long to get spoiled. I think I'm already used to having a wife make such a fuss over me," he said softly.

The way he looked up at her from his chair sent a warm tide of pleasure spilling over her middle. She felt a blush rising out of the unglamorous neckline of her robe.

She tugged on her hand, "I, uh, don't want it to burn."

He released her hand and she scurried toward the range. Moments later, she was bearing a platter of aromatic food to the table. She set it down, then stood by, nervously awaiting his reaction.

"Eggs Benedict!" he exclaimed in delight. The dish had been arranged appetizingly on the platter and garnished with fresh orange slices and sprigs of parsley.

"Do you like them that way? I didn't know."

"I'll eat just about anything that doesn't move off the plate. And rutabagas. Don't ever try to feed me rutabagas."

She laughed. "I think that's the only thing that wasn't stocked in the pantry or refrigerator."

During this exchange she had carried the coffeepot to the table and refilled his mug. As she set it on a trivet, Trevor rose from his chair and pulled hers out for her. She looked up at him in surprise and when she did he pecked a quick kiss on the tip of her nose. "Thanks for breakfast."

"You're welcome." She sank into her chair. Her hands were trembling slightly, but she filled his plate, then her own.

"Delicious!" he pronounced after taking an unabashedly huge first bite. "Where did you learn to cook like this?"

"My mother taught me the basics. And I took a cooking course while—" She stopped abruptly. Trevor's head came up, a question in his expression.

"While?" he prodded.

"While my hus…while Richard was overseas."

She had never mentioned the cooking class in her letters. Why, he wondered.

"What did Richard think of your cooking classes?" Had he missed some letters? He was suddenly, unaccountably, furiously jealous of anything she might have written to her husband that he, Trevor, hadn't been privy to. What else had he missed?

"I didn't tell him."

Trevor's grip on his fork relaxed. "Why?"

She took a drink of juice and blotted her mouth with her napkin before answering. "I wanted to surprise him with all kinds of exotic recipes when he came home," she said, cutting into the slice of Canadian bacon. "Babs and I took the class together. It was great fun. Babs was the worst student. She ruined everything she tried, but it wasn't a total waste of her time because she ended up dating the chef."

She was chatting now because she was nervous. Trevor could tell because she wouldn't look at him directly, but glanced at a spot just off his shoulder. They weren't even at the point where she could mention Richard's name without feeling awkward about it.

"I'll bet you were at the top of the class, because this is great." Her head came up and she blessed him with a shy smile that melted his heart and made up for the hellish night he'd spent alone in the guest room. Well, almost. "I've always ridiculed the former jocks who get married and go to fat. Now I can see how it happens." He winked at her.

"Were you a jock?"

"In school."

"What sports?"

"Hmm, let's see." He sipped his coffee. "Track. Basketball. Rowing."

"Rowing?"

"I don't think you have it in Texas."

"That must be what developed your shoulders and thighs."

When her gaze dropped to his long legs, she noticed the scars. There they were, ugly pink raised seams in his flesh, running the length of his left leg, intersecting and meshing like railroad tracks.

Trevor lowered his fork to his plate and watched her.

Bracing his elbows on the table, he folded his hands in front of his mouth and waited for the revulsion he prepared himself to see in her expression. It never came. When she raised her eyes to his face, there was only compassion in her brown eyes.

"I told you it wasn't pretty," he said, a definite edge to his voice.

"It's not so bad, Trevor."

"It's not so great, either."

She looked at his leg again. "It must have been awfully painful."

"It was."

"You've never told me what happened to you."

He shifted uneasily and she attributed that to self-consciousness. "It doesn't matter."

"You once said you were embarrassed to wear shorts. You shouldn't be."

A wry grin slanted his mustache upward. "You don't think all the ladies on the beach would cover their eyes and run in terror?"

"Not at all. You're too attractive."

He sobered instantly. Leaning forward, he speared her with his green gaze. "Do you think so?"

"Yes."

Several moments ticked by while Kyla was held transfixed by the gruff intensity in his voice and the hypnotizing power of his stare.

She willed herself out of the daze and stood up hastily, bumping the table with her thighs hard enough to rattle the glassware. "If you're finished, I'll clean up the dishes."

She spun around, but was brought up short when Trevor dug his fingers beneath the tie belt of her robe at the back of her waist. Giving it a swift tug, her turned her around and pulled her between his wide-spread thighs so that her middle bumped into his chest and his face was on a level with her breasts.

"Thanks for breakfast." The words, spoken in a low, rumbling voice to begin with, were almost completely muffled by the fabric folded over her breasts.

"It was the least I could do."

She lowered her eyes to the top of his head where the dark wavy hair swirled from the crown. It wasn't easy, but she resisted the urge to thread her fingers through the ebony strands to see if they felt as alive as they looked.

Her eyes battled to stay open when he rubbed his hard cheek against her breast, but they lost the contest and flickered closed. She felt the vibration of the moan that issued up out of his chest as his nose nuzzled her.

"You bathed this morning." It wasn't a question.

"Yes."

"You smell good. Like soap. And powder. And woman."

He made gentle gnawing motions with his mouth that sought and finally found the peak of her breast through the cloth. He didn't actually kiss her. He didn't actually suckle. What he did was rub his open mouth back and forth over her until he felt her flesh respond, then he touched her with his tongue.

"Breakfast was delicious," he whispered. Her skin became damp where his breath filtered through the robe. "Is there any dessert?" He pressed his face deeper into her softly giving flesh. But he pulled back almost immediately and looked up at her. "Hmm?"

When he saw her tremulous expression, he chuckled and stood up, pushing her gently away from him. "Never mind. Let's get dressed and go get that kid of ours before your parents spoil him rotten." He checked the clock on the oven.

"By the time we get there, they should be getting home from church. I'd like to take everyone to lunch. The Petroleum Club goes all out on its Sunday buffet."

"We're not members," Kyla found enough voice to say. She was still feeling aftershocks of delight at having Trevor's mouth on her breasts.

"But I am." He tweaked her nose. "I'll clean up the kitchen—you go get ready. I want to show you off." He kissed her swiftly and gave her rump a husbandly pat.

Kyla left the master bathroom twenty minutes later, after having applied her makeup and arranged her hair. That was when she came to the startling realization that she and Trevor might not be sharing a bed, but they were still sharing a bedroom.

She caught him in the act of stepping into a pair of dress slacks. A fleeting impression of light-blue briefs registered on her brain before she spun around and said, "Excuse me." She almost made it to the bathroom door before his stern voice halted her retreat.

"Kyla."

"What?"

"Turn around."

"Why?"

"Because I want to talk to you."

Slowly she came around, studiously keeping her eyes aimed at a point above his head. Casually he zipped up the trousers and, still shirtless and barefoot, crossed the room toward her. "I showered in the guest bath so I wouldn't disturb you, but my clothes have all been stored in the drawers and closets in here. It will be damned inconvenient to move them."

She wet her lips rapidly. "That's fine, fine. We'll just, uh, try to stay out of each other's way."

"I won't." He laughed, but when he saw her frown he said,

"Okay, we'll split the differences. You can get in my way any time you like, and I'll try to stay out of yours. Deal?"

It was too complicated to think through, especially looking at his bare chest as she was. So she merely parroted, "Deal."

"Good." He turned his back—a smooth expanse of darkly tanned skin stretched tautly over rippling muscles—and returned to his closet, where he proceeded to take out a shirt and pull it on with the nonchalance of a person alone.

Kyla forced her feet to move to her own closet. She stood there motionless, working up her courage to take off her robe.

You're behaving like a child, she told herself angrily. The nightgown she had faced him in last night was a thousand times more revealing than the bra and half slip she had on beneath the robe. Swiftly, before she could change her mind, she whipped it off.

"I've been thinking."

At the sound of Trevor's voice, she jumped as though she'd been shot in the back now exposed to him. "About what?"

She willed her fumbling hands to hang the robe on a hanger properly and return it to the metal bar in the closet. It required tremendous concentration because she knew he was probably looking at her back and the slender ivory satin straps of her bra.

"About Aaron."

She hazarded a glance at him over her shoulder. He wasn't looking at her at all. He was tying his necktie, using the mirror he had had mounted over the bureau that was built into his closet. His shirt had been buttoned, but he hadn't tucked in the shirttail yet. The stiff collar had been flipped up against his square jaw. "What about him?" She reached for the dress she had chosen to wear.

"Maybe we should be locating a proper day-care center for him."

"Do you think he's old enough?"

"You're more expert on that than I am. I was just wondering what we'll do with him during the day if Meg and Clif get that motor home and strike out for parts unknown."

That had been a concern of Kyla's, too. "I suppose he should be around other children his age. There's an education in that."

"No doubt. How else will he learn all the dirty words?"

She laughed with him. "But I'd want to investigate the school's reputation."

"Absolutely. It will have to be sterling. We both have to be sold on the facility and faculty before we enroll him. Need any help?"

Before she could formulate an answer, his hands were pushing hers aside. They had been at her waist in back grappling with the lowest button on her dress. How could a man of his size move so silently? She stood ramrod straight as his fingers negotiated the buttons. After securing the top one, his hands smoothed down her back and settled on her hips.

"No one would ever guess you'd had a baby. Was it a difficult pregnancy?"

"Not at all."

"You're so slender," he said softly, squeezing her hips lightly before his hands fell away. "Can you give me some help here?"

Unwisely she turned to face him. Only a few inches separated them. "Help you? How?"

"Check to see if my collar is turned down properly all the way around. Sometimes I don't bend it down just right and my tie peeks out from underneath."

She gave it a hasty inspection. "It's not quite folded down all the way in back."

"Would you fix it for me, please? It's hard to reach."

"Sure." She spoke with far more carelessness than she felt. Actually she was wondering how she was going to keep her hands out of the black hair that curled beguilingly over his collar if she came that close to touching it.

No sooner were her arms raised and her hands occupied adjusting his collar over his tie than he flipped up his shirt-tails and unzipped his trousers. Her hands froze. Her eyes sprang up to his. His expression was bland as he casually began stuffing his shirttail into his trousers. Occasionally, too occasionally, his knuckles bumped into her middle.

"Anything wrong?" he asked.

"No, no, nothing," she gasped and quickly folded his collar down. She patted it firmly into place just as the rasp of his zipper reached her ears. Her arms slid from his shoulders. He finished fastening the fly of his pants.

And then they stared at each other while time was held in suspension.

"Thanks," he said after a long, still while.

"Thank you, too." His eyebrow quirked with humor. "For doing up my buttons," she added hastily.

"Oh. You're welcome."

They fell into another staring spell. Kyla was the first to move away, and she did so by turning her back to find her shoes in the closet.

It took the familiar pandemonium that went with corralling Aaron to restore her equilibrium. But even that didn't erase an image in Kyla's mind of light-blue briefs stretched over tight, rounded buttocks.

The Powerses were impressed with the number of people who greeted their new son-in-law as they ate lunch at the exclusive Petroleum Club. Even Aaron seemed awed by his surroundings. His behavior during the meal was above reproach.

After lunch Trevor drove the Powerses out to the house he had built for Kyla and Aaron. After a tour that left them speechless, Trevor followed them back to their house in his pickup. The remainder of the afternoon was spent packing and loading Kyla's things that still had to be moved.

"He's a tired little rascal tonight," Trevor said of Aaron as they tucked him in. He patted the boy on the seat. Aaron's eyelids were already at half-mast. His stuffed animals were lined up around the slats of the baby bed like sentinels.

"Which is probably just as well," Kyla remarked, pulling a light blanket over her son. "The first night in a new place might be traumatic if he weren't so ready to go to sleep."

"Don't you think he likes the room?"

She heard the anxiety in Trevor's voice and looked up to find that he was genuinely concerned about it. "What little boy wouldn't like it?"

She gazed around the bedroom, which had been decorated in a railroad motif. The Little Engine That Could was puffing up the hill painted on the wall. A steam-engine-shaped toy chest, filled to capacity, took up a good portion of another wall. A miniature track had been run around the molding six inches below the ceiling. At the flip of a switch a tiny freight train circled the room at a clicking pace, belching puffs of white smoke every so often and tooting its horn periodically. Aaron had clapped his hands in glee and only frowned in frustration when he realized he couldn't reach it.

Her gaze returned to Trevor. "What I meant was that sometimes when a child sleeps in a strange place it upsets him. Apparently Aaron isn't bothered by it." Aaron was already snoring softly. Kyla covered a huge yawn with her hand as they left the room.

"You're worn out, too." Trevor clasped her shoulders and within seconds his strong fingers were working the knots out of her shoulder muscles. His thumbs magically pressed the tension from the base of her neck. Moving closer and laying his cheek against hers he said, "Want to spend a few minutes in the hot tub? Does that sound good?"

It sounded heavenly. She couldn't think of anything better than being immersed in hot bubbly water.

"I'll meet you out there."

Or anything more dangerous than sharing such a sensual experience with Trevor.

She eased from beneath his massaging hands. "If you don't mind, Trevor, I think I'll just go to bed. This weekend has been so hectic. It's taking its toll."

"All right."

She could tell he was trying not to let his disappointment show. This man had taken her as his wife, knowing she still loved another man. Wasn't she being a rather poor sport? "Unless you really want me to," she added.

He shook his head impatiently. "No. I know you're tired. Good night."

He bracketed her neck with his hands and tilted her head back with both his thumbs beneath her chin. He planted his lips firmly over hers, parted them, waited for her to accommodate him and, when she did, slipped his tongue into her mouth like a velvet sword.

It was a torching kiss that conveyed all the passion that smoldered within him. His practiced technique ignited her desire until she could swear that tiny tongues of flame were licking at her body.

When he released her at last, she all but sagged against

him, so totally had his kiss depleted her. "Good night," she said huskily and moved away toward the bedroom in what she hoped wasn't a staggering walk.

Trevor sat in the dark, idly rocking the porch swing with his heels against the decking.

A terse expletive summed up his mood of the moment. He tossed the remainder of the whiskey he'd been sipping onto the ground. He didn't need alcohol. He didn't need anything to make him any warmer, nothing to increase the heat that simmered in his loins.

He needed Kyla. Naked. Beneath him. Sheathing that part of him that ached with its need for her.

Cursing again, he thumped his head against the thick chain holding up the swing until it hurt badly enough to feel good.

Would she ever love him? Would she ever want him as he wanted her? So far he'd accomplished everything he had set out to. She and Aaron were living under his roof, sharing his life, enjoying his protection.

But she wasn't in his bed yet. Would she ever return his love?

Possibly.

But never if she knew who you were.

He had had every intention of telling her he was the legendary Smooch before they got married, but he had talked himself out of it. Better to be legally bound before breaking the news.

Then he had decided to tell her the morning after their wedding night, after she had had a night of his loving and they were bound not only legally but physically. So much for good intentions.

Well hell, it wasn't his fault that they hadn't had a wedding night, now was it?

But you should have told her by now, his conscience argued.

"Yeah, I know," he answered it out loud.

But how? When? What time was ever going to be right to say, "We didn't meet by accident. I orchestrated everything because I knew before I ever saw you that I was going to marry you and provide a home for you and your son. Why? Well, because I'm responsible for your husband's death and I felt like I owed it both to him and to you. Oh, but I do love you."

He repeated that curt obscenity and pushed himself out of the swing.

Would Kyla believe that he loved her after he told her who he was? Hell, no. *He* wouldn't believe it were the tables to be turned.

Propping his shoulder against the outer wall of the house, he stood at the edge of the deck and stared sightlessly into the near space.

"What the hell am I going to do?" he asked the night.

He knew that with just a little finesse on his part, he could get her to surrender to his sexual advances. He knew enough about women to know that she wanted him, if only she would admit that to herself. But that was the key to it, she had to admit it to herself. When they came together—*Lord, don't let it be too much longer*—she would have to initiate it. He wouldn't be accused later of taking advantage of her that way, too.

You've got to tell her, he was reminded by that relentless conscience.

"But I've got to win her first."

He didn't have to tell her tonight. Or tomorrow. Or even next week. He would take it one day at a time. When she knew he loved her, he would tell her. When the time was right he'd know it.

And if there's never a right time? his conscience taunted him.

But he didn't listen anymore. He began thinking of the woman sleeping in his bed. He envisioned an hourglass with sand the color of her hair sliding through its slender passage. One grain at a time. One kiss at a time. One caress at a time. And her resistance was lessened that much more.

"Your time's running out, Kyla." The hoarse whisper wasn't a threat. It was a promise.

"Sorry, I'm late," Kyla said breathlessly as she sailed through the back door of Petal Pushers. Her arms were full of order blanks and ledgers and catalogs. All were slipping to the floor despite her efforts to keep them secured between her arms and her chest. She piled them on the desk and paused to draw a breath. Her hair had been whipped to a fiery madness by the wind. Aaron had slobbered on her blouse.

"What kept you?" Babs asked sweetly. "Did something come up this morning?"

Kyla pretended not to catch the double entendre. "You can't imagine what a circus it was trying to get the three of us dressed, fed and off for the day." Kyla eased herself down into the chair behind the desk and drew a deep breath.

Babs laughed. "Honeymoonitis?"

"What?" Kyla frowned as Babs hiked a hip over the corner of the desk and leaned forward with an eager expression on her face.

"I know what made you late this morning. Is he as good as he looks?"

Kyla pushed herself out of the chair on the pretext of picking up the papers she had dropped. "Who?"

"Who? For God's sake, Kyla, whom did you just marry? Trevor, of course."

"Oh, Trevor," Kyla said absently, deliberately keeping her back to her perceptive friend. "Good at what?"

"You aren't going to tell me, are you?"

Kyla faced her friend. "About my sex life? No."

"Why?"

"In the first place it's none of your business. And in the second place I can't imagine why you would want to know."

"But I do," Babs said, hopping off the desk and stalking Kyla into the shop. "Every scintillating detail."

"Do we have any orders today?"

"Is he the rowdy, reckless, tempestuous type?"

"Maybe we should change the window displays this week."

"Or the slow, leisurely, languid type?"

"I'm not listening."

"Is he a moaner?"

"Has the mail arrived?"

"Does he talk to you? I'm sure he does. What does he say?"

"Babs!" Kyla shouted to stop the barrage of questions. "We haven't had a conversation this ridiculous since we were in the eighth grade."

"And then you told me everything."

"I've grown up. Why don't you?"

"You even told me what Richard's kisses were like when you first kissed him. Can't you at least tell me that much? What are Trevor's kisses like."

"Indescribable," Kyla said truthfully. "Now can we please change the subject?"

"One more thing."

Sighing, Kyla crossed her arms over her chest and feigned boredom. "What?"

"Is he positively breathtaking naked?"

Kyla swallowed. Then, because she couldn't even imagine what Babs's reaction would be if she told her she didn't know, she simply retorted, "What do you think?"

And from that Babs had to draw her own conclusions.

Chapter 11

They learned to live together. Kyla discovered that her husband existed on very little sleep. He enjoyed staying up late, but he was a jovial, early riser. She had always dreaded getting up in the morning whether she had slept three hours or thirteen. Trevor learned to give her a wide berth in the mornings until she had had at least one cup of coffee.

He was prone to drape clothes over the nearest piece of furniture as he disrobed, and to scatter sections of the newspaper as he finished with them, and to leave empty glasses on end tables. But he was also conscientious about picking up after himself and helping her with household chores without even being asked.

The first week they were married, Kyla wore herself out trying to keep Aaron quiet and well-behaved around Trevor. He wasn't accustomed to having a young child underfoot. She was afraid Aaron's constant activity and incessant racket would disturb him.

But Trevor never showed signs of irritation, not even

when Aaron was behaving at his worst. He spent a great deal of what psychologists called "quality time" with the child, doing everything from playing with him on the deck while she prepared dinner, to reading him books, to bathing him when she had both hands full. As for being a good father, Kyla could find no fault with Trevor Rule.

As for his being a good husband, she could find little to complain about, either. He was considerate and good-natured. Each night he left her alone in the master suite while he slept in the guest bedroom. He exercised no modesty in changing clothes in front of her. Often one surprised the other in various stages of undress by opening the wrong door at the wrong time. Such scenes never failed to disconcert Kyla, but Trevor seemed to take them in stride.

He was generous with his embraces and kisses, too. Anyone would think they were a happily married couple madly in love with each other. He would frequently slip his arms around her from behind and nuzzle her neck, complimenting her on her hair or her complexion or her figure. He never asked permission for a kiss, but took them as his due. Often his good-night kisses were so tantalizing that as she closed herself up in the bedroom alone, she would curse herself for a fool.

"He's my husband. I owe him conjugal rights. And if being with him would alleviate this jittery feeling inside me, why not?"

Then she would open the drawer in the bedside table where she had placed Richard's picture. (She had had enough sensitivity toward Trevor's feelings not to display it openly.) Gazing down into the beloved face, she would promise him again that he still lived in her heart, that she would never betray his memory by falling in love with another man, and that he would always be her *true* husband.

But her body wasn't so easily convinced. As she lay alone in that wide, empty bed, it wasn't Richard's face that haunted her, but Trevor's. His smile. His hair. His rugged, sun-baked features. His kiss. All vivid.

As the days merged into weeks, that jittery agitation inside her continued to brew until, like all boiling kettles, it had to blow.

It happened after a particularly arduous day in which she had haggled with a wholesaler in Dallas who had billed her for a shipment of roses that Petal Pushers had never received. To top that, she had argued with Babs over her offer to keep Aaron for the weekend while Kyla and Trevor treated themselves to a Dallas hotel's weekend getaway package.

"I think you need the time away. You look like a tightrope walker who has just lost her knack for it," Babs had observed badgeringly. "I keep waiting for you to lose your balance and fall off."

"I'm fine."

"Something is wrong with you, and I intend to find out what it is, if I have to ask Trevor."

"Don't you dare!" Kyla shouted, spinning around to confront her friend. "Stay out of my business, Babs."

She regretted her sharp words the moment they left her mouth and apologized for them. But for the rest of the day, Babs was sulky. Trevor had offered to pick Aaron up at his day-care center, but the job of marketing fell to her. She couldn't find everything she needed because the clerk had rearranged the shelves; the lines were impossibly long and the checkers incredibly slow. Several times she was tempted to leave the groceries in her basket and walk out without them.

By the time she arrived home, she was physically and emotionally exhausted. To save herself a trip back to the car, she tried to carry all three grocery sacks at one time. She was juggling them as she stepped up onto the deck and headed for the back door.

Her turbulent mood wasn't improved by the sight that greeted her. Trevor was lounging in the hot tub, a cold beer near his hand. And Aaron—

"Aaron!" she cried angrily. "What in the hell is *this*?"

"This," Trevor said, smiling, as yet unaware of her bad temper, "is pudding painting. The teacher at the school said he loved it, so I decided to try it out at home."

Her child, who was sitting at the small table Trevor had bought for him and placed in the shade on the deck, was covered from head to toe in dark sticky goo that Kyla was monumentally relieved to learn was chocolate pudding.

Thankfully, he was wearing only his diaper. His chubby hands were scooping the pudding out of a bowl and slapping it onto the sheet of butcher paper Trevor had provided for him. He smeared it around, then raised his hand to his face and licked the pudding from between his fingers. Apparently that wasn't the first time his stomach had taken precedence over his artistic endeavors. His face was covered with pudding. He smiled at her through the chocolate mess and chattered something.

"I think he said 'bird,'" Trevor explained. "At least that's what I suggested he paint a picture of."

"He's filthy!" Kyla cried.

She could feel her anger rising as surely as the mercury in a thermometer. Knowing it was unreasonable to get so upset over practically nothing, she nonetheless couldn't control the inevitable eruption of her temper.

"He'll wash," Trevor said pleasantly. But between his arching brows a V had formed and was deepening. "The teacher said it was a very creative exercise for him."

"The teacher doesn't have to clean up the mess," she retorted vituperatively. "And neither do you. I'll be the one who has to. Or didn't you and teacher get around to discussing that in the cozy little chat you no doubt had together?"

She stalked to the sliding glass door and tried to wedge her foot through a crack so she could open it. It wouldn't budge and with her hands full of the grocery sacks, which were beginning to sag under the slipping contents inside, she was helpless.

Finally, gritting her teeth, she looked at her husband. "I hate to interrupt your bubble bath, Trevor," she said with brittle sweetness, "but I think the least you could is get out of the hot tub and help me."

"Any other time, Kyla, but—"

"Well, never mind then!" she shouted. "I'll do it all myself."

He shot out of the hot tub then, angry and—

Naked.

His feet slapped against the redwood decking, slinging water with each long stride. Kyla stood rooted to the spot, even when he reached her and yanked the grocery sacks from her arms. He secured all three of them in one fist and slid open the glass door with such impetus that it rocked in its track. Heedless of both his nakedness and the water he was dripping everywhere he stormed into the kitchen and virtually slung the sacks of groceries onto the tiled countertop.

Then, with one hand propped on his hip and his right knee slightly bent in an arrogant, belligerent stance, he turned to face her. She read his expression loud and clear. If she could have captioned it, it would have said, "Well, you asked for it, lady."

Furious with herself for making such a scene and furious

with him for letting her, she fled into the bedroom and rattled every pane of glass in the house when she slammed the door behind her.

"Am I still in the doghouse?"

Dusk was thick and purple just beyond the plantation shutters on the bedroom windows. Kyla lay on her side, her knees drawn up to her chest. After a long bout of crying, she had showered and put on her nightgown. The sheet was pulled as high as her waist. Her cheek was resting on her hands, which were folded, palms together.

She raised her head slightly. Trevor was at the door, peeking around it as though he might be pelted with flying objects if he dared go any farther into the room.

"No. I'm sorry."

He came in. He was dressed in nothing but a pair of cutoffs and Kyla closed her eyes before returning her head to the pillow. All too well she remembered how his body had looked, soaking wet, the sunlight flickering through the trees and falling onto every silver rivulet that trickled down through that forest of hair on his chest. She recalled the hard, corded muscles of his stomach, the length of his limbs, the impressive sex nestled in a thatch of dark hair.

She had wept hot, bitter tears of regret—regret because she had noticed just how magnificent his nakedness was, regret that in spite of her best intentions she wanted him, and regret that she had denied him to herself for so long.

Now she felt the mattress sink with his weight as he lay down behind her and curved his body around hers. His fingers sifted through her hair, lifting stray curls off her cheek. He arranged the loose strands on the pillow just so. His ministrations were soothing.

"Hard day?" His breath was warm and soft in her ear.

"A bitch."

He chuckled. "Then I guess you weren't ready to see your son looking like something out of a minstrel show, were you?"

I wasn't ready to see you rising out of that hot tub like a male version of Venus, either. "I'm sorry I made such a fuss. It was a combination of things."

He was propped on his right elbow, leaning over her. His index finger swept back and forth over her cheek. "Now you understand why I didn't jump out of the hot tub to help you with your load right away."

"Yes."

"I wasn't expecting you home so early or I would have already been out and had Aaron bathed and ready for supper."

"It wasn't your fault, Trevor. None of it. It was mine." She sighed. "I don't feel well and—"

"What's wrong?" He was instantly alert, his body tensing behind hers.

"Nothing."

"Something. Are you sick? Tell me."

She turned her head up and back and stared at him in a way that conveyed her message.

"Oh," he said in a chagrined voice. "That."

"Yes, that." She turned to her original position.

"When?"

"I discovered it when I came in. I should have known. I was acting like such a viper."

"You're forgiven." He touched her tentatively, laying his hand in the shallow of her waist. "Do you...does it hurt?"

"Some."

"Did you take anything?"

"A couple of aspirin."

"Will that help?"

"A little."

"Not much?"

"No. It has to wear off."

"I see."

Moving slowly, he eased down the sheet. The nightgown was short and had narrow straps. It was made out of some thin, white material that reminded him of his most expensive handkerchiefs. There were flowers, white also, embroidered on the hem. Beneath it, he could see the outline of white panties. She looked vulnerable, virginal, and his loins began to ache with desire.

He touched her waist again. She didn't stir. Gradually he slid his hand down and around, giving her time to protest. When she didn't, he pressed his palm warmly over the lower part of her abdomen. "There?"

"Uh-huh."

Moving his hand in slow circles, he massaged her. "Better?"

She nodded.

"Poor baby." He kissed her temple lovingly.

She sighed and her eyes closed sleepily. "Trevor?"

"Hmm?"

"Have you ever lived with a woman?"

His hand paused, but so momentarily that the hesitation was barely discernible. "No, why?"

"Then what do you know about this?"

"Only that I'm glad I don't have to go through it every month."

Without opening her eyes, she smiled. "Typical male answer."

"But honest." He took a love bite out of her bare shoulder.

She didn't actually think about moving her legs. A message to them wasn't consciously transmitted. They just moved, unfolding away from her body, straightening and providing him greater access to her swollen, cramping tummy.

"Did you and Aaron manage dinner without me?"

"Like clockwork."

"What did you do?"

"Well," he said, sliding his legs against hers, catching the backs of her knees with his and filling her insteps with his toes, "first I hosed him down to get all the chocolate pudding off."

She laughed. "By the way, I approve of the idea of pudding painting. He was certainly having a good time. On any other day, I probably would have put on a swimsuit and joined him."

"As we both know by now, you had a right to be out of sorts."

"I shouldn't have yelled at you."

"I liked the part about Aaron's teacher and me having a 'cozy little chat.' The way you said it made me think you might be jealous." This time his mouth found her ear. His tongue delicately stroked the lobe. "That's so soft. A little fuzzy."

"Go on," she said in a breathy voice.

"I forget where I was."

"You…you…hmm…You, uh, hosed him down."

"Oh, right, yeah, and then I fixed his dinner."

"What did he eat?"

"His favorite."

"Hot dogs?"

"Uh-huh."

"Without the buns?"

"Of course." He kissed her neck and she moaned softly. "Tomorrow morning the birds in our woods will have three hot dog buns for breakfast. I hope they like mustard."

A low laugh issued from her throat and she didn't know whether it was because of his joke or because his mustache was dusting the column of her neck as if it were an object made of rare porcelain. "Did you—"

"I know what you're going to ask and yes, I did. I watched Aaron take every bite and made sure he chewed it."

"Thank you." Her mouth searched for his.

"You're welcome." His lips found hers.

The kiss acted like a spark at the end of two very short fuses. He ground his mouth against hers hungrily and her lips parted for the introduction of his tongue. Her body followed her head around until they were lying face-to-face.

Her arms locked around his shoulders. The tips of her breasts strained against the front of her nightgown until they touched the furry wall of his chest. He pressed her down, covering a side of her body with his own.

"Kyla, you—"

"Trevor, I—"

"What?"

"Trevor?"

From the bed came sounds. Gratified groans. The silky shifting of linens. Soughing breaths. Incoherent whispers. Whimpers of pleasure. The music of mating.

His hands moved with restless greed. He touched her thighs; for a fleeting second her calf filled his palm. He ran his fingers along her fragile collarbone. He cupped her breast.

"Ahh." Her back arched and she tore her mouth free of his kiss.

"What's the matter?"

"It's tender."

"Oh. I didn't…it is?"

"Yes."

"I'm sorry."

"No, it…actually it felt good."

"It did?"

"Oh, yes." She sighed as he gently caressed her again.

"Like that?"

"Hmm."

"And the nipples?"

"Yes, yes."

"Tell me, if—"

But he never finished the sentence, because her fingers wove themselves through his hair and drew his head down for another avaricious kiss.

When it ended, he lowered his head. It moved from side to side ardently pressing hot, random kisses into her breasts. His hands formed a brace for her ribs. He shifted her beneath him. His knee separated hers. The nightgown was pushed to her waist. She tucked his hard thigh high between hers. She moved against it. Rotating. Rubbing. Reaching.

"Damn!"

He lay atop her, his breath thrashing like a strong wind in her ear. She could feel the rapid thudding of his heart where his chest crushed hers. Between his powerful hands, he was holding her head immobile. His fevered face was buried in her hair.

"Don't move, sweetheart."

"What is it?"

"Please don't move, my love," he groaned. "Be still for just a minute."

She did as he asked. Several moments later, he slowly raised his head. His face was infinitely sweet and his expression compassionate. One corner of his mustache crawled up to form a rueful grin. "Wouldn't you know it? I get you just where I want you and it's the wrong night."

Embarrassed, her eyes fell away from his face. He kissed her cheek and moved away, coming off the bed completely. Bending at the waist, he laid his palm against her flushed cheek. "Are you all right?"

She wasn't in pain, except for the lower part of her body, which was aching abominably, and not with the miseries of menstruation. "I feel better," she said inanely.

He straightened and uncomfortably shifted his weight from one foot to the other. His fingers raked strands of ebony hair off his forehead. "You skipped supper. Are you hungry?"

"No. Did you eat?"

"I nibbled. I'm fine." They looked at each other briefly, then away, realizing at the same time how banal this conversation was after the passion that had seethed between them only moments ago. "Well, I'll leave you alone now. Good night."

He turned and headed for the door. The muscles of his back rippled beneath the smooth skin. The cutoffs gloved his buttocks.

"Trevor?"

He spun around. "What?"

"You..." *Don't stop now. You've gone this far.* She swallowed her pride and her better judgment. "You don't have to go."

Trevor looked at his wife. She was propped up on her elbows. The nightgown's embroidered hem was riding her upper thighs. Her tousled hair was tumbling over her shoulders like spun pink gold. His kisses had left her lips wet and berry-colored. The fabric of her nightgown was damp where his mouth had been. It clung to her breasts, transparently molding to the tips, which were making rosy inverted dimples against the soft white fabric.

He grimaced and rubbed his moist palms down the legs of his cutoffs. "Yeah, I do. I have to go. If I stay..."

If he touched her again there would be no stopping him from consummating his marriage and quenching his raging desire. Hell, he wasn't fastidious. But the first time they made love, he didn't want her to feel embarrassed or uncomfortable or to regret it for any reason.

"But hold the thought," he added on a husky whisper seconds before he left the room.

Aaron was already in his high chair and Trevor was turning strips of bacon in a sizzling skillet when Kyla warily approached the kitchen the following morning.

"Good morning, baby." She leaned down to kiss Aaron. He affectionately bopped her on the nose with a soggy piece of bacon. "Thanks a lot," she muttered.

"It was either get him up or let him jump in his bed until all the springs broke," Trevor said, taking the skillet off the burner and moving toward her.

"Thank you for seeing to him."

"My pleasure."

He clasped her waist lightly and drew her forward. He gave her one of those morning kisses that smelled like aftershave and tasted like teeth recently brushed. Kyla wouldn't have minded if it had lasted longer, but after smacking another quick kiss on her mouth, he said, "Sit down. You must be starving."

She glanced worriedly at the clock. "I've got to hurry. I overslept."

"Take your time. I called Babs and told her not to expect you on time this morning. Aaron's school isn't expecting him until around ten."

He set a platter of bacon and homemade waffles in front of her and sent her salivary glands into delirium. "I am starving."

"How are you otherwise?" He bent down and slid his hand past her waist. "Tummy still hurt?"

"It's much better."

"And here?" He palmed her breast and gently rolled her nipple between his thumb and finger.

She could barely breathe and gasped out, "Fine... much fine... I mean much better."

"That's good." He kissed the top of her head and sat down across from her. While she fumbled with her napkin and tried to remember how to use a fork, he buttered a waffle for Aaron and slid the plate onto the high chair's tray. "Here, Scout. Attack."

They laughed at the child's atrocious table manners and Kyla remarked, "We've got to start doing something about that." When she realized she had included Trevor in that statement, making the "we" sound so permanent, she glanced up at him. His expression was warm and flooded her body with a golden heat.

"How did you sleep?" he asked.

She noticed that his fingers were so long and strong that they barely fitted in the crook of the coffee mug's handle. Yet they could be so gentle when they touched her body, as they had been only moments ago. Getting a bite of waffle past her thickening throat was no small task, but when she did she answered, "Fairly well."

She had dreamed of him and awakened perspiring, with her heart pounding and her breath coming in short, rapid bursts. At least she could now satisfy Babs's curiosity and tell her without any exaggeration that Trevor was breathtaking naked.

"I didn't sleep too well last night," he said.

"I'm sorry. What was wrong?" He had certainly taken

her breath when he came out of that hot tub. His chest and thighs and—

"It was too hard."

Kyla's fork clattered to her plate and when she reached for it, she knocked over her orange juice.

Aaron pointed and said, "Uh-oh! Uh-oh!"

Trevor scraped back his chair and lunged for a dish towel. He blotted it against the spreading puddle of juice. "I was referring to the bed in the guest room."

"What?" Kyla's head swiveled around. His mustache was twitching with his need to laugh.

"The *bed* was too hard."

Her cheeks were bathed with hot color. Thankfully she was spared further embarrassment when the telephone rang. Trevor answered it.

"Dad!" he exclaimed.

Kyla lifted Aaron, who had polished off his waffle in record time, onto her lap. He reached for the food left on her plate and between her kisses, he ate that, as well. She glanced at Trevor, who was smiling broadly into the receiver.

"Sure, no problem. What time...? For how long...? Is that all...? Well, that's better than nothing.... Okay, we'll be there. Bye." He hung up.

"Your father?"

"He's flying down today to spend the night with us. That's all right with you, isn't it?"

"Certainly. I know you were disappointed that he couldn't come down for the wedding."

"I want him to meet you and Aaron. He can only stay one night and then he has to make a trip to L.A. for some case he's working on." He popped a piece of bacon into his mouth and chewed vigorously. "I want to drive him around town and show him some of my buildings. You know we— Say, I'm sorry. I didn't mean to get carried away."

Actually she was enjoying his enthusiasm. "Go on," she urged. "What were you about to say?"

"We didn't get along very well. Not until after my accident."

"He wanted you to be a lawyer?"

"And I had other ideas. But while I was in the hospital, we came to an understanding and now everything's great between us."

Her smile was genuine. "Are you driving to Dallas to pick him up?"

"If you don't mind. He gave me his flight number. I thought we'd all have dinner in the city."

"Aaron included?" she asked worriedly.

"Of course, Aaron included. He's part of this family." He scooped the child out of her arms and held him high over his head. Aaron squealed in delight. "Dad loves to eat Italian." He named a famous Dallas restaurant. "Should I call and make reservations?"

She hated to dampen his excitement, but apparently he didn't realize what a risk it was to take a fifteen-month-old child to a sedate restaurant for a leisurely meal. "I don't know if that's a good idea, Trevor. I'm not sure they welcome children there."

"Hey, if they don't want our kid in their restaurant, we'll take our business elsewhere."

From the maître d' to the lowliest dishwasher, everyone in the family-owned establishment was charmed by the three men, George Rule, Trevor and Aaron. Kyla's anxiety was all for naught because Trevor had spoken with the maître d' personally when making the reservation and the staff was prepared for Aaron before the party arrived.

Her initial meeting with Trevor's father, amidst the confusion at the airport, had gone more smoothly than Kyla had had any right to expect. At first Aaron was shy with the tall, white-haired man with the authoritative voice. But no more so than George was with the child.

Deliberately Trevor seated them in the backseat of the car together and by the time they reached the restaurant, located in Dallas's prestigious Turtle Creek area, the two were fast friends. In fact it was George who carried Aaron inside and showed him off to everyone as his grandson.

"Trevor tells me I'll miss meeting your parents," George said on the drive back to Chandler.

"We got a postcard from them yesterday from Yellowstone," Kyla said. "They're having the time of their lives."

She explained to George that the Powerses had sold their house within days of her marriage to Trevor. What furnishings Kyla didn't want, they had sold at auction. Trevor had helped Clif pick out the motor home that best suited their needs. Meg had furnished it with the giddy excitement of a little girl with a new dollhouse. Two weeks later they had left.

"She gets homesick for them," Trevor said teasingly, reaching across the front seat to tug on a lock of Kyla's hair. "They spoiled her rotten."

"So do you."

His head swung around. She had been as surprised as he to hear herself make that statement, but she realized after vocalizing it that it was the truth. Trevor glanced out the windshield to make sure he wasn't endangering them, then looked at Kyla again.

"I'm glad. That's what I want to do."

They continued staring at one another until George coughed loudly and said, "I don't know about you, Aaron, but I'm beginning to feel like a fifth wheel."

There was enough daylight left when they reached Chandler for Trevor to walk George through some of the building projects he was working on. Kyla remained in the car, watching their silhouettes move against the darkening sky. Trevor had hefted Aaron to his shoulders where the boy rode, his legs straddling Trevor's neck. They made a poignant picture.

"But that should be Richard," Kyla whispered, fighting the tears that blurred her eyes.

She wept because she couldn't convince herself of it. If the man should be Richard, why did it look so right for her son's fat fists to be trustingly clenching handfuls of Trevor's black hair? Why did it touch her heart so achingly to see Trevor swing Aaron down carefully and unabashedly give him a hearty hug? And why did she want to feel those same strong arms holding her?

George was justifiably impressed with the house and heaped unqualified praise on his son. Kyla carried Aaron off to bed and after a brief visit with George, excused herself to give Trevor and his father some time alone.

"I've got a bruise on my shin the size of a fifty-cent piece," George said. "Any particular reason why you kicked me under the table when I mentioned your stint in the Marines?"

Trevor had been glad Kyla was involved wiping spaghetti sauce off Aaron's mouth and had missed his father's inopportune comment at dinner. "I'd rather Kyla not know about that. She doesn't know how I got hurt."

"Any of it?"

"No."

"Hmm."

Trevor knew his father well enough to know that even a "Hmm" was never casually spoken. "You certainly fell in love and married quickly, didn't you?"

"Is that so odd?"

"For you it is." His son looked at him sharply and George smiled. "Your reputation with women reached even your ol' dad's ears, Trevor. This sudden romance is out of character."

They were sitting out on the deck in the comfortable chaise lounges. George was puffing on a cigar, which his doctor had advised him to give up. Trevor was glad the darkness covered his uneasiness. He didn't like the direction the conversation had taken. "I love her, Dad."

"I don't doubt that now that I've seen you with her. It's just strange that 'Smooch,' as your buddies used to call you, fell so hard and so fast."

"I've been in love with her for a long time," Trevor said, almost beneath his breath.

George rolled the cigar between his fingers, studying its glowing tip. "She wouldn't have anything to do with those letters you pored over and wouldn't let out of your sight while you were in the hospital, would she?"

Trevor should have known better. Nothing, not the most trivial scrap of evidence, slipped past the shrewd George Rule. To him nothing was insignificant. Trevor got out of his chair and walked to the edge of the deck. He propped his shoulder against the wall and stared out at the darkness as he had done weeks before while ruminating on how to tell Kyla who he was. "Dad, I'm going to tell you a story you're going to find hard to believe."

When he concluded his tale, several ponderous moments of silence followed. Finally George said, "I promised never to interfere in your life again, Trevor, but you're playing with fire."

"I know," Trevor admitted, turning around to face his father.

"How do you think this young woman is going to react when she learns the truth?"

Trevor hung his head and slid his hands into his trouser pockets. "I hate to think about it."

"Well, you'd better think about it," the older man warned, "because she *will* find out." He pulled himself to his feet and ground out his cigar in the ashtray Trevor had provided for him. Laying a hand on Trevor's shoulder, he said, "But who knows? It might work out. If you love her enough."

"I do."

"Does she love you?"

Trevor hesitated, his eyes slicing toward the darkened master bedroom windows. "I think she might be coming to. Or maybe she's just getting used to having me around. Hell, I don't know."

George smiled. Then his fond gaze rested on the eye patch and he was reminded once again of how valuable his son was to him and how close he had come to losing him. Moisture gathered in his eyes and he pulled Trevor forward for a fiercely emotional, if short-lived, embrace. "After what you went through, son, you deserve to be happy."

"No, Dad," Trevor said roughly over his father's shoulder, "after what she's been through, she deserves to be happy."

Soon afterward they said their good-nights and George ambled toward the guest room where Trevor had placed his suitcase.

Trevor approached the door to the master suite with the dawdling, shuffling footsteps of a boy who had been sent to the principal's office. His stomach was doing handsprings. His heart was thudding.

Just what the hell was wrong with him? Was he excited at the thought of her welcoming him into bed? Or frightened at the thought of her rejection?

Frightened? Of a woman weighing no more than one hundred and ten pounds? Don't be ridiculous.

Then why are you standing out here like a moron, staring at this door with your stomach in knots and your heart pounding and your palms sweating and your groin...

Oh, God, no, don't think about your groin.

Were his knees really shaking? Why, for God's sake?

He was a grown man, not a schoolboy. This was his house. He had built it. He had financed it. He had a right to sleep in any damn room he pleased.

She was his wife, wasn't she? And yeah, he *had* been spoiling her for the past few weeks. He'd walked around on eggshells, doing and saying everything he could to please her and nothing that might upset her.

Hadn't she been pleased when he installed her old re-painted swing set in the backyard for Aaron? Hadn't she been pleased when he built that sandbox? And hadn't she laughed when he engaged her in a tickling match as soon as they had filled it with soft, cool sand? And hadn't she returned the kiss that wrestling match had resulted in?

Hell, yes she had! His nickname hadn't been Smooch for nothing, you know.

But he hadn't carried that or any other kiss further than he thought she wanted it to go. He had been acting like a lackey to win her approval. He'd slunk around with his tail between his legs until it was getting damned uncomfortable. Well, it was high time he started letting her know that he was the man in the family and that as such, by God, he had some rights!

The door burst open under his hand and he closed it with a resounding slam. Kyla bolted upright in bed and clutched the sheet to her breasts. "Trevor? What's happened? What's wrong?"

"Nothing's wrong. All right, I'll tell you what's wrong," he snarled as he stalked into the room, armed to the teeth with righteous indignation. "My dad is sleeping in the guest room. So for tonight, Mrs. Rule, we share this bed."

Chapter 12

"All right."

Her softly spoken concession effectively disarmed him. His inflated wrath went as flat as a fallen soufflé. He rolled his shoulders to collect himself. "Well, good," he said tersely. "I'm glad you see it like that."

For some reason, her obliging conciliation only served to make him madder. He didn't need her to patronize him. No, sir!

He tore off his clothes with jerky, angry pulls and pokes and punches. One by one the garments were slung away from him. They were left wherever they happened to fall. When he was down to his briefs, he yanked back the covers and thrust his feet between the sheets. After brutalizing the pillow with his fist, he ground his head down into it.

"Good night."

"Good night, Trevor."

He turned his back to her, rocking the entire bed while

he adjusted himself into a comfortable position with all the querulousness of a fairy-tale giant.

There! Guess I showed her.

If that were the case, why was it *his* body that was stiff and burning with lust? Why was it *his* heart that ached with love denied release?

Kyla awakened to find him watching her. He lay on his side facing her, his tousled dark head pillowed on a bent elbow. Silent and still, the only part of him that moved was that single green eye that wandered over her face and hair as though cataloging every detail.

She didn't realize she had lifted her hand until she saw it move into her range of vision. Lightly she touched the black eye patch. "You never take it off."

"I don't want you to see it."

"Why?"

"It's so ugly."

"It wouldn't matter to me."

"Curious?"

"No. Sad. I was just thinking how pretty your eye is and what a shame it is that the other one was lost."

"I'm grateful that one was spared."

"That goes without saying."

"If for no other reason than for this moment. I wouldn't trade looking at your face right now for anything in the world." His voice was rough with emotion.

Kyla's throat ached with the need to cry. Her hand moved from his eye patch down to his mustache. Her fingers coasted over it lightly. Then she touched his upper lip.

Trevor's breath hit the back of his throat. Heat filled his sex.

She had never touched his face. Now she engaged in an

orgy of touching. The bones in his lean, dark face were pronounced. His brow bone jutted over his eyesockets. The
wing-shaped brows were sleek and thick. A bristly beard
stubble covered the lower half of his face. His mustache,
which her fingers couldn't leave alone, was amazingly soft.
With her fingernail, she languidly traced the shape of his
lower lip.

"Be careful, Kyla."

She withdrew her finger a fraction. "Why?"

"Because for almost seven hours I have been lying here
wanting you. Do you understand?" She nodded. "I don't
think it's too smart of you to touch me now. Unless..."

He left the condition unspoken, but they both knew what
it was.

Outside, bright sunlight was already filtering through
the leafy branches of the trees and casting wavering patterns against the closed shutters. Birds were chirping happily.
Squirrels chased each other through the upper branches. Butterflies flitted from flower to flower. Redbirds and bluejays
looked like brightly feathered arrows as they darted among
the trees.

The activity in the bedroom was considerably less obvious, but no less energetic. Emotions seethed between them
like huge swells in the Atlantic. Longing was so thick it was
palpable, desire so potent it could be breathed. If auras could
be seen, the air around them would have shimmered with a
red glow of mounting passion.

Her body didn't demonstrate its longing as blatantly as his,
but she suffered from the same affliction. At that moment,
Kyla thought of nothing more than satisfying her need to be
cosseted, caressed, covered, completed.

She touched his lower lip again.

In one fluid motion, he brought them together, positioned

her beneath him and captured her mouth in a hot, hungry kiss. Hard and bold, his manhood sought the heart of her femininity. Found it. Favored it with urgent caresses.

"God, I want you." He frantically groped for the hem of her nightgown. Her hands plucked at the elastic waistband of his briefs. One hand slipped inside and touched the taut curve of his buttock.

Groaning, his mouth found her nipple and closed around it while he enjoyed the silky smoothness of her panties and the contours they confined. She sighed his name and raised her knees. His fingers slipped into the waistband of her panties.

The bedroom door flew open and with the impetus of a miniature cyclone, Aaron came bounding into the room. He was chattering as raucously as were the bluejay and squirrel outside.

The breath leaked out of Trevor's body in a slow steady hiss, relieving the tension in his chest. He pressed his forehead against Kyla's and wished he could relieve the pressure in his loins as easily. A laugh began deep inside him and left his lips on an expulsion of air against Kyla's mouth. "Remind me to throttle him later."

Kyla, too, was feeling the agony of forcibly subduing passion. Sighing, she pressed her face into the warmth of Trevor's neck. "If I don't get to him first."

Trevor rolled off her, but kept her locked in the security of his arms. Together they turned their attention to Aaron.

"He must have talked his indulgent grandfather into releasing him from his crib," Trevor observed.

Attuned to the adoration of his audience, Aaron took center stage and performed some of his cutest tricks. Their laughter only encouraged him. Wearing a sappy grin, he started turning in slow circles. Heedless of their warnings that he was going to get dizzy, he circled faster until, drunk, he reached out to break his fall.

What his hand grasped was the decorative pull of the bedside table drawer. Gravity tugged at Aaron and he was too dizzy to counteract it. His bottom landed solidly on the carpeted floor and the drawer came out of its mooring to drop into his lap.

He wasn't hurt, but the two adults reflexively sat up when they saw that the inevitable was about to happen. Aaron stared at them in stunned surprise, then glanced down at the drawer lying in his lap.

The framed eight-by-ten picture of the Marine in full dress uniform was the only thing in the drawer. Aaron slapped the nonglare glass with his hands and said, "Da. Dadadada." He smiled up at his spectators, fully expecting an ovation for his brilliant performance.

The arms still holding Kyla in a loose, affectionate embrace went as hard as steel. Gradually they released her. She felt their warmth being taken from her by slow degrees. Then, with one violent motion, Trevor came off the bed on the far side and swept up the trousers he had left lying on the floor the night before. He shoved his legs into them and zipped them with a vicious tug as he strode toward the door.

"Trevor, please!"

He spun around, bare-chested, barefoot and furious. His jaw was bunched with rage and there was a cold glint in his eye as it took a bead on the woman now sitting up in the bed, her hair a mess, her face pale, her lips tremulous, her eyes pleading.

"I won't be a stand-in," he growled. "As long as there's another man living inside your skin, madam, there's no room for this." He crudely cupped himself. His chin bobbed once for emphasis before he stormed out.

★ ★ ★

"It's Lynn Haskell," Kyla reported, holding her hand over the mouthpiece of the telephone receiver. "She's invited us to a picnic at the lake on Labor Day. Do you want to go?"

It had been a week since George Rule's visit. The most miserable week of Kyla's life. The tension in the house crackled like old paper and was just as flammable. The suspense of not knowing what would touch off the inevitable conflagration was nerve-racking in the extreme.

Trevor never lost his temper, never raised his voice. Kyla would have welcomed it if he had. He was rather like a brooding, dark thunderstorm that refused to break. It lurked overhead, ominous and threatening.

He treated her no less politely than he ever had, but there had been a noticeable suspension of his demonstrations of affection. He rarely touched her, and then only out of necessity. With Aaron he behaved in the same loving way. With her, he was remote and mechanical.

Which was the way I wanted it in the first place, she rushed to remind herself every time she had a yearning for his brilliant smile…or a meaningful glance…or a touch…or a kiss.

Now, in response to her inquiry, he shrugged noncommittally. "I'll leave that up to you, Kyla. Whatever you want to do."

She shot him a withering look. He ignored it and bent back over the wooden puzzle with the oversize pieces that he was patiently working with Aaron for about the tenth time that evening.

She couldn't keep Lynn on the phone indefinitely. She had to tell her something. But what? The Haskells were Trevor's friends. Whether he said so or not, she was certain he wanted to go. Lynn was too astute to see through a lame excuse. Getting outside and spending a day at the lake would probably be good for all of them. Hopefully it would relieve some of the tension.

"Lynn, we'd be delighted to join you." From the corner of her eye, she saw Trevor glance up at her, but he immediately returned his attention to Aaron. "What can I bring...? No, no, I insist."

Invariably, the first Monday in September in Texas was cloudless and blisteringly hot. This Labor Day proved to be no different from its predecessors.

"Kyla, they're here," Trevor called from the front porch where he had hauled their gear and stood waiting with Aaron. The Haskells had suggested that they all travel to the lake in their van since it would hold both families and the picnic paraphernalia, as well.

"Coming." She went through the house checking to see that doors were locked and that she hadn't forgotten anything vital. When she reached the front porch, Trevor and Ted were loading the back of the van and Lynn was giving Aaron a "pony ride" on her knees.

"Hi. Climb aboard while there's still room for you," Lynn said, her holiday spirit showing.

During the drive to the lake Ted teased Kyla about her packing. "If I'd known you were going to bring along that much stuff, I'd have rented a trailer."

She wondered if the other couple noticed that she and Trevor could banter and joke with them, but that they had little to say to each other.

He had dressed in faded cutoffs, jogging shoes in sore need of retirement and a gray sweatshirt with the sleeves cut out. He had also enlarged the neck so that the crisp, dark pelt on his chest filled the jagged, uneven V.

Kyla had pulled her hair back into a ponytail. She had

worn a pair of old shorts over her bikini trunks and had tied
the tails of a matching shirt at her waist. It gapped open to
reveal the bikini bra underneath. She was glad she hadn't
tried to look nice. By the time they reached the lake, she had
been mauled by Aaron, who had caught the infectious holiday mood from the rambunctious Haskell children.

They reached the lake, found a spot they all agreed was
perfect and began the chore of unloading the van. When
they were finished, Trevor celebrated by taking a can of beer
from the cooler and gulping it down in three swallows.

He drank another to squelch the flames of desire that
licked his belly when Kyla stripped down to her bikini after
Lynn suggested that they work on their tans.

They trekked to the water's edge with the children. Aaron
splashed about happily and wasn't satisfied until his mother
had been showered with the cool lake water. When her nipples pouted against the cold, Trevor grumbled a feeble excuse
and went back to their picnic spot for another beer.

He carried it down to the lake and offered Kyla a drink.
When she accepted it, she accidentally touched his hand. And
when her head tilted back, he wanted nothing more than to
open his mouth over her exposed throat.

While he and Ted stayed in the shallow water with the
children, Lynn and Kyla swam out to the dock that was
buoyed in deeper water. Trevor watched every graceful arc
her arms made through the water. His gaze was trained on
her when she pulled herself up the ladder. Standing up to
wave to Aaron, her slender body was silhouetted against the
summer sky. Water sheeted on her thighs and coursed down
her flat tummy.

"I'll be right back," Trevor muttered.

"Where are you going this time?" Ted asked him, shading
his eyes against the sun and looking up at Trevor.

"I, uh, I think Aaron wants a cookie."

He picked up Aaron, who was perfectly content piling lake mud onto his knees, and carried him up to the van. Aaron got a cookie and Trevor drank another beer.

After a lunch that would have fed a caravan of gypsies, the children napped in the shade. When they woke up, everyone walked to the baseball diamond. The annual citywide "Skins and Shirts" game was a tradition among local businessmen. Anybody who wanted to play was to bring his equipment and meet at the diamond where they were divided into teams.

Trevor had just one eye and he walked with a limp, but months of physical therapy and a daily exercise program that he kept to religiously had put him in far better physical shape than the pencil pushers who had thirty or more pounds of sedentary living to lose.

Kyla gnawed on the knuckle of her index finger when he stepped to the plate in the ninth inning. The Skins, the team both he and Ted were playing for, were behind by three. The bases were loaded. There were already two outs. It all depended on Trevor. He rose to the occasion, knocking in a grand slam home run.

Kyla, like everyone else rooting for the Skins, went wild. Trevor received the hearty congratulations of his teammates. Then he and Ted came jogging toward their families.

"You were great!" Lynn said enthusiastically to Trevor.

"Hey, what about me?" Ted asked, affecting hurt pride.

"You were great, too." Lynn wound her arms around her husband's neck and kissed him soundly.

"I was holding my breath," Kyla said, laughing excitedly. As she smiled up at Trevor, her face was bathed with sunlight and her eyes were squinting against the glare. Behind a thick screen of curling lashes, he could see that they were shining.

Her hands were pressed against her chest as though she were trying to contain her jubilance.

"It was a lucky shot," he said modestly.

They took hesitant steps toward each other. Paused. Then Kyla flung herself against him and, coming up on tiptoe, pressed her mouth against his for a kiss befitting the hero of the day.

Trevor, reacting instinctively, wrapped his arms around her waist. The taste of her delicious mouth for the first time in over a week sent a shaft of pleasure spearing through him. It exploded like a fireball in the bottom of his belly. Lost in her taste, drowning in it, his tongue thrust deep. Heedless of the daylight, the crowd, everything, his hands slid to her derriere and lifted her against his swelling manhood.

Something, possibly Ted tapping him on the seat with his baseball glove, but something, reminded him of where they were. He raised his head and, looking down at Kyla, laughed shakily.

Kyla gazed up at him, a bewildered expression on her face. Her eyes were smoky. Her breasts were rising and falling rapidly with each breath. Her lips were red and wet and slightly roughened by his mustache. Lifting three fingers to them, she touched them tentatively, as though they'd been scorched.

"Ready to get back?" Ted was standing with Lynn, their arms linked loosely around each other's waists. Each had a child by the hand and Aaron was terrorizing a doodlebug at their feet. "How 'bout a beer, Trevor?"

"Yeah, sure, a beer."

He drank that one in two swallows, went swimming to rinse off the sweat and grime of the game, then chased his swim with another beer.

They nibbled on leftovers for supper and gradually a healthy tiredness settled in. Trevor was mellow and feeling no pain by the time the van was loaded and they started the drive home. Traffic was congested. He was happy to relinquish the responsibility of coping with it to Ted.

In fact, he relinquished every responsibility except that of finding a resting place for his head against Kyla's shoulder. He leaned against her heavily and let his arm slide down her side until his elbow nestled in the valley between her thigh and lap. His hand curled around the inside of her thigh. He stroked the smooth skin with a lazy thumb and found that it felt good to move his arm slightly so that the hairs dusting it dragged against her smooth flesh.

Once he thought he turned his head and kissed her neck, but he wasn't certain if he actually carried out the intention or just thought about it so hard that he imagined he did.

When they reached home, he concentrated on not appearing tipsy—as he had a sneaking suspicion he was—in front of their hosts. He soberly thanked the Haskells for a great time and bade them good-night.

He realized just how rubbery his arms and legs were as he tried to carry their picnic gear up to the porch. After taking a few staggering steps and dropping the picnic basket twice, he mumbled, "Think I'll wait till tomorrow to put all this stuff up," and dropped it all onto the ground.

"That's fine," Kyla said, pressing her lips together to keep from laughing. "But could you please unlock the front door?" Aaron, who was asleep in her arms, was becoming heavy.

"Sure, sure."

Stupidly, he just stood there looking at her while the seconds ticked by.

"You have the key, Trevor."

"Oh! Of course I do." He went on an uncoordinated search through his pockets until he produced the key.

Holding it up inches in front of her nose he said, "Ta-da! See, I told you I had it."

She suppressed another laugh, but he seemed not to notice as he wrestled with the lock.

"Someone has changed the lock!" His exclamation was spoken just as Edison must have said of the first light bulb, "It works!"

"Turn the key so the teeth are up."

He did as Kyla instructed. When the lock clicked open and the door swung wide, he gazed down at her and said, "You're wonderful. Did you know that? Wonderful."

She rolled her eyes with a long-suffering expression and pushed her way past him, going straight to Aaron's room and putting him to bed with dispatch. Minutes later when she came back through the living room, Trevor was sprawled on the sofa, one arm and leg dangling. She checked to make certain he had relocked the front door, then moved toward the couch and bent over him.

He was asleep. She brushed back a strand of wavy black hair that had fallen over his forehead. He awoke. "Kyla?"

"Hmm?"

"You're sweet."

"Thank you."

"So sweet and beautiful."

"Oh, yes, I know."

He missed the wry inflection in her tone. He had no idea he was being humored. All he knew for certain was that the pale moonlight, spilling through the glass doors, looked beautiful on the face of the woman he loved.

He hooked her behind the neck and pulled her head down for a kiss. Kyla, not prepared for this sudden move, much less the passion behind the kiss, lost her balance and fell atop him.

Trevor struggled to right the situation but only succeeded in rolling them both to the floor.

For several moments, he didn't comprehend that the soft pillow his head was lying heavily on was Kyla's breasts. Not until he lifted his head and gazed down at her. Then he lowered his face and nudged aside the shirt she had retied at her waist before the trip home. He touched her with his lips.

"You smell like sunshine." His nose rooted in the valley between her breasts. "I love the smell of sunshine."

He shifted so that his thighs came to be settled between hers in a snug fit. If it registered with him that her arms were lying listlessly at her sides and that her hands were turned up in an attitude of surrender, he didn't comment. He merely rearranged them so that they rested above her head, then with his index finger traced the inside of her arm from palm to armpit as though drawing a path for her veins to follow.

"If sunshine had a taste, it would taske like you, too." His mouth moved over her breasts, lips opening and closing as though taking bites. He got caught up in what he was doing and made a savage attempt to untie her shirttails. When they finally came undone, he cast them aside and attacked the front fastener of her bikini.

When she lay bare beneath him, he whispered huskily, "God above, you're beautiful."

He touched her reverently, his fingertips brushing back and forth across the soft flesh. He took his time. He made no apology. Because he was convinced she was just another dream. One of many about Kyla. But God, this one seemed real!

He cupped a breast in each hand and reshaped them with kneading motions of his fingers. Lightly he pinched her nipple between his thumb and finger, then lowered his mouth and entrapped it.

The sounds he made were those of a starving man who had just found sustenance. He suckled both breasts. He rubbed his mustachioed lip over the nipples now made glossy by his kisses. He made a sharp point of his tongue and played with them, tempting them to shrink, to become harder. And they complied.

Vaguely he became aware of the writhing movements beneath him, speaking to his body in a language it understood even if he wasn't translating too clearly.

He levered himself up and unfastened her shorts. Unerringly his hand wedged itself past them and into the damp bikini trunks. He cupped the delta that fitted his palm to perfection. He rubbed it, pressing, luxuriating in the soft fleece that covered it. His fingers curved down into the sweet mystery below.

His groan started in the bottom of his soul and rumbled through his entire body. "You're wet for me."

Passionately he kissed the throat from which a sobbing sound emanated and introduced his fingers into the fount of that seductive wet heat.

His breath rushed in and out of his body. Or was it Kyla's? He wasn't sure. He solved the riddle by clamping his mouth over hers and kissing her until neither of them could breathe at all. His tongue reached for her throat.

Her shorts came off easily. The trunks required considerably more patience and skill, both of which had deserted him by the time he whipped them from her ankles. Frustrated and clumsy, he freed himself from his clothing.

God, her skin was cool.

And he was so damn hot.

Her body accepted him. He sank into her silky wet femininity and shuddered with the pleasure. He was enveloped by warm, creamy womanhood, and it was the best it had ever been.

His mouth settled against her ear. "I've waited for this for so long. I've wanted... But it's much better... You're...my love...."

With his hands beneath her hips, he lifted her higher against him and moved with swift, sure thrusts. Her body began to quicken around his. The breasts beneath his mouth trembled and the nipple against his tongue pearled into a hard round button.

And just as he felt the sweet rush of her release pouring over him, he came in a torrent.

Huntsville, Alabama
"I'll never move again. We're living here for the rest of our lives."

"Fine with me," the man said tiredly. "Helluva way to spend Labor Day. Laboring!"

"But we got everything put away. Finally. Everything except that box with all your Marine junk in it."

"It might be junk to you, but some of it means a lot to me."

She patted his hand. "I know. I was only kidding. Come to think of it, did you ever send that picture to that guy's widow? Stroud, wasn't it?"

"Yes, and no, I never did. I'll do that tomorrow." His brow wrinkled. "But I don't know how to find her."

"Why don't you send it to the Marine Corps? I'm sure they could forward it to her."

"Good idea." He stood up and offered his hand to help her up. "Let's go to bed. I'm exhausted. But don't let me forget to fish that picture out and send it off tomorrow," he added as he switched out the light.

Chapter 13

It took her a moment to remember why she was sleeping on the floor. Without pillow or blanket or anything to alleviate the discomfort, she had slept a dreamless sleep for the first time in weeks.

Moving nothing but her eyes, she looked through the glass doors and saw that it was still very early. Hesitantly she stretched her cramped legs and tried to sit up. His fingers were snared in her hair.

It took some gentle tugging, but at last she was free. She picked up her discarded shorts and tiptoed toward the hall. On the way to Aaron's room, she refastened her bikini bra, the cups of which had passed the night bunched up under her arms.

Aaron was still asleep and showed no signs of waking up anytime soon. He had had a strenuous day yesterday and it was taking its toll. Kyla was thankful. Right now, she had to think and needed no distractions.

She pulled on her shorts and crept back through the house.

Trevor hadn't stirred from his place on the floor in front of the living-room sofa. He wasn't snoring, but his breathing was deep and steady. Kyla slipped outside without awakening him.

She took a towel from the stack they kept in the closet near the hot tub and walked through the woods toward the creek. The morning was still. The new sun hadn't yet penetrated the dense branches of the trees. The undergrowth was cool and damp against her bare feet.

The creek flowed lackadaisically. Heavy rain turned its current into a series of rushing swirls. Otherwise it was calm and provided a great breeding ground for crawdads. Aaron had clapped his hands in delight over one when Trevor—

Trevor.

His name echoed through her mind, eradicating all other thought. Sighing, Kyla spread her towel on the deep grass near the creek bank and sat down. Raising her knees to her chest, she propped her chin on them.

It had happened.

She closed her eyes as tremors of pleasure shimmied through her at the memory. Pressing her forehead against her knees she tried not to recall the splendor of his lovemaking, but her efforts were to no avail. Her brain might not want to remember, but her body was relishing every sweet recollection.

Why hadn't she resisted? She could have. He'd had too much to drink. When he collapsed on top of her, she could have shoved him away from her and he probably wouldn't have known the difference. Why hadn't she?

Because I wanted to make love with him.

There. She had admitted it.

She raised her head and stared at the creek as though expecting it to debate with her. It continued on its unconcerned trickling course toward lower ground.

Kyla had wanted him to make love to her since the kiss following the baseball game. That kiss had been a turning point. Even now, she could remember exactly how he'd looked as he came jogging toward her, limping more than usual after the exertion of the game.

His grin had been a wide, white swath beneath his mustache. Pointed clumps of black hair, wet with perspiration, had striped his forehead. The waistband of his cutoffs had been damp with sweat, stretched and slightly curled away from his navel. His legs, even the scarred left one, rippled and bunched with sinewy muscles as he came toward her.

Never had she seen a man so rawly masculine. Trevor epitomized the male animal and everything inside her that was woman gravitated toward it as surely as the creek flowed toward the lake.

The kiss he had pressed onto her mouth had been salty, gritty. The sweat that had plastered down his chest hair also plastered her to his chest. When she felt his hands, powerful and manly, anchoring her against his aroused manhood, she had known then that she wanted him, and that she would have him, by her own design, if not by his.

Later, when he had started kissing her breasts, she wished with all her might that nothing would interrupt this time.

Call it wicked.

Call it unfaithfulness to Richard.

Call it what you like, but she had wanted to feel Trevor Rule inside her.

"Kyla?"

She jumped and whipped her head around. Trevor was standing behind her wearing only his cutoffs, the shadow of a beard and a wary expression.

"Hi."

"Are you all right?"

She returned her gaze to the creek, finding it difficult to look at him after last night. Her chest hurt with the effort to breathe. "Yes, I'm fine. I woke up early and the morning was so pretty.... Is Aaron awake?"

"He wasn't when I left."

"I guess yesterday wore him out."

"I guess so."

He crouched down beside and slightly behind her. Idly he plucked bunches of grass, examined them, then scattered the blades back onto the ground. "What time are you going to work this morning?"

"I'm not. Babs and I traded off, last Saturday for today. That's why I was in no hurry to get Aaron up."

He acknowledged the information with a brief nod and stood up again. He was restless. Neither was talking about what was uppermost in their minds.

From the corner of her eye Kyla saw him wander toward a tree. He stopped. He turned and looked back at her. When he finally got to the tree, he raised his arms and propped them on one of the lowest branches slightly above him. He draped his wrists over the rough bark and hung his head to stare at the ground.

She laid her head back on her knees and prayed for something to break the silence.

"Did last night really happen, Kyla?"

Just as she had always thought, God had a sense of humor. Be careful what you pray for.

She glanced in Trevor's direction. He was now pinching pieces of bark off the oak and flicking them into the water. "Don't you remember?"

"I remember either an incredibly erotic dream—" he took

a deep breath "—or the best thing that's ever happened to me." Her head came around quickly, swinging her hair like a red-gold cloak around her shoulders. He saw the tears standing in her eyes. A spasm of monumental regret twisted his features. "God, I'm sorry."

"It's all right."

"The hell it is."

"No, really."

"I was drunk."

"You were relaxed."

"Did I hurt you?"

"No."

"Force you?"

"No."

"Was I abusive?"

"No."

"Because I could never forgive—"

"Trevor, I wanted to!"

The hundred and one apologies he had cataloged in his mind, died on his lips. "You did?"

"Yes." She drew a shuddering breath and started plucking at the same grass he had deserted. "I've been doing some thinking."

"About what?"

"That you might…might want other children, other than Aaron, I mean. Some, at least one, of your own. It would have been unfair of me to…to withhold—"

Her lips were stopped by a long, tanned finger being laid against them. No longer could she avoid that piercing green eye. It beamed straight into her soul. "I would like to have at least one child of my own. And I appreciate your willingness to accommodate me. But is that the only reason you wanted to make love to me?"

"No," she whispered, shaking her head. "I just didn't know what else to say."

"Why did you want to make love with me, drunken and stupid as I know I must have been?"

She turned her cheek into the palm that had provided a resting place for it. Her eyes closed and two of the tears that had collected in her eyes rolled down her cheek. But when she opened her eyes, she was smiling. "You weren't drunken and stupid."

"Could've fooled me."

Laughing, she reached up and touched his hair affectionately. "You were as you've been since I first met you."

"Which is?"

"Kind, generous, fun to be around."

"Please, no more. I don't want to get a swelled head. But are you describing me or Santa Claus?" He assumed the wheedling expression of a little boy asking for one more piece of candy. "Don't I have any attributes of a more romantic nature?"

Her laughter was as sparkling as the creek water in the sunlight. "Need your ego stroked?"

"For starters," he drawled.

She shot him a shy look, but continued playing the game. "All right. What do you want to hear? That you're dashing and as handsome as the devil? That my best friend thinks you're a hunk and a stud, but a nice stud and that's rare?"

"Your best friend? How she'd get in here? I want to know what you think."

"All of the above," Kyla confessed in a raspy voice.

"Is there more?" His nose got lost in the loose curls above her ear.

"Should I go so far as to say that the mere sight of your body sets my blood on fire?"

"Sounds good to me."

Her head fell back when his lips found her throat. "You're incredibly good looking and sexy and—" She clamped her lower lip with her teeth.

"And?" he prodded, bringing her head up to meet his gaze.

"And," she added slowly, "I'm very glad I'm married to you."

He called upon a deity, whether in prayer or vain, Kyla was never sure. He applied the lightest pressure to her shoulder and she lay down on the towel. He followed her down, partially covering her body with his.

"I love you, Kyla Rule."

Her arms folded across his back. Their bare legs entwined. What their bodies had done only hours before, their mouths now reenacted.

"You're taking the day off?" he asked gruffly several moments later.

"Uh-huh."

"Then so am I. But let's get Aaron up, feed him and take him to the day-care center anyway."

"Why?"

Her husband grinned down into her face with a roguish gleam that made her heart flutter and her thighs liquefy. "Because I want to spend all day in bed tumbling my wife."

"...Yes, yes..."

"Like that?"

"Yes!"

"I'm afraid when I press so deep, I'm hurting you."

"No... It...ah...Trevor...yes..."

"Sweetheart... Kyla... I can't... How much longer do you think?..."

"Not yet. I want it to last forever."

"So do I, but…"

"Now, now, now…"

"You're so beautiful."

"You make me feel beautiful. And naughty."

"Naughty?"

"I've never been set in front of a mirror to be admired. It's decadent, isn't it?"

"Purely. But this way I can see all of you at once. Lift your arms."

"How? Like this?"

"Perfect. Did you breast-feed Aaron?"

"For a while. Why?"

"Just wondering. Your breasts are so pretty. Did I say something wrong?"

"No, it's just—"

"What?"

"Some of the things you say embarrass me."

"Don't be embarrassed. I love you. Does it bother you for me to touch you like this?"

"Bother me? Hardly, I…ah…"

"Oh, God, look at you. I barely touch you and…"

"You know just how to touch me…how to…"

"You taste like milk."

"Use your mustache—"

"Sweet, sweet milk."

"And your tongue—"

"You taste like Kyla."

"So don't say it's ugly."

"Every man should have a left side with a racetrack carved into it."

"Do the scars ever hurt?"

"No."

"Never?"

"Well, sometimes."

"Why does this one curve all the way from your spine to your sternum?"

"Right now I'm glad it's there."

"Glad?"

"Yes. Because your lips feel so good against my chest."

"I'd kiss it even without the scar."

"Would you, love?"

"Yes. I've wanted to kiss your chest for a long time."

"That's not my chest any longer. That's my navel."

"Close enough."

"Speaking of close…hmm, hon…"

"You got me off the subject. Why did they cut you like that?"

"I was bleeding internally from several organs."

"Oh, Lord."

"It's all right. Just keep doing what you're doing and I don't even remember it."

"Like this?"

"Oh, baby, that feels good. Kyla…Kyla…Oh, sweetheart, oh… That's the first time you've touched me."

"The first time I saw you—"

"Yes?"

"When you got out of the hot tub—"

"Yes?"

"You were breathtaking."

"No, this is breathtaking…. The way you're touching me now…that's breathtaking."

★ ★ ★

"…but I told Babs there was no way I would sneak onto the bus with the football team."

"You were a good girl."

"I was a coward, always afraid of getting into trouble. So I rode home with the band where we belonged."

"And Babs?"

"How did you find that little patch of freckles?"

"Just lucky, I guess."

"That's my birthmark."

"Yes. Now tell me about Babs."

"Well, when we got back to the school, she came off the bus with this guy she had previously called an 'ugly moose.' She was wearing a…I don't know…a *look*, and I knew what had happened. That's also when I knew that she and I were different. I couldn't just have sex for the sake of sex."

"Damn! Sure about that?"

"Trevor, stop it now. I thought we were going to talk."

"Then stop lying there looking so delectable. All right, I'm sorry. Let's talk."

"I forgot what we were talking about."

"Were you a virgin when you got married?"

"The first or second time?"

"Very funny. Answer the question."

"That's not what we were talking about."

"You're right. Sorry I asked. It isn't any of my business."

"Yes, I was a virgin."

"You almost sound ashamed of it."

"I'm afraid you'll be turned off by my lack of experience."

"Would I be doing this if I were turned off?"

"I don't know which I like best. What you're doing or the expression on your face while you're doing it."

"Look at the way it curls around my fingers. It's such a pretty color. And soft. And so is this."

"Trevor…what?…"

"Relax."

"But what… No!"

"I want to."

"No, I…"

"Please, Kyla, let me love you."

"But…oh, my God…Trevor?…"

"Yes, love, yes. You're infinitely sweet."

"No more, please. I can't stand it. My sides are hurting."

"One more. This one's about a man who goes into a pet store to buy a parrot."

"Trevor, I mean it now, no more of your dirty jokes."

"You're laughing."

"That's my point. I shouldn't be. I'm a lady."

"How can you pretend to be a lady while you're straddling my lap and I'm making lunch out of your nipples?"

"Trevor!"

"Ouch, hon. Be still or you'll cripple me more than I already am. On the other hand, go ahead and squirm. They look damn cute when they jiggle."

"You're outrageous."

"Wait till you hear the joke."

"There's no stopping you?"

"No. Now be a good wife and listen. This guy goes into the pet store and… Kyla, I thought I told you to be still. This guy goes into the pet store and the owner says, 'I've got this terrific parrot.' 'Can he talk?' the man asks. Kyla, you're asking for big trouble. Now stop that. 'Sure he can talk,' the pet store owner says, 'but there's one problem.' Kyla, I'm warning you. 'What's the problem?' the guy asks. 'The parrot can talk, but he hasn't got any feet.' Kyla... So the guy says, 'Then how does he stay on his perch?' And the pet store owner says... Oh, to hell with it."

"That's the joke?"

"No, but I just thought of a better punch line."

"That was the hardest part to accept. There was nothing the Marines could send me. No mementos. Nothing. It was as though he had never existed. That broke my heart. There wasn't even enough of him to fill the casket."

"Don't, don't, sweetheart."

"He deserved a better death. And dealing with the military was frustrating. They couldn't or wouldn't tell us anything for security reasons. The details were so sketchy."

"For instance?"

"Richard wasn't even in his own bunk that morning. Why? Why didn't a single thing belonging to him survive the blast? I wanted something tangible, something of his that I could hold in my hand. A razor. A wristwatch. Anything."

"Shh, shh. If it's going to upset you, don't talk about it anymore."

"It's not as painful as it sounds. In fact it feels good to talk about it. And you're a dear to listen."

"I love you, Kyla. We've needed to talk about Richard. I wanted both of us to have the freedom of speaking his name out loud."

"I loved him, Trevor."

"I know."

"And do you know that I love you? I didn't think I could ever love another man, but I love you. I just realized it. I love you! Trevor, are you crying?"

"I love you so much, Kyla."

"You won't ever leave me, will you?"

"Not a chance."

"Swear it."

"Never."

"I can't believe it's raining."

"Just an afternoon thundershower. It'll be over soon. Then we'll dress and go get Aaron."

"But not yet. Let's enjoy the rain."

"Rain is no fun unless it can be shared."

"How do you do that?"

"What?"

"Read my mind."

"Do I?"

"From the very beginning, you seemed to know what I was thinking. How?"

"Because I love you."

"Yes, but—"

"Turn around, Kyla."

"I don't understand how you—"

"Are we going to make love one more time before we go get Aaron or not?"

"Hmm, Trevor, not fair. You know when you touch me there I melt."

"Where? Here?"

"Yes, yes."

"And when I kiss you there?"

"I die a little."

"Then kiss me at the same time and we'll die a little together."

Huntsville, Alabama
A letter was mailed.

★ ★ ★

Humming, Kyla checked the pot roast. Even Meg Powers would have been proud of it. Kyla replaced the lid on the roaster and turned off the heat in the oven. It would keep warm until Trevor and Aaron returned. Trevor had taken the child with him to run an errand, leaving Kyla at home to prepare dinner, a task she now took pleasure in.

In fact she was finding pleasure in just about everything she did these days. For the past three weeks, since Labor Day and the night following, she had lived in a bubble of happiness.

"A few days off has certainly done wonders for you!" Babs had exclaimed the day Kyla went back to work after the holiday. "You're shining like a new penny. And I'd be willing to bet that Trevor is the one who polished you to that glow."

Kyla's laugh at the ribaldry had been lusty. "You're right, I'm in love."

"Well it's catching, because Trevor has already called twice to see if you'd arrived yet, and he said to give you a kiss for him when you did, which I refused to do. What's happened to the two of you?"

"Nothing," Kyla lied airily, as she reached for the telephone to return Trevor's call. It had been all of half an hour since she had seen him.

"I'll bet you've been renting X-rated movies for the home VCR."

"Nope."

"You ordered that kit of marital aids I showed you in *Playgirl?* What did Trevor think of the edible panties?"

"Will you hush!" Kyla had said, laughing. "I did no such thing." Then into the telephone she said, "Hi, darling. You called?"

"You're taking ginseng tablets?" Babs had persisted. "Feeding him oysters on the half shell every night?"

"No! I'm sorry, Trevor. Babs just wanted to know if I was feeding you oysters on the half shell every night…. What?… No, I can't tell her that…. No… Oh, all right. Babs, Trevor said to tell you that if he were eating oysters on the half shell every night, we'd have to buy a new mattress. Now be quiet, please. I told you I'm in love and I want to talk to my husband."

And I am in love, Kyla thought happily, as she now went through the living room, picking up the toys Aaron had left in his wake. Noticing the unopened mail lying on the hall table, she took it into the kitchen on her return trip and sat at the bar on a high stool to sort through it while waiting for her men to come home.

One envelope in particular caught her eye. It was from the Marine Corps. Slashing it open, she found another envelope inside with *Please forward* stamped on it. The name printed in the upper left-hand corner sparked her memory, but she didn't recall why until she noticed the return address. Huntsville, Alabama. Hadn't one of Richard's friends been from Huntsville, Alabama? Curious, she slit open that second envelope and took out the single sheet of plain white stationery. A photograph dropped to the bar.

The letter was brief. It introduced the sender, who expressed sympathy over Richard's death. It explained that the sender had recently found the photograph and thought that Kyla might like to have it. It ended with a heartfelt wish for her future happiness.

Laying aside the letter, she picked up the snapshot. Smiling at her from the center of a trio of Marines was Richard Stroud. He looked just as she last remembered him. He had a military haircut, high over his ears and short on top. He was in his full dress uniform, but there was a jocular smile on his face, as though someone had said something exceptionally funny just before the shutter was snapped. The lens had captured Richard's sweet, spontaneous smile.

He was standing between two other Marines. Their arms were companionably resting on each other's shoulders. The sender of the picture had considerately captioned it for Kyla. He had identified himself as the man on Richard's right. He had an open, down-home face, a toothy grin and big ears. One wouldn't hesitate to buy a used car from a man with a face that honest.

Kyla's eyes slid to the other side of the picture. "Smooch" had been neatly printed under the man on Richard's left. One would be wise to exercise caution before buying a used car from him.

Could anyone that good-looking be trustworthy? He had the grin of a hungry alligator, a brilliant white smile that slashed across his darkly tanned face. Mischievous green eyes viewed the world through spiky black lashes. He looked ready to wink, and Kyla got the distinct impression that he had made the funny remark that the other two men were laughing at. Smooch's smile was smug, unapologetically arrogant, indubitably conceited.

And familiar.

It was her husband's smile.

There could be no mistake. Even with the skinhead haircut of a Marine, without the eye patch, without the curving mustache, there was no mistaking that smile.

Kyla dropped the photograph as though it had burned her fingers. She stared down at it where it lay on the bar, but couldn't bring herself to touch it again.

There had to be a logical explanation. Richard and Trevor arm in arm? Trevor a Marine? How had a picture of Trevor come to be captioned "Smooch," a nickname she remembered well from Richard's letters to her from Egypt?

Smooch was the womanizer. The shameless playboy. The friend of Richard's she knew she couldn't stomach should they ever meet.

And she was married to him.

The implications associated with that rushed at her like a swarm of killer bees. She covered her head. She bit her lower lip to catch the sob that rose out of her chest. She forced down the scalding bile that suddenly filled the back of her throat.

There had to be some explanation. Of course there was. Trevor would come in and see the picture and say something like, "Gee, that's spooky. Can you believe that guy looks so much like me?" Or, "They say everyone in the world has a twin. Guess this Smooch is mine." Or, "It's amazing what they can do with trick photography these days."

It had to be a mistake.

But there was no mistake and she knew it.

She heard his pickup pull into the driveway. Her insides were roiling, her blood was churning, her head was thundering, but on the outside, she looked as immovable as a wood carving.

"Before you get mad," Trevor began the moment he stepped through the door, "Aaron and I took a vote and decided unanimously that it wasn't too close to dinner for him to have a cookie. So we broke open the package on the way home. That's why his shirt—What's the matter?" He had chanced to glance up and noticed her condemning expression. Cookie-smeared hands didn't warrant the intensity of it. "Kyla?"

He moved toward her and when he reached the bar, he saw the picture. He muttered an obscenity and spun around.

Reciting a dictionary of curses, he went to stand in front of the windows. Shoulders hunched, he slid his hands, palms out, into the back pockets of his jeans.

"Come here, Aaron." With much more composure than she felt, Kyla picked up her son. She felt like screaming until she couldn't draw another breath, like bashing her head against the wall, like bashing Trevor's against it.

Lifting Aaron to the sink, she washed his face and hands, then set him on the kitchen floor and surrounded him with brightly colored plastic measuring cups, which were among his favorite playthings.

Finally she returned to the bar, picked up the snapshot and studied it for a moment before she said, "You take a good picture."

Trevor came around slowly, pivoting on the heels of his Western boots, which Kyla knew now were as false and phony and affected as everything else about him.

"So now you know."

"Yes, I know," she snapped. "It's true what they say, isn't it? Clichés always have an element of truth to them. The wife is always the last to know."

"I would have told you."

"When, Trevor? When? When we're old and gray? When I was too feeble to hate you with every fiber of my being as I do now?"

"Me or what I've done?"

"Both! I can't stand the sight of you. *Smooch!*"

She uttered the name as though it were the most loathsome epithet. He winced. "I knew how you felt about Smooch. That's why I never came right out and introduced myself to you."

She laughed, a bit hysterically. "Smooch. I'm married to Smooch, a man known for his sexual conquests. A man who would tumble anything in skirts because all cats are gray in the dark."

"Kyla—"

"Didn't you tell Richard that once?"

"Yes, but that was before—"

"I don't want to hear it," she shouted, slicing the air with her hands. "I don't want any explanations from you except one. Why did you do this? What purpose did it serve? What sick, sick game have you been playing?"

"It isn't a game." His reasonable tone contrasted jarringly with her shrill one. "It was never a game. Not from the beginning."

She reined in her temper and drew in several restorative breaths. "And just when was that? I assume our meeting wasn't accidental."

"No."

"Then when did this start?"

"When I woke up in a hospital in West Germany and discovered I was alive. Missing an eye, injured almost beyond repair, but alive."

"What did that have to do with me?"

He took a step toward her. "You wanted to know why Richard wasn't sleeping in his bunk." She nodded, though no question had actually been asked. "I came in drunk the night before the attack on the embassy. Richard helped me get undressed. I barely remember it, but I do remember falling into his bunk. He was sleeping in mine when that bomb went off."

One hand flew to her mouth, the other gripped her stomach. Tears sprang to her eyes.

"My sentiments exactly," Trevor said grimly. "When I realized that Richard had been killed in my place I didn't care if I lived or died." He looked away, reliving all the pain, literally feeling it rack his body again, reducing him, making him less than a man. "But I lived. With the help of an orderly who befriended me I found out about you and Aaron. When I was well enough to leave the hospital, I came looking for you."

Kyla folded her arms across her stomach. She paced the length of the bar, rocking slightly forward and back from the waist, as though excruciating pains were tearing her insides to shreds.

When she rounded on him, she cried, "In my opinion you have carried your military duty too far. You went above and beyond the call. I don't want a husband who married me out of a sense of obligation, thank you very much!"

Her voice was so loud and vitriolic that Aaron stopped tapping the cups against the floor and looked up at her. His bottom lip began to quiver. "Ma-ma."

Wrested from a pit of humiliation by the tremulous sound of her child's voice, Kyla knelt down beside him and smoothed her hand over his head. "It's all right, darling. Play with your cups. See? Oopsy-daisy. They fell over. Stack them back up for Mommy."

Temporarily mollified, Aaron went back to his play. Kyla faced Trevor again. His face was almost as stony as hers. His lips barely moved. "It isn't like that."

"Then tell me what it's like," she sneered. "Tell me what motivated you to move here and seduce me into—"

"*Marriage,* Kyla," he said with angry emphasis. "What's so dishonorable about that?"

"Because it was all a setup. I can't believe I was gullible enough to fall for it, to fall for you. Your manners, your concern for Aaron, your instant attraction to me, your...your everything. Your damn conservative car! You stepped straight out of the Widow's Guide for A Dream Second Husband, didn't you? Why did you go to so much trouble? What made you do it?"

"I love you."

She stretched her arms out in front of her as though warding him off. "Don't...don't you dare play word games with me." She virtually spat out the words because she didn't want to alarm Aaron with her loud voice again.

"I'm not, Kyla. I was and am in love with you."

"That's impossible."

He shook his head adamantly. "There's one essential part of this story that you don't know yet."

"Then pray tell me what it is."

"Your letters."

She fell silent, dumbfounded by what he'd just said. "My letters?"

"Your letters to Richard."

She sank onto the stool as she stared up at the man who had reverted from a loving husband into a stranger again. It had happened so quickly. Seeing the picture of him had ripped the rug out from under her. Now she felt as though the floor had just dropped away. When would she hit bottom?

"You read them?" she asked with an inflection that clearly indicated she thought that was the most heinous crime he had committed so far.

"They were sent to me by mistake when I was in the hospital." He told her about the metal box and of his granting Richard the favor of using it. "When they sent me my belongings, that box was among them. I opened it and, yes, Kyla, I read your love letters to your husband."

He reached across the bar and covered her hands with his own. "I don't expect you to understand, but I swear to you, I credit those letters with keeping me alive. Every precious word did me more good than any medicine, any surgery, any therapy. They made me want to live again, so that I could meet the woman who wrote them. I memorized each one of them. I could recite them word for word to you now. They're engraved on my mind more deeply than the Pledge of Allegiance or the Lord's Prayer. They—"

"Oh, please. Save it for your next victim." She snatched her hands from beneath his. "I don't want to hear it. Do you think I'd ever believe another word you said after the way you've tricked me?"

"I didn't think of it as tricking you, Kyla."

"No? The orchids, the house." Coming off the stool she began to pace again. "Everything. It all falls into place now. The way you seemed to read my mind. And all the time you *knew*. You knew because you had read my letters."

"And responded to what they said."

"No wonder you could manipulate me so effortlessly."

"I was giving you what was in my power to give."

"Courting me and being so nice to my parents and—" Suddenly, her body yanked to attention. Her brown eyes narrowed as she glared at him. "My parents. *You* managed to get their property rezoned at such a propitious time, didn't you?"

He closed the space between them in three long steps and laid his hands on her shoulders. "Now, Kyla, before—"

She flung off his hands. "Didn't you?"

"All right, yes!" he shouted back.

"And the sale of their house? The sale that we all marveled over because it commanded such a premium price. The sale that went through in record time without a hitch just in time for our wedding. You arranged all that, too, didn't you?"

His face was closed and hard and as guilty as sin.

"I see," she said on a soft laugh. "Well it's no wonder you

felt like you could marry me and take Aaron to raise. You had bought and paid for us, hadn't you?" Her hands were running up and down her arms vigorously, as though washing away a feeling of uncleanliness.

"Stop that. Damn it, I've told you that I love you."

"I can't tell you what a comfort that is coming from a man known to his cronies as Smooch."

"Those days are over."

"No doubt they are. But you went out with a bang, didn't you? You made certain that your final conquest was a woman who was most unlikely to refuse you, a poor lonely widow lady with a child to raise. Come on, Trevor, confess. Didn't you think, in that manipulative, conniving, devious mind of yours, that I might accept you when other women would scorn you now that you aren't quite so handsome? Widows are more desperate for a man, aren't they? Wouldn't poor little Kyla Stroud be so anxious for a man to take care of her that she would overlook an eye patch and a limping, scarred body?"

She wouldn't let herself feel ashamed for the flicker of emotion that crossed his face.

"That's not true."

"Isn't it? When you were once again sure of your sex appeal, how did you plan to dispose of Aaron and me? Or did you plan to? Was I to be so grateful for what you did to me in our bed, that I'd overlook what you did in others'?"

His head dropped forward. "What do you want from me, Kyla?"

"I want you to leave me alone." She picked Aaron off the floor, protectively hugged him to her chest and stormed to the back door. "You've done so much for me, Trevor. You've lied and manipulated my future. You married me out of pity and because you were afraid that I was the only woman who would have you now. But there's one more thing you can do for me, Mr. Rule. You can get the hell out of my life."

Chapter 14

"You're just plain stupid, you know that?"

Babs had sat enthralled while Kyla poured out the entire ugly story. She had arrived on Babs's doorstep an hour earlier. To say she was upset was putting it mildly. Aaron had been fed a grilled cheese sandwich, bathed, dressed in one of Babs's T-shirts and diapered from a supply that Babs kept for his visits. He was sold on the idea that it would be great fun to sleep in Aunt Babs's bed, and that was where he was.

In the living room of the small apartment, Babs sat on the floor, legs crossed, while Kyla occupied a corner of the short sofa. Two glasses of white wine stood on the coffee table.

Kyla had fully expected Babs to share her outrage over Trevor's treachery, taking up arms if necessary to railroad him out of town. "Stupid?" she repeated, thinking she'd heard Babs wrong.

"Stupid. Dumb. A real... Oh, never mind," Babs said irritably, getting to her feet. "I'm going to bed."

"Wait a minute," Kyla exclaimed. "Haven't you listened to a single word I've said?"

"Every self-pitying syllable."

"And that's all you can say about it?"

"That's all I'm going to say about it. If you expect me to sit here with you and hash over what a louse Trevor Rule is, then you're in for a disappointment."

"But he is! Didn't I just tell you—"

"Yeah, yeah, you told me all about it. About how he woke up in a military hospital on foreign soil, half-blind, half-paralyzed, not knowing if he was going to live or die, and if he did live, if he'd be able to crawl, much less walk, much less make love or anything else a normal man has the privilege of doing. He woke up to find out that his friends had been blown to kingdom come by a bunch of fanatics, but miraculously his life had been spared. But to an insensitive cad like our Trevor, I doubt that bothered him much."

Scorn dripped from her voice like the water from the wineglass she had just rinsed out in the kitchen sink.

Stung by Babs's sarcasm, Kyla said, "All right, I'll concede that physically he had a difficult time."

"Now don't go exaggerating things, Kyla."

"It was *hellish,* okay? But what about the letters? Reading them, memorizing them like some pervert."

"The creep! How could he do something like that? Even Van Johnson never did anything that sentimental in his movies. Imagine Trevor doing something that horrible. Imagine him having the nerve to rearrange his future just so he could be near the woman who composed those letters. Imagine him, a man who could have had any woman he wanted with a crook of his finger and a come-hither look, going to all that trouble to meet you, his soul mate. And he didn't even have the decency to lure you into his bed first. No, he had to go and marry you!"

"Only out of pity," Kyla tightly reminded her unsympathetic friend. "Only to pay me back for Richard's death because he felt responsible."

"Right, so he'd be considered a martyr. Any other man would have come to see you, paid you his respects, humbly apologized for being alive when your husband was dead, offered you his help, probably his money, and when you refused he would have gone away with his conscience salved. But not Trevor. Oh, no. No doubt he wanted the world to think he was a do-gooder. So he hung around and got to know you, married you, took your son under his wing and built you a house a Rockefeller wouldn't be ashamed to claim." She made a tsking sound and shook her head. "What a creepy, sneaky heel. What a rat."

"You don't think it was sneaky the way he manipulated the rezoning of my parents' property?" Kyla exploded angrily. "You don't think it was underhanded the way he helped push the sale of their house through?"

"What a dastardly deed," Babs cried, shielding her eyes with her arms and feigning horror. "He handled all the dirty work so they wouldn't be bothered with it. He exacted a top price for their property, closed the sale and got them on their way to doing what they'd been wanting to do for years. The man has no heart. And the way he treats Aaron is positively sickening. Doesn't he know that most fathers don't treat their natural children that well? If he wanted to be a real father to the boy he should throw in a few harsh words, a little neglect, a lot of impatience."

"Enough, Babs. Soon I'll have to roll up my pant leg." Kyla rubbed her throbbing temples. "I might have known you'd take up for him."

"Take up for a louse like that? No way. If I were doing that, I'd probably tell you straight out what a selfish bitch you are."

"Selfish?"

"You wouldn't know something good if it came up to you on the street and bit you in the butt. If I were taking Trevor's side, I'd point out that some people prefer martyrdom to happiness."

"Stop it!"

"It's safer. There's no risk involved. When you don't love, you don't risk losing."

"You've got stars in your eyes for him. That's what this sermonizing is about. You've had a crush on him from the beginning."

"Granted. I've always had a weak spot for hunks with a sentimental streak."

"Well, the two of you would get along great. You both think with your genitals."

Babs sucked in her breath and held it for a long time. Gradually she let it go, but her body remained rigid. "Before I smack you, which is something I've miraculously restrained myself from doing so far tonight, I'm going to bed. Aaron, whose mature company I much prefer over yours, can sleep with me. You, my friend, can fend for yourself."

"Come back here. You can't just walk away from a fight."

"Watch me."

"I'm sorry for what I said. That was dreadful and I didn't mean it. Babs, please, tell me what to do."

Babs spun around and confronted her. "All right, you asked for it, here it is. You're not fighting with me, Kyla, you're fighting with yourself. And it's not me you're angry with. You're not even angry with Trevor. You're mad at yourself."

"What do you mean?"

"You were the Honor Society student. You figure it out. Now, good night."

Babs went down the hall and closed the bedroom door behind her. Tears smarted in Kyla's eyes as she returned to the living room. She prowled it aimlessly, nursing her indignation with self-pity.

So much for friendship. She felt betrayed. Murky waters could be closing over her head for the third time while she waved frantically at the shore where Babs stood mocking her, and she wouldn't feel more forsaken.

She had counted on Babs's unqualified allegiance. She had expected Babs to rally to her side and chant like a cheerleader, "That's a girl, that's telling him. Way to go. Right on." Instead Babs's sympathy had lain solely with Trevor.

Kyla flopped down on the couch and took a hefty draft of wine. "No wonder," she mumbled. Babs was female. She had fallen under *Smooch*'s spell. She, like hundreds before her, had been dazzled. That was it. Babs had become a traitor over a pair of muscular biceps and a dark curving mustache. What was loyalty to a friend when weighed against the way Smooch filled out his jeans?

Scoffing, Kyla took another sip of wine.

And what had she meant by the crack about Kyla being mad at herself?

Nothing. Absolutely nothing. Babs loved to drop little half-finished, underdeveloped tidbits of thought like that into conversations, like spoonfuls of cookie dough onto a baking sheet. And that's what they were, half-baked.

But if that were so, why did she keep dwelling on it?

Why was she giving any thought to the possibility that she *was* angry with herself? What did she have to be mad at herself for?

For falling in love with Trevor.

She slammed the glass of wine onto the coffee table and stamped to the window. Pulling viciously on the cord of the blinds, she raised them to peer out. She saw nothing but her own image reflected in the glass. Face-to-face with herself, she was forced to argue.

Admittedly she was smitten by him. She wasn't immune to a nice pair of biceps, either. And what about his generosity? And his constant kindness? And his lovemaking?

To stifle a sob, she crammed her fist against her lips. She didn't want any reminders of the way she had gloried in his tender loving. Guilt had a brassy taste. Somewhere along the way, living with and loving Trevor had become more important than keeping Richard alive in her heart. She had let the signal fire go out and that was an unpardonable offense.

Babs was right. She was angry with herself for loving him despite it all.

She couldn't hold it against him that he'd been in Richard's bunk the morning the embassy was bombed. That had been a quirk of fate. He hadn't used her letters to exploit her, but to grant her her heart's desire. He was an exemplary parent to Aaron. He was ambitious and successful, but not one of those men enslaved to his work for the sake of making a buck.

True, he had lied by not telling her that he had known Richard. Yet if he had introduced himself as Smooch, she would have run just as hard and fast as she could, and forever been without him. If he had married her out of a sense of duty, then he was an actor of Olivier's caliber.

Love like that which Trevor had given her couldn't be faked, nor could it be summoned on command. It had to come from the heart.

If a love was that strong, what could be wrong with it?

She fled Babs's apartment. Once in the car, a thousand

possibilities flickered through her mind like the insects caught in the headlights' beam. What if he had already left? What if she had lost her love for the second time? The first time, she had had no control over the loss. But this time she would have thrown it away.

As Babs had said, she was just plain stupid.

She released her pent-up breath on a wave of relief when she saw both his car and his pickup still parked in the driveway of the house. Entering through the front door, she saw that there was a feeble light on in the bedroom and rushed toward it.

Trevor was sitting on the edge of the bed, his head bent over a sheet of paper, which had been folded so many times that the creases were worn thin. She recognized it as one of her letters. Others were untidily stacked at his side. The light she had seen came from the fireplace where an unseasonable fire was burning. He was reading by firelight.

He glanced up when he heard her come in. His inquiring gaze held hers until she reached him, then she looked down at the frayed letter. Taking it from his hand, she read it. When she came to the line that said, "He sounds like the kind of man I detest," her eyes clouded with tears.

Moving quickly, she snatched up the scattered letters one by one, envelopes included, until she had them all. Crossing the room, she moved aside the brass fire screen and threw them onto the dying fire.

"Kyla, no!"

The paper caught, crackled and curled, making a pastel pyre atop the logs. The flames were short-lived. Within moments the letters burned themselves out, shooting sparks up the chimney.

Kyla's face was streaked with tears when she turned to face him. "You don't need another man's leftovers, Trevor. If you want to know what I think, what I feel, ask me. Let me open my heart to you. Richard..." She paused and drew a deep, rattling breath. Her nails bit into her palms. It was the most painful thing she had ever had to say, but she finally voiced the truth that she had ignored for so long. "Richard is dead. I loved him. We created another human being through that love. I'll always be grateful that Aaron is a living testimony to it. But Richard is gone. I love you."

"Kyla." His voice broke on her name.

She threw herself into his arms. They wrapped around her, drawing her small frame against his. He buried his face in her neck. "I love you, Trevor. To know it, all you have to do is look at me. Read it in my eyes."

"No, don't leave me," she protested. With amazing strength, she clasped his thighs between hers.

"Aren't I getting heavy?"

"I like it."

"You're weird." He raised his head from the pillow to smile down at her.

"*I'm* weird? You're the one who fell in love with a woman through her letters to another man." She angled her head back to see him better. "What if I'd been a troll?"

"If you'd been a troll, if you'd been anything except exactly what you are, I would have introduced myself, offered my condolences, offered my financial assistance and bade you farewell."

"That's what Babs said."

"She did?"

"When she was still speaking to me, that is."

"Have I missed something?"

"I'll tell you all about it in the morning. Right now I'm

busy." She allowed her tongue the unbridled pleasure of investigating his ear.

"I presume our son is safe," Trevor murmured around the tip of her breast, which responded beautifully.

"He's sleeping with Babs."

"You consider that safe?"

They laughed and when they did, Trevor grimaced. "Does that hurt?" she asked.

His lips tilted into that hungry alligator grin. "Laugh some more."

Instead they kissed. When she felt his body filling with renewed desire for her, she clasped his head with both hands and raised it above hers. "Forgive me. I said some terrible things to you. About your scars."

"I knew you didn't mean them."

"And about your eye patch." She touched his cheek lovingly. "I think I know why you chose that over a prosthesis."

"Why?"

"You wear it out of defiance of the disability it represents. It would have been easy for you to wear a glass eye, to cover your scars. But you never take the easy way, do you, Trevor?"

"Not anymore. I used to. Before this happened to me, I didn't take anything seriously. I thought life was a series of parties held in honor of me. I found out the hard way it just ain't so." He pondered his next thought as he let strands of her hair slide through his fingers. "Or maybe I used the patch as a shield. Beneath it is the ugliest scar of all. Maybe I was afraid that if you saw that, you'd see the ugliest part of me, which was my deception."

"No more secrets between us, Trevor."

"None. Never. All my defenses are down."

His fingers got lost in her hair and his voice turned soft and raspy. "You were justifiably furious, Kyla. I *did* trick you into marrying me. But after I saw you, and you were even more beautiful than the things you had written, I simply had to have you, by fair means or foul. It was never my intention to replace Richard in your heart, but to create a place there for myself."

"I guess your biggest transgression was impatience."

"How's that?"

"If you had introduced yourself as Smooch—"

"You would have hated me on sight."

"Initially, maybe. But not after I got to know you. What I'm trying to say is that I feel like this was inevitable."

"You mean that no matter how it came about, we would be married, lying here, doing this?" He moved inside her.

"Yes," she gasped softly. "Remember when you said that as long as there was someone else living inside me there was no room for you?"

Chagrined, he smiled lopsidedly. "Very crudely put, if my memory serves me."

"Crudely, but accurately." She touched his mouth with hers and left it there against his mustache. "You fill me completely, Trevor. Body, mind, and soul."

Then very gently, and with no interference from him, she threaded her fingers up through his hair and removed the eye patch.

★ ★ ★ ★ ★